*Gabriela Houston*

# THE BONE ROOTS

ANGRY
ROBOT

ANGRY ROBOT
An imprint of Watkins Media Ltd

Unit 11, Shepperton House
89-93 Shepperton Road
London N1 3DF
UK

*angryrobotbooks.com*
*twitter.com/angryrobotbooks*
From whence it came

An Angry Robot paperback original, 2023

Cover by Alice Coleman, illustrations by Gabriela Houston
Edited by Gemma Creffield and Alice Abrams
Recipes cited from *Salvic Kitchen Alchemy* by Zuza Zak, Watkins 2023
Set in Meridien

ISBN 978 1 91520 258 1
Ebook ISBN 978 1 91520 263 5

Printed and bound in the United Kingdom by TJ Books Limited

9 8 7 6 5 4 3 2 1

MIX
Paper from
responsible sources
FSC
www.fsc.org    FSC® C013056

# PRAISE FOR GABRIELA HOUSTON

"Gabriela Houston's writing is both economical and evocative – a rare skill."

*SFX Magazine*

"[Gabriela Houston] truly is a writer to look out for, and one that I think will go far."

*Libri Draconis*

"As twisted and intricate as the bone roots themselves, an intimate portrait of what it means to become a mother and the fight to protect – at any cost. Be prepared to be gripped, chilled, and lulled deep into this mythic world with Houston's lyrical prose."

Caroline Hardaker, author of *Composite Creatures*

"Gabriela Houston's *The Bone Roots* is an exuberantly told story that weaves together the lives of two mothers and their daughters. This enthralling tale is filled with dark magic, intriguing monsters, and a tension that holds until the very end."

Chris Panatier, author of *The Phlebotomist*

"A powerful tale of two mothers and the lengths they'll go to protect their children, set against a richly detailed backdrop of Slavic folklore. Wonderful!"

Shona Kinsella, author of *The Vessel of KalaDene* series

"[Houston] creates a realistic, enchanting fairy tale with real-world themes."

Ginger Smith, author of *The Rush's Edge*

*To Cameron*

# AUTHOR NOTE

*The Bone Roots* is influenced by the folktales and folk traditions from across the many Slavic nations. Since I'm from Poland, the majority of the "Slavic" words used throughout the book are actually Polish, anglicised for the ease of reading. For those readers who might be curious about the cultural and linguistic context, I have prepared a glossary of some of the phrases used in the book as well as notes on the creature names. While the creatures often have slightly different names depending on which Slavic language you use, I tend to go with the Polish versions. So, if you come across a differently named, yet a very similar creature in Croatian, Bulgarian or Czech folktales, chances are the difference is merely linguistic.

# PROLOGUE

*They'd walked for days.*

*The noblewoman's fine clothes snagged on the brambles and twigs, their silver thread pulled and unpicked. Her black hair came undone from the four braids she wore down her back, and she smelled like sweat and dead leaves. None of it mattered. It was a long way to go on a promise, but the hope which sustained her lent her strength.*

*"How much farther?" she asked her companion. The vedma turned to look at her, her green eyes flashing in the evening light filtering through the thick canopy. Her curling red hair stuck with sweat to her forehead. The vedma didn't reply with words. Instead, she gave a little smile, giving a glimpse of her white teeth, as sharp as razors. The bone roots curled around her feet, and she pointed ahead.*

*There, in front of them, rose a tree, more magnificent than anyone could have imagined. Taller and more awe-inspiring than Tsarica's Summer Palace.*

*Goddess Zemya's tree was white like ivory, the bone of its trunk and branches reflecting the reds of the evening light. No worm worried its smooth surface. No decay touched its leaves. The tree was not content with keeping to a single season, its colours shifting and changing, the little buds unfurling into a pale white-green of spring, and filling with the lushness of summer right in front of the women's eyes, before turning blood red and falling to form a thick carpet under their feet.*

*The forest was filled with life here. A multitude of birds flitted about, nesting within the embrace of her branches, and filled the air with their chatter.*

*But for all the wonders before them, the two women's eyes were fixed on the twin fruit, hanging low and ripe from a lower branch, just low enough for their trembling hands to touch. And within the fruits, visible through the finely veined, translucent skin, were the two babies, as pink and perfect as any newborn, though much quieter. The twins' eyes were watchful, their gaze unnervingly fixed.*

*And for the two women, there were no more questions, and no doubts either.*

# CHAPTER 1

It's been fifteen years since Kada sharpened the bone dug up from her father's grave. Fifteen years to the day since she used it to cut the stem connecting her baby daughter to Goddess Zemya's great tree.

Today, like every year since, Kada stood on the crossroads, bleeding into the ground. The Great Tree's bone roots reached far and wide, spreading all over Fiesna, and their tendrils were nowhere as close to the surface as where the human path above intersected. Kada stared into the horizon as dawn coloured the sky above the tree line. She chewed slowly on a piece of honey cake as she counted in her head. The blood trickled slowly like molasses from the shallow cut in her arm. It dripped onto the ground, where it stained the earth briefly, before seeping through the sand to where the white roots soaked it in. The pulsating marrow sap within them pulled Kada's payment towards Zemya herself.

Kada didn't begrudge it. It was a small price to pay for her child. Her beautiful daughter she once thought she'd never have. This, this small pain, was nothing.

As the sun rose, exposing the misty fields on either side of the road, Kada carefully put a piece of clean cloth on the cut to stem the bleeding. She recoiled at the tiny white tendrils twisting out of the soil, searching greedily for any drops that might have pooled on the ground.

A rooster sang in the morning light. The people of Torlow would be waking soon, emptying their night-pots behind their houses, the smell temporarily drifting into the road where Kada walked. She took care to avoid the gnarled roots poking here and there. The dust kicked up by her heels stained the hems of the wide trousers she wore under her knee-length skirt.

The earth rose and sank again. Kada felt the movement through the woven soles of her *bast* shoes. The thin ribbons of the bone roots brushed against her feet, as if to smell their woven bark. Kada tensed, even though she knew she was safe. She had made her shoes herself after all, from the bark of the linden tree, the least beloved of Zemya's children. If there'd ever been a blasphemer who'd dare peel the white skin off the silver birches growing in the holy groves, Kada never met one.

Zemya was disturbed that morning. It could be that the blood Kada fed her was deemed an inadequate offering, or perhaps the earth goddess mourned the end of summer, preparing the bones beneath the ground for the winter's long slumber. Kada shivered. She always preferred the seemingly endless winter nights. The calm of the land soothed her. The fox never came in the snow, everybody knew that. Zemya only sent it when the trees greened, and the grasses sent their thirsty shoots towards the sky.

The milkman rolled his cart past her, casting Kada a judgemental look. The road belonged to him this early in the morning. What business could a vedma working for a fine house such as Gorcay's have with the dawn's world? As a vedma contracted to look after the town, Kada was simultaneously considered too high to share the early hours with the servants and too low to escape the judgement of the townsfolk entirely. Kada paid the man no mind. Her business was her own, and she owed nobody an explanation. Tongues would wag even if she spent her life sitting as still as a statue; there was no avoiding the evil minds of men.

The main street of Torlow was cobblestoned like in some of the finest cities in Fiesna. It was a small vanity of the townsfolk, who were all proud of their home, with its pretty new brick homes, built next to the older stone dwellings. The reds and the silvers of the walls were sometimes broken with blue paint, informing all who passed that there were unmarried women living within. Sometimes the paint was white, trailing in a vine around the door frames, a wordless message of grief and death. Sometimes the inhabitants painted sunflowers on their doors to welcome a new child into their home.

Kada passed many doors on the way that morning, reading the messages with the absentmindedness of one who usually was first to learn of all that happened within the homes and hearts of Torlow's folk.

The street was still quiet when Kada entered the hall of Gorcay's house. More of a palace, really, though only Tsarica's own home could ever be called that. And yet names mattered little, where the beauty of the painted turret roofs towered above the rest of the town. It took years for Gorcay to have enough dead wood to build the ceiling supports for the multi-level house, as well as the front facade, the fallen trees carefully transported and stored before being planed and cut to shape, each piece carved with swirling patterns.

Stone and the fast-growing tail-reed would have been easier, and cheaper, but anybody could have a stone house. Gorcay would have nothing but the best. The wood was the heart of the land, after all, and Gorcay wanted to get at the heart of things, always.

Kada had little time that morning to check on Secha, who'd be getting dressed by now, so she went straight to the kitchens, where the disgruntled cook was just shouting at the baker's boy.

"What's the matter?" Kada said, taking her shawl off and hanging it on the hook close to the doorway.

"Ah, there you are! Finally!" the cook turned on her, like she knew he would. The baker's boy sent her a grateful little smile. "The daybreak's come and gone, Master Gorcay will be wanting his tonic with his eggs and bread, and you're off, Zemya-only-knows where, so that neither voice nor bell can call you!"

"A vedma doesn't respond to a bell." Kada gave him a playful look. "And I have the tonic half prepared already, Motik. Don't worry on my behalf. I'd be more concerned about that ham you're cooking."

"What?!" Motik rushed off to the other side of the room, where the big pot was bubbling over the fire.

"Go on there, shoo," Kada whispered and winked at the boy still lingering at the entrance. He needed no further encouragement and bolted, just as Motik turned around.

"My ham is fine! What do you think you doing, putting the fear in me!" His eyes widened. "Oh, so you're in cahoots with the boy, are you? Everyone's against me!" He shook his head and returned to grinding the last of the dry parsley sprigs, turning his back on Kada.

She laughed and leaned forward, planting a kiss on the man's cheek. "There now, Motik, it's like you have a wasp buzzing between your ears this morning. Tell Kada what worries you."

The cook tsked and made as if to push her away, though his cheeks reddened. "Oh, it's all at once today, and then you add to it by saying my ham's not cooking right. I swear, my heart nearly stopped!"

Kada stood next to him and pulled a small wooden chest on the long worktop towards her. Nobody but Kada ever touched it and even Motik, who saw it every day, shrank away as she opened it and took out the three trays from inside. The chest was made of some foreign wood, red like poppies, and fragrant from the herbs and salves stored inside. This wood did not look like the kinds allowed for harvest by Zemya, but it didn't look like any wood that Kada had ever seen in Fiesna either. All in all, Kada felt it lent her a mystical air.

"So, when you say 'all at once'..." she said, pulling out a small clay pot of goose fat. She opened the seal and wrinkled her nose at the smell.

Motik was glad to turn the attention back to his concerns. "First of all, Master Gorcay woke early today. His toe hurt something awful last night, and he was horrid cross when he got up this morning. Then the baker sent down the wrong bread, like I can't tell the difference – as heavy as an anvil it was! The man grinds in acorns, you can bet your little finger he does and if he wasn't the miller's second son, I'd give him an earful! But who listens to old Motik? Nobody." He jutted out his lower lip, like a wrinkled toddler. "Look, even you're sniggering at me!"

Kada patted his shoulder. "I'm not! And the baker wouldn't dare mix in the cheap flour for Gorcay, you know that very well. Probably sent you the pumpernickel meant for widow Zonia. She likes to chew on her bread like on a sap piece. Makes her bones and teeth harder, so she believes.

Anyway–" she lifted a finger as Motik was about to begin another complaint, "–it wouldn't do Gorcay any harm to forego his fluffy bread rolls for a day."

"Master Gorcay, you meant to say, my girl." Motik raised one owl-like eyebrow. "Don't get too used to the disrespect. The fine men will bear it with a smile for a time, then strike you down for it, just when you get all comfortable!" The cook made as if to pounce, his hands like claws raised above his head. Kada just laughed, tucking her greying red hair behind her ear.

"I'm no girl, and haven't been for many years now," she said, winking at Motik. "And Gorcay is too clever a man to strike a vedma. Besides, to strike me, Gorcay would have to catch me first, and your pastries got him too fat and slow for that!" She laughed at Motik's outraged expression. She transferred the ground herbs into a cup, and picked up the iron kettle from the fire, her hand carefully wrapped in a piece of cloth. When the hot water hit the herbs, a bitter smell came up from the cup.

Motik's nose twitched, but he said nothing.

"And where is your daughter this morning?" he asked, as Kada placed the cup on the tray, next to Gorcay's breakfast. "Is she joining the girls in town for the celebrations?"

"I haven't decided. I'll take the breakfast tray to Gorcay's room myself. Let the maid breathe a bit," she said, picking up the tray. It was pure silver, and cold to the touch. Her skin tingled as she carried it upstairs.

# CHAPTER 2

Sladyana glanced at her tea, cooling on the tray by her bed. The sun was already high, but the house was quiet, eerily so. Her day usually started early. There were plans to be made, people to be visited, estate work to be overseen.

Her grand ancestral house was eerily quiet. Sladyana knew there was work going on where she could not see it, yet her servants, understanding their mistress' wishes, kept out of sight on this day, communicating in whispers, as if a single word could shatter her peace.

At least beyond her gardens, the usual trade work continued uninterrupted. Carts rolling in, carts rolling out, their wheels' creaking as they passed the cargo to the river rafters. They took the precious wares through the turbulent waters, faster than any road, and cheaper too, which Sladyana appreciated whenever her own estate's produce was shipped to the far-off markets of Fiesna.

But none of that today. One day a year, she allowed herself a remembrance.

She sighed and reached for the fine porcelain cup, decorated with the painted blue flowers of Fiesna's mountains. At the foot of the bed Tula still slept soundly. Sladyana smiled and nudged the child with her foot. Tula just turned on her back and snored.

Sladyana drank her tea in three gulps then rolled off the

bed. She washed her face in the warm scented water laid out for her and ran her fingers through her long hair. Still black, even if only thanks to the powders sold to her maid.

On any other morning, Sladyana would ring a bell and the maid would come hurrying in, to fix her mistress' hair, and help her get dressed. But not today. Sladyana needed no attendants and hangers-on to witness her sad little tradition.

A rustling in the sheets alerted her to Tula. The girl rubbed her eyes and made a little motion with her hand.

"Good morning to you too, *slonechko moye*." Sladyana came up and stroked the girl's soft brown curls. "Get ready now, we have things to do."

Tula looked up at Sladyana with a question in her eyes. Tula could have been no more than six. She'd been a member of Sladyana Goroncheva's household for just over three years, having arrived barefoot and hungry. The servants were about to chase the child away, but Sladyana interjected. She wasn't sure why herself. Tula wasn't the child's real name, if she ever even had one. A mute, she had been most likely rejected by her own family. The farmers living in Fiesna often had trouble feeding themselves. A child that could not speak was likely to be judged a drain on the already meagre resources.

A game? The child moved her hands below her chin and tapped her wrist. She spoke in the language of their own, which Sladyana made sure remained a secret between them.

"Not quite a game." Sladyana pulled on a simple dress and quickly braided her hair, for comfort, not vanity. Nobody would see her in her garden, she had made sure of that. Not even Aunt Kasimira would dare disturb her on this sad anniversary. "There is winning in a game. In this one, the best you can hope for is not losing entirely."

* * *

They walked down the stone staircase of Sladyana's house. The woman rested her hand on the marble bannister, then raised it again, as if scalded. The stone was beautiful, yet so cold to the touch, her oversensitive skin couldn't bear it. The ghastly ancient portraits of the Goronchev family members haunted the quiet corridors, their features exaggerated to fit whatever the fashion of their day required. Tula trailed behind Sladyana, holding onto the hem of the woman's dress. The only noise came from the kitchens, and even that was subdued: some clanking of the utensils and the noise of the mortar grinding the herbs for Aunt Kasimira's bitter tea.

Tula pulled on Sladyana's skirt, trying to catch her eye. The woman ignored her. They went out the back into the private walled gardens. The hedges were yellowing already, the summer days nearly at an end.

Sladyana looked up at her house. When looked at like this, there was something rather ridiculous about the place, in spite of all its sombre grandeur. Sladyana and her aunt lived there alone, except for Tula. There were the servants, of course. But they couldn't give the house life, not really. There used to be friends and distant cousins, staying for months at a time sometimes. But not anymore. Sladyana still enjoyed her parties and the occasional guest, but she valued silence more now. A fact which didn't blind her to the fact that her house resembled a mausoleum more than it did a home these days. Perhaps it would have been different if... She didn't want to finish the thought. Such thoughts brought tears to her eyes, and she had things to do.

Tula found Sladyana's hand and squeezed it. The moment

she caught the woman's attention her hands started moving at a rapid speed.

Sladyana made a slashing gesture with her palm, cutting off any further questions. "Watch quietly if you wish or play over there. You're old enough to understand now."

Tula stared at her for a moment and then nodded sagely. She sat crossed legged in the grass, her hands resting lightly on her knees.

Sladyana sighed and sat opposite her. She wasn't sure why she brought Tula with her this time. After all these years, maybe she just wanted some reassurance that she wasn't entirely mad. She took out a small paring knife from the pocket of her skirt and rolled up her sleeve.

She paused for a moment, staring at the yellowing grass. She swallowed and ran the blade over her forearm.

Tula gasped, her small hands flying to cover her mouth. She began to gesture wildly.

"It's ok, *slonechko moye*, you will see." Sladyana forced a smile to her lips as the blood welled up in the slash on her arm and began to trickle down to the ground.

At first nothing happened. The red drops fell on the blades of grass and dribbled into the soil. A fear squeezed at Sladyana's heart. It had been so long. Perhaps the worst had happened.

Fifteen years was a long time. Enough for Sladyana's once taunt skin to begin to show fine lines, no matter how much she powdered her face. Enough time for her breasts to droop and small freckles to appear on her hands. Enough for her heart to shrivel to a cold hard thing. Enough for a child alone in the world to grow into a young woman. And bad things happened to young women alone in the world.

Sladyana shut her eyes tight.

Something tickled the side of her thigh and she turned back towards the ground, the weight of her despair from the moment before lifting from her shoulders.

The little white worms of the bone roots twisted out of the ground and soaked up Sladyana's blood. A sob escaped her throat.

Zemya still accepted her payment. That meant her Luba, her baby girl, was still alive, and still out there to be found.

For a moment longer Sladyana watched as the roots of the distant Great Tree pulled the red drops of her life deep into the earth. Then a movement caught her eye. She looked at Tula, whose fingers hovered above the ground. A filigree network of the bone roots twisted around the child's fingers and tickled the palm of her hand. Tula's brown eyes seemed to darken as a smile spread across her lips.

"What are you doing?" Sladyana said in a hoarse voice, her mouth suddenly dry.

Tula startled, as if awakened, and lifted up her hand. Something like guilt passed the child's face, and the bone roots receded back into the ground. Tula hung her head and hid her hand behind her back.

"What just happened?" Sladyana reached out. "Show me your hand."

Tula jutted out her lower lip, and, slowly, held out her palm for her guardian's inspection.

In the girl's hand, nestled like a pearl, was a single drop of hardened sap.


The lunch was a quiet thing. Sladyana liked to entertain, and the large dining room was designed to be filled with neighbours and friends, with musicians, and storytellers.

But today the food was already served when Sladyana walked into the darkened parlour. There was no music and nobody but her and Tula, who was already waiting in her usual place. The girl sat with her back rigid and straight, her eyes firmly glued to the plate in front of her. The sight softened Sladyana's heart somewhat.

"Sit next to me," she said.

Tula's face instantly broke into a huge smile, and the girl dutifully picked up her plate and cup and trotted around the long table to sit to Sladyana's left.

*Can I have it back?*

Sladyana raised an eyebrow and Tula's hands fell back in her lap.

The woman sighed and pulled out the piece of paper she kept in her pocket. She unrolled it between her index finger and thumb and picked up the piece of sap which the bone roots had given Tula. Sladyana looked at it for a moment more, holding it against the light of the candle. The sap was hardened to a pebble, its surface part porous, like some ancient chunk of honeycomb. Orange and red flames twisted within, with a black thread running through the centre. As black as coal, as black as a raven's wing, as black as Luba's fine downy hair, as it was when she disappeared. Sladyana's gift from Zemya. Her baby, the fruit of the life tree. Plucked from its branches with her own hands, paid for with blood.

Sladyana knew the moment she saw Luba that this child was meant for her. Behind the veined skin of the fruit, the baby was nestled like a stone, all smooth and perfect, with black hair, and eyes of blue, staring straight at her mother's face. She was surprised then, how natural it seemed. The two pods growing out of a single branch, shining with life. And from inside of one of them, Luba called to Sladyana. Sladyana became a mother the moment she laid eyes on her. Her baby, not grown in her belly, but meant for her, made for her.

"Did I miss anything?"

Sladyana raised her eyebrow and didn't look to the side, shaking the memory out of her head. "Only the warmth of the food, aunt."

"Well, a cold meal never hurt anybody, but if I've learnt anything over my long years it is that there's no hurrying three things in life: love, a decent meal and an old woman's shit."

Kasimira Krall settled herself beside her niece and leaned her walking cane against the table. "I see it's just as miserable and despondent an afternoon as I expected. I'm glad I didn't rush for it." She poured herself a glass of wine and glanced at Sladyana. "Are we to have some talk, or am I to depend on the mute for a conversation?" She nodded towards Tula who scowled. The child's survival instinct was intact, however, and she had the sense to partially hide under the table.

"Always happy to talk with you, Aunt."

"Well, of course you are, I'm delightful." Kasimira winked at her. Her once dark pupils were now paler and blue-rimmed, but she could still see inside the pocket and heart of any noble from a hundred paces away. She paused for a moment, scraping the side of her plate with her two-pronged fork. "So how was it?"

"She's still out there."

Kasimira closed her eyes and nodded. "That's my girl."

Sladyana reached out and squeezed the old woman's hand.

"We will find her one day, Aunt. She chose me, you know that. She chose me, and if she chose me then she will find her way back to us eventually."

# CHAPTER 3

Inog stretched his back, the crack of his bones loud enough to startle a finch off the pine bough. Inog rooted through the ground with his long snout, nostrils flaring at the tangy scent of the tubers and bulbs under the ground, along with the sweet smell of earthworms wriggling under the soil. Inog shook the last bit of dew off the bristles on his grey-black mane.

Another scent, old and faint as it was, assaulted his senses from the hut where he slept when in his human form, which was not often these days. It had been a while since his lover came to him, and when she wasn't there, he preferred the power and the strength of his boar body. It forced a kind of simplicity of thinking on him, chasing away the doubt and the loneliness. Things were clearer this way.

He pushed his head against a pine tree. The bark cracked and gave way, satisfying an itch as it went. He chewed on the fallen bark slowly. He hadn't the need to hurry, to cast around a furtive look. Neither wolf nor lynx would dare approach God Inog.

He overturned the earth one more time, this time to listen more than to satisfy a hunger. The bone roots whispered to him, his mother's voice urgent and displeased. A piece of the root broke off and curled around his left tusk. It twisted its body in a pattern, Zemya's idea of a caress.

Inog shook the bone root off, gently, so it wouldn't fall far to the ground. He grunted and trotted off into the woods, ignoring the goddess' exhortations. She could deal with her own problems; he needn't make them his own.

# CHAPTER 4

Gorcay's room was the finest in a very fine manor. Gossamer fabric hung in the windows, the glass panes keeping the fresh air out. Kada wrinkled her nose, as the sour night-sweat stench hit her nostrils.

Gorcay was still in his bed, large enough to fit four of him. He occupied himself by looking through the documents sent down every week from his warehouses, which speckled the land from Torlow to the great Emerald Sea in the south. His small over-the-lap desk, designed to sit over his legs, had an ink stand and was wide enough to allow for clean work. Still, Gorcay's mind worked too feverishly to control all the small nervous movements of his hand, and so the lovely fabric of both his nightshirt and his bedding had speckles of the black ink.

"Ah, finally," he said, raising his eyes as Kada entered the room. "Thought you got lost on the way somewhere."

She nodded and smiled, ignoring the complaint.

"I woke up early and you were not here to attend me. Where were you?" Gorcay shifted a bit, making space for Kada to sit on the bed beside him. He was not an old man, perhaps even a few years younger than Kada, but liked to play the role of an aged invalid, if only to be fussed over.

"As Torlow's vedma, I'm often needed by people other than yourself, as improbable as it might seem to you." Kada smiled and put the tray with Gorcay's breakfast on the small side table by his bed. "But today I was on my own business, as every woman ought to be before the dawn breaks."

"What business could you possibly have away from me?" he grumbled, as she gently took the pen out of his hand and picked up his work desk, to then replace it with the breakfast tray. "If you lived in my house instead of that ridiculous mud hut outside, I would be able to call you whenever I need you, day and night, and not suffer as I do now."

"And what an appealing prospect that is." Kada raised her eyebrow at him.

"Well, *I* find it appealing." Gorcay laughed at her expression. "Now, my foot's been hurting something awful. Been afraid to look at it."

"Then let me be brave for both of us." Kada sat on the bed and lifted the end of the down-filled duvet. She winced.

Gorcay threw his arms in the air, almost overturning his breakfast tray. "Well?"

"You're not going dancing anytime soon, that's for sure," she said, taking a small jar out of her apron pocket.

"I bet I could if you went with me." Gorcay picked up the cup with Kada's tonic, smelled it and put it back on the tray. "How about we give it a go?"

"Tonight's dancing is for the young." Kada smiled and gently began applying the honey and hemp salve onto the swollen skin around the toe joints. "And I have more pressing things to occupy my time."

Gorcay tucked into his breakfast. "Such as?"

"Such as looking after those who refuse to look after themselves. Forego that extra egg, if you will." She narrowed her eyes in disapproval. "Don't think I didn't notice Motik ladling it on."

Gorcay rolled his eyes. "You nag like my dearly departed wife used to."

"You pay me to nag you."

"And it costs me deep in the pocket! Don't think I don't know that!" Gorcay winced as Kada poked the swollen skin around his big toe. "Yet I don't mind it so much when it's coming from you. It's a talent of yours."

"I have many useful talents." Kada smiled, wrapping a clean bandage around Gorcay's foot to keep the salve in.

"So you do," Gorcay said with a smile. He somehow still had all his teeth, miraculous considering the number of sweet things he liked to eat. His blue eyes twinkled with humour. "I guess you were really made for it."

"For what exactly?" Kada stood up, picking up her things. She noticed the still-full cup on Gorcay's tray. "Drink that while it's hot."

"Why, for being a wife, of course." Gorcay sipped at the drink. "So how about it?"

"How about what?" Kada walked towards the window and opened it wide, letting the fresh air in.

"How about marrying me?"

Kada chuckled. "And be torn apart by your heirs? No, thank you. You can have your pick of the unmarried maids of Torlow. At least the ones who still don't know any better."

"Eh." Gorcay waved the notion away. "Who needs a silly young goose flouncing about. I'm no dancer and the girl would soon cast her eye about for a more vigorous partner than an old man like me. I'd rather have your company. And never you mind my heirs. My son doesn't care either way. I'm not sure he has the capacity to look beyond tomorrow, which at least means he doesn't worry unnecessarily. And my daughter would welcome the surety of their inheritance, with none of the burden of my old age wrestled upon her."

"I'd rather the surety of pay, with none of the burdens myself." Kada laughed and took the fork out of Gorcay's hand as he was about to tuck into the last fried egg.

Gorcay sniffed as if offended, though they'd had much the same conversation every morning for the last seven years. "You know," he said as Kada walked towards the door. "Your Secha will no doubt start her own life away soon enough. What will you do once she accepts one of the countless suitors lining up for her pretty green eyes and shiny red hair? Or else once she leaves flying on the wind as you vedmas like to do?"

"I'll worry when that time comes and no sooner," Kada threw back, as in jest, though the thought pained her. If she'd shown it though, Gorcay would needle the point endlessly. "I'll be back in two hours to check how the salve is working."

# CHAPTER 5

The thread ran silken-smooth between Secha's fingers. The wheel spun and spun, a blur in the early morning light, its steel surface gleaming. Secha's lips curved upwards, as the twisted floss poured through her hand. A strand of the thread caught on her sharp nail and the spell was broken. The wheel ground to a stop.

A scratch on the door startled her.

Secha stilled her breath. The scratch came again.

She didn't ask who it was. She didn't have to.

She sat on the dirt floor of the hut, her back to the woven reed door, her ear to the fabric stretched upon it. The breath on the other side. She could almost feel it in on her cheek.

A rustle sounded in the grass, and it was gone.

But it would be back.

# CHAPTER 6

Sladyana stood flanked by her servants on top of the steps overlooking her courtyard. The view stretched for over a mile and from the distance the column of carriages looked like a procession of ants, slowly making their way towards her home. The guests for the day were arriving in droves, their gilded carriages looking somewhat ostentatious in the daytime. By torchlight though, she knew they would glitter and sparkle like the finest jewels. Some of the carriages were adorned with the crests of Fiesna's finest families. Others made up for their lack of heritage with a show of wealth in the sumptuous decorations. Many of the horses wore plumes on their head harnesses after the Western fashion.

"I wonder how many roosters are freezing off their behinds for this decoration." Aunt Kasimira's thoughts seemed to mirror Sladyana's, as the old woman hobbled over, impatiently waving away the servant's offer of help. She turned back to her niece. "It seems a good horse is not enough for the fine people of Fiesna; they would have them fly next."

"Be nice, Aunt," Sladyana said with a crooked smile. "They are my guests after all."

"And what good would they be if they didn't provide an old woman with a chance of some sniping commentary?" Kasimira grinned, then shifted her weight with a wince.

Sladyana stayed quiet, knowing her aunt would hate being seen as feeble.

"I see you are wearing your finest threads for this picnic. Is he coming then?"

Sladyana self-consciously smoothed the front of her blue brocade dress with a peacock pattern on the belt.

"Be careful," Kasimira said. "He's either in it for the fun or your money. Neither makes it prudent for you to get too attached."

"Since when are you opposed to a little bit of fun? We have important guests tonight, not all of whom share my bed. Besides" –Sladyana brought a hand to her earlobe, checking the earring with the tips of her fingers– "a dress is just a dress, not some soppy declaration."

"A dress maybe not," Kasimira nodded and inclined her head closer to her niece. "But those ridiculous gold butterflies in your braids certainly are. You're a woman of five and forty, not fifteen. Be careful is all I'm saying." She put a huge smile on her face and spread her arms wide at the sight of the first guest, a fat woman in a loose green gown coming out of a particularly gaudy carriage. "Nadia Idlichevna! What a rare pleasure!" To Sladyana, however, she whispered, "How you enjoy spiting me. Why would you invite that halfwit?"

Sladyana chuckled and said with a smile on her lips, "So that you can gossip with her and about her all afternoon and leave me and Makail alone. Oh, and there he is."

A young man of twenty years-old or so trotted up the steps, overtaking the red-faced Idlichevna without as much as a glance. Tall, with thick blond hair, he wore a military-cut kaftan, expensive in its simplicity, with embroidered belt ends swishing around his knees. "Lady Goroncheva! Finally, you allow me to enter your presence, after banishing me so cruelly last week!" He took a deep bow, and kissed Sladyana's outstretched hand with a mischievous twinkle in his eye.

"And what about my presence?" Kasimira noted. "Have you missed it any?"

"As the ripe wheat misses the rain!" Makail made a low bow.

"Which is to say, not at all. Careful, young man, this old mare has a kick or two left in her." Kasimira gave her niece a wink and moved towards the other guests, who were by now crowding into the courtyard.

Makail stood next to Sladyana. "I was very happy to receive your invitation, having spent the last week fretting that I offended you." He nodded towards the other guests. "Though now I suspect I might have been right."

"Offended me?" Sladyana gave him an askance look. "How could you have possibly?"

"First you banish me from your presence on the flimsiest of excuses–"

"My excuses are never flimsy!" She offered a hand to a portly man with an impressive moustache, who was wiping his forehead after the exertion of climbing the few steps. "General Slovatchov, I am so glad you could make it!"

"I wouldn't have missed it for the world, *piekna moya*." The man gave Sladyana a sloppy kiss on her hand, his lips leaving a wet mark which she discreetly wiped against the skirts of her dress as he turned towards Makail. "And I see you have invited the merchant's son! Very well, I'm sure there will be a young filly or two at the party to be entertained, so that we grown people can talk in peace." He twirled his moustache in a self-satisfied way, the thumb of his left hand hooked casually behind his belt.

"I see you have done rather too much growing in the last few months, dear General," Makail flashed his teeth as the older man reddened. "In any case, I have already promised Lady Goroncheva I will escort her to the picnic tents, so I suppose we will have to enjoy your conversation later?"

Makail offered his elbow to Sladyana, who took it, but with her other hand gently touched Slovatchov's shoulder. "As always, the best for last, old friend."

The older man's expression instantly brightened, and he bowed deeply.

"Why do you insist on encouraging that man?" Makail said through gritted teeth as they led the procession of the guests towards the garden. Tents and parasols were already set up by a small army of servants, hired especially for the occasion. Long tables were laden with picnic fair: small pastries, cold cuts and thick-sliced bread featuring prominently. "He must be the most unpleasant man this side of Solevo. And he means to make you a stepmother to his brood of equally unpleasant children, you know."

"I merely invite him. He's an influential man, and amusing in his own way," Sladyana chuckled. "And his presence irritates you, which is only ever an added advantage."

"So, you admit you're trying to make me jealous?" He picked up a pastry and offered it to her.

"Nothing as common as that." She hid her face behind her fan and took a bite.

"I see your little pet is joining us?" Makail ate the rest of his pastry and licked his fingers. "I noticed her sneaking a slice of cheese off the table."

Sladyana looked to where he pointed and indeed Tula's bare foot was sticking out from under the tablecloth of one of the tables. She tsked. "She wasn't meant to, but I suppose it is too much to ask of a child to forego such an attraction. She's hardly in the way."

Makail wrinkled his nose but seemed to think better of disagreeing.


The afternoon progressed in pleasant and occasionally vicious chit-chat. Everyone was keen to make the most of the last warm days of the season, and the guests' laughter was heard above the music.

Once the guests had eaten their fill, Sladyana stood from her rug and clapped her hands to get everyone's attention. The servants walked among the assembled and handed out woven baskets. "And now for the mushroom competition. You all know the rules! Only the pine milk caps, and the brown and red caps. Toadstools and the like mean an instant forfeit. I will have no poisonings at my party!" She winked at an old matron sitting on one of the chairs provided. The woman, a four-time widow by the latest calculation, laughed and bent her head back towards her newest companion, who was clearly yet to be warned off.

Sladyana put a sheer shawl over her hair and took one of the baskets, hooking it over her arm. "The trumpet will sound at the passing of an hour! Good luck to you all!" She took Makail's arm. As they passed Tula, she winked at the child. "Take Nasha with you, *slonechko moye*! Pick me the biggest milk caps!" The girl jumped with excitement and grabbed the servant's hand, following the guests towards the tree line.

The woodland behind Sladyana's gardens became filled with the shadowy figures of her guests, who walked with their eyes fixed on the ground, hoping to spot a familiar shape hiding among the moss. Those intent on picking things other than mushrooms moved discreetly towards the thicker parts of the oak forest, leaving the rest to their meditation.

"She's joining the game as well?" Makail whispered.

"And what harm could it do?" Sladyana raised her eyebrows at the young man, who made a face. "There's one!"

"That's a beauty!" Makail bent down and picked the brown cap, partially hidden by the fallen leaves. He cut the stem with a small knife and placed it in his companion's basket. "Only I wish I didn't feel you use the foundling's presence to keep me at arm's length."

"I also wish you wouldn't feel such nonsense." A soft gasp caught Sladyana's attention. She peered into the forest, but all seemed calm. There was little wind and only the tops of the trees swayed gently above their heads.

Makail scratched his head. "It must be one of our competitors." He flashed a smile. "Either they found a particularly impressive mushroom or abandoned the search altogether for more pleasant pursuits."

Sladyana ignored him and walked ahead to investigate.

"It's nothing! Where are you going?"

There was something there, a flash of colour, a jolt of movement. She squinted, trying to see beyond the shrubs and wild rose bushes.

And there, by a fallen oak, stood Tula. The broken forest giant dwarfed the child, the bare branches arching above her small frame. Her basket lay on the ground, and her arms hung limp at her sides. The servant meant to look after her was nowhere to be seen.

Something like fear squeezed Sladyana's heart. Her head

was swimming, and she couldn't focus her eyes. A hint of red moved by the tree. Crystal blue eyes, and a long snout. And the bone roots. They came out of the ground, cradling Tula's feet; their filigree cage closing around her ankles.

Sladyana screamed.

The noise seemed to shake Tula out of her stupor and the roots receded back into the ground.

The fox looked at Sladyana and barked, a strange screeching sound, so unlike that made by Sladyana's hounds. Makail jumped out of the woods, swinging a large branch.

"Away with you! Shoo!" He shouted at the fox.

The fox appeared unafraid, a calculating look crossing its eyes. When Makail got closer, the animal shot like an arrow between the man's legs, quickly sinking its teeth into the flesh of his calf. Then the fox ran in a red blur, disappearing into the woods.

Sladyana knelt next to Tula, ignoring Makail's loud swearing.

"What happened, *slonechko moye*? Why were you alone? What did the fox do? Are you hurt?" She stroked the girl's hair, her cheek, and showered Tula's face with kisses.

Tula gazed up into Sladyana's eyes, a strange look in her face. Her hands moved through the air, in a pattern so quick, Sladyana could barely follow. The same words repeated over and over.

*It called me. It will be back.*

# CHAPTER 7

Kada watched her daughter as Secha attended her hives, checking them ahead of the winter months which, in the land of Fiesna, always arrived sooner than expected. The Autumn was now in full swing, and the wet soil squelched under Secha's woven soles. The girl wore a simple tunic and trousers for the task, puffing on a long pipe and occasionally releasing clouds of smoke which lulled the bees to a stupor, stilling their buzzing.

The clouds rolled by above them, their grey bellies full and heavy. Kada wrapped her shawl closer around her shoulders, grateful for the good roof on their home. The hives stood in the gardens behind Gorcay's house, tucked away behind a tall hedge. Far enough that his workers didn't complain, yet close enough that he could claim patronage of Secha's efforts.

No honey in Torlow was sweeter than Secha's and no bees had a more powerful sting. They had patients coming from as far as Ortovo hoping Secha's bees' venom would heal their rheumatism. They'd leave with their skin red, itchy and pockmarked and claim they'd never felt better.

"You're hovering, *mamusha*," Secha said, without looking back. She reached inside the hive with her bare hands and pulled out a brood comb, which she inspected carefully before slotting it back in.

"I like to watch you work with them," Kada said, perching on an old tree-stump used for splitting wood.

"It's not that interesting, really," Secha said through the corner of her mouth, though Kada could see the twinkle in her daughter's eye as she put her index finger into the hive. She pulled out the queen, who sat there content and fat, surrounded by a couple of anxious workers. Secha brought the queen close to her lips and whispered something Kada couldn't quite make out.

"All in order?" Kada asked.

Secha frowned and shook her head. "There's a blight on the fields beyond Morshe."

"The earth is readying for winter sleep," Kada said, skewing her head to the side. "Not even the bees could possibly know that."

"Mine can," Secha said, putting the queen back in the hive. She picked up the painted lid and carefully replaced it on top.

"I don't know that I like you talking to them." Kada flexed her toes, turning her face towards the still-warm-sun.

"I don't talk much, I mostly listen."

"Not sure that's much better."

Secha came up to her mother and squeezed herself onto the stump next to her. "You were the one who gave me my first hive, remember?"

"I do."

Secha leaned her head on her mother's shoulder. "It calms me to be around them." She looked up and smiled at Kada. "I feel complete here."

Kada tensed up and put her arm around Secha. "No reason for you to feel incomplete anywhere."

"Tell me again how you chose me," Secha whispered.

Kada looked at her with surprise. "How come?"

"I haven't heard it in a while," Secha said. "I feel like I need reminding."

"I hadn't thought to bring you back with me," Kada said. "I went to the tree for another. And yet, in the twin pod, right beneath its leafy skin, there you were."

"There I was," Secha repeated in a whisper.

"I was about to turn around and leave."

"But I couldn't let you."

"No." Kada kissed Secha's head. "You looked down at me, your eyes green just like mine, your hair my exact shade of red."

"Like I was grown for you," Secha offered, a grin stretching her face. She emptied the contents of her pipe on the ground and ground out the embers with her heel.

"You looked at me and I knew I couldn't leave you there on that tree, no matter what." Kada nodded. "Took me a while but I went back, cut the stem of your pod, and saw it pop open, your lovely face looking straight at me. Then I brought you home."

Kada held her daughter's hand. "Do you remember? Any of it?"

Secha focused her eyes on the beehive, her shoulders tensed. "I try not to." She went quiet.

"Good." Kada's shoulders sagged with relief. She rubbed Secha's back and forced a smile to her lips. "The less you remember, the farther the fox. And soon my love," she said into Secha's hair, "soon you will forget it all. I promise."

# CHAPTER 8

"It's lovely, mama." Secha twirled round, the beads on the hem of her wide belt knocking against each other. Her bare feet pounded the bare dirt floor of the hut they shared. It was a small stone building leaning against Gorcay's great house. It was simply furnished, with a single bed, a bench and a small table where the mother and daughter often shared their evening meal. It held no finery, their home, but it was tidy, and always warm, with plenty of fuel for their fires. Since Gorcay had been unsuccessful in convincing Kada to move to the great house, he at least made sure they did not lack for the simple comforts.

"You're dancing already!" Kada laughed. Seeing Secha like this, laughing, happy, light on her feet, was everything. Even if Kada would have to pay for it later with an anxious heart.

"I wasn't sure you would let me go." Secha sat heavily on the bench in the corner, her bare feet hovering off the ground for a moment.

"Why not?" Kada nibbled on a piece of bread she'd liberated from Gorcay's kitchens. Motik was right after all, the good dark bread was not quite fancy enough for Gorcay's taste.

"Because you *told* me you might not let me go." Secha raised her eyebrows at her mother. She ran her fingers through her curly red hair, so much like her mother's when Kada was younger. Remarkable really, the similarity between them. Kada often marvelled how the tree knew to tailor Secha just for her, carving her face till the rounded cheeks and the almond eyes were just like Kada's, so nobody could say Secha didn't grow from her womb.

"I can always change my mind. There's still plenty of time to do nothing of interest whatsoever," Kada said, battling the smile that was already twisting her lips.

"You could, but then think of all the hearts I will fail to break!" Secha put her hand dramatically over her eyes, like an actress from the market-day plays.

"Take care not to entice *too* many." Kada managed a smile.

"Don't worry, mama. I'm not as stupid as that." Secha kissed her mother on the cheek. "I will be heavy of foot and dull of wit." She twirled, her green eyes sparkling in the evening light.

"Somehow I'm not sure you can manage that," Kada laughed, in spite of herself.


Kada walked her daughter to the market square, which was decorated with sprigs of pine, cut with gold sickles by the priestesses. Their sap sanctified the ground where the young and the old alike celebrated the last of the warm months, and together braved the onset of winter. Secha waved at her friends and ran off, leaving her mother a coin lighter and a heartache heavier. Kada walked towards a hot mead stall and bought some of the spiced drink. The taste of honey hit the back of her mouth and tickled her throat as she sipped slowly, looking at the crowd.

"I see Secha with her friends," The woman at the stall,

ruddy-cheeked, doubtless from consuming too much of her own wares, leaned forward with a conspiratorial tone. "It's good you brought her this year. There was talk about whether you would, you know."

"And who did the talking?" Kada sipped the drink without looking at the woman. Mead drank on the night of the Mokosy celebrations was said to allow those drinking it to see into the invisible world of Ort, of the soul of everything. But Kada suspected that even if that were true, then this watered-down brew would be barely enough to do so. "Secha's only fifteen. I'd be well within my rights to hold her back another year if I wished to."

"Your rights, yes, but it would be hardly sensible to keep your daughter home, like she was a child still. Not with the news that's been spreading across the whole of Fiesna these past few months." The mead seller raised her eyebrows and tapped the side of her nose conspiratorially, pleased at Kada's surprised expression.

"What do you mean?"

"Those who meet and are not above chatting with the common folk of Torlow could tell you," the woman said. "Looks like there's some news don't reach the fine people of Gorcay's household!"

"If the news is worth knowing, share it," Kada said. She glanced towards the crowd of revellers. Too many people for Kada to spot Secha, who was no doubt getting ready for the dance.

Kada's throat felt dry and scratchy all of a sudden. She took another sip of the heated mead, but the sweetness and the pleasure of it was gone somehow and all she felt now was burning liquor.

"I'm surprised you don't know, tell you the truth." The

stall woman wasn't about to let go of this opportunity for crowing. "Zemya's not happy, they say. There's talk of trees falling by the borders, rot spreading through their leaves, the bark peeling. The fox is coming for the children again."

"The fox is always coming," Kada said. "Sooner or later." She turned her head away and looked at the crowd over her steaming cup.

A familiar figure moved towards her, dressed in a moss-green tunic and rough-spun trousers, with a gold-thread belt running across his trim waist. Some looked up at the strange man, noticing his broad shoulders and dark eyes. Most looked away quickly though, something about the man not encouraging a closer inspection.

He locked eyes with Kada and smiled. She didn't speak until he was right in front of her, so close she could feel the smell of moss and dead leaves on him.

"I wasn't expecting you," she said, resisting the temptation to put her hand on his chest.

"It appears I need to go where I'm not invited just to get a glimpse of you these days," he said.

"A glimpse of me is all you'll get if you get the townsfolk's tongues wagging." Kada looked at him, then shot her eyes to the left to signal for him to stand beside her. He obeyed quickly so to anybody passing they might seem strangers, both enjoying the anticipation of the impending celebrations.

"And why are you concerned about the townsfolk knowing you're admired by tall handsome men?" Inog whispered, looking at the crowd. He ran his fingers through his thick, greying black hair, which immediately flopped right back over his eyes. "I'd have thought you'd enjoy the notoriety."

"I enjoy people not knowing my business." Kada sipped a

bit more of her drink and continued looking for Secha. She thought she got a glimpse, only for another young woman to move in front and block the view. "So why are you here?"

"Can't I enjoy the celebrations intended for my brother and sister?" Inog turned slightly away, as if his attention had been caught by something in the crowd, but at the same time stepped closer towards Kada, without touching her. He was so close she could feel the heat emanating off his body.

"More like very distant cousins," Kada said with a small smile.

"Careful now, lover," Inog said. "We gods are touchy. Now–" he peered around the crowd. "Where's that sharp-tongued child of yours?"

"I'd like to see her myself." Kada stood on her tiptoes. The musicians were tuning their instruments, the discordant sounds of tightened fiddle strings almost lost in the hum of people talking and laughing. "There!"

She pointed towards a flash of red curls. Secha was standing third in the girls' line as the music started. Now the crowd had separated, Kada could see her daughter clearly. She shone, separate from the others like a rose in a cabbage patch. Kada's heart swelled with pride.

The pairs moved rhythmically to the march music, each third beat a low dip, which lengthened the step as they wove in and out of the intricate figures. Sometimes their arms were arched above the fellow dancers' heads, sometimes clasped in a chain weaving through. The music rose as the sky turned dark, the moon giving the revellers an eerie look.

The bonfires were lit. The music changed rhythm, getting faster and faster as the drums joined in. The dancers separated from their partners and each young woman spun in a circle, their skirts puffing out with the movement, opening like night lilies. Kada smiled, her hands moving, seemingly of their own accord, clapping out the time. Even Inog seemed transfixed by the performance.

The dancers jumped over the bonfires, flames licking their feet. Each jump was accompanied by a collective gasp from the crowd, followed by appreciative hollering and whooping once the dancer hit the ground safely.

Kada caught Secha's eye. Her daughter's cheeks seemed to glow in the light, her sharp white teeth glistening as she grinned. Kada held her breath when Secha lowered her body in a run-up to the jump. She sped up and leapt high above the bonfire. Kada could feel the heat from the flames on her face, though she stood a few good paces away. The fire distorted her vision, but in the split moment it took Secha to glide above it, Kada's eyes locked with another's on the other side. The glint of narrowed pupils was there and in the next moment was gone. Kada called out to Secha, but her daughter was already hidden in the crowd, once more spinning with the others.

"What's wrong?" Inog turned to her, his face serious, but she didn't look at him.

A rivulet of cold sweat ran down Kada's back. She dropped her drink and ran between the dancers, upsetting the movement, the rhythm of the drum unmatched by her frantic movement.

"Secha!" she screamed, but no reply came, as the girls and boys of Torlow twirled around her, their laughter and whooping drowning out Kada's voice.

A glint of the face, the almond eyes, the narrow smile getting wider. She saw it, there, and then there. A dancer passed in front of her, and the face was gone. Had she imagined it?

"Watch it!" an angry voice called out, as someone's shoulder brushed hard against her. Once more she called out, her voice thin and weak to her own ears. A blind fear caught her, and she struggled against the pull of the dancers, tears streaming down her face, her red hair escaping from the tight bun on her head and falling around her shoulders. She must have looked like a wild thing, her eyes wide and her mouth twisted, but she didn't care. Her arms outstretched, she battled her way through the crowd which seemed to barely register her presence, the unwelcome trespasser on the holy celebrations.

Someone's hands grabbed her by the shoulders and pulled her out of the crowd. She struggled like a hare against the snares, but the hands only dug deeper into her flesh.

A voice called out to her, but Kada couldn't make out the words. She turned her sharp nails on her assailant, pulling and tearing. The arms held her tight though, and a soothing voice kept repeating something into her ear. "Kada, Kada, stop. Stop now."

Stop what? She couldn't. She looked for her daughter, her daughter was lost. She was gone, she was taken, she was right in front of her.

"Mama, it's OK, it's OK, I'm here." Secha's moon-round face was in front of her own, showering kisses on Kada's wet cheeks. The relief shook a sob out of Kada.

"Let's get her out of here," Inog said, holding onto Kada.

She was pulled roughly out of the crowd, people watching her as she went, her hand holding on tight to Secha's.

She barely knew where they were leading her. She leaned on them both, the warmth of their bodies a soothing comfort. She focused on that, her feet moving mechanically. Vaguely aware they'd left the festivities behind them, Kada sighed as the calming darkness enveloped them. She wasn't quite aware how much the light of the torches and bonfires bothered her till they'd left them behind. She was lulled by the rhythm of walking, not allowing herself to think of what had happened. Not till the familiar woven door closed behind them, and she was sitting on the bed she shared with Secha.

"Don't worry, *mamusha*, I'm right here, I'm not going anywhere," Secha said, as she pulled her hands out of her mother's tight grip. "I will build up the fire and boil the water for some tea. Chamomile will calm you." Panic once more began to build up in Kada's throat and she once more moved to grasp Secha's hand in hers.

"Let her go. The girl has sense. And she's right here, where you can watch her."

Kada looked up through tear-hazed eyes. For a moment she didn't recognise the severe-looking face. Then her hands flew to her mouth. "Inog!" Shame pushed its way to the front, the relief she felt fading away as the full realisation of what she'd done washed over her. "I'm so sorry, I–" Her eyes darted around, as she struggled for something to say.

"'Sorry' is a word for strangers." Inog pulled himself up a small stool and sat, taking Kada's hand between his own. "You don't need to apologise to me. But tell me what it was. Was it a zmora? An upior you saw in the crowd?"

"No, it was nothing, just..." Kada hesitated and closed her eyes for a moment. "It was nothing at all. I got confused and overreacted."

"That's interesting," Inog said, letting go of her hand and leaning back, folding his arms on his chest.

"What is?"

"You have never lied to me before," he said.

"That you know of," she said, forcing a light-hearted smile.

"Yes." Inog didn't smile at the joke. "The first lie that I know of." He stood up and walked up to Secha, who stood very still, more so than any girl Kada had ever seen.

Inog gently lifted the girl's chin with his index finger and seemed to inspect her face. Secha stared into the god's eyes fearlessly, her eyebrows knitted together in annoyance. He nodded and pulled his hand away. "She'll have to watch out for that. No human born can be as still as this. A stillness like that could betray her all on its own." He scratched his chin, looking at the ceiling of the hut. "Have you had signs of the fox?"

"Not any more than usual." Kada looked at the floor.

"Is that another lie?" Inog stared hard at her. "You know I only want to help you."

"Until you don't."

Anger flashed across Inog's face. He seemed to grow, his tall frame filling the small hut, the teeth in his mouth elongating. And then, in a moment, he was back to how he was.

"I care about you. About your daughter."

"Until you don't." Kada repeated, watching his face.

"I'm more than Zemya's son." Inog sat on the bed next to Kada and it creaked under his weight.

Kada put her hand on his cheek. He leaned his face into it, and they touched foreheads. "Secha is nearly sixteen. I must keep her hidden till then. The fox's eyes will turn to yellow and the blood in my daughter's veins will turn red and then I can be open with you."

"I would never betray you," Inog whispered, his eyes closed. Kada's heart filled at the pleading in her lover's voice.

"And I trust you," she said. "As long as Zemya doesn't test you."

"And eventually she tests us all." He moved away and stood up.

"She does." Kada nodded and locked eyes with Secha, who stood as still and as pale as a candle in her white dress, her red curly hair a flame around her face.

# CHAPTER 9

"So how was it?" Gorcay asked Kada, as they walked around his warehouse. It was an impressive red brick building, and he was proud of it. Some of the rich men liked to distance themselves from their roots. The great families' professions, once they'd served their purpose in elevating them, were often neglected, sometimes right to the point of ruination, in the hope that the Fiesna families of a more exalted lineage might accept the newcomers into their social circles. "Fools and idiots," Gorcay would call those families. "If you don't know who you are, others will be more than happy to tell you anyway." He himself was never happier than when among his wares.

"Well?"

This shook Kada from her thoughts. She eyed him carefully. "Why d'you ask?"

Gorcay quietly counted the bales of linen on the shelf and jotted the number down with a pencil before replying. "I'd like to know how the celebrations I have largely funded went, is all." A curious expression crossed his face. He rubbed his chin, where a scratch rose in an angry welt. "Do I need an ulterior motive beyond satisfying a curiosity?"

"Of course not, sorry–" Kada looked down, flustered. How much did the man know? Everything, most likely.

"I forgive you for the impudence," he said with a smile, his eyes once more on Kada's face. "So?"

"So, it was a lovely celebration." She stared him down. "The food was excellent, if the mead was a bit too watered down; the dancers were graceful and the Mokosy bonfires licked the skies."

"All sounds very normal and rather boring," he said. "These spices are going straight to Zonvrost, man, you can't keep them so close to the window!" He shouted at the two workers who were about to place a heavy chest in the dampest part of the building. "If they make their way to the Imperial Court covered in mildew, I will send you with the next batch for the roast!"

"Yhmm," Kada muttered.

"That is interesting to me, you see," he said, turning to her again. "Because I heard it was not as boring as you make it out."

"Accounts vary." Kada walked up to an open chest and ran her fingers across the embroidered silk inside. It had an intentional coarseness to it, which better exposed the fineness of the thread.

"Beautiful, isn't it?" he said. He'd walked up to Kada quietly without her noticing. She pulled her hand away, startled.

"Yes," she said, feigning indifference.

"It would suit you," Gorcay said, picking up the fabric, which turned out to be a wide shawl, the colour of the sea, neither completely blue nor green, shimmering in the light. With one quick movement he threw it around her shoulders, so it fell in a drape over her red curls. "See?" He smiled. "Beautiful."

Kada reddened, aware of the eyes of the men working.

"Ridiculous." She pulled the fabric off. "Even if I could afford such luxuries, what would a vedma do with something like this? Women in labour and men breathing their last rarely care what I wear."

"No, perhaps not," he said, eyeing her strangely.

She folded the shawl and passed it to him. He put it back in the chest. "Why did you call me here this morning?" she asked.

"It's an exciting day for me," he said. "We've had our biggest order yet from the Imperial Court. The fineries passing my warehouse today are such as have rarely been seen in Fiesna. I thought you might want a look."

She arched an eyebrow.

"And I'd hoped you'd share with me what exactly happened last night." He turned his face away but from the reddening of his neck Kada could tell he was annoyed. "But I see keeping things secret is rather a habit with you these days."

"What have you heard?"

He laughed mirthlessly. "Is there a chair I can use here or am I to stand on attention till the rooster crows?" he called out and a nervous-looking clerk ran up with a stool.

Gorcay sat down, his large frame straining the wood till it creaked. He folded his hands over the notebook in his lap and looked up at Kada.

"I was told the vedma I employ suddenly turned into a real shrieker, a klikusha, who ran through the crowd as if the dead possessed her body." There was not a shred of a smile on his face as he spoke. "I heard she interrupted the celebrations, possibly causing offence to the gods, which–" he raised his hand in case Kada was to interrupt. "–for myself, I neither believe nor would care about if I did. But

I do care about the reputation of those I employ. Because it rather reflects upon me and my business, you see."

Kada's eyes darted around the room. She slowed her breathing and forced a smile to her lips. "It was just silliness. A moment of madness overtook me. I must have drunk too much mead and I thought I saw Secha trip and hurt herself."

Gorcay straightened his legs, watching Kada carefully. He was still a handsome man, though overindulging in food and drink had softened his once powerful figure. Still, as he eyed Kada, he seemed more like a bear and not her less-than-resilient patient, and she didn't like being the one under scrutiny.

"You're a sensible woman," Gorcay said, taking out a small pipe, hooking it over the fold of his wide belt. "And I know I've given you cause to think me less so. But have I given you cause to think me stupid?" He slowly filled the pipe, and held it out, his eyes still on Kada. One of the clerks hurried over with a flaming splinter from the fire in the corner of the warehouse. It was always ablaze to keep the damp out.

After a while, Kada shook her head.

"Good." Gorcay nodded. He took the first puff and coughed. "Though it took you a moment longer than my vanity would have liked." He leaned forward, resting his elbows on his knees, and used the tip of his pipe to point at Kada. "You're not so silly as to go into a panic over a grown daughter's fall. You were screaming Secha's name like the Homen was after you, I have heard as much." He narrowed his eyes "Do you know why I have asked you to speak to me here?"

Kada hesitated. "I'm sure you have more than one reason."

Gorcay laughed. "Indeed. But let me divulge one at least." He made a sweeping gesture around the warehouse's handsome interior. "I have built this. All of this. The connections, the good will of the townsfolk, of the magistrates. I have set up trading partnerships from the Green Sea to the Tolusian steppes. This warehouse is just one of many, dotted along the road that leads right to our Tsarica's door. So, take it in, look around you."

"You want to impress me?" Kada raised an eyebrow.

"No." Gorcay looked at her strangely. "I assume you already are impressed, or else you haven't been paying attention these last seven years. I am reminding you that so much of what I have depends on what I know and what I find out. And so, after yesterday I find myself in a highly uncomfortable situation, and, moreover, one quite unfamiliar to me." He took another puff. "So, my vedma, since when are the wolves at your door and why haven't I heard of them before?"

"There are no wolves–"

"Don't lie to me," Gorcay said, a dangerous edge in his voice. "You bring trouble to my town, to my door, I will know of it. Don't think to lie to me again."

Kada and Gorcay stared at each other for a while.

"You're right," Kada said, finally. "I have been hiding things from you. As I have the right to. But" –she raised her hand as Gorcay's face began turning red– "I owe you an explanation. There's someone who means me harm, from my old life, before I came to Torlow." She lowered her eyes, and wrung her hands, as she felt Gorcay begin to soften. "I thought I saw his face in the crowd. I thought he meant to hurt Secha."

"That makes sense," Gorcay nodded. If he doubted Kada's

word, he didn't show it. He rubbed his chin where the shaving nicks itched still. "Why didn't you just tell me?"

"I thought we were safe and that he was either dead and gone or else had forgotten all about us," Kada said, keeping her eyes low.

"Are you sure it was him then?" Gorcay asked. "I will have my men look for him. If he's there, I will root him out!"

"No," Kada shook her head. "I really think it was a trick of light. There's no way he'd know to look for us here."

"I don't like it," Gorcay said, chewing his lip. He sat up straight and smacked his leg, an idea occurring to him. "You will move to the big house! That way if it *was* him, you'll be safe."

Kada opened her mouth to protest, but Gorcay was already standing up. "I will not have my people murdered in the ramshackle huts mere feet from my home, not when I have rooms and servants' quarters aplenty, and food to feed you and fuel to warm you. No," he said. "Don't think of protesting. There's young Secha's safety to think of as well. Collect your things and come over to the big house. There's a bedroom free on the top floor you can take."

"I–" Kada started. She lowered her face so that Gorcay would be unable to see her smile and whispered. "I accept."

"Very well. That is one problem sorted." Gorcay laughed, wincing as he put his weight on his swollen foot. "Collect your things and come over. Motik will show you to the room."

Kada nodded and turned towards the door.

"Oh, and Kada?" Gorcay's voice stopped her. He spoke quietly, as if unsure of himself all at once. "I also heard... Well, I heard there was another man there. A tall man who carried you out of the crowd..."

"A stranger," Kada said, without looking back. "Just a kind stranger."

"Very well." Some cheerfulness came back to Gorcay's voice. "Very well, be off then."

# CHAPTER 10

The hounds sniffed at the ground, pulling on their leashes. The moon shone brightly, but the forest was a black cave, the dense canopy obliterating all traces of light.

"It might be more prudent to go in the morning." General Slovatchov scratched his head under his hat. "It's never wise hunting in the dark." The general's servant carried his master's gun behind him, jumping every time one of the dogs barked.

"If you wish to turn back, General," Makail said, leaning the long nozzle of his rifle on his shoulder, "I am sure nobody will count it against you. Old eyes can't adjust as well to the dark after all. You might accidentally shoot yourself in the foot. In any case," he spread his arms wide to indicate the half dozen or so hunters gathered, "as you see we don't lack for able-bodied men. I'm sure you wouldn't wish to slow us down."

"I hunted long before your mother first spread her legs, pup, and I will hunt long after the world strips you of that white smile." Slovatchov's moustache twitched, as it always did when he was annoyed. "Just be sure you don't stand between me and the quarry."

Makail looked like he was about to say something, but stopped himself at the sight of Sladyana, flanked by two torch-bearing servants, striding towards the hunting party.

She wore wide trousers tucked into her knee-high boots, and a short *kontush* jacket with a gun tucked behind the wide woven belt. She carried a long rifle in her hand and her braided hair was tied up high on her head.

"Are you adamant, then, that you wish to come with us?" Slovatchov shifted uncomfortably.

"You are coming with *me*, old friend," Sladyana said. She didn't smile to soften her words. Her eyes were focused on the tree line, her jaw jutted out. "Friends!" she called out to those gathered. "Thank you for joining me tonight! The blight of the thieving fox has come to my land once again, and this time it will not live!"

"We have children too, Sladyana Goroncheva." One of those assembled, Sladyana's neighbour, tipped his hat. "And we will not let the fox take them!"

"It's dark so we must be careful," Sladyana said. "The fox might have its tricks too. We hunt together, the hounds at the front. We will comb through the forest in a line. Make sure the beast can't escape." She took the leash of one of the hounds and led the party toward the forest.

Sladyana signalled to the servants walking on either side of her to move forward, the light of their torches casting an orange glow on the gnarled branches of the trees. She walked carefully, placing the toes first, not trusting the ground. The mosses and the leaves underfoot released their wet scent as Sladyana trod on them.

A few bats flew overhead and Sladyana's hound twitched its ear at their squeaking. There was no talking now, all the hunters focused on their task. A nervous energy filled the air.

A spiderweb brushed against her face and she flinched, pulling the sticky strands from her cheek.

Suddenly, one of the dogs to her right let out a little whine. She snapped her head around and saw it pulling on its leash, paws worrying the ground. The pressure built in its throat till it was released as a bark.

"It's got the scent!" The man holding the leash called out in triumph. Sladyana's dog then picked up the scent too, its whole body turning rigid with excitement. It began pulling Sladyana along the path, a sense of urgency in its soft barks and growls. The hunters walked closer together now, forming a curved line, like the blade of a sickle.

A feeling of excitement washed over the party and there was a nervous laugh from one of the Sladyana's neighbours. Her face remained immobile though, the rush of blood in her ears making her deaf to all else.

A stifled scream came from Slovatchov, as he tripped on a branch; his hand released the leash when he made contact with the ground. His hound instantly shot into the forest in the pursuit of the prey.

"After it!" Slovatchov called out as his servant pulled him up. He rushed ahead, the twin flames of the servant's torches lighting the way.

"Wait! We should stick together." Makail made as if to follow, but hesitated, looking towards Sladyana for guidance. She mouthed "go" and so, with a loud curse, he ran after the general.

Some others of the party took it as a signal to release their hounds as well. They rushed into the woods baying loudly, a horde of invaders in the quiet space of the night. They tore through the undergrowth, their owners struggling to keep up behind them. More than one of the hunters tripped in the pursuit, scratching his hands and face.

Sladyana breathed in quick and shallow breaths as she

ran, her hand gripping the rifle for comfort. She caught the sight of Slovatchov, his balding head bare, his hat lost somewhere in the excitement.

The small man, gripped by the excitement, seemed to forget his age and trotted at a respectable pace. He pointed and shouted "There it is! I saw the scoundrel's tail! It's not far!" He whooped in triumph.

And then Sladyana saw it. A movement between the gnarled roots, a hint of eyes reflecting the torchlight. Grey on grey; the darkness confusing. "Stay together!" she called out, but her voice was lost among the furious barking and the excited cries of the hunters. The bloodlust gripped the party as they broke their line formation, running into the darkness.

Makail appeared close to Sladyana and gently touched her elbow. They exchanged a look and both broke into a run again, holding their rifles close to their sides, their servants trotting close by, lighting the way.

"What is this?" Makail whispered, as they came to a clearing, where no clearing should have been. The tree line itself seemed to shift and undulate, as if pulled and pushed by some invisible force.

Sladyana felt bile rise up in her throat as she looked to the earth. Zemya's bone roots twisted like worms under her feet. "Where are the others?" she said.

"My Lady, there!" Her servant pointed. A shot rang through the air and then another.

Makail's face brightened as a number of orange torch lights floated in the distance. "They're all there! They must have got it!" He took a step forward, but Sladyana pulled him back, so hard he nearly fell over.

"Look closely," she said. "There are too many."

He peered into the dark again and counted. Even if their party had been doubled, there were far too many lights ahead.

"And look!" She pointed to the ground in front of him. The man squinted. A deep hole had opened up in front of Makail's feet.

"You would have broken your neck if you'd gone."

He nodded, his expression grim. "At least we know we have the right fox." As he was saying the words, the trees seemed to shift again, and rose around them once more, the illusion of a clearing gone.

"It's too dangerous to stay here," Makail said. "The fox knows too many tricks."

"No," she said. "I won't lose it again. You go back if you like. I'm going." And she motioned for the torchbearers to follow her, giving the hole a wide berth.

Makail hesitated for a moment, and then followed with a curse.


They walked quietly for a while, following the distant barking. Sladyana's own hound whined on its lead, nearly bursting with the pent-up energy. She gave its head a pat.

Sudden shouting broke the silence.

"It could be another trick," Makail said, clutching his rifle in a white-knuckled grip.

They proceeded carefully, testing the ground with each step.

Shots rang out one after another, and a blood-curdling scream echoed through the forest, followed by dogs' whining.

Sladyana could feel Makail's eyes on her, but she wouldn't

show fear. She was close, she knew she was. She could taste metal in her mouth, and she realised she'd bit the inside of her cheek.

The voices were getting closer, and she called out to make sure the overzealous hunters wouldn't shoot at them.

After a few more steps, a scene of chaos revealed itself among the moss-covered stones and trees. One of the hunters was on the ground, bone protruding through a wound in the leg.

"Sladyana! Makail!" Another hunter turned to them, something like a relief crossing his dirt-smeared face. "Modlichek thought he spotted the damned beast and tripped."

Modlichek grimaced as his attending servant tied a piece of torn cloth above the wound.

"I myself barely escaped with my life, the hounds turned on me."

"Your hounds?" Sladyana's eyes widened.

"My Bolt. I hand-reared him from a pup. He saw me and went straight for the throat." The man wiped his forehead, his hat lost somewhere in the woods. "If I didn't have my rifle ready that would have been me gone. My man servant hasn't been so lucky. The dogs tore him to shreds before we got to him.

"The forest is playing tricks on us," Makail said. "It favours the fox thief tonight. We should go back. Return at first light. With a bit of luck, the hounds would have torn the creature apart by then."

"Where's Slovatchov?" Sladyana said, casting her eyes about the group.

"The idiot ran off alone. I say leave him!" another hunter piped in.

"No," Makail interjected. "We leave nobody, isn't that right, Sladyana? Sladyana?" By the time he turned around Sladyana was gone.

Sladyana placed her feet carefully, slowly. The sound of leaves and pine needles crackled underfoot, raising the small hairs on her back. She didn't take a torch, leaving the servants and the hunters behind her. Stupid, perhaps, but she wouldn't let the fox get away. Not again. "You can't have her," she whispered through gritted teeth.

The others could leave if they wanted. The fox had taken too much already. Her Luba, her baby. And now it came for Tula, as well. It wouldn't leave without her, Sladyana was certain of that. It would await its chance, and no locks and no hard doors would keep it away.

She clutched the gun and tried to steady her breathing.

Something moved between the trees, and a sound reached her ears. Dripping, like melting snow falling off the branches. She came out from among the trees and there it was. A large, overturned oak, its autumnal foliage still attached, drawing strength from its dying mother. A sharp branch protruded like a spear. And impaled upon it, the body of General Slovatchov hung limp and lifeless in the moonlight.

Sladyana stared motionless, every fibre of her body yearning to run, to escape this place. But a movement in the corner of her eye stopped her.

The fox sat close to the pool of Slovatchov's blood, staring at Sladyana, the bone roots blooming in a flower around it, forming a concentric pattern, like ripples on a lake.

Sladyana took a breath and in one smooth movement

brought the rifle to her cheek, her finger to the trigger.

The fox seemed unperturbed by this, its eyes gleaming with a strange intelligence, as it dipped one paw in the black pool of blood. As it did so, the bone roots shot up into a cage of the most exquisite pattern, surrounding the fox, caressing its fur. The roots slicked their way between its shoulder blades and slithered across its head. As they continued their dance the fox itself began to change, its blue eyes staring at Sladyana, its limbs elongating.

Sladyana's gun fell to her feet, and she reached out with one trembling hand. The fox sat very still, watching her, till her fingertips nearly brushed against its nose. But then the voices of the hunters grew closer as the barking of the hounds pierced the air.

In an instant, the fox was once more nothing but a fox again, and a moment later it was gone.

# CHAPTER 11

"Congratulations, it's a girl," Kada said, gently wiping the blood off the baby's forehead before putting her in her mother's outstretched arms.

"Thank you," the young mother smiled. Her face was pale, and her hair stuck to her forehead with sweat. Kada knew a day or so of rest was all the girl would be allowed before she had to strap the baby to her back and join her husband, clearing and ploughing the fields before the winter set in. The father sat by his wife, kneading his hat between his hands like it was a loaf of bread. He looked up at Kada shyly from below his straw-coloured hair. "Thank you so much, Vedma Kada. For helping my Tanya. And we being of no importance in the town…" He reddened. "I can't pay you much. I have little beyond the seed grain this year."

"People of the town pay Gorcay with the town tax and he, in turn, pays me." Kada smiled. "My services are paid for and are for all of the townsfolk. You owe me nothing." She stood up and stretched her back, which creaked like an unoiled hinge. It had been a long labour and she got no sleep in the night.

"And… the other thing?" The young man looked down at his feet, too ashamed to meet Kada's gaze. "We live too close to the marshes for the roots of Mother Zemya to keep us safe. I hate to ask…"

"And yet you do." Kada tied her shawl around her head. She took pity on the young father, barely more than a boy really. "I would have done it anyway. You can sleep easy."

She walked out into the dark. The morning was coming soon though, as the blackbirds were already singing their love-tunes to the day from their perches high up in the still-bare alder. The ground was wet under her feet, and she winced as her shoes sank with each step. She had to hurry, before the pale pink face of the Dadzbog appeared over the horizon, chasing away the creatures of the night.

The marshlands were indeed close to the young parents' hut, closer than most people chose to settle. Most folk never ventured there, considering the unrooted land cursed. But Kada loved it, for the presence of Goddess Zemya, which felt like a constant buzzing under her skull whenever she stepped over the bone roots of the Great Tree, stilled here.

Kada walked by the bank where the lichen-covered willows dipped their rods in the water. The ground was still muddy there, but less likely to sink under her entirely. When she ran out of the obvious path, Kada took out the ground-up widow flower from the pouch by her belt. She whispered a prayer and blew at the powder nestled in the hollow of her hand. A pink ribbon of dust flew above the water, showing the way. Kada followed exactly, as any misstep in the green algae-covered water would see her sink in the bog in a matter of moments. The local people called the algae "green lashes", for the way it dimmed the eyes of the marsh pools, their delicate film both lush and deadly, hiding the safe paths from the travellers.

Bog beacons, tiny orange mushrooms, tightly wrapped their closed cups around their thin white stalks as they poked out in the shallower spots, a pretty flash of colour.

Kada's feet were cold and wet, but she didn't care. She missed this. This feeling of being unobserved. A flame blazed for a moment above the yellowed swamp grass, and then went out again. Kada took out a crust of bread from her pack, careful not to drop anything into the water. She whistled low, the bread resting on her outstretched hand.

For a moment nothing happened. Kada glanced to the East, but the sun was still hidden from view. There was still time.

The water in front of her swirled, and a hulking figure, taller than any man Kada ever saw, with pupil-less white eyes, dripping lichen that hung in strands off its bulbous head, rose before her. It lifted its hand, each finger ending with a wide-tipped, shining pad, like a lure, hypnotising those too ignorant to look away.

"Hello, shvitzosh," Kada said. The creature reached for the bread in her hand, but she closed her fingers over it.

The shvitzosh's eyes blazed a brighter white, anger flaring his nostrils. "You brought the bread. Give it to me."

"Not yet." Kada smiled. "I give it to you now, you will eat it and then pull me into your swamp."

"I might drown you now and take the bread anyway," shvitzosh said, swaying gently in the wind blowing through the marshes. The eerie glow of his fingers lit up Kada's face as she stared up at him, unafraid.

"Bread is not just bread, my friend." She stared right into his eyes. The wind had pulled her shawl off her head, and it billowed like a sail behind her shoulders.

"What is it then, if it is more than it seems?"

"Bread is a story shared, bread is a promise of friendship and peace," she said. "If you tell all."

The shvitzosh stared at her for a moment, then he fell to

his knees, the water splashing the front of Kada's skirt. "You will not listen." His head was now on a level with Kada's, and she dared not look away from his eyes.

"That is why I'm here, to hear all."

The creature shook his head. "You lie. You will listen for a moment, then turn your head away, and leave. They all leave."

"I will not."

"My crimes are too great." Kada could hear the pleading in the creature's voice. He wanted to believe her. Wanted to trust her so badly. "You will turn in disgust and leave me here."

"I'm not an innocent," she said. She reached out and placed her left palm on shvitzosh's head. It was wet and spongey. It gave a little under her touch, like moss after the rain. "I will hear all."

And then he spoke. Kada breathed slowly, as the crimes of the creature's human life unfurled before her. Nothing was hidden, nothing was glossed over. The shame and the pain and the cruelty, and violence, all spoken in the voice of thunder.

Revulsion and hatred fought in Kada's breast, but she didn't lose sight of her task. As the creature spoke, soft strands separated from its body, floating around like spring spiderweb. Kada carefully plucked each strand from the air, her fingers weaving a tapestry of colour, each thread pure light.

*—I cut—*

Her fingers knotted a thread, hanging in the cold air in front of her.

*—the blood ran down her face—*

A new thread flowed across her palm like silk.

*–lies–*

The colour solidified as a line after line of the tapestry ran closely together.

*–Buried him there–*

A thread cut Kada's finger, but she paid it no mind. She kept weaving as the shvitzosh spoke.

*–Just a baby–*

Tears came to Kada's eyes. She blinked them away. She had to see clearly, she had to complete her work.

*–The blinding blow–*

The creature shrank with every strand pulled off. First a giant, it became Kada's height. Then he only reached her shoulder, her breasts, her navel.

When the words slowed to a trickle and the shvitzosh was no taller than her knees, Kada tugged on the shining cloth hanging suspended in the air and threw it over the creature's body.

A sigh of relief escaped him, as soft ears grew from its head. The cloth tightened around his body, moulding itself to him, pulling and stretching, till a large red cat stood in front of Kada, his green eyes reflecting the pink light of the morning sun.

Kada bent down and held out the bread to the transformed shvitzosh.

The cat ate the offering and then allowed himself to be picked up. He purred in Kada's arms.

"There's a family with a new baby waiting on you. There's a sprig of this year's heather on the door and a bowl of milk on the step in front," she said.

The cat purred at the words, his body vibrating under Kada's hand. She walked back the same way she'd arrived, stepping carefully where the green lashes of the swamp were disturbed in the night, following the ribbon of her own footsteps.

"You will serve them well and keep them safe and then once they pass on you will serve their children's children. Love them well and earn the company of the good once more, domovoy."

"*You* were the one to free me." The newly transformed house spirit looked at her with his shining eyes.

"And I tell you to help them." Kada's hand stroked the cat's head absentmindedly. "But a day may come when I call on you. And you will answer." She looked the domovoy in the face to make sure he understood.

The cat blinked once, slowly. Kada smiled, in spite of herself.

"Your crimes will weigh heavy on my dreams. Make sure to make your new life worthy."

They had reached the dry path and the domovoy jumped from Kada's arms and trotted towards his new home.

Kada stretched her back. The morning was now truly here and she'd pass many a curious glance on her way back to Gorcay's house.

She sighed with pleasure at the thought of the food Motik would have left out for her, as he always did when she was easing a child into the world. There'd be soft dark bread and sausages and an egg, and plenty of hot pine tea with honey. And Secha would be sitting by her, all the while, chatting excitedly while sewing.

It was going to be a good morning, Kada decided. A good morning of a good life, filled with quiet comfort. And she was the one who made it so.

# CHAPTER 12

A low hum wove its way into Kada's dream. The afternoon light danced over her closed eyes, as she stretched her fingers and toes, and then the length of her arms. She turned to her side, luxuriating in the warmth of her covers, before opening her eyes.

Secha sat on a stool, her back straight, her unbraided red hair falling in a wave over her back. She didn't notice her mother waking, and Kada enjoyed looking at her girl, unselfconsciously enjoying the task of spinning a thread. A humming came from the spinning wheel, which turned in a blur, faster and faster.

A smile stretched Secha's mouth, her small razor-sharp teeth glinting white. Her hands moved gracefully through the air, but they neither spun the wheel nor held the floss. They moved in a rhythm to a music only Secha could hear, and the thread, Kada realised, was pulling evenly from the rays of orange sunlight coming through the window.

"Secha?" The small hairs on Kada's arms stood up. "What are you doing?" She rose up on her elbow, suddenly wide awake.

Secha turned to her, unblinkingly, with a smile still stretching her lips and her green eyes wide, like she was suddenly pulled out of some pleasant dream.

"You can't do this," Kada said slowly, trying to keep the trembling from her voice.

Secha turned her head to the side, puzzled. "I'm just..." She looked down at her hands, uncomprehending. Then towards the floor, where the wool floss lay, ready for spinning, untouched next to the reels and reels of shining orange thread. "Oh..."

Kada sat on their bed and rubbed her eyes. "Is this the first time this happened?"

Secha's face was inscrutable.

"You're considering whether you should lie to me," Kada said. She laced her fingers together and rested her chin on them. The heat kept in by the covers was quickly dissipating and a shiver went down Kada's spine. "I try to protect you, but I can't do that if you're intent on betraying yourself."

Secha hung her head. "I didn't notice at first."

"No," Kada whispered. "You wouldn't. There's too much wood in this house. I can feel it though the floor and the facade out front. Zemya is pulling on you. The fox is calling on you. It will draw you out and then let the common folk do his job for him."

"Nobody will find out." Secha walked over and sat next to her mother, resting her head on her shoulder. Her hair smelled like moss and wet leaves. Kada closed her eyes, breathing in her baby's scent.

"There was a marriage offer for you yesterday," Kada said, straightening up. "Can you guess?"

"Lulek Tychek?"

Kada laughed humourlessly. "No, but I suppose I'm to expect the brick-maker to offer his son as well?"

Secha nodded. "He said as much."

"And did he hear from you to discourage him, I wonder?"

Kada shook her head. She didn't wonder at all, in fact. No words Secha could say would convince the boys who saw the light in her eyes and her smiles were anything else but encouragement for them alone. "It's Botrik Lelechek this time. That one is not going to be so easy."

Secha jutted out her chin and rolled her eyes. "'No' is just as easy a word, whether you're a Tychek or a Lelechek, *mamusha*."

"That's a child's notion, Secha." Kada reached for her socks and her woven shoes. "A vedma might well consider her child above a match with a brick-maker's son. Nobody in Torlow would wonder why I wouldn't want a life of hard labour for you. They might even laugh at Lulek's father, that he hadn't sense enough to knock such a notion out of his son's head. But a Lelechek…" She pulled the socks on. They provided the warmth as well as a welcome insulation from the floor where, just below the mud-covered reed structure, sat the thick wooden support-beams. Trees, even in death, were all Zemya's spies.

"Why should he be different?" Secha nudged her mother's shoulder with her head, like a cat. "Botrik is half the man Lulek is anyway, and all can see it. He snivels and simpers and struts around like a pasha. It shouldn't surprise anyone that I wouldn't have him."

"Botrik Lelechek's father is a learned man. He works for the Imperial tax office. I might be a vedma, but I'm still employed by Gorcay. I might work for the good of the town, but as far as Artek Lelechek is concerned, I'm not much above a servant and as such I am beneath him. Meaning you're beneath him."

Secha laughed. "Well, that's the problem solved then. I'm too beneath him to ever dream of marrying his son!" She put one hand dramatically over her eyes.

Kada smiled, in spite of herself. She bent down to tie her shoes. "You're too young to understand the arrogance of men, Secha. A refusal will be a slight Artek Lelechek is not expecting. One he will not easily forgive or accept, for that matter."

"Gorcay is above Lelechek." Secha put her finger to her lips, as a cheeky smile curved.

"Gorcay considers himself above most men," Kada said, not noticing her daughter's impish expression. "But I'm not Gorcay."

"No... but you *could* be his wife," Secha said.

Kada looked up, her mouth hanging open.

"Who would ask for me then, as Gorcay's stepdaughter? Who here is equal to him?" Secha leaned forward. "Nobody, that's who. And I'm not his actual daughter, I couldn't expect a dowry or an inheritance, so the folk of his station wouldn't give me a second look! It's perfect!"

"Except for one thing," Kada noticed, raising one eyebrow. "I'd be required to marry him."

"So?" Secha leaned back, her hands laced behind her head. "He offered. Several times from what you told me. And you like him."

"I like most people."

"No, you don't."

Kada chuckled. "Fine, you got me there. But I still don't want to marry him."

"And I don't want to marry *anyone*." Secha leaned forward, serious all of a sudden. "Not as long as I bleed sap, and hear the bone roots sing."

Kada's smile died on her lips. She put her hand over Secha's knee. "And you won't have to, my girl. I will make sure of it."

# CHAPTER 13

"Here's where the nasty sod lives. I won't go farther," Ostoja Hospod said, pulling his hat over his eyes, as if to say the problem was not his to sort out anymore. "You do your vedma tricks now, yeah?"

Kada looked at the miedza, the thin line dividing two farms, covered in yellowed grass.

"My wife said you made a bit of a show during the Mokosy night." Hospod let his eyes roam over Kada, a smarmy grin stretching his face. He pressed one nostril and blew out a globule of snot onto the grass. He used his sleeve to wipe his nose. Kada recoiled and turned away.

"Nah, don't take offence at the honest words there." Hospod laughed and hooked his thumbs over his wide belt. He was a well-to-do farmer with plenty of land and cattle, and his fashion imitated that of the merchants. "Folk talk, you know."

"So I'm told." Kada pulled a pouch from inside her over-the shoulder bag. Her fingers were cold and struggled with the string. After the night in the marshes, she would have liked a bit more rest before going out again, but there was no helping it.

"Pity about your girl, though," Hospod said. "There might have been more offers for her, but folk get scared off, with the mother making a spectacle. Not me, though."

"What?" Kada was momentarily confused.

"My boy, you know." Hospod puffed out his chest. "I have big hopes for him, as clever as his old man, everyone says. Chip off the ol' block and some such."

"I have heard," Kada said. And indeed she had. Hospod's son had already managed to make a name for himself for being as pleasant as a rusty nail in a butter bun, only less intelligent. She took a step towards the miedza. She could feel the wrongness from the ground. Zemya's bone roots shifted under the soil, twisting away from the spot Hospod had pointed out before, leaving a tear-shaped gap, darker, lifeless – a piece of soil with no grass, no wheat, nor weed.

"So?" There was a tinge of impatience in Hospod's voice.

"So what?"

"My boy. Your daughter."

"I have a daughter and you have a boy," Kada said with a smile. "Perceptive."

"My boy wants to marry Secha." Hospod slapped his thigh. "I'm making you an offer here! A better one that you're like to get elsewhere!"

"Is that so?" Kada sprinkled salt on the ground in front of her. The bone roots shrank away, and the ground rumbled, a vibration Kada felt in her fingertips.

"You think your girl's above us maybe?" Hospod grew red. "You might be a vedma, and that might mean something now, but times are changing. I'd take a good piece of land over your potions and mutterings any day!"

"Much good will your land do you if you can't grow on it." Kada crouched on the ground and watched as the salt wove a white ribbon to the bare patch of ground, where the soil shifted, ever so slightly. "You have a miecnik there, and he will grow fat on your harvests till the ground is bare and deadly to walk on."

The man's jaw hung open. "But you can fix it? You can chase it away?"

"With my mutterings?" Kada turned to Hospod and raised one eyebrow. "Possibly. But best you're not here when I do. The miecnik might pounce out at you and drag you away with him." Kada made a snatching motion with her hand.

Hospod's eyes were as round as a copper coin. "It'd do that?"

"You never know with a miecnik," she said, struggling to keep a serious expression.

"Right..." Hospod took a step back. "My son's offer we can discuss at a later stage."

"Much later," Kada nodded. "You never know, but the miecnik might follow me to try and take his revenge on you for chasing him away. I'd stay away from me if I were you, at least for a while."

"Right, smart." Hospod nodded. "And you're paid for this" –he made a sweeping motion towards the miedza– "by Gorcay, right?"

"Right," Kada said. "Your generosity is noted. I'd run fast if I were you. This next thing I'm going to do will be hard to watch."

"Very well, very well," the man muttered to himself as he quickly backed out of the field, before turning away and trotting back home with as much dignity as he could muster.

When he was out of earshot, Kada leaned forward and whispered to the ground "I know you're here. Come out now, and chat with me awhile."

Grey-white fingers dug their way from under the ground in the bare spot, the flesh peeling away from the bone of the many-jointed fingers. A head sparsely covered with hair pushed through the soil, till two watery eyes blinked at Kada. The rest of the face and the creature's body was still covered.

"I'm hurt at the lack of trust," Kada said, hand on her chest. "Won't you come out properly to talk, miecnik?"

"I find your lack of trust in *me* equally shocking," the miecnik said. "Why so far, with the nasty, nasty salt like a wall between us? Come closer to me so I can see you better and smell the moss and wet leaves that left their scent in your hair?"

"So you can pull me under like you did with Hospod's chicken?"

The miecnik laughed, his black gums and needle-like teeth exposed. "That as well!" He wriggled out of the hole in the ground, revealing a ringed white body like an earth worm's, and propped his arms up on their elbows. His hands cradled his corpse-like face. "What now?" The miecnik drummed his fingers on his protruding cheekbones.

Kada crouched down. "Now I need you to leave."

The creature stroked his chin, pretending to consider. "No. I don't think so." He put his hand palm down on the soft wet ground and smiled. "A counterproposal."

Kada cocked her head to the side.

"I eat you, starting with your pretty hands." The miecnik laughed and shifted his weight. His rib-less chest shifted in a glutinous mass.

Kada wordlessly flicked a pinch of salt at the miecnik.

He hissed as the salt burnt and sizzled on his skin.

"I thought you might be uncooperative," she said. "I think you will find I have you at a disadvantage though."

"You have nothing," the miecnik scoffed, narrowing his eyes. He moved a bit farther from the hole, revealing another pair of arms. "And what little you have, I will take, bones and fat and sinew all. Your bit of salt will not protect you." As the miecnik pulled himself out of the hole, the grass of the miedza rotted under his fingertips.

"You have the maws and the claws." Kada smiled. "But I have allies." She tapped the earth one, two, three times. The bone roots twisted and curled out of the ground, and then away, shifting around her, moving in and out in swirling patterns. The stretch of the miedza's grassy surface rumbled and rolled up and down, like waves on a lake.

"Bastooks!" The miecnik laughed. "You call the bastooks, who I can rob at will? The weak and the feeble – you have chosen poor protectors, moss-witch!"

From the ground ten figures rose. As small as a child, with faces wrinkled, the bastooks, the rightful guardians of the miedza, appeared. Their eyes were small pitch-black beads in the deep folds of their faces, and they watched the miecnik apprehensively.

The smallest among them took off his hat and bowed to Kada. "We're here." He cast a furtive glance at the miecnik, who was baring his needle teeth, fingers digging into the soil.

"And I have brought the promised gift." Kada reached into her pocket and pulled out a folded handkerchief.

"What have you there, girl? Show me!" The miecnik, curious in spite of himself, pulled out farther from the hole and hissed as his hand touched some of the sprinkled salt.

Kada unfolded the handkerchief and inside revealed small black seeds. She smiled at the bastooks and blew the seeds into the air around miecnik.

The miecnik winced and then, when nothing happened, relaxed and laughed. "A bit of dust is all you have?" He locked eyes with Kada and smiled, stretching the corners of his mouth till they nearly reached his ears. "My turn!" Two more pairs of arms came out of the hole containing the rest of miecnik. He used two left arms to sweep a cloud of dirt onto Kada, covering the salt she'd spilt. Then, the miecnik hurled himself at her, his long worm-like body popping out of the ground with a wet squelching noise. He fell on top of Kada, maw open wide.

She held him at arm's length, pushing at his neck. "Now!" she shrieked, turning her face to the bastooks.

The bastooks, as one, stomped their feet and clapped their hands, beginning a little dance. Their small compact bodies twirled like spinning tops, kicking up the dust.

The miecnik turned to them with a snarl, which turned first into a look of surprise, then shock.

The tiny black seeds spread by Kada sprouted, releasing thorny tendrils, which crept along the ground, till they reached the miecnik's pale body. The bramble branches twisted their way around the creature's soft flesh, their brutal thorns digging into the pale grey-white skin, drawing blood as thick and yellow as pus.

Miecnik screamed in pain, releasing Kada, who rolled away and rose to a low crouch.

"I did ask nicely, Miecnik," she said with a smile. She pushed some stray hair off her face and winced as the back of her hand smeared a little blood from a fresh scratch. "You were stupid enough to reveal yourself."

The Miecnik swore and raged, as the brambles grew thicker, their ropes tearing his skin. "I'm sorry, I will go!" he shouted. "I will go from here, and you will neither see nor smell me again. I will be gone, I promise!"

"You belong to the bastooks now," she said, straightening her blouse. "This is their land and you have stolen it from them. Now they will do as they wish."

The miecnik shrieked as a tendril of the brambles forced its way across his mouth.

"We thank you." A bastook with a particularly fine beard stepped forward. "You have done as promised. And now we will as well." He snapped his five-jointed fingers and two younger-looking bastooks stepped forward. They bowed to Kada. "Torto and Morli will keep a boundary around you and yours and misdirect any who mean you harm."

"And the fox?"

The bastook looked at her strangely. "My brothers will keep it out with their lives, if need be."

"Thank you. May it not come to that." Kada smiled at the two bastooks, who bowed and burrowed into the ground so fast one would be forgiven for thinking they'd never been there at all. "What will you do with the miecnik?"

"The thief ate three of my brothers and poisoned a strip of our land," the ancient bastook said, locking eyes with the creature, still struggling against the bramble branches. "We will leave him out by the forest, for the birds to peck him and for the nocnice to devour him."

Kada nodded. "It's no more than he deserves."

"May we none of us get a similar comeuppance." The bastook laughed and in a blink of an eye he, his brothers, and the miecnik all disappeared, leaving behind overturned turf and a few broken bramble leaves.

# CHAPTER 14

A heady smell of herbs and flowers hit Kada's nostrils long before she reached her old hut. The sun had barely risen in the sky, and a cold and distant thing it was. There was a dusting of snow on the ground, which lay quiet and sleeping under Kada's boots.

Kada smiled in anticipation of a companionable morning with her daughter. The hut was claimed by Secha for her mead-brewing and candle-making, and so she would be there, pouring her wax of such bright yellow, that candles made of it lit up a room with or without flame.

Kada had taught Secha how to pick and melt the wax from her hives, how to make the wicks and how to hang them to drip down. But to it Secha added a magic all of her own. Anyone lucky enough to buy her candles would have a house filled with summer in the coldest of winters. And it wasn't from oils of lavender and thyme. These were scents such as any candlemaker might purchase – poor imitations of the real thing, as close to the summer bloom as a shadow is to a warm body. No, Secha's candles completely overwhelmed the senses, bringing a full summer with the smell of fresh-cut hay, forest moss and wildflowers blooming between sheafs of barley. The crackling from the wick was like dry grass bending and breaking underfoot, and the wax brought the memory of honey to the tongue.

Kada loved watching Secha work. The deliberate, slow movement, the concentration in the girl's face – it centred Kada and gave her a sense of hopefulness.

A suppressed laughter came from the open door of the hut. Laughter that didn't belong to Secha.

More curious than alarmed, Kada stepped a little closer. It wasn't that she wanted to spy, exactly, but the desire to catch a glimpse of her daughter's life that was outside of her mother's was too much to resist.

By the large vat where Secha dipped her candles, stood one of the serving girls from Gorcay's household, holding the stick with candles tied to by their long wicks. It was Aleenka, a girl a year or so older than Secha, who only recently came to Torlow looking for work. Aleenka wore her plain linen skirt and shirt with a stained apron tied around her waist. She was not a plain girl, though not a pretty one either, but the smile she beamed at Secha lit up her face, flashing a hint of beauty that went deeper than her features.

Secha stood by Aleenka's side and instructed her how to dip the candles, slow enough to get an even new coat of wax, but not so slow as to melt the part already solidified.

Kada watched Secha whisper something in Aleenka's ear, her hands on the maid's, her thumb gently caressing the calloused skin on Aleenka's fingers. Whatever it was Secha said made Aleenka redden and lower her eyes.

Kada realised with a start that in this scene she was an interloper. She backed out carefully, keeping that moment of gentleness she witnessed like a gem inside her heart.

# CHAPTER 15

The fox waited as the white roots slowly receded into the ground. They moved sluggishly now, the late winter's cold lulling the earth and its goddess to sleep. The fox dropped the bird it was holding onto the ground and allowed Zemya to take it. The fox was hungry, exhausted from its long journey, but there were more important things than the demands of its stomach.

The fox sniffed the air. Zemya offered it something important, it understood as much. There was a service rendered, and a service deserved a payment, no matter how severe the pangs of hunger. The animal's blue eyes watched dispassionately as the white roots again rose up and wove their way across the bird's yellow breast, climbing over its torn body. Suddenly they pushed in, crushing the bird and pulling it beneath the soil.

There was a hunger on the air, and the fox responded to it. Its long ears pricked up at the noise in the distance – a plough ripping open the thawing ground to prepare it for the seeding. Zemya giving just as eagerly as she took.

The birds, hardy enough not to leave for the white-cold season, were drawn to the field where the ground worms had been revealed by the upturned earth, and to the smell of seed in the linen bags. They waited patiently, eyeing the farmers. The scarecrows and shouts did nothing to deter them. But a fox could come and cull the feathered thieves, a hero for a moment, before the farmers remembered their own chicken coops and free-roaming geese. Before the narrow limits of their alliance were reached.

The fox could go as far as the field, and no farther. Though the one beyond called to it, though that call pulled on its heart and promised a wholeness the fox could scarce believe.

Still, it could go no farther. But it would find a way. Zemya would help it find a way.

All the fox had to do now was wait.

# CHAPTER 16

Sladyana lay naked in the bed, wrapped in nothing but a sheet, her clothes strewn across the floor, the veiled *kokoshnik* she wore to General Slovatchov's funeral thrown across the chair. She pulled her knees close to her chest, head pounding as she sincerely wished death upon the loudly cooing pigeons roosting in a crevice of the outside wall.

The door hinge creaked as it swung open.

"I don't want food," Sladyana said, shutting her eyes tight. It was enough she would be expected to host a dinner tomorrow, in Slovatchov's memory. They'd look to her to make sense of what happened that night. As weak men often did, they'd look to her to give them a sense of purpose and with her words and flattery wash them free of the stench of failure.

She had no stomach for it. There was a gaping emptiness inside her, and her very skin felt like an unbearable weight, pulling her down, as if she would fold in on herself.

A sound of footsteps shuffling across the floor failed to draw her attention. She'd used the last of her energy and she had no strength left to repel this unwanted visitor. Maybe they would leave on their own.

The mattress bounced, and a little figure crawled up to Sladyana. *Tula.*

Tula pulled on the sheet and crawled underneath, wedging herself in the space between Sladyana's stomach and knees, pushing her back against her guardian's stomach, as Tula's head dug uncomfortably into her neck.

Sladyana felt a moment of panic. The linen of Tula's tunic irritated her bare skin, and the smell of the girl's hair filled her nostrils. The inescapable intimacy of Tula's hands held onto Sladyana's forearm, so close to her chest so that Sladyana could feel the rhythm of the child's heartbeat.

Tula's hair was brown not black, her scent different to Luba's. The two were nothing alike; they were separate and different. And Sladyana knew it. She didn't resist that knowledge. Yet somehow, in the space between grief and comfort, a warmth welled up inside her. That warmth pushed at her till Sladyana released a sob that shook her whole frame. Tears poured down her face and dampened the child's hair.

Sladyana pulled Tula closer and in a while they both drifted off to sleep.

# CHAPTER 17

Kada shook the dried stem of last year's yellow rattle plant. The small black seeds inside their pods made a sound as they bounced around. The air was cold enough to pinch the inside of her nostrils. Winter nights were Kada's favourite. Calmer, and cleaner somehow, than the days; they carried different scents and sounds. She sat on a stone marking the edge of Torlow; neat brick houses loomed at a distance behind her. A moon-lit ribbon of a path lay to her right, and there was nothing but the darkness of the trees and undergrowth to her left.

She didn't cross the boundary of the forest, of course. There were many there who would not care she was a vedma, and so one of Zemya's chosen. Zemya liked to think she knew all, with her root spies. But knowledge and control are not always the same thing.

Kada shook the plant again. The rattling noise would call them soon, the bozhontkas. The little ones gone too soon, holding onto a world they never got to know.

Then, they appeared – bluish lights hovering above the bushes. Kada hummed a lullaby, no words yet, for words could scare them off. The bozhontkas listened to the tone, to the emotion of those addressing them; the words often confused them. They would listen only once they felt safe and comfortable.

One of the lights floated a little closer. It split into two burning eyes, watching Kada's every move. She didn't turn to it just yet though. Instead, she continued to hum a tune to the rhythm of the rattle.

A moment later the spirit's face showed, blossoming around sad eyes. Kada hummed still but wrinkled her eyes with a smile. The boldest of the bozhontkas seemed to have come to a decision and approached Kada. It was a little boy, no older than three, with a mane of curly hair, and arching, tufty eyebrows. He placed his head in Kada's lap, tentatively, slowly, holding the breath he no longer needed to take.

She placed her hand on his head, let him get used to the weight of it, and then stroked him gently. Touching a bozhontka was a strange experience. A tingling travelled across her palm, and she could feel it all the way up her arm. The child spirit let out a satisfied sigh.

More bozhontkas came forward now, their faces clear in the night air. They were most of them under the age of five when they died. The confusion of their last moments forever carved into their memories and faces. They all needed something. They all stayed for the hope of something they could not define. Some would find their way to their family homes, when the Dziady celebrations called to them in the late Autumn. There, fed and comforted, they might brave the long journey to the stars. But there was no hurrying them.

Their families, of course, would never understand. Kada knew that, of course, and so the little spirits' existence was her burden to carry, and her secret to keep. She knew, with a mother's certainty, that one last look at one's child's face would never be enough. And the temptation to keep your beloved dead with you, even if only as spirits, would be too much for the grieving folk to resist.

It would be unkind to keep the bozhontkas from their path. And it would be wasteful to not use them when it suited her. And a true vedma was never wasteful.

Kada put the rattle plant down next to her and uncorked the bottle of buttermilk she brought with her. The stopper came out with a quiet "pop" which was enough to frighten the spirits who scattered in an instant, all but the boy in her lap.

Yet in a moment they were back again, emboldened by the absence of a catastrophe. Some made small mewling noises. They began to crowd around Kada, a few jostling for a place in her lap, a couple more interested in the rattle plant.

Kada took her hand off the boy's head and held it out, palm up. In a trickle, she filled the cup of her hand with the buttermilk. The bozhontkas approached her carefully, and took turns sipping at it, though the amount never grew less in her hand. But the spirits seemed satisfied, and a couple burped as if they'd had a jug of the stuff. The burps were met with giggles, and soon they all sat relaxed next to Kada.

And only when the last of the spirits curled at her feet, happy and content, did Kada speak to them.

"The fox is sniffing the air. The fox is coming," she began. "The thief of milk and crust. The tail that swishes, the whiskers that twitch and the eyes that see all."

"Who is it coming for?" a little girl spirit asked, while chewing on the memory of a fingernail with the memory of her tiny teeth.

"The fox comes for the children," the boy who had his head in Kada's lap said, nodding sagely. "My papa said the fox comes for the children."

"Your papa told you the truth," Kada said, stroking the

boy's cheek with her finger. She felt his pleasure at the praise like a nettle sting on her fingertip. "The fox is the liar in the hearth and the thief among the grass. It will lie to you when it comes."

"What should we do when it comes?" A little girl leaning on Kada's knee looked up at her with wide eyes, so light they must have been blue once.

Kada smiled and embraced the child, though the spirit's skin shot a lightning of pain across Kada's body where they touched. The other bozhontkas flocked around, their ghostly faces earnest, and their arms outstretched.

# CHAPTER 18

Kada was roused by muffled voices, carrying across the top floor of Gorcay's house. She'd always been a light sleeper and she woke up with a start. It took her a moment to calm her breathing as her eyes adjusted to the dark.

"Secha?" she whispered into the musty air of the room. She sat up in their bed, but even as her hand reached for Secha's covers she knew her daughter wasn't there.

Kada stood up and put a shawl over her shoulders. The cold of the house made her flesh pucker up like a freshly plucked chicken. She opened the door and followed the voices along the hall, her bare feet making no sound.

Kada paused in front of the door to Aleenka's room. She considered not opening it. She could just go back to sleep after all. She pushed it open.

The dark outline of her daughter and another girl on a narrow bed stood out stark against the moonlight filtering in from the outside.

"Secha?"

The girl Secha was kissing turned around sharply and squealed, trying to frantically pull the covers over her chest, and knocking Secha to the ground in the process. Secha grunted in pain as her side hit the cold floor.

"Shhh, Aleenka, it's ok," Kada said, glancing to the hall awkwardly, as the poor maid began to sob in fright.

Secha stood up, naked. She tried to hush the girl, who was now shivering. "It's ok, Aleenka, she won't tell."

"It's fine, child, go to sleep." Kada nodded. "Secha, put your shirt on and come with me."

Secha stood very still watching her, green eyes wide and shining in the dark like a cat's. Kada tensed, thinking for a moment that her daughter wouldn't obey. But then, Secha did as she was asked, kissed Aleenka's lips as her mother looked away, then followed Kada out.

They walked silently to their room.

Only when the door shut safely behind them did Kada relax. She turned to Secha, the anger taking the place of the fear which had begun to leave her body. "Are you a fool?" she said. "Do you want to be discovered?"

Secha shrugged. "Who will discover me?" she said, looking at her mother sullenly. "Children of Zemya's tree are no more than stories to girls like Aleenka. She's too worried about losing her job to turn her mind to where I'm from."

"That's a naive thing to say." Kada shook her head. "And naivety is a dangerous thing. Until you turn sixteen, and your blood turns red, there will be a million and one things for someone to notice about you if they're looking closely enough. And if you make that girl fall in love with you, nobody will watch you closer than her."

Secha stretched in a lazy feline way. "Not if I keep her close enough. She kisses me with her eyes closed."

"And what of Aleenka's feelings?" Kada sat heavily on her bed.

Secha's mouth tensed to a line. She folded her arms. "I thought you'd be happy I chose so well."

"Chose?" Kada looked at Secha for a moment, studying

her daughter. Secha's features seemed sharper, somehow, in the near dark of the room. "What do you mean?"

"If I'd picked one of the townsfolk, they'd convince themselves we were engaged before the rooster crowed." Secha seemed quite pleased with herself, leaning against the wall. "But a servant like Aleenka knows she can't lay a claim on me. So nobody gets hurt."

"Is that what you think?" Kada studied her daughter's face. "The girl cares about you! Anyone who cares to look can see it. Do her feelings mean nothing to you?"

"You're one to talk!" Secha stuck out her chin petulantly.

"What do you mean?"

"Now we live under the same roof as Gorcay, somebody is bound to notice you coming back in the night with forest moss in your hair." Secha rolled her eyes at Kada's shocked expression. "I'm not a child. And Gorcay cares about you. I think he'd be pretty upset if he found out about your woodland adventures."

"I'm a vedma, child," Kada said quietly. "I go where I please, and nobody would dare question what errand I'm on." She sighed and approached Secha. "You're not like the others. And it takes a great deal of my skill and energy to keep the fox from our door." She reached out and tucked a stray lock behind her daughter's ear. "Just two seasons more, that's all I ask of you."

"That's a lot." Secha looked away, the defiance leaving her body.

"I know it is." Kada put her arm around her. "But if I keep you hidden from Zemya's spies until your next birthday, if I can placate her with my blood and my gifts, if I can trick and misdirect her, then one day your blood will turn as red as the poppies, and your eyes will no longer shine in the dark, and your hair will not smell like wet leaf-buds in the Spring and frost in Winter. You will be free to love and live as you like." She put her index finger under Secha's chin and pushed her daughter's face up to look in her eyes. "But if the news of who you are spreads, the fox will come and take you away from me. Is that what you want?"

Secha held Kada's gaze. "It's difficult, mama."

"Is that what you want?"

"No." Secha's eyes filled with tears. "I chose you."

"And I made my own choices to have you." Kada nodded and hugged Secha. "And now you are mine to protect."

# CHAPTER 19

"Don't go yet." Inog put his hand on Kada's.

"I must," she stroked the top of his hand with her thumb before slipping away. "It's nearly morning and they will look for me." She quickly pulled on her socks and blouse. The fire Inog started to keep the cold from their bones was not enough once she pushed the furs off her.

The light filtered into his small shelter between the twigs and the moss of its walls. It was a poorly constructed dwelling, perhaps, but a dwelling he built for Kada's needs, not his own, and so he didn't notice its shortcomings.

"They will look for you not for your own sake, but so you can soothe their aches and scratch their every itch." Inog sat up and hooked his elbows around his knees. "I've got an itch you could scratch for me." He traced the outline of her ankle with his finger. "And an urge that needs soothing." He grabbed the edge of her blouse and gave it a pull, so she fell on top of him.

She chuckled and rested her chin briefly on his chest. "I have a job to do, Inog, you know that. And a daughter to look after."

Inog's salt and pepper hair fell across his forehead, covering one brown eye. She smoothed it away.

He frowned. "Your daughter belongs to the forest." He leaned back, putting one arm behind his head as he stared at the holes in the roof of his forest shelter. "And you belong with me, so the forest will claim you too. Why fight it?"

Kada pushed herself up and stared at him. "I belong here, do I? Are these your words, or Zemya's?"

"My mother thinks we all belong to her, you know that," Inog said. "But no, she's laid no claim."

"Not yet." Kada sat with her back to him.

He reached out and stroked the ends of her greying red hair. The skin on his hands was rough and calloused and Kada winced as a few strands caught on them. "What are you afraid of?"

Kada said nothing.

"That's how I first saw you, you know." He grinned and took a leaf out of Kada's hair.

"How?" Kada's eyes flitted to him.

Confident he'd gotten her attention, he once more pulled her closer and looked into her eyes. "You had this look, this determination. You stood over a creature you killed, and I smelled no fear on you. No anger either. You had a purpose all of your own, and I was certain in time you would let me uncover it. And sometimes I even fooled myself into thinking I did."

"Indeed? And what do you think my purpose is?" She put one finger on his cheek, as he turned to it and snapped his teeth as if he'd want to bite her hand. She giggled, in spite of herself.

"You're protecting your daughter."

She scoffed. "Well, that's a little obvious, don't you think?"

"Yes." He nodded. "But your actions confuse me. You keep the gift of Zemya's among the ordinary folk, where she is exposed. The fox wouldn't take her if she was here.

Among the friends and the allies of her mother." He sat back up and kissed Kada's shoulder, breathing in her smell. "Your people don't know you; they won't stand up for you."

"I'd rather stay where Secha and I can blend in, than be here where I'm at the mercy of Zemya's changeable whims."

"Why is it you trust the deals and allies you make, but not the natural bonds between things?" Inog grunted in exasperation.

Kada shot him a look. "You sound like a boar when you make that noise."

He shrugged. "I *am* a boar. The *god* of boars!"

"Well, stop." She smacked his shoulder and chuckled. "It's unattractive." She looked down at her bare feet. "I can't stay here," she said, suddenly serious again. "I understand the bonds I forge. I know how far I can trust them. I can't rely on deals whose terms I can't negotiate. And it's only a few more months till Secha turns sixteen. I can keep her safe till then."

"And when will you be back to see me?"

"I'm not sure yet." Kada picked up her skirt. "I have a thing or two to deal with back home. Give me a ride to the treeline?"

Inog huffed. "I thought you just turned a ride down." He smiled at her in his lopsided way as she narrowed her ayes at him. "Fine. Killjoy."

Inog stretched lazily. He knew she watched him from beneath her lashes and he smiled. He stood up naked in front of her and laced his fingers with hers, pulling her up. She traced a pattern on his chest and kissed him, before gently pushing him away.

He groaned, his eyes still shut. He turned and walked out of the hut, then spun on his heel, and smiled at Kada. Then he bent in half, like taking a deep bow. There was a moment when his muscles rippled across his back, before his flesh rose and fell like waves under his skin. In an instant, the shape of his spine changed, rough hair growing from the shortening neck as his face elongated into a snout and two brutal-looking tusks wormed their way out of his jaw.

It took an instant and where Kada's lover was a moment before, Inog the Boar God stood.

"Show-off." Kada snorted and lifted the edge of her skirt as she climbed on top of his back. She lay low, grabbing handfuls of coarse grey-black mane to steady herself.

They rode off, and neither of them noticed the blue eyes watching from between the snow-covered trees.

# CHAPTER 20

The fox was confused.

Spring had come, and with the waking of Zemya's roots, the hunt was once more on. Yet, the fox couldn't join it.

There was a straight path in front of it a moment before, which now twisted and split into three, each one leading it straight back to the clearing.

It tried following its nose, to the human smells of the town, the sweat and waste and overflowing shallow gutters. The compost heaps behind the houses, with their heat and stink.

But even that sense let the fox down. A hint of rose, out of season, and an appetite-inhibiting stench of putrefaction, all out of place, all a barrier.

The fox barked out, a guttural cry of frustration and anger, as it pawed the ground. Yet, the bone roots moved away from view, deaf to the fox's pleas.

There was a border around the town. One the fox had been unable to penetrate. It could feel the tremors of the earth under its feet, as some creatures burrowed and twisted underground. It could feel their mirth, their contempt for its efforts to avoid their spells of misdirection.

The fox finally sat down on its haunches, exhausted. It looked at the sky, and the columns of smoke coming from the stoves inside the neat brick houses.

Calling and taunting both.

It would rain soon. The fox could see it in the low flight of the swallows, chasing flies which buzzed ever closer to the safety of the ground.

It rose up and pattered off in search of a shelter.

It would be back. Not today, but soon.

# CHAPTER 21

"You were gone this morning," Gorcay grumbled, as Kada put a fresh poultice on his foot. "I thought if you moved to my house then at the very least, I'd know where to find you."

"And why did you think that exactly?" Kada raised her eyebrows at him. "I recall making no such promises."

"What if I need you at night?" Gorcay's chin jutted forward. "If my leg gets worse."

Kada smiled. "Then I suppose I should just tell the sick and the birthing mothers they should reserve *their* needs for the waking hours?"

"You make me sound unreasonable. You always make me sound so damned unreasonable." Gorcay threw his arms up in the air in frustration. "Eh, never mind that. Leave it." He pulled his leg away from Kada and stepped onto the floor, the untucked bandage partially unravelling from around his foot. Kada moved to help him, but he raised his hand. "Oh please, Gorcay the invalid can deal with this small crisis." He picked up the end of the bandage and tucked it in, then made a sweeping gesture. "You see? Gorcay the inept has somehow managed. Anyway," he stood up and hobbled to his desk. "I have work to do. Can't mess around all day with your salves and medicine and incantations."

"Incantations?" Kada moved her hand to cover her smile.

"If I knew how to heal gout with a spell, I would be the richest vedma in Fiesna. Think of all the rich folk who'd be willing to cover me in gold to find a solution beyond adjusting their diets."

Gorcay picked up a new quill and started sharpening its end with a special knife he kept on his desk. He paused and wagged his finger at her. "Careful now! I noticed my cream was gone from the breakfast tray this morning!" He smiled. "Never trust people who don't enjoy food, Kada. People who don't enjoy food don't enjoy life. And you can't get anywhere with that sort for they've already given up."

"I'm glad that description doesn't fit you at least." Kada stood up and began collecting her things.

"Have you seen any more signs of that… person?" Gorcay didn't look at Kada.

"What person?"

"The one who caused you so much concern during the Mokosy night."

"I told you what it was." Kada's fingers tightened around the bedpost till her knuckles turned white. "Just a trick of the eye. An old fear."

"You did." Gorcay nodded. "And I was happy to accept your explanation. But it makes me uneasy that there is someone out there causing you so much worry."

Kada looked to him in surprise. "Why?"

"Why should it surprise you?" He sounded annoyed now, pressing the sharp knife too hard to the edge of the quill, breaking off the tip. He threw the ruined pen down in exasperation. "I gave it some thought, you know. It has occurred to me you might have concealed some crucial information. About who this person was. And I thought, after all, Secha must have had a father, so it follows there was a lover in your life before you came here, as distasteful as the idea might be to me." He coughed.

"Just one?" She quirked an eyebrow, thinking to make him laugh. But he just sat there sullenly, not looking at her.

*Jealous.* Kada held her breath.

"Is that... person," Gorcay said, avoiding her eyes completely. "Is he a powerful man?"

Kada considered for a moment. "Yes, yes he is."

"I thought so," Gorcay said to himself. "Of course it would be. I'm a fool for not seeing it earlier. The way you talk, the way you hold yourself. And you won't tell me who it is, I suppose?"

Kada shook her head.

"Hmpf." Gorcay leaned back in his chair. The wall behind him was plastered over and painted pale blue, like a duck egg, nearly perfect except for a narrow crack running from the ceiling to the floor. Kada focused her eyes on it.

Gorcay cleared his throat. "Were you married to him? Can he lay a claim on you through Zemya?"

"No." Kada shook her head again. "I've never been married."

Gorcay seemed to brighten at that. "That's some good news at least. So, would you like to be?"

"I don't understand."

"Yes, you do." Gorcay nodded. He stood up and walked up to Kada. She tensed her shoulders. "If you marry me, my name alone will protect you."

"You really want to marry me?" Kada said. Her mouth went suddenly dry. She flinched as Gorcay reached out and stroked a lock of her hair which escaped from under her headscarf.

"I want to keep you safe." Gorcay avoided her eyes.

"By marrying me."

He smiled at that. "As I have often told you." He pulled his hand back. "I'm still young. I've been told I'm not hard to look at. I'm also rich. That is often counted in my favour. And I would treat you well, you know I would."

"It's a generous offer," Kada started.

"Don't." Gorcay shook his head. "It *is* a generous offer. So, think about it before you say no. I don't want the answer just yet. Unless," he muttered. "Unless it's a 'yes', of course."

"I will think about it," Kada nodded and turned to the door.

# CHAPTER 22

Secha hummed, the noise in her throat 76armonizing with the buzz of activity within her hive. The air felt warm in the sun, though the still-thawing earth would need some days more before it gave up on Winter's sleep entirely. The scent of the opening linden tree blossom filled Secha's nostrils. She stood in a grove of an estate close to Torlow. She'd brought six of her hives with her, tied to the back of a hay cart, padded well for the journey. It was a long way to go, but the honey from linden blossom had the woody, spicy aroma that made for the best mead, and additionally linden honey was excellent for pulling the poison out of wounds, and so Kada always needed a steady supply of it. Secha could feel the throbbing of her bees' anger and confusion, as she opened the hive entrances to allow them to explore their new temporary home.

She reached inside one with an ungloved hand, as she often did when nobody was watching. She pulled out her hand slowly, the fat queen crawling along her index finger. Secha smiled and brought the queen close to her ear, ignoring the agitated bee attendants, circling round their exposed queen.

"Is she telling you anything useful?" A gruff voice behind her startled Secha and she almost dropped the queen.

She turned around and saw Botrik Lelechek in a grey and

black *kontush* reaching below his knees as was fashionable among the rich. It suited his tall frame, and he knew it, puffing out his chest, covered in embroidered fabric. Secha's mouth quirked in a contemptuous smile at Botrik's finery, so incongruous with their surroundings.

Botrik noticed and bared his teeth at the unspoken insult. His hand tightened on the deer-horn pommel of his sabre.

"Can I help you?" she said. The buzzing about her head became just a little louder, undulating to match the rush of blood in her ears. She let the queen crawl across her palm, soothed by the touch.

"I sure hope so." Botrik rubbed his hands and smiled. The smile stretched his lips, exposing a pale scar running across his mouth, though his eyes remained cold. "You and your mother haven't given me the answer yet."

"What answer would that be?" She glanced around. There was nobody there, and even if there was, the farmer who owned the orchard would be a poor defender. Shouting would be as effective as trying to move a haystack with a wooden spoon.

Botrik reddened, but kept his voice level, as if trying to contain his emotion. "I have made you an offer of marriage, and it's been weeks with no answer."

"Silence is sometimes an answer in itself." She cocked her head to the side. A breeze picked up, as her eyes sparkled with mockery. "You want a formal answer, get it the proper way. Come calling when my mother is with me. Don't follow me when I'm alone and stand there glaring."

"I decided to remind you of the honour I'm doing you," he said, a growl building up in his throat. "So, what's your answer?

Kada had warned Secha that brutal men take offence

easily. That it was always safer to make a man like this not feel slighted till absolutely necessary. And Secha was going to be polite and deescalate. She truly was. But then the bone roots snaked across her feet and the buzzing of her bees filled her ears, clouding her mind. The buzzing matched the beating of her heart, and a shadow fell across her face.

She pretended to think for a moment. "I don't think so," she said, a wide smile exposing her teeth.

Botrik snarled and took a step forward. "I thought you were a smart girl," he said "You think marriage is the only way to have a girl like you? Nobody would care if I had you right here. Nobody would blame me, even if they believed you." And now, finally, his smile reached his eyes. As he looked Secha over, he seemed to come to a decision.

Secha brought the queen closer to her lips and whispered something softly.

Botrik raised his eyebrows. "You think you can frighten me with this vedma nonsense?" He snorted. "One liar to another, your play isn't convincing." He opened his eyes wide and put his hands to his heart. "Oh! What's that?" He looked to the sky with a dramatic pretence of shock. "Is it the sky falling on my head because a girl cursed it?" He straightened up and laughed. "I'm a Lelechek, Secha. No dirty-handed peasant is going to fool me."

Secha closed her eyes for a moment. "Do you know why my hands are dirty?" A cloud of bees rose above her head. The bees nestled in her hair took flight too, for a moment making her hair rise up like a flame above her head. "Under my hives I bury a wolf's throat." She looked back at the man. "I dig between Zemya's roots, and give her a predator's windpipe, which her bone roots crush and grind into a powder I feed my friends. It makes their venom strong, you see." The other hives released their swarms, the bees' anger pulsating on the air. "It reminds them not to fear the snarling wolf, the angry bear." She placed the queen gently back in the hive and grinned. "For what is one" –she spread her arms wide– "against the many."

She brought her palms together in a wide arc, and all at once the swarms hit Botrik. He stumbled backwards, a shriek escaping his throat. The moment he opened his mouth though, a dozen or more furious insects entered his throat, choking, stinging. They were in his nostrils, crawling into his ears, stinging his eyes. He tried to run, blind, gasping for breath, coughing, his throat closing.

Secha stood there quietly, an absent-minded smile stretching her lips.

When the last of the swarms finally rose from the bloodied, swollen mess of Botrik's corpse, Secha knelt next to him and gently brushed the bodies of her fighter bees off him. She'd mourn them later. She pushed her fingers into the hard ground. Bending down she placed her forehead to the cold soil and did not recoil when the bone roots caressed her face.

By the time she stood back up, the soil and the turf were already shifting back over the man's body, pulling him down towards the hungry goddess.

Secha brushed some of the dirt off her skirt and went back to preparing her hives, whistling softly as she worked.

# CHAPTER 23

Kada stepped out of her shoes and let her toes dig into the soft damp moss. She unknotted the scarf holding her hair back and let it drop to the ground, aware of the eyes watching her. She closed her eyes and breathed in, drinking in the comfort of the clean, cold air in the heart of the forest, the mutter of the trees the only sound. Still, she knew she was not alone.

Easing into the afternoon's soft light, she undid the string of her skirt and let it fall to the ground. She stepped towards the stream and dipped her toes into the freezing water, finally free of the ice. The folds of her long linen blouse tangled between her thighs. There was a stillness in the air.

"Untie your hair," she heard the low voice from between the trees. She smiled, and, without turning around, pulled off the tie of her braid and loosened her curls with her fingers. Her greying red hair cascaded down her back.

She closed her eyes again, listening to the footsteps behind her. To the cracking of the small twigs and the rustling of the crushed dry leaves. She waited, till she felt breath on the back of her neck, and the warmth of his body behind her.

"Take it off," he said.

She threw her head back and fumbled with the buttons of her blouse. She smiled as she heard him inhale the scent of her hair. She pulled the fabric off her shoulders and let it fall down.

He slid his hands over her arms and suddenly pulled her towards him, so she half stumbled backwards. Her breath caught in her throat when their skin touched. She could feel the coarse black hair that covered his chest and smelled the moss and the soil on him. She flinched when he bit her shoulder, then leaned into the pain and pleasure of it.

She opened her mouth to speak, but all that came out was a gasp, as his hand travelled down her belly and his fingers parted the lips of her.

Kada raised her arms up and wrapped them around his neck as he leaned his head forward, resting his chin on her shoulder.

"Is this what you needed?" Inog whispered.

"More."

She turned to face him and, hands on his shoulders, pushed him down.

"You don't stop till even the gods kneel before you," Inog said with a smirk, placing his hands on her hips.

"And would you be satisfied to stop there?"

His reply drew a gasp from her. Kada buried her fingers in his black hair and looked up at the canopy. The wind picked up and cooled the sweat that trickled down her back.

A shiver went through her body and her legs buckled under her. Inog's hands broke her fall to the moss, and he laughed as she moaned holding his head between her thighs. She stretched, and dug her fingers into the ground, but then flinched, repulsed, as the bone roots instantly wrapped themselves around her hands.

"What's wrong?" Inog asked, lifting himself up towards her.

She shook her head and pushed him down onto his back. He flashed his teeth as she climbed on top of him and guided him inside her.

An ash leaf fell down, spiralling in the warm breeze, till

it settled in Kada's curls. She smiled as Inog's hand brushed it away, his fingers tangling up her hair. The soft gentleness transformed into something else entirely when he grabbed a fistful of her hair and pulled her towards him, her mouth on his, as she moved her body to the pulsing rhythm of the woodland's heartwood.

Inog moaned and placed his hands on her hips, digging his fingers into her flesh. She pulled away from the kiss and arched her back. A bead of sweat rolled down under her collarbone and followed the curve of her breast.

Inog propped himself up with one arm, to bring his face close to her. He bit into the skin between her shoulder and neck, just hard enough to hear a whimper escape from Kada's throat. She wrapped her legs around him and allowed his hands to hold onto her waist to lead the rhythm of her movement.

A glimpse of red among the trees made her stop.

Inog looked up at her with glazed-over eyes. "Don't stop,' he said.

"There!" Kada pointed.

He groaned as she climbed off him. "What are you talking about?" He sat up and reached for her. "There's nothing in this forest you need to worry about when you're with me. Now come here…"

She pushed his hand away. "I saw it! The fox!"

"So?" He looked at her curiously.

She looked at him, shocked. "What do you mean? You knew?"

"The fox is my mother's business." He shrugged. "Nothing to do with me."

Kada narrowed her eyes. "You didn't think it might have something to do with me?"

"Why would it?" He leaned forward and kissed her shoulder. "The fox comes for those who get on my mother's bad side. And those who do can look after themselves. You'll be fine."

She froze. "And what if the fox came for me and mine?"

"Would you just relax?" He rolled his eyes and huffed. "Nothing's going to happen."

"And what if it does?" she insisted.

"Why?" he looked at her warily. "What did you do?"

"It's not about what I did," she said. "If the fox comes for me, where will *you* stand?"

He shifted uncomfortably. "The fox is my mother's. You know I can't interfere."

"You mean you *won't* interfere."

He looked at her, silent.

"Very well." She stood up and walked to her clothes.

"Where are you going?"

"You said those who have cause to fear the fox can look after themselves." She pulled on her blouse and turned to the forest. "And I can look after me and mine!" she called out. She couldn't see the fox now, but she could feel its eyes on her. "Do you hear me, fox? I will look after mine!"

# CHAPTER 24

Kasimira Krall sat on the low wall in the wide courtyard behind the house. She waved away a servant girl's offer of a warm blanket. "The summer's breathing down our necks, girl. How decrepit do you think I am that you offer me a wool blanket in the full sun?" she said without deigning to look at the girl.

"Stop terrorising the servants, Aunt. We both know you'll be needing that blanket a moment from now," Sladyana said, sitting herself next to her aunt and smiling at her affectionately. "And how come I find you here? I thought you would join me for the Volochoy visit."

"I'm closer to the death every moment. Why would I waste my morning talking to the Volochoys?" Kasimira shot Sladyana a look. "No, I thought I'd sit here awhile. Watch this strange child you love so much."

"Tula?" Sladyana cast her eyes towards Tula. The maid instructed to look after her gave a half-hearted smile when the girl brought over what looked like a caterpillar on a leaf. Tula set the leaf on the ground and gestured at the maid, who "hmm-ed" and nodded, without the slightest clue what the child was trying to communicate. "Why?"

"There is a puzzle there. A secret you won't reveal to me." Kasimira adjusted her hand on her stick and narrowed her eyes. "And I like neither."

"A secret?" Sladyana watched as the child chased after the butterflies with a little net. She dug into the earth with her grubby little hands, to look at the startled worms, twisting around the grass roots. A jay fluttered down beside the girl and watched her for a moment before flying away again. "From you, Aunt? I wouldn't dare."

"Don't think me stupid, child," Kasimira chuckled. "Ever since the hunt... No, even before that... This foundling dug up some hope in you. And then the fox didn't take the child. Tula was with the fox at the picnic, you've said that yourself. And the fox always takes the child, given half the chance, everyone knows that."

Sladyana shifted uncomfortably. She stared at Tula, watching the way the dandelions' heads snapped beneath the girl's fingers, their seeds flew on the child's breath. There was something in what her aunt said, of course. "I can't guess the fox's intentions," she said finally. "But if I have some renewed hope... Hope of getting our Luba back..."

Kasimira winced. "We don't say her name. Not outside of the anniversary."

Sladyana exhaled sharply. "But that is what you mean, is it not?" She looked to her aunt, who refused to meet her gaze. "You worry I still hope to find my daughter."

"The very old can't afford to have too much of hope." Kasimira cradled the top of her walking stick, resting her chin on her hand. "It can break your heart, hope. Luba is alive still, which is the only comfort I allow myself."

"What does it have to do with Tula?" Sladyana wanted to reach out, and hold her aunt, but knew the woman wouldn't like that.

It was a moment before Kasimira spoke, so long that Sladyana thought her aunt wouldn't say anything at all. "This child has changed something. Unbalanced our balanced world." Kasimira turned to Sladyana. "There is a sort of pact I have agreed with the universe. That I won't ask for more, as long as you are alright."

Sladyana swallowed. "What makes you think I'm not?"

"I've known you since you came out from between your mother's legs, smeared in blood, blue and wrinklier than I am now." Kasimira chuckled and shook her head. "I can see how you are with this child. I didn't object to you taking her in—"

Sladyana made a face.

"Fine, I did not object *too loudly,* when you took her in," Kasimira continued. "You ached for a child. But now… Tula is like a doll, a breathing, living doll, speaking only to you, only the words you made for her."

Sladyana frowned and opened her mouth as if to speak, but Kasimira lifted her index finger which was enough to silence her.

"I don't approve of this secret language between you. And not only because you make this living, breathing child reliant on you alone, which the girl will grow to resent no doubt." Kasimira looked down. "But because it makes it easy for you to see what you want to see. It's easy to do, after all, with this child who speaks no words except those you taught her. To assume what you wanted to assume and tell yourself the stories most comfortable." She reached out and held her niece's hand. "And I disapprove of it, I won't lie to you. I have always taught you to see things for what they are."

"I do, Aunt," Sladyana said. "I don't pretend I have a new reason to hope. I *have* a reason. And, though I don't understand it, Tula can help me find the answer.

A shadow fell over Kasimira. She looked up with a start to see Tula had approached her.

"What is it?" the old woman asked.

The child smiled shyly and, first shooting Sladyana a glance, held out a perfect round dandelion head towards Kasimira. Tula's other hand shielded the flower from any gusts of wind, and not a single seed had been disturbed. A little globe of temporary perfection.

Kasimira shifted uncomfortably. "I have few enough breaths left in my body, child. What reason do I have to waste one on a pointless game?" She added, "The dandelion spreads weeds across the garden, you know. Brings more bees and insects too, to sting you if you place a foot wrong."

Tula chuckled without making a sound and continued staring.

"But maybe... Just once?" Sladyana said.

Kasimira looked at her. "There are so many reasons not to, child. But for you..." She took a breath and blew at the little dandelion, sending a swarm of the little seeds flying through the air. The old woman laughed, and brought a hand to her mouth, surprised at the sound.

"Very well," Kasimira said, gruffly, avoiding Tula's eyes. "I did it. You be off then."

Tula grinned and ran off. Kasimira stood up and shivered.

"How about that shawl?" Sladyana called out to her maid.

# CHAPTER 25

Kada shook the rain off her scarf, as she entered the town store, the only one open outside the market days. The shelves were always filled with assorted goods, some holding bottles filled with Secha's own mead, Kada noticed with some small pleasure.

There were pewter cups and iron pots and rye flour, not milled locally and most likely crawling with weevils. There was a shelf of multicoloured scarves and painted wooden beads hung from a rack, just tantalisingly out of reach of the girls giggling in the corner.

"Ah, Vedma Kada! A pleasure seeing you here today." The shopkeeper, Matook, clasped his hands together and rubbed them like he was trying to crush a walnut shell. "What brings you to my shop?"

Kada smiled at the man. He had seven children by his wife, and at least four that Kada knew about borne by others, mostly helped into the world by Kada herself. This was common knowledge, of course, and while one might expect some sourness on the part of the wife, the whole affair was carried with such an absence of guile and with such a cheerful openness, there was little left to criticise. In any case, Matook's wife, Ada, gave as good as she got. At least three of her children's faces were so dissimilar to their father's that nobody could feel hard done by.

"I need a new iron pot, with a long handle if you have one."

Matook smiled broadly and went in the back to look. As he did so, Kada leaned against the counter, and looked out of the open door, at the rivulets of rain digging a pattern in the dirt ground outside. The summer storms had finally found Torlow, and they soaked the earth with a savage ferocity.

A man walked in and shivered. He fixed his eyes on Kada and she stiffened when she recognised Artek Lelechek's servant.

"Vedma Kada, I was told I'd find you here," the man said, taking his hat off in respect. He smiled shyly.

"Gotrik." Kada nodded. "What can I do for you?"

The man's face brightened instantly. "You remember my name, Vedma Kada!" His fingers moved constantly, turning the hat over and over in his hands.

"Of course." How little some expected. "How is your wife? Your little boy must be coming up on three years?"

"Three and a half nearly, if it please you, Vedma Kada," the man said, beaming with pride. "And as strong and bright as any boy you ever saw! Don't know where he gets it from, I'm sure. Not from his poor parents, that's for certain!"

"I'm sure he's a credit to you." Kada smiled at the man's proud chattering. "And why were you looking for me?"

"Oh yes!" The man smacked his forehead as if herding his thoughts back to the pen. "My master, Artek Lelechek, sent me to request the" –The man furrowed his eyebrows– "'the pleasure of your visit'. He told me to repeat it exact. 'Pleasure of your visit.' Yes."

"I see." Kada sighed. "Please tell him I will be over tomorrow after breakfast."

"Only, if you please, Miss," Gotrik sniffed and wiped some

of the rainwater dripping from his eyebrows. "My master was very firm he wanted to speak with you straightaways."

Kada leaned on the counter and massaged her temple. "It's late. It's wet. Is he sick?"

"No, Vedma Kada, he's as well as ever." The man looked down at his feet. "Only he was very clear he would see you today."

Kada sighed. There was no stalling Artek Lelechek, even though the pleasure of whatever visit she was forced to pay him was more than likely to be entirely one-sided. "Matook, can you bring the pot to Gorcay's house when you find it? If I'm not there, just leave it with Motik in the kitchen."

A clatter of falling metal came from the storeroom. "As you say, Vedma Kada!" Matook looked out from the door behind the counter. "I must tell you, Master Gorcay's house must be a deal comfier than that old hut you used to live at! A sensible move, my wife said!"

Kada set her lips in a line. The downside of moving to Gorcay's house was the inevitable avalanche of gossip that was likely to spread through the town. Couldn't be helped, she supposed. She nodded curtly, to let Matook know her displeasure, and followed Gotrik back into the rain. By now, the rain had abandoned its torrential aspect and had settled into a type of drizzle that would comfortably last a fortnight and still not rid the clouds of their load.

They marched through the wet, unpaved streets, the houses on both sides of them shuttered up in spite of the early hour. Nobody who could help it ventured out in such weather. The only reason Kada herself was out was because the shop was on her way back to the house. She now sighed as each soggy step took her farther away from the warm comfort of her room. Artek Lelechek lived in a very fine brick building on the exact opposite side of Torlow to Gorcay, a good twenty-minute walk. When they finally reached the house, Kada was shivering under her soaked shawl, her red hair sticking to her face.

Gotrik moved as if to lead her to the servants' entrance, but she ignored him and headed to the main door. Small slights would add up if you let them, and they would do so quickly with a man like Lelechek.

She entered the large hall, with a grand staircase leading to the family rooms downstairs. A foolish waste of space that hall. She looked around at the ornate plaster decorations after the Western fashions. As out of place in a Fiesna brick house as a velvet cushion under a donkey's behind.

"I will let the master know you're here," Gotrik said, bowing quickly.

"How about you let me in somewhere warm first." Kada raised her eyebrows at him. "Or I might be in no state for conversation once he does arrive."

"Of course!" Gotrik blanched. The poor man looked around him like he wasn't quite sure which way was up, and after a gratefully brief moment of hesitation he led Kada to what was a very comfortable sitting room, with imported padded seats and a large fireplace. Kada allowed herself a smile as Gotrik seemed torn between gesturing to the fabric-covered seating and the bare chair by the fire, and she waved him away.

"Don't worry, I won't drip all over any of your master's fine seats. This rattan chair will do me just fine. You go and let your master know I'm here." She sat herself close to the fire and allowed the heat of the flames to warm her fingers.

Barely a moment passed before she heard footsteps on the hard floor of the hall.

"Vedma Kada, thank you for taking the trouble to visit me," Artek Lelechek said as he strode into the room. Kada thought she'd never actually seen the man walk in any other way. No dawdling and soft stepping for him. She suspected Artek marched right out of his mother's womb and hadn't stopped marching since.

"Since I'm told it couldn't have waited a day..." Kada allowed an edge to enter her voice. "What can I do for you, Lelechek? Are you ailing?" She looked him up and down. "You seem as hearty as ever."

"And I thank Zemya for that favour every day," Artek said. He sat in the chair opposite to Kada. He was an old man by the local reckoning, but still as straight-backed as any young boy, though his flint-coloured eyes had no innocence of youth left in them, and little good will either.

"So, what can I help you with today, Lelechek?" she said. "If you and yours are well, what need have you of a *hungry* vedma's services?"

"Oh yes, forgive me," Lelechek said without a smile. "Gotrik, fetch some cake and tea for our guest!" he called out into the corridor where, judging by the shuffling noise, Gotrik still stood, shivering and wet, awaiting further instructions.

Kada felt sorry for the manservant. "No need. Let the man dry himself," she said to Lelechek. "I'd rather not make the trip again tomorrow to nurse him from a chest cold."

"As you wish," Artek nodded. "Gotrik, you're dismissed!"

The man muffled a thanks and left Kada and the master of the house alone.

"So, I should better get right to the point," Lelechek said, leaning forward in his seat.

Kada didn't reply beyond raising her eyebrows.

"There is of course the private matter of my son's proposal," Lelechek cleared his throat. "But that is not why I have asked you here."

"It's not?" Kada had to admit she was surprised.

"Of course, I'm eager to get things moving on that front…" The man shot her a look. The delay in Secha accepting his son's offer of marriage was clearly an unwelcome irritant in Lelechek's life.

"It would be an insult to Zemya to pick the apple before the blossom's done falling."

Lelechek grunted. "We both know Secha's not likely to get a better offer."

It was Kada's turn to be annoyed. She narrowed her eyes at Lelechek. "And why are you so eager then, if you're confident of that?"

"Now, I meant no offence." Lelechek held up the palms of his hands as if he wanted to show he held no weapon. Which was a lie of course, except men like Lelechek didn't ever stoop to using a weapon one could actually see. "You are eager to make the best possible match for your daughter and I can't fault you for being a good mother." He paused, as if to make clear he absolutely could and did fault her for this. "In any case, I have a request to make of you."

"Which I'm still patiently waiting to hear." Kada rested her cheek on her fist, placing her elbow on the woven armrest of her chair.

"Indeed, forgive me this delay." Artek cleared his throat. "As loath as I am to come to you with this, my son is missing."

"Botrik?" Kada blinked twice but then quickly composed herself. "What do you mean he's missing?"

"It's been weeks now." Artek nodded. "My son has been

known to go off for a while in the past, without much notice, you know how boys are…"

Kada fought to keep her face straight.

The man shook his head, "…But never so long, and without a word too. I thought at first he went to visit his friends in the capital. He's done that often enough, so I didn't worry. But my friends from the city have disabused me of the notion. I have sent servants around, to look for him in the nearby inns, but nobody has seen nor heard of him."

"I'm very sorry to hear that," Kada said, a bit more kindly. "Do you suspect him hurt? I've heard of gambling and brawls. Could he be involved in something like that?"

Artek looked up sharply. "You've heard of that, have you?" He rubbed his forehead. "Well, I suppose there is no point in denying it. My son grew up rich, handsome and popular, and that can turn a boy's head." He cleared his throat. "No doubt marriage, to a good girl like your Secha, would calm him and keep him home more. No man wants to leave his wife for long, especially should she be as pretty as your daughter."

Kada's mouth twitched. She took a deep breath and let the air out through her nose before replying. "I am sorry to hear of your worries, Artek, but what are you asking of me exactly?"

"Can you help look for him?" he said, lacing his fingers in front of him. "Discreetly?" He looked up at her and Kada's heart softened somewhat at the worry in his face. "You have friends in the spirit world. Could you ask them? He's not a perfect man, but he's my son. Please help me find him."

# CHAPTER 26

It was late by the time Kada walked up the steps to the room she shared with Secha, and the whole house was asleep.

Kada liked the house like this, quiet, empty. In the daytime it was always bustling with activity in one way or another. Doors slamming, Motik scolding a scullery maid. In the night it was just Kada and the domovoy she had secured for Gorcay. It walked up to her now and purred as it rubbed itself against her leg. She smiled absent-mindedly. She never stroked it. She knew forgiveness was necessary, but this particular one's confession as a shvitzosh was hard to forget, in spite of its soft fluffy silver tail and large yellow eyes. It blinked at her slowly, a sign of affection she couldn't reciprocate. The domovoy was happy to make do with a crust of bread instead, luckily, which she pulled out of her skirt and threw to the floor.

She walked down the corridor of the servants' floor. She looked forward to taking her wet clothes off and slipping into her warm bed by the sliver of moonlight which would illuminate a patch on the wall. She liked to watch it as she drifted off to sleep. It cleared her mind and chased away dreams.

She placed her hand on her door's handle and paused. A noise. Was it a rat scuttling across the floor? She glanced back to the domovoy, as content as ever, as it sat guard at the top of the steps. No, not a rat then.

There it came again, a low whimper down the corridor. It was muffled but she heard it clearly this time.

She tiptoed to the room it came from and slowly pushed the door open. Aleenka lay on her bed, curled up into a ball. She'd buried her face in the covers, to stifle the sobs which even now shook her frame. Her naked body gleamed blue in the moonlight, except for the eight deep lines running across her back, dripping black into the blankets.

"Aleenka?" Kada said, her hand flying to her mouth.

The maid let out a strangled yelp and sat up, pulling the covers to hide her body.

"No, wait it's just me, it's OK," Kada whispered and closed the door behind her. She reached a hand and approached the bed slowly. Aleenka's eyes grew wide. "What happened to you, child? Who hurt you?"

"Go away!" Aleenka shut her eyes tight. Her face was swollen from crying.

"It's OK," Kada said. She noticed more scratches elsewhere on Aleenka's body, not as deep, crisscrossing on her arms and neck. A weeping bite mark on the shoulder. "I'm a vedma, I can help you."

"Help me?" Aleenka snickered. "You're not going to help me! You're a monster!"

"I know you must be scared. You don't have to be scared of me," Kada whispered. A blind panic caught her throat. The smell of sex in the room, the scratches, the look of hatred in the maid's eyes...

Oh Zemya, please no...

"You're a monster. Both you and your daughter. And she's the worst of them all!"

Secha was sleeping, or pretending to be, by the time Kada came into their room.

Kada sat heavily on their bed and pulled off her soggy clothes. She was chilled to the bone; she told herself that was why her hands were shaking. She took off her wet shirt and threw it over a small stool in the corner. It would dry or it would not, she didn't much care in that moment.

Sitting naked on her bed, she tried to remember what she was meant to do. The cold penetrated Kada's flesh, but her mind barely registered it. She stared at her hands, trying to think what to do. The long nightshirt. She had to put on her long nightshirt. It slipped over her head, the edge of the fabric catching a few small hairs on her neck.

She looked at her daughter. Secha's blankets covered her up to the neck, and her round face rested on her hands. She looked like a child, till you noticed the dried blood under the long fingernails. A sick feeling settled in Kada's stomach. She helped her daughter cut her nails less than two days before. Yet now Secha's nails were long once more, and sharp at the ends. Little oval blades, pale pink.

Could it have been longer than that? But no. Only two days ago they laughed and joked in the morning, as Secha placed her hands in Kada's lap. Just like when she was a small child, looking into Kada's eyes with that boundless love and trust.

"I have failed you," Kada whispered, brushing a lock of hair off Secha's forehead. "Though I don't know when or how." A sob caught in Kada's throat. She placed her palm on Secha's cheek, as soft as a baby's. "I'm so sorry, my girl."

"It's not your fault." Secha's eyes opened in one go, all bright and wide in an instant, her voice unslurred by sleep.

"You were awake?" Kada pulled back her hand.

"I couldn't sleep." Secha pushed herself up till she sat cross-legged against the wall.

"I imagine not." Kada closed her eyes. She could still see the light of the bright moonlight through her eyelids. The rain had cleared the clouds away after all.

"You spoke to Aleenka." There was a pause. "Does she hate me?"

Kada turned to Secha. There was confusion written all over Secha's face, like she was trying to solve a puzzle she didn't have all the pieces to.

"She should. I hope she does. It might keep her away from you."

"It wasn't *me*!" Secha hid her face in her hands. "It was me, of course, but it wasn't either. I couldn't see. I was kissing her and then I was tearing at her, and I *wanted* to hurt her, I wanted to kill her, I think. But it wasn't me." She looked to Kada. Tears were rolling down her cheeks. "I felt strange today. Like there was something scratching at me, just behind my eyes. And so, I went to her, I wanted to be held, I wanted to feel safe and loved."

"You *are* loved." Kada couldn't help herself. She moved as if to embrace her daughter.

"I know *you* love me! And you love me entirely, and you love me as I am, and you love me like you did the day you plucked me from that damned tree. And you shouldn't. You shouldn't love me." Secha sniffed and wiped her nose with her sleeve. "I killed somebody. Weeks ago, I killed a man, and I didn't tell you."

"What?" Kada sat up straight.

"Botrik." Secha looked at her hands. "He was angry, came looking to scare me. To hurt me."

Kada covered her mouth and closed her eyes.

"You're not surprised," Secha said. "Why are you not surprised?"

"I–I was told Botrik is missing," Kada said before taking a breath. "I was asked to help look for him. But–" She looked up in alarm. "Did I just hear you say you killed him?"

"Well, technically my bees did." Secha wiped her eyes. The moon shining in through the window hit her face in a funny way, and Kada's eyes widened for a moment. But then a cloud passed through, and it was gone.

"Your bees?"

"He wanted to hurt me, mama, I could tell he did. I smelled it on him." Secha's nose twitched as if she wanted to shake off an unpleasant scent.

"He wouldn't have dared." Kada reddened. "You're my daughter."

"He meant to." Secha watched her mother, her pupils wide and shining.

"Oh, Secha." Kada rubbed her eyes. She was so tired. "What have you done with the body?"

Secha made a popping noise with her mouth as with both hands she mimed a sinking motion in the air.

"It would have been better to burn it or leave it to the wolves." Kada looked away.

"It's cleaner this way."

"The bones shouldn't so readily listen to you. We want the bones to forget about you, remember?" Kada looked at her daughter. "The more you talk to the bones, the more you talk to the bees, the closer you get to… The harder it becomes to keep you here with me, do you understand? And it lets… the other one… in. As you've found out for yourself."

"Botrik deserved it. But" –Secha looked down at her

hands– "I didn't mean to hurt Aleenka. I don't know why I did this, I only know I didn't mean to." She shot a glance at her mother. "Is she alright?"

"No." Kada raised her eyebrows. "Of course she's not. You mauled her. I told you to stay away. Stay away till you can stay. Then you can marry her if you want, though she wouldn't have you now, truth be told. But you can't afford to lose control again."

"Is she…" Secha chewed on her lip. "Will she tell?"

"No, of course not." Kada sighed and then something made her sit up again. She rubbed the skin on her chest with her palm. "But you knew that. You chose her because she'd be more scared of being found out than anything else."

Secha stayed silent.

Kada swallowed hard. "It's not a bad thing to be wily, but don't be cruel, Secha." She looked at her daughter, at her beautiful girl, as still as a statue. "If you change too much, then you will not be mine anymore. And you will have to leave." Her voice dropped to a whisper. "Please don't leave."

"I'm staying with you, Mama." Secha moved forward and wrapped her arms around her mother's neck. "It's not long now and then I can't be taken away."

"Not long is long enough if you lose control." Kada stroked Secha's hair, which blended with her own. She picked up a strand of her hair and a strand of Secha's and curled both around her finger. It fell down, a single ringlet joining mother and daughter. "Stay the way you are a little while longer. And then there will be no more need to pretend."

# CHAPTER 27

"So will you come with me to the wedding?" Makail stretched lazily, the line of golden hair leading down from his navel catching the light from the candle by the window. The curtains around the bed had been drawn on all but one side, to allow both the moon and the flame to illuminate the space. The curtains were made from heavy, but tasteful cream brocade, handpicked by Sladyana, who now absentmindedly ran her hand over the draping fabric, enjoying the feel of the silk thread.

"I'm not sure your father will appreciate you bringing an older lover to his house. Not for such an occasion for sure. The gossip would be brutal." Sladyana let her hand rest on his chest, her other hand propping up her head.

He frowned, like a child unaccustomed to being denied something he wanted. "And what can they say that would matter anyway?"

"You are your father's only son," Sladyana chuckled. "And while your older sister will take over his business, you are expected to make your own way. I'm old enough to be your mother, and I have Tula too. Your father might get the idea that instead of creating your own family, you're looking to marry into someone else's."

"That would imply he doesn't know me at all." Makail nibbled on her shoulder, smiling at the sigh it elicited.

"Families of any kind are of no interest to me. And why should they be? Bratyava will take care of my father's heirs with her million brats, and I will take care of me. It has ever been the case with us, and so it will remain."

"Perhaps." Sladyana shrugged. "Far be it from me to manage your affairs. But then why should I bother with the nuptials of strangers, when I know I will be seen as nothing but an aged interloper seeking to seduce a younger man?"

"Can't do anything about the seduction part," Makail flashed his teeth at her. "But it's promising to be more entertaining than that. My father's not marrying some fancy woman, you know. She's a vedma!"

Sladyana's eyes widened for a moment. "A vedma? A real one, do you think, or one of the hedge witches selling mud ointments to the naïve?"

"Oh, she's the real deal, or so my father tells me!" He pulled the sheet off Sladyana's chest and used his finger to trace a pattern on the skin of her breast. "Drives my dear sister crazy. In her letters she insists we should stop the whole thing. That our inheritance is on the line." He laughed. "By which she really means her inheritance. She thinks I've spent more than my share already."

Sladyana raised her eyebrow. "Is she wrong?"

"Oh, not one bit." Makail edged closer and nuzzled Sladyana's neck. "But perhaps if my father has something to occupy his mind aside from the business for once, he might lay off me. Besides, I'm not bothered by the red-haired vedma."

With a start, Sladyana sat up in the bed. "What did you say?" Her breath caught in her throat. "What is this vedma's name?"

He looked at her quizzically. "Kada. Why? Do you think you know her?"

"No, of course not." Sladyana squeezed the bridge of her nose with her thumb and index finger, trying to release the pressure building behind her eyes. *The name was wrong, but names could be shed like old clothes.*

"I'll come with you," she said, distracting Makail with a kiss.

"Excellent!" He brightened. "You could even bring your foundling! That way you can keep an eye on her."

"I thought you didn't care for Tula?"

"I don't. Not particularly." He laughed. "She takes too much of your attention, which could be bestowed on me. But I know if I make it a competition between us, I would risk looking very petty and silly indeed."

"Never stopped you before." Sladyana looked at the window. *After all this time...*

"Now then!" He made a face and wagged his finger in front of her face. "You can't object, as I've already made such concessions. And don't worry, my father will adore you. He always enjoys the company of clever people."

She stroked his face, thinking how she was quite possibly older than Makail's father himself, and that the man might be less than thrilled at his son bringing her to a family event. But out loud, she only said, "I think that will suit me very well."

# CHAPTER 28

"So, this is our room now?" Secha looked around the fine chamber. "Because I could get used to this!" The room had a four-poster bed with gossamer curtains drawn up and tied with ribbons to keep insects out in the summer months. Once the winter's cold set in, those would be replaced with a thicker fabric to keep the warmth in. There was a little side table with a candle holder and drawers filled with spare candles, Secha's own, scented with flower oils.

Secha stood entranced, her fingertips tracing the pattern on a painted chest. The floral motif curled and swirled, leaves unfurling and flowers blooming under her touch. Kada looked on, mesmerised, before letting out a startled gasp. She grabbed Secha's hand, and pulled it away, as another painted vine grew along the surface of the chest.

Secha looked up and bit her lip. "Sorry, Mama."

"Soon, mila, just a little while longer." Kada tried to put on a smile. It was all a joke between the two of them. Nothing to worry about at all, certainly nothing to bring a cold panic into a mother's heart. "So," she said, wrapping her arm around Secha. "What do you think of our quarters?"

"Very fine," Secha said, looking around. "And the bed has real down quilts! Not just blankets!"

Kada nodded. "Gorcay insisted his wife-to-be and her daughter couldn't possibly sleep in the servants' quarters."

"Oh, I quite agree," Secha said, a twinkle returning to her eyes. "If I'd known I would be given a real down quilt, I would have told you to accept him a long time ago! Even if he *is* a gouty old man."

Kada's mouth hung open. "He is *not* an old man! He's younger than me, I'll have you know!"

"Gouty though," Secha made a face. "I once saw his foot – it looked like a cooked crab, all red and swollen!"

"You're too young to understand, Secha." Kada grew serious. "The young are often cruel about ageing bodies, thinking it will never happen to them. That they alone are immune."

"I kind of am." Secha looked down. Kada understood her meaning.

"Not for long." Kada squeezed her daughter's shoulder. "But Gorcay is a good man, and I will not have you mock him. If his affliction is not improved, that is my failing not his. I'm the one who's been treating him all this time, don't forget. And he is quite attractive too, in his way."

Secha made a face.

Kada laughed. "Right, which side of the bed do you want!"

Instead of answering, Secha flung herself onto the side by the window, making the old frame groan. She wrapped the ends of the quilt around her and rolled around. "It's so soft!" She peeked out. "Try it, mama!"

Kada laughed, then hesitated for just a moment before she too flung herself next to Secha. The mattress was freshly restuffed, and the smell of sweet, dry hay penetrated the thick quilt. Kada stretched out on her back beside her daughter.

"Do you remember when I was little? The room we slept

in?" Secha turned to her mother, her face cradled in the palm of her hand.

"Which one? There were so many before we came to Torlow." Kada closed her eyes. She felt some tension leave her body. It was already late afternoon. Would she be missed and judged if she allowed herself to luxuriate in the soft, clean sheets a while longer? If she didn't emerge till the morning came? She carried more than she admitted to herself and only in this proximity to her daughter, in this room of warmth and comfort, did she feel all the fatigue nestled deep within her body.

"I don't remember the name of the place. I think I was quite small." Secha stuck her nose out from the cover and reached out for her mother's hand. "I remember flowers in a vase."

"That could be my drying herbs," Kada said in a murmur. "Doesn't narrow it down much." Sleep was close and unless she got up soon the day would disappear in a blink of a tired eye. She clasped Secha's hand between her two palms and brought it close to her face to feel the warmth of her daughter's fingertips on her cheek.

"The room was bright and airy," Secha said with a yawn. "There was a pattern on the wall. Blue and white. There was a large bed, white sheets with an embroidered edge. I remember touching that embroidery, how it felt on my skin."

Kada's eyes snapped open. "Secha, *this* is the finest room I have ever had." She propped herself up on her elbow. "That room you describe... You were never in that room. You never felt those sheets."

"I remember it though..." Secha muttered. "I can see it now..."

"No!" Kada pinched Secha's chin between her index finger and thumb. "This isn't your memory, Secha. Forget it. Don't dwell on it. Don't open that connection. It's done, it's gone, it's severed. You're here now, you're with me, baby. You have always been with me, ever since I plucked you from Zemya's tree, and I will be right here by you. Now remember something real, Secha, can you do that for me?"

"Tell me something to remember, Mama," Secha said. "Tell me something real."

Kada lay down on the bed and pulled Secha closer. Her daughter's body felt thin and limp by her. She kissed the top of Secha's head and stroked her red hair as she talked. "There was a room in Sechovo, a tiny village, more than thirty miles to the East of here. We shared a hut by a small fishpond. I showed you how to fish with a rod and a line, and you caught your first pike. There was a path leading towards a large granary, and two big cats to guard the wheat from vermin. And one time…"

And so, they continued, for a long time, spinning memories from broken edges. They stayed there till the evening darkened the streets outside their window and the squeaking of the bats sounded above the cooling homes.

# CHAPTER 29

Kada and Secha sat at the kitchen table, shelling green peas, pulling the little pods out of a large basket that stood between them. The pods would snap with a pleasant pop between their fingers, and the peas would yield under their gentle touch, rolling one after another into a bowl.

The sun was streaming through a narrow window high up on the wall, and the whole kitchen was warm with the steam rising from Motik's pots. The cook himself was making a *pashtet*, the finest in all of Torlow, if he was to be believed. The mixed meats were all cooked with vegetable stock in a large pot, with selected herbs measured out by Motik himself, proudly secretive on this occasion.

He would later mince the meats and mix them with liver, milk-soaked bread and eggs, then he'd bake it all in tins till every single member of the household made an appearance in his kitchen, drawn in by the aroma. Only then would Motik, with the absolute authority of a lord in his keep, bring out the smallest tin of his *pashtet*, baked separately from the ones for the party. He would let it cool on a rack, and ignore the pleading eyes, as well as the progressively more desperate excuses the staff had to make to hang around the kitchen.

When he was ready, and only then, would Motik bring out a board with the coveted *pashtet* on it and a cut crusty loaf. He would slice the bake thinly, as carefully as a city surgeon. He'd place a slice on each piece of bread and top it off with the tiniest smear of horseradish, freshly grated that morning.

Everyone in the household, from the youngest stableboy, right up to Gorcay himself, would get the same portion. None ever dared complain. And for a short while, the entire household enjoyed a strange form of camaraderie, only ever achieved with great food.

The first portion of the *pashtet* was already browning in the oven and Gorcay, in his simple white linen tunic and wide peasant trousers, walked down the steps, wincing whenever he put too much pressure on his left foot. Kada raised one eyebrow at him.

"But it's the *pashtet*..." Gorcay looked down at the floor like a boy caught sneaking cookies from the jar.

"Very well," Kada said. "But don't come crying to me when that gout keeps you awake tonight."

"My *pashtet* never made anyone feel bad," Motik said without turning around. "Of course, everyone is free to forfeit their share, Vedma Kada."

"Not on your life!" Kada laughed. She turned to Gorcay, who had picked up an empty bowl and was seating himself on a chair between her and Secha. "And what are you doing?"

"Helping," he said. He picked up one pea pod and inspected it close to his face. He smashed it between his hands with a loud clap, making the peas shoot out across the kitchen. Secha snorted and glanced at her mother.

"You realise you have servants for that?" Kada asked. She picked up another pod and showed Gorcay how to neatly split it.

"If my fiancée and future stepdaughter are not too fine for the work, then I'd consider myself no man at all if I couldn't lend them a hand."

"Will you lend us a hand tiding the peas you spill on the floor too, *future stepfather*?" Secha asked innocently, amusement twinkling in her eyes. Motik gasped loudly by the pot, his chest puffing out with the barely suppressed outrage.

"Secha..." Kada said but couldn't stop herself from chuckling. She turned to Gorcay. "You sure you want us? Still time to back out..."

"No, no there isn't!" Motik called out. The man took the large pot off the heat and wiped his hands in his apron. "Not with the amount of food I've ordered and prepared for the engagement feast!"

"You heard him." Gorcay threw his hands up. "And, as we know, insulting our esteemed cook would be akin to insulting the gods themselves. No sane man would do that!"

Kada froze for a moment. Luckily, nobody noticed, as Gorcay stood himself up and walked to collect the little green peas scattered on the floor.

"Here, Secha!" he said. "Nobody can say I don't clean up my own messes!" He bent down and hoisted the pea up high above his head.

"I'm impressed and consider myself well-instructed!" Secha said. She stood up and did a theatrical curtsey.

"Very well, no more of that!" Motik said, bringing the wooden board and the small tin of cooled-down *pashtet* to the table. "Secha, clean the peas away. Soon the whole house will descend upon us!"

And just as if they'd all heard him, the staff of Gorcay's house started appearing, one by one, watching in respectful silence as the cook parcelled out their portions.

Once all stomachs had been satisfied, Kada scaled the narrow staircase out of the kitchen behind Gorcay, noting the difficulty with which he stepped. She thought of Inog's lithe body, the sheer strength of him and something like regret balled up in her stomach.

Without turning around, Gorcay said, "I'm sorry I can't walk any faster."

Kada took in a sharp breath, as if he could hear her thoughts. "I don't mind!"

"Hmm." Gorcay made a noncommittal grunt.

"Will you be well enough for the party?" she asked.

"As long as you douse me in some of your tonics and don't expect me to be too vigorous a dancer. I will try to not bring shame upon your head," he said, half turning around, and this time she sensed a smile in his words.

They emerged in the main hall of the house. As her footsteps echoed in the empty room, she suddenly realised they were alone. Gorcay turned to Kada and when their eyes met, she knew the same thought crossed his mind.

"You don't regret it, do you?" he said quietly, all his usual confidence drained from his voice. "Agreeing to marry me?"

She glanced to the door. Out there was a whole world, with wild meadows and untamed forests, lovers still to meet, monsters to conquer. But beneath her, in the kitchen, was Secha. Secha with fingers that could spin golden thread from sunshine, and ears that could comprehend the bees, and eyes that contained a madness.

"I have no regrets, Gorcay," Kada said. She took a step towards him and lifted up her face, placing a honey-flavoured kiss on his lips.

He took in a sharp breath, then leaned into her. When she moved away his eyes remained closed for a moment.

She smiled at him and cupped his cheek in her hand.

"Maybe…" He cleared his throat. "Maybe all things considered you might call me by my first name? I think I'd like to hear you say it."

Her mouth hung open. "You know, I never actually thought about you having a first name. Never heard anyone use it!"

He shrugged and looked at her shyly. "It's 'Sobis'. I suppose I always encouraged people to use my family name. In business, it pays for people to think of you in the way you direct them. Letting them get too comfortable with you is risky. But I'd like you to have a different name for me."

"Sobis." She nodded. "I'd like that. I better go now, though." She laughed at the disappointment in his face. "I'll be back soon enough! I have some vedma business to attend to."

"I wouldn't dream of keeping you from it then." He smiled and Kada knew he hoped to kiss her again, but he made no move towards her. She placed a palm on his chest, both as an endearment and a barrier between them.

"I will see you this evening."

As she turned to leave, Gorcay called out. "Oh, on another note… I've been told some of my associates have been having trouble finding my house all of a sudden. You wouldn't know anything about that?"

Kada's hand moved to her mouth. "The bastooks! I have a pair of them protecting us. But only from those who wish us ill."

"I'm a merchant, Kada. A successful one." Gorcay gave her a funny look. "Most of those I do business with wish me ill. And there will be plenty of those at our engagement as well."

"I will clarify." She nodded.

"You do that." Gorcay nodded as he walked towards his office. "Clarity is a valued commodity in life."

# CHAPTER 30

"You shouldn't go," Kasimira said, quietly, so that the servants carrying the bags to the carriage wouldn't hear. Sladyana looked at her aunt. The old woman looked strangely small, standing alone in front of their great house. "Or else at least leave Tula with me. A child has no business at an event like that. You risk making yourself into a laughing stock, parading your foundling around like that."

"Tula is coming with me." Sladyana smiled and waved at the child, who was receiving a small basket with some pastries from the cook's assistant. How like Kasimira, not to actually admit she wanted the comfort of the child's presence for its own sake. And Sladyana would have indulged her aunt, were the situation any different. "I can't spare her."

"And why not?" Kasimira said, thumping the end of her walking stick on the ground, kicking up a small cloud of dust. "There are things you're not telling me. And you never keep things from me."

Sladyana froze for a moment. "I saw something. During the hunt."

"You saw the swamp fires and a number of foolish men tripping over their feet till one of them met with a stupid death." Kasimira shook her head and cut the air with her hand for emphasis. "You were scared, and angry and full of bile, trying to get that fox. You don't know what you saw."

"Aunt." Sladyana walked up to her and placed her hands on her shoulders. "The fox wants her. It showed me something. I don't know if it meant to trick me or hurt me. But I saw something." Sladyana looked down. "If that vedma is the same one... Aunt, she could be our way to finally finding my girl. It can't be a coincidence. Tula might be the key to solving this puzzle for us."

"I see." Kasimira pulled Sladyana into a hug. "Of course you must go. I only wish I could come with you." Kasimira looked wistfully towards the house, its stone walls her chief comfort and armour for many years. Sladyana thought how much older the woman looked when not surrounded by their fine furnishings. It was like the house itself kept the years at bay. But a house needed a family to be a home. And Kasimira, perhaps, could understand it better than most.

"Just think, Aunt... I might be coming back with my daughter," Sladyana whispered. "The vedma might help me bring Luba home."

# CHAPTER 31

Kada's hand lingered above the exposed roots of the great oak. She didn't touch it though. She worried if she did, she would hear its scream.

"It's not well," Inog said behind her, stating the obvious.

"No, it's not." She didn't dare turn around. He was standing so close to her, she could feel the heat of his naked body on the exposed skin of her neck. "All these shoots," she said, crouching down. The tree was hundreds of years old, with the canopy blocking most of the light. The bottom of its trunk, just where the roots bulged out of the ground, was covered in small shoots, no higher than her knee, the odd whiskers of a desperate tree. "It knows none of them will survive."

"But it hopes still." Inog came forward and touched the ancient bark. A blue spark of electricity passed between the god and the oak. A message between old friends. Inog turned to Kada and smiled sadly. "A lot of the trees are sick, Kada. Are you here to tell me why? And why you won't meet my eyes?"

Kada looked up at Inog and reddened. "One doesn't have anything to do with the other, if that's what you're asking."

"It wasn't." Inog sat down on the oak roots, his back to the trunk. "Though now I'm wondering."

She laced her fingers together behind her back and

tightened them till the knuckles turned white. There was no use prolonging it. She stiffened her back. "I'm getting married," she said. "I came to let you know."

"Congratulations." Inog watched her for a moment. "What does that mean?"

Kada grimaced. She wondered if he could actually be that obtuse. But he was the god of boars, she reminded herself. Of course, he would be slow to understand her meaning. "It means I'm getting married. To someone who's not you."

Inog raised his eyebrows. "Did you *expect* to marry me?"

"No, what–" Kada stood there for a moment with her mouth open. This was not going how she'd expected. But indifference was surely the better of two options, wasn't it? "Don't you care?"

"Why would I?" Inog stretched out, his hands laced behind his head. "I'm a god. If you play games with the humans you insist on living with, what is that to me?" A furrow appeared between his eyebrows, as if a thought had just occurred to him. "What is this marriage to you? Do you expect a change to occur between us?"

"I–" She threw her arms up in exasperation. "Of course there will be a change. I'll be married. That means I agree to be a partner to someone else. *Only* to them."

"Oh." Inog's face fell. "Why?"

She almost laughed at his crestfallen expression, but that would offend him. And she didn't trust his affection for her enough to offend him. Kada sat next to Inog. "Well, for one, my husband might object if I leave in the middle of the night to meet a lover."

"So, you're not getting a husband." Inog straightened up and brushed his knuckles against Kada's shoulder. "You're getting an owner. Why would you do that?"

"You don't understand." Kada covered her eyes.

"Gorcay." Inog sniffed. "The rich man whose brick house is decorated with dead trees. It looks like it's built of blasphemy and murder. Strange choice."

"Fallen trees are expensive." Kada leaned forward and rested her chin on her knees. "Humans like expensive things."

"And you do too now, apparently." Inog sniggered. "Why don't you come live with me here then if you like the sight of wood when you wake up?" He gestured around him. "Do you think he can protect you better than I?" As if to illustrate the point, his teeth lengthened out into brutal twin tusks, capable of tearing through man or beast.

Kada turned her face towards him and watched him from beneath her lashes. "If that was the sort of protection called for, I'd have no need for you nor any other man for that matter."

Inog watched the green glint in her eyes for a moment and returned fully to his human form. "No, I suppose you wouldn't. What do you need then?"

Kada chewed on her lip.

"It's Secha, isn't it?" Inog huffed and stood up. He walked a few paces away and stood with his back to her. The sun was high up in the sky, but the forest floor beneath the oaks was dark, only speckles of sunshine lighting up bits of his skin. Kada longed to reach out and touch him. She didn't, of course. What would be the point?

"You should bring her here," he said. "She doesn't belong out there."

"No, she doesn't. But she will. Soon she will."

"You've waited this long. What's the point in marrying someone if she's so close?"

"My reasons are my own and don't concern you," Kada said. "But Secha isn't the only reason I'm marrying Gorcay." She looked Inog slowly up and down. "You might choose not to believe it, but I do have feelings for him."

Inog snorted. "You're right. I don't believe a word of it." He walked up to Kada and crouched next to her. She avoided his eyes again. It would do her no good to look. He put his hand under her chin and turned her face towards him. "You said the forest's ailing had nothing to do with it. But I look at your face and see it's a lie. What are you not telling me about Secha? She is unusual, I grant you. Even for one gifted from my mother's tree. But is there more to it?"

She pushed his hand away. "She is my daughter. That's all you need to know. That's all that matters. Being married to Gorcay will make me more than a vedma. Nobody will dare touch me. *Or* Secha."

"Well, at least you will be alright then." Inog scoffed. "Not a thought for me. Not a thought for the forest and all who depend on it. You could use your powers to help me. You could join with me to protect the land, to serve Zemya with your strength." He lowered his voice to a growl. "But you know that. You just don't care."

"That's not true." Kada shook her head stubbornly.

"You should bring Secha to the forest."

"Never!" Kada's eyes flew wide open, and she jumped up as if ready to charge at him.

"That's it, isn't it?" Inog narrowed his eyes. "That's why you're holing up in a ridiculous ceremony with some ridiculous merchant. You're keeping Secha like some garden rose. But she is Zemya's. The roots of a cultivated tree are broken and damaged in ways you can't even fathom. The connection Secha has to Zemya will be severed if you continue as you are."

"I *want* it severed!" Kada shouted, her raised voice scaring the starlings. "I want her safe! To be just another vedma if she chooses, just another woman." Kada turned away and started walking towards the road.

"You can't protect her, Kada!" Inog's voice rang between the trees as Kada walked on. The brambles and wild rose bushes pulled on her skirt, the long arms of the forest grabbing her, as if to keep her there. Slow her down. She set her lips in a line. They'd not have her.

"Zemya takes everything and then asks for more still! I'm done here," she said, without looking back. "And I'm done with you."

# CHAPTER 32

The music played softly in the background. Gorcay had brought in a famed gusla player from two towns over. Now the old man plucked the strings of his lovingly painted instrument, harmonising with the crackling of the fire pit.

Most of the chairs and other furniture had been carried out of the hall – the biggest room in Gorcay's house – to make space for his illustrious guests to dance out of the view of the common folk celebrating at his cost outside.

Kada smiled politely when introduced to Gorcay's guests, mostly rich merchants and Imperial officials, all hoping to find Gorcay in an unguarded moment, as well as to ogle his vedma bride-to-be. Engagements were a big affair in Torlow, and Kada had to suffer through it whether she appreciated being made into a spectacle or not.

Her hand kept flying up to the *kokoshnik* she wore for the occasion. A cumbersome thing, made of a woven frame, with fabric pulled tight over it. A glasswork veil sat at the back, covering her coiled up hair with a translucent film, which caught the light whenever she moved. It was beautiful and so Kada didn't fight Gorcay on it when he proudly unwrapped it in front of her. Kada chuckled at the memory of him, all giddy with excitement as he prepared for the engagement party. There was an innocence to his joy she hadn't expected.

"Dear Vedma Kada." A voice behind Kada made her flinch. Kada swallowed the bite of pastry she'd been chewing and turned around to come face to face with Gorcay's only daughter, Bratyava. The woman was in her early twenties, and already swelling with her fourth child, which, if her other offspring's appearance was anything to go by, would share little more than their roof with her husband, who trailed miserably behind his wife. If Gorcay was to be believed, Bratyava chose the man herself, carefully picking the most weak-willed from all her suitors, which told Kada all she needed to know, really.

Bratyava's intelligent blue eyes regarded Kada carefully. "I was enthralled with the news of your conquest of my father, and naturally I couldn't wait to speak with you!"

"A conquest suggests a design," Kada said, a polite smile on her face. "I assure you there have been no spells or potions involved."

"Is that so?" Bratyava took a cup of watered-down wine from her husband without looking at him. "I was naturally curious, seeing how little your sisterhood tends to mingle with us common folk."

"Nothing common about you or your father, Bratyava."

"No, I suppose not." Bratyava nodded. "But in the end, he is a man, and rich men seem sometimes unable to discern the difference between a younger woman's true affection and more mercenary motivations."

Kada's anger flared up and she opened her mouth to answer Bratyava, but then closed it again and sighed. What was the point. The heat of the room was oppressive, and the smell of so many bodies in such close proximity made her want to claw her way out. "Incidentally, I'm older than your father."

"By how much?" Bratyava said without skipping a beat.

"By enough," Kada said, with a meaningful look at the younger woman's pregnant belly. "I could eat eggs stuffed with salmon roe till I grew gills and there'd still be nothing fertilising this field."

The women's eyes met and Bratyava broke into a grin. "I'm most glad to welcome you to the family, dear Kada!" She leaned forward and planted a cold kiss on Kada's cheek. "Husband!" Bratyava called out. Kada was somewhat startled to find the man was still there, so close to invisible was he rendered by his wife's presence. "Find me a place to sit and a plate of food." Bratyava walked off without so much as a backward glance, her prospective stepmother instantly forgotten now that she was satisfied Kada couldn't chip away at her inheritance with a late-bloom baby.

"There you are!" Gorcay appeared by Kada's side and offered her his arm.

"You say that as if you'd been looking for me," Kada said, one eyebrow raised. "When I know perfectly well you've been hiding behind that fat Ostrovich merchant."

"What can I say, my Bratyushka scares the skin off my bones." Gorcay laughed. "She is so much like I was at her age!"

"A frightening thought." Kada looked around. "Where is my daughter?"

"Don't fret, she's here." Gorcay pointed towards the end of the room where the fire blazed in the pit.

Kada saw Secha then, her red hair braided and blazing like the sun. How could she stand the heat of the flames; she stood so close to it. A shiver ran down Kada's spine, the small hairs on her neck standing up. Secha turned to her and smiled. Her beautiful face lit up like a lamp. Some of the guests seemed to have noticed and watched Secha, transfixed. Secha reached out towards her mother, her other hand holding onto a basket with a cloth thrown over it.

A relief washed over Kada, as understanding pushed away her unease. She walked up to her daughter as the guests made way for her.

"Come, Mama, it's my favourite part," Secha whispered into her ear, an overexcited child. Kada stroked her hair affectionately and took the basket from Secha's hand. She gestured to Gorcay, who walked up to them, amusement fighting with curiosity in his face.

"I take it it's the time for the engagement promise?" he said in a low voice. He looked around. "Everyone seems to think so now anyway, so I guess we have no choice."

Kada nodded and took a step closer to the fire. Gorcay's hand touched the small of her back as he looked on in interest. A small gesture of possessive affection. Kada caught the angry flash in Secha's eyes and stroked her daughter's hand in a movement so subtle nobody else would notice it. But the flame in Secha's green eyes subsided.

Kada reached inside the basket and pulled out a small doll. It was no longer than her palm, a simple effigy of hay and rags, with a painted face. All engaged women were expected to give one like it to the flames of their home. It was usually a largely symbolic gesture. But Kada was a vedma, and a show was expected.

"In this doll lies my old life," Kada said, loud enough for everyone to hear. "The life I leave behind now as I promise to marry this man and start a new life with him." She turned to Gorcay. He held out his hand to her. With a small dagger from the bottom of the basket Kada slashed a small shallow line across his palm. She expected Gorcay to wince, or else to whine and whimper, like he did in front of her whenever his foot bothered him. But here, in this hall, Gorcay blinked slowly at her like a cat, and flashed his teeth in a grin. Kada rolled the doll in the blood pooling in his hand and turned back to the flames. "Just as he promises his blood and life to me. May I be just and fair so I can steer this union." A trickle of sweat ran down Kada's cheek.

Nobody in the room stirred, she believed they barely dared to draw breath. Kada was Zemya's, a vedma. Would Zemya take it as an insult, one of her servants promising her loyalty to another?

Kada threw the effigy onto the flames, which spat and hissed as the small seeds that were wrapped inside burst open and crackled, filling the air with a strange aroma.

Kada let out a breath of relief. She was herself unsure what she'd been expecting.

Then Secha's yelp made her spin on her heel.

The bone roots were pushing up between the stones of the floor, searching for Kada as the flames leapt higher. The roots of Zemya crawled along the floor, wrapping themselves around Secha's ankle and creeping towards Kada. Kada knelt on the floor and held out her hands, trying to ignore the roots touching Secha. She whispered to Gorcay to kneel next to her. Kada nicked her hand and pressed it against Gorcay's bleeding palm, their blood dripping together towards Zemya, drop by drop. A streak of lightning lit up the night, flashing in through the open windows. Thunder came soon after.

The bone roots retreated. Kada's blood offering had appeased the goddess' hurt pride.

The guests erupted in cheer, their need to see a spectacle satisfied, the relief at the absence of the divine presence in the room palpable.

Kada glanced at her daughter above the heads of the guests. Secha's face was slightly paler than before, but calm. Kada called to her, but somebody moved in between them, and grabbed Kada's outstretched hand to shake it.

Secha tried to move towards her mother, but some women elbowed their way between them, their faces still enraptured.

The crowd moved like the sea, waves of people rippling in and out, those who had done their duty and congratulated the betrothed pair instantly replaced by those who hadn't yet said their blessing over the happy couple's head. It seemed like an age before Secha managed to reach her mother again. She stood next to Kada, their full skirts hiding their clasped hands, as Kada took Gorcay's elbow.

"With the formalities over, I suppose I ought to feed you all!" Gorcay called out above the hubbub. He paused as the guests obliged him with laughter. "And for you, fine people, only the best would do!" He gestured towards his cook, Motik, who was wringing his hands, trying to hide his head between his shoulders, a blush of pride spreading across his face. He was both uncomfortable with the attention, and excited to show off his skills, Kada didn't doubt.

Motik winked at her and cleared his throat. "In honour of our illustrious Master Gorcay, and our beloved Vedma Kada, I have prepared a special treat for you all." He gestured towards the door. "A whole roast boar!" Motik clasped his hands, his eyes twinkling with pride as the dish was carried out.

Kada blanched. Secha squeezed her hand.

Some of the guests gasped and clapped, while others expressed their appreciation with nods.

"It's OK, Mama," Secha whispered. "Look how much

smaller it is. It's just a boar, just an ordinary hog, one of many."

And Kada could see it. It was alright. It wasn't him. Of course it wasn't him. She was being stupid. The boar, carried out on a large platter by three men, was indeed just an animal. The fat on the glazed crackling skin glistened in the light, and its sunken eye sockets were filled with dark shadows.

And yet, when the platter was placed on the table and the aroma of roasted flesh filled the air, Kada's stomach churned. The smell of meat filled her mouth with saliva in spite of herself and she suppressed a gag.

"You've outdone yourself, Motik!" Gorcay patted the old cook on the back. He turned to Kada, glowing with pride. "I wanted to surprise you! I went out with a few of the men, and I hunted it myself."

Secha squeezed her mother's hand and Kada nodded, forcing an appreciative smile onto her lips.

Wild boars were the most dangerous of the forest game, and not everyone got to taste them. But Gorcay had to have the best in all, she knew as much. She should have predicted this.

He approached the table and picked up a carving knife. He grinned at his guests and said something to Bratyava. It must have been funny because she threw her head back and laughed. Kada could hear it over the ringing in her ears.

Gorcay approached Kada with a piece of the still-steaming meat speared with the tip of a knife. He paused, confused, once he noticed the blind panic in her eyes.

"You have to, Mama." Secha's voice soothed and settled Kada.

Kada blinked and steadied herself. She opened her mouth

and bit into the morsel proudly proffered by Gorcay. The juices ran down her chin, and the smell of it hit the back of her throat. She wiped her mouth with a handkerchief Secha passed her. Again, Kada smiled, and allowed Gorcay to kiss her cheek, to the cheering of the guests.

"Vedma Kada?" A woman's voice made Kada turn around, a welcoming smile still plastered to her face.

The woman standing in front of Kada was around her age, with long black hair braided and looped above her shoulders after the Eastern fashions. She wore a rich brocade dress and a *kokoshnik*, which encircled her face with the sparkling of a coloured glass mosaic.

Kada smiled at her politely, till recognition all at once drained the blood from her face. The thought to pretend she didn't know the woman crossed Kada's mind but was rejected immediately. They knew each other and neither could convince the other otherwise.

"Lady Goroncheva..." she said.

Sladyana Goroncheva inclined her head in a greeting. "I'm pleased and flattered you remember me. You must have helped many women over the years."

"Not like you," Kada said, forcing a grimace she hoped looked like a smile to her lips. "None of them quite like you."

"Yes, I wouldn't expect them to be, really..." Sladyana said. "I understand congratulations are in order." She reached one gloved hand towards Kada.

"They are indeed." Kada nodded, reluctantly shaking the proffered hand. She cleared her throat, eyes darting about the room. Secha was chatting to someone in the far-off corner of the room. Good. "So," she continued, focusing her attention back to Sladyana. "How have you been these past... What has it been? Fourteen years?"

"Fifteen years, eleven months and three days," Sladyana replied without a moment's pause. "Not as well as I'd hoped."

She wasn't releasing Kada's hand, her blue eyes searching the woman's face for... something.

"I'm sorry to hear that." Kada shook her head, assuming the look of gentle concern. "When I left you with Zemya's gift, I saw nothing but a happy future for you."

Sladyana narrowed her eyes for a heartbeat but, finding no obvious untruth written on the vedma's face, she released her hand. "A disaster befell my family soon after. In fact, I'd hoped to ask your help back then, but you had vanished."

"As my kind do," Kada said. "We don't often settle for long."

"But *you* did!" Sladyana picked an invisible speck of dust off Kada's shoulder. "I hear you've been in Torlow for seven years or more! And now you seek to settle even more permanently, marrying Makail's father."

"Makail?" Kada said weakly.

"Did someone call my name?" Makail Gorcay walked up to them with an easy grace, and kissed Kada's hand. "Congratulations, Vedma Kada! I expect I'll be calling you 'mama' soon enough!" He turned a beaming smile towards Sladyana. "And I see you have met my friend, Sladyana! She kindly accepted my invitation." He winked at Kada. "I know father has rooms, and believe me, allowing me companions will keep me out of mischief."

"I'm sure there would have been no mischief either way," Kada managed to say. Her throat was dry, and the words came out like a croak to her ears. "But I'm very happy you have Lady Goroncheva here."

"We have met before, you know," Sladyana said with

a flash of her teeth, her arm lacing through Makail's, as if anybody there could be in any doubt as to their relationship.

"A long time ago." Kada nodded. "Briefly."

"Now, Vedma Kada." Sladyana eyed her carefully from below her long lashes. "You made a great impression on me then. Though your name has changed since…"

"Oh, has it?" Makail perked up. "That sounds mysterious!"

"No mystery." Kada's voice had a sharper note in it now. One that accepted the challenge. "My full name is Roskada. Some in my life called me Ros, some called me Kada." She turned her eyes towards Sladyana. *I have nothing to hide*. The words remained unspoken, but were understood nonetheless. "I'm very glad to meet you again after all this time. Now, please excuse me, but I need to attend to our other guests."

"That is quite all right," Sladyana said. "Since I'm staying the full month until your wedding, we two will have plenty of time to talk."

# CHAPTER 33

"I can't tell you how happy I am to have both my children at the breakfast table with me!" Gorcay said, reaching for another bread roll. "And I have a whole month of it to look forward to!"

Kada smiled weakly. They all sat together at a long table in the dining hall. The room itself was filled with light from the large windows overlooking the garden. The windowpanes were not entirely smooth, with the angle-cut edging which created small rainbows on the walls and the furniture.

Bratyava was picking at her food, occasionally shooting her husband disapproving looks. Kada wasn't sure what it was that had offended the woman. Whether it was the way the poor man chewed his food, or how much he ate, or how friendly he was, Bratyava looked upon him as if he was something unpleasant she had stepped in on a country road.

On the opposite side of the table to Kada and Secha sat Makail and his lover Sladyana, with a brown-haired girl of no more than six sitting next to her. Makail caught Kada looking at him, and raised his cup to her, though it contained nothing but spiced dandelion tea, as far as she knew.

"I was surprised to hear yesterday, Vedma Kada, that you and Lady Goroncheva are old friends!" he said, casting a sidelong glance at his companion. "How did that happen? I wouldn't have thought you'd have been thrown together much in life." He nodded towards his rapidly reddening father. "Not until recently at least."

"People from all walks of life are lucky to have a vedma with them in their time of need," Gorcay said. He reached out and clasped Kada's hand, startling her. "Especially one as skilled and powerful as Kada." He gestured towards Sladyana. "And your guest might not thank you for bringing up whatever private matter she had in the past."

"Oh, but do tell," Bratyava piped in, dabbing her mouth with a linen cloth. "We're among family, after all!"

"Perhaps it's a delicate matter," her husband objected weakly. She shot him a warning look, and he went back to being very interested in the bread roll before him.

"It *is* a delicate matter," Kada said. "One perhaps not suited for breakfast conversation." She locked eyes with Sladyana, who had narrowed her eyes, lacing her fingers under her chin. She took on an almost feline aspect, the illusion so strong for a second, Kada half expected a tail to pop up behind the woman, swaying gently, warning of trouble.

"They'll think you've treated me for something dreadful now!" Sladyana said with a soft drawl. A growl, if Kada ever heard one. "I simply wanted a child, and Kada helped me carry one."

Kada tensed her shoulders. She noticed the intentionally ambiguous word used by Sladyana. How much did Makail know? Was it a trap for Kada, to either lie about the nature of the assistance offered to Sladyana, or else to disclose her actions?

She picked up a teapot, wrapping a linen cloth around the handle and poured more tea into Gorcay's cup. "Here, your cup's empty."

She ignored his questioning look. He took her queue and

his intelligent, and usually lively, face assumed a neutral expression. "Thank you, *moya mila*."

Secha snorted, and then started coughing to cover it up, unsuccessfully, judging by the blush spreading across Gorcay's face. It was the first time he'd tried out the endearment on Kada, and Secha had clearly hurt his feelings. Kada glared at her.

"Oh, how hard for you, dear Lady Goroncheva! To wish for a child, when the world denies you one!" Bratyava exclaimed, a smug expression instantly settling on her face, as she stroked her distended belly. "My husband and I have of course been blessed in that department. This one will be our fourth baby in as many years!" She beamed a predatory look at her husband who shrunk into himself further.

Like a snail aching for a shell, Kada thought.

"So, is this the blessed child?" Bratyava pointed at Tula, who shot her guardian an amused look.

"Sadly, no," Sladyana said. "Though I have taken Tula in when she was little, she is not mine. No, my child has been stolen away."

A cup slipped out of Gorcay's hand and spilled the hot tea all over the table.

"Oh, I'm clumsy today," he said. "But I'm shocked, Lady Goroncheva! Shocked and saddened!"

Kada glanced a look at Makail. He didn't seem surprised at the revelation. Good to know. But he was now watching Kada and Sladyana, a curiosity entering his eyes, so much like his father's. Kada could do without it.

"I had no idea, Lady Goroncheva," Kada said, setting the teapot down. She passed a napkin to Gorcay without looking. "I wish you'd have contacted me at the time. Perhaps I could have helped."

"Yes," Sladyana nodded. "I wish I'd been able to. But by the time it had happened, you were already gone. And so it went."

"And nothing was ever uncovered?" Gorcay said.

Sladyana shook her head.

"It's been so long now, who knows if I will ever see her again," she said. "She must be, well, about Vedma Kada's daughter's age now. How old are you, again... Secha, is it?" She turned her searching blue eyes towards Secha. Kada had to fight the urge to claw the woman's eyes out.

"I'm nearly sixteen," Secha said brightly.

"Ah... I see..." Sladyana raised her eyebrows and said nothing else, though a steely expression entered her face.

"Yes, Secha was born soon after we parted ways," Kada said quickly. They locked eyes. Sladyana was there, she saw the twin fruit of Zemya's tree.

"It is lucky she looks so much like you, Vedma Kada!" Makail said. "Or else one could suspect you!" He laughed awkwardly. Nobody joined in. Kada held her breath. If Sladyana was going to expose Secha's origin, she would do so now. But the other woman just sipped on her tea, her expression carefully blank. Kada exhaled and allowed her shoulders to drop. After all, to expose Secha would be to expose Sladyana's own child's provenance. And she was clearly unwilling to do so.

"Was it the fox then?" Bratyava said, her mouth agape. "The thief? Was it the fox do you think?"

"*Moya mila*, that seems rather a stretch," Bratyava's husband piped in. She swatted at him like a particularly cumbersome fly.

"Oh, but not at all," Sladyana said. "It was the fox. The night it stole my child, I saw it. The fox thief standing there in my house. I saw it as it ran. And no bullet could hit it."

A silence fell over the table, only Bratyava's husband's chewing broke the silence.

"I'm no stranger to that blight myself," Kada said, her eyes lowered. "My younger brother was taken from my parents forty years ago."

"That's awful! You never said!" Gorcay's eyes widened. He instinctively reached out across the table and squeezed Kada's hand.

"It was my late parents' wound, not mine. I was too little to have a bond with him. Though the sadness that his disappearance left behind lingered," Kada said. "I am very sorry, Lady Goroncheva. May Zemya strike the fox and restore your child to you."

"Indeed. May she strike down the thief," Sladyana replied.

# CHAPTER 34

Thunder rang out its warning in the distance. Kada had kept count under her breath since the last lightning and there was no danger close. Not yet anyhow.

The sky seemed angry that night. The path to the graveyard was lit up with the fire zigzagging across the sky.

Kada walked on in spite of the storm, as her soon-to-be-groom already slept in his bed, alone and hopeful. She walked because there were five goldfinches on Secha's bedsheets in the morning as she slept. Just hopping along the side of her body, staring at her without making a sound. Kada had shooed them away, and then closed and shuttered the window behind them. But then four wrens were waiting for her outside Gorcay's house when she left to make her rounds that morning. Digging in the ground with their little clawed feet, as Zemya's roots rose and fell around them, seemingly in play. The roots were waiting for Kada, beckoning, demanding that she stop and listen. She ignored the summons. She was not ready.

And so, she now found herself walking across the rain-soaked dirt road, trailing fear behind her like a bad smell, calling the predators of the night who were kept in check by little but the mantle of her authority as a vedma.

She finally reached the graveyard, a sad and musty place. The grave markers were all flowers and shrubs. One could learn much by what was planted and where. Hollyhock for a husband, dill and foxglove for a wife, poppies and sunflowers for a child and wild strawberries for the lonely and the forgotten, so that perhaps a passer-by might stop and whisper a message of thanks for the sweet red fruit. There were special plants for those who died in winter, buried shallow in the frozen earth. There were plants for the cruel and plants for the kind. For those who hoarded and those who toiled for the benefit of others.

Every time anyone in Torlow died, Kada would be there at the burial, and it would be her hand that would place a seed in the ground. With her palm to the soil, she'd wake the roots in the ground to accept the body, to grow the flower, to wake up the Baba Cmentarna to shepherd the soul of the departed.

Kada stood at the border of the hedge-bordered graveyard, the perfume of its many flowers overpowering and cloying even in the night, even in the rain. She stepped within and whistled a low tune to wake the one who hated her.

But she would not be hurried. She knew Kada had come to her and though she thirsted for the vedma's flesh and the sweet marrow in her bones, she didn't attack. For Baba Cmentarna was old and she knew to be cautious.

"I'm here and I'm unarmed, *Babushka*," Kada said. "I'm here to talk."

"Oh, but how will you be able to talk with no tongue in your mouth?" Baba Cmentarna crawled out from under a dogwood bush, planted for a maiden who had shone brightly for her short time on Zemya's land, and had been loved by many. Baba Cmentarna wore her human aspect, or as near to humanity as she cared to get. Her mandibles worked relentlessly underneath her thinly stretched lips.

The skin she wore seemed too tight on her; it had burst in places on the joints of her knees and elbows, leaving raised red welts on the inside and trickling blood and puss on the outside. The woman-creature was naked, of course, the human disguise being enough of a covering in her many-faceted eyes. Baba's hair grew long both on her head and her womanhood, in yellow-grey clumps covered with the soil she'd dug her way from.

Yet Kada didn't shrink away from the creature and neither did she acknowledge her threat. She bowed her head as if Baba was just an old woman, full of knowledge and kindness, owed respect even from a vedma.

"You have some trap laid out for me, Zemya's wench?" Baba Cmentarna stopped a few paces from Kada, close enough that she was nearly certain of the kill, yet far enough so as not to startle her prey. "I am not so foolish as to listen to one of your kind for the second time. So tell me. Is this prison of a bone and flesh garden not enough then?" She swept her arms wide. "What other yoke does your mistress seek to tie me to?"

"My mistress didn't send me tonight," Kada said, and sat down on a wet stone as if she was coming for a visit to an elderly relative. She held out her hand and noted with pleasure that the rain had all but stopped. "I came on my own."

"Then more fool you." Baba Cmentarna sat on her haunches and scratched her head, pieces of scalp, rotting and pungent with decay, falling to the ground. She was now so close she could easily capture Kada, and they both knew it. "The night is my time in this little kingdom of dust and weeds that your predecessor trapped me into. Any Vedma who enters my realm at night is mine by right."

"A kingdom of dust, I will grant you." Kada took her handkerchief off and wrung out the water. "But of weeds you say? Look around you!" Kada raised her eyes and met Baba's piercing gaze. "If there are more beautiful flowers somewhere, I'm sure I've never seen them."

"They are weeds if I don't want them here," Baba said. Her long black tongue flicked out and pulled a stray woodlouse crawling out of her nose into her black maws. "And you're a weed yourself – a flower in a place you're not wanted. Your mistress didn't send you, you say? Then you're a traitor of sorts too, for none of your kind would speak to the likes of me without Zemya's permission."

"That need not concern you," Kada said. "It just so happens I need a friend and naturally I thought of you." She grimaced in spite of her best efforts. There was nothing natural about this creature. Nothing friendly either. But Kada needed her.

Baba Cmentarna leaned forward and sniffed the air. Kada didn't flinch, though she saw how the bones and teeth moved under the creature's ill-fitting skin and smelt the stench of death upon her. Then Baba Cmentarna unfurled herself, towering over Kada. She threw her head back and laughed, an inhuman sound. "You forget who I am, little girl. I don't blame you entirely. I've been diminished and hidden away here for so long, tied to this patch of ground, shepherding your dead. I am but a fraction of who I was, but that fraction is enough to squeeze the life out of you, one drop of sticky sap at a time!"

"My blood runs red. And I know exactly who you are, and what you are, and what you're capable of. That knowledge is why I stand here tonight." Kada jutted her chin out, and something like anger flashed in her eyes. "Reject my offer, and you will continue as you are unless another vedma releases you. And none but me ever would!"

"Then you *are* a traitor. And traitors have no allies, and no honour either. But… I suppose you're right." The ancient creature in front of Kada stood very still for a while, swaying on her long legs. She began to shrink, just a little, till the skin on her stomach folded in on itself and she was no taller than any old woman, though nobody would ever mistake her for one. She walked up to Kada and sat on the stone next to her. "None but a traitor to her people would free such as I. But don't you care what happens to the dead of your town? Who will lead them onwards in their journey?"

Kada shrugged. "Another will take your place. Willingly or not." *That could be taken care of later, after all.*

"So, tell me," Baba said. "What do you need of me?"

# CHAPTER 35

Aleenka picked off the dry sheets from the line behind the high wall of Gorcay's garden, carefully inspecting the fabric for any tears that might need repairing, before placing them in the basket. She breathed in deeply the smell of clean laundry and a small smile curled her lips. The whistling call of a bullfinch made her pause. She looked up, adjusting the hair scarf that kept her dark blonde hair out of her face. She observed the bird for a moment, taking in the colour of its wings, hoping to hear its flute-like song again. But the bird just stared at her, for a stolen moment in their lives.

Secha stood unobserved by the stone gate, watching Aleenka's deliberate movements. She wondered at her lover's ability to notice things with a gentleness, in spite of the seemingly never-ending tasks that hardened her muscles and toughened her skin. Secha curled a lock of her hair around her finger, as she did when nervous, which was rarely, or whenever she felt mischievous, which was more and more every day.

She stepped out into the light and waited for Aleenka to notice her. The servant girl, seemingly finished with her daydreaming, picked up the laundry basket with a huff and propped it against her hip, the curve of which made Secha's mouth go dry.

Aleenka turned around and froze. "Miss Secha," she

said slowly, glancing around to see if there was anyone else about. "Is there anything you need help with?"

"Aleenka..." Secha stepped forward but paused when Aleenka took a step backwards, keeping distance between them. "I want to–"

"To what?" The mask of calm slipped from the young woman's face. "To hurt me again? Knowing I can't tell nobody?"

"I didn't mean to..." Secha looked to the ground. "It wasn't me; you have to know that! I don't know what happened... Please believe me, I never meant to hurt you..."

"But you did! And how! I still have the marks your teeth left on me. The claw marks. I could listen to you till the cows came home, and try to believe you, but then my body would tell me the truth every night." She moved to go past Secha.

"Please..." Secha tried to step in her way, but Aleenka spun around and smacked her in the face, a small iron ring on her finger leaving a red welt. The laundry basket slipped from Aleenka's grip, spilling some of its contents onto the grass.

"Look what you did!" Aleenka bent down to pick up the folded sheets. Secha looked at her, shocked, her hand to her cheek.

"I loved you, you know," Aleenka said without looking at Secha. "And I know you can't say the same, and, you know, I was so stupid, I didn't mind that. I couldn't believe it, the flame-haired daughter of the vedma, the girl every boy and girl in town chased after, the beautiful Secha choosing *me*!" She laughed, shaking her head. "I know what I look like. Not many would give me a second glance. My face is just like a million faces out there: forgotten the moment I turn away. And I know fancy folk look down on me: on my strong arms and legs, my thick waist." She whipped up her head, her chin jutted out. "Well, I don't care. I *like* my body. It's strong, and it needs to be strong for the life I have. It might not be beautiful like yours, but it deserves to be loved. And I will not let you bleed me and hit me and abuse me, just because you think yourself better than me!" Aleenka picked up the basket again.

"I don't think myself better than you..." Secha whispered.

"No?" Aleenka brought her face closer to Secha's. "Then why did you think you had the right to hurt me?"

"There's something inside me, Aleenka..." Secha avoided the woman's eyes. "I can't explain it and I can't control it, but I care about you."

Aleenka laughed. "If that's what your care looks like, I'd rather have your indifference, thank you very much." She walked past, and this time Secha stepped aside, letting her through. "Oh!" Aleenka exclaimed at the sight of a figure watching them from behind the stone gate, on the path leading towards the house. "Lady Goroncheva, do you need anything?" she curtsied. Secha watched as Aleenka effortlessly slipped back into the role of obliging servant.

"I was looking for someone to draw me a bath in my chamber," the old woman said, watching Secha and Aleenka with a searing intensity. "I understand you're the one to handle such matters?"

"Yes, my lady," Aleenka nodded. "Straight away, my lady."

Secha met Sladyana's gaze. She then deliberately turned towards Aleenka and said, "Thank you, Aleenka, for your assistance. I will let you go now."

A flash of pain crossed Aleenka's face. "Thank you, miss,"

she said in an even tone. She readjusted her grip on the basket and walked towards the house.

Sladyana gave Secha a curious glance before following Aleenka.

Secha turned around on her heel and ran, barefoot, towards the orchards.

# CHAPTER 36

Kada groaned inwardly as a familiar voice called out to her on the main street of Torlow. She pretended not to hear, as she wove her way between the market stalls hastily set up every other week against the brick walls of the long rows of houses.

A smell of mushroom dumplings hit her nostrils. She'd usually stop and indulge in one, in defiance of Motik's elevated senses which would doubtless smell the betrayal on her breath. Yet, while she was happy to forgo the treat to avoid contact with Rotik Moglovy, clearly there was no escaping the man today. She cringed as she heard the hurried footsteps and the heavy breathing behind her.

"Dear Vedma Kada! What luck that I have come across you today!" Rotik Moglovy caught up with her and patted her shoulder, whether to convey familiarity or steady himself after the short run, she couldn't be sure. "I have great need of you! Have you not heard me calling you?"

"I'm sorry, Rotik, I was lost in thought!" Kada lied. The *pierogi* seller snorted. Kada shot her a warning look and the seller busied herself rearranging her wares. "What's the problem? Did the tonic I prescribed you not help?"

"Oh, but dear Vedma Kada, how could you even think that! You know as well as I do that you have no equal in all of Fiesna when it comes to healing skills! No, but of course your tonic was *most* effective. My dizzy spells have simply disappeared a few doses in!"

*Almost as if they were never there to begin with*, thought Kada, but not a muscle moved on her face. "Then whatever is the matter?"

"Ah, but you yourself know, I'm the most unfortunate of your patients." The man wrung his hands. "I don't know how I insulted Mother Zemya this time, but offend her I must have, for she keeps on sending these ailments my way! I truly believe, nobody in Torlow suffers quite like I do!"

"Not quite like you, that's true," Kada said with a straight face. "So, what is this newest malady?"

"Ah, this one is of most sensitive nature." His voice dropped to a whisper, still loud enough for the sellers on the other side of the road to hear and roll their eyes. "You see, I have suffered great pains and aches all over, but most of all in my guts."

"I'm sorry to hear it." *In more ways than one.*

"And with such sweats and such trepidations!" Rotik shook his head. "And the gasses that escape me are of most noxious nature. Even my dearest wife complains, and you know how she never complains!"

*There was hardly any space for her to do so.* "And does this affliction tend to happen mostly after a meal?" Kada asked.

"Oh yes. You are always so quick to get to the root of it!" The man nodded vigorously. "These days a man can barely eat a goose and cheese stew without the kind of pains that twist him till he can hardly breathe."

"Have some yarrow infusion for the stomach complaint." The man looked visibly disappointed. Kada sighed. "And I will send you over some May hawthorn nalevka. For the 'trepidations.'"

"Of course, of course, dearest Vedma Kada!" he said. "I do thank you!"

"Don't mention it. And avoid the stew." Kada said and turned around. She walked a few more paces before another call stopped her in her tracks. "Yes?" she turned around with a practiced smile. But it wasn't one of the townsfolk this time. It was no other than Lady Goroncheva standing in the road, her fine slippers already covered in dust, utterly unsuited as they were for anything beyond the carpeted floors of grand halls.

"How odd to meet you here!" Sladyana said, a strange twinkle in her eye.

"Is it?" Kada reached out and shook the woman's gloved hand. "I do live and work here, after all."

"Oh yes, that!" the grand woman laughed, covering her mouth. "I do forget." Unasked, she laced her arm through Kada's. She brought her face close and dropped her voice to a conspiratorial whisper. She pulled on Kada's elbow, forcing her to walk beside her, as if they were the closest of friends. "I was sorry to have missed you at breakfast, you know."

"I'm sure Makail was not!" Kada said. "I wouldn't want him to think I'm monopolising his friend's attention."

"Oh, I wouldn't worry about that!" Sladyana laughed. "His attention comes and goes, and it's best to not rely on his time too much. Just this morning he insisted on going hunting with Lady Bratyava's husband, what is his name again?"

Kada opened her mouth to answer, then closed it again. "Orlovitz, I think?" She laughed, in spite of herself. "You know, I'm not entirely certain. Oh, that is awful of me."

"I wouldn't say so," Sladyana said smoothly. "I suspect

that poor man's own mother needed reminders. There is not enough personality there to hold one's attention for long."

"That's not very kind," Kada said weakly.

"I suppose not. In any case, the poor man was dragged out of the house by Makail this morning, as Makail's own father had no intention of obliging his son. They both rode off to the marshes, vowing to bring back some wild fowl for the cook to prepare tomorrow. And as I found myself this morning with a bit of time on my hands, I decided to go exploring." Sladyana's words came out with the practiced ease of an accomplished socialite, though her hand, clasped tight over Kada's forearm, dug uncomfortably into the vedma's skin.

"I'm afraid you might find Torlow a little disappointing," Kada said. "It lacks the fine shops of the capital, and entertainment is mostly limited to holiday days."

"Then I must rely on your company!" Sladyana winked at her. "We have a lot to catch up on. Nearly sixteen years..."

"A lifetime."

Sladyana turned a sharp eye on Kada. "For our daughters, for sure."

"Yes." Kada took a deep breath. "I'm still shocked. I can't imagine the pain you must be going through." She shook her head. "My family never recovered from their own loss. The fox hurts so many more than people would wish to think."

"Of course. Your brother." Sladyana stopped for a moment, and nearly made Kada trip over. "Oh, sorry." She began walking once more. "May I ask... Have your parents attempted to find him?"

"They did. But it was too late." Kada said. "He was never recovered."

"Your poor parents..."

"Yes." Kada cleared her throat. "My father, especially, never got over it. He had always wanted a boy, you see. He was one of those men who see little value in girls. He wished it had been me who disappeared." She closed her eyes for a second and she rolled her shoulders back. "He resented me for staying, for being alive." They walked for a moment in silence. Two carts rolled by them; a guard seated beside the driver at each. Only sensible, really, when transporting the goods to one of Gorcay's warehouses.

"That is awful." Sladyana squeezed Kada's arm, this time more in sympathy than threat. "I hope your father didn't harm you."

"No," Kada said. "He was a little afraid of me, I believe. My gifts manifested early."

"Yes." Sladyana watched her curiously. "And is your daughter similarly blessed?"

Kada swallowed. "I see some promise. Too early to tell. And even with the gift, she might choose a simpler life. I would not begrudge her. Vedma life is not easy."

"No, of course not." The women were approached by a beggar child, barefoot and dirty in the face. Sladyana reached inside the pocket of her skirt and pulled out a small coin, which she tossed to him, then turned back to Kada. "But you give so much. Vedma Kada, I won't lie to you. When Makail told me his father was marrying a red-headed vedma, I couldn't rest till I saw you. When Luba..." She brought her hand right under her nose and closed her eyes. Once she composed herself, she started talking again. "When my child was stolen, I looked for you. To ask for your help. But you had moved on and I confess I was angry, unreasonably so. I'm sorry if some of that old anger came out during our breakfast yesterday. I apologise."

"Really, there's no need–"

"No." Sladyana waved the objection away. "I must apologise for my rudeness. You gave me the greatest of gifts. The happiness of those days after Luba came home with me, the joy... I had wanted a child so much. I never quite believed I could have one, not till the moment I saw her growing in that strange pod on Zemya's tree. Not of my blood, but so much like me. Made for me, intended for me... Like nothing else in the world. I could feel her from the inside of that fruit."

Kada hesitated, before putting her hand on Sladyana's shoulder. "I wish I could help. I do. But the fox never returns the stolen children. Your daughter is gone."

"But that's just it!" Sladyana faced Kada, a feverish hope in her eyes. "I believe my child is looking for me, just as I'm looking for her!" She let out a mirthless chuckle. "You don't believe me. I wouldn't blame you for thinking me quite mad. But I know what I saw. The fox came back. And the roots have left a message for me, through Tula."

"A message?" Kada kept her voice level, though her heart was beating so hard she was sure it was going to burst out of her chest at any moment.

Sladyana pulled out a small purse from within her overdress. She emptied the contents into her palm and held it out for Kada to see. Inside her palm lay a small drop of sap. "The roots gave this to Tula. On the anniversary..." Sladyana looked to the ground. "I have kept up with the offerings, you see. I hoped you could interpret it for me?"

"I can try." Kada picked it up in two fingers. She held it against the light. "Sap," she said. "Not much to go on, I'm sorry." She handed it back. "But–"

"Yes?" Sladyana's face brightened.

"I could try to uncover more. If you find me a week from now in the kitchen once Motik's gone for the day, I will see what I can rustle up."

Sladyana's face broke into a smile, and she grabbed Kada's hands between hers. "Thank you! You don't know…" She paused, suddenly conscious of the curious eyes of the passers-by. She smoothed the front of her dress and kept her eyes on Kada as she said, "I will be forever grateful."

"I can't promise anything." Kada raised a finger in a warning. "I can only do my best."

"That's all I ask," Sladyana said, nodding.

Kada's heart broke a little at the lie there. The woman was asking for her family whole again, the time lost restored, and her daughter back in her arms as she was when she had been ripped away: a baby with her mother's features.

Kada said nothing to that and forced a sympathetic smile to her lips.

# CHAPTER 37

A scratch on the door woke Kada. The night was still outside her window and the air was still, undisturbed by breeze.

Secha slept soundly beside Kada, snoring gently. Her legs stuck out from underneath the quilt, though she liked to keep her shoulders covered.

The scratch again. Kada sat up in the bed and rubbed the sleep out of her eyes. She rolled to her side and let her feet fall to the floor.

Outside the door, sitting perfectly still, with its cat eyes shining, was the Gorcay household domovoy.

The moment Kada stepped out into the corridor, the creature began rubbing itself against her legs.

"What is it?" she asked. She never spoke to this one at the house, normally, but the hour was late, and everyone was long asleep.

"You have a visitor," the domovoy said with a purr. It blinked at her slowly, once, twice. She sighed and motioned for the creature to wait for her.

She grabbed a shawl and closed the door behind her, taking care not to make a sound. She crept along the corridor and down the steps, following the creature closely. The floor creaked beneath her bare feet. The house spirit cast her a judgemental look, one that cats reserve for the clumsiest of beings.

"Who is it?" she asked, as the domovoy led her towards the *banya*, the bath building outside of Gorcay's house. It should be empty and cold at this time of night, but candlelight shone from the crack beneath the door. The domovoy stopped right outside the door and sat on its haunches, watching Kada.

"You haven't forgotten what you owe me?" Kada asked the creature.

"Relax. Neither I nor the bastooks would have let him through if he wished you harm." The domovoy seemed offended, even more so than cats usually do. "Though why you'd need those nasty, dirty little creatures to protect you when you've got me and my kin is hard to understand." The domovoy began grooming its paws, then lay on the ground, resting its chin down.

Kada sighed and pushed the door open. A burst of steam hit her in the face.

Inside the large bathtub sat Inog. Just as Kada stepped in, he seemed in an animated conversation with the bannik, the bathhouse spirit, who casually threw bits of wood into the fire.

"What are you doing here?" she said with a hiss.

Inog glanced up at her. "I would have thought it obvious," he said. His dark hair stuck to his forehead, and the drops of water glistened on his skin.

"You shouldn't be here!" Kada closed the door carefully behind her. "And you!" She turned her anger on the bannik. "You should know better than to let him in here! Never mind you're treating him like a guest of the house!"

The bannik looked ashamed for a moment.

Inog winked at him. "Don't you worry, little one. Kada's anger burns fast but is gone just as quick. You will get your morning milk and bread, I'm sure."

"Make your own promises and you keep them too," Kada said to Inog, shooting the bannik a furious look. "I told you I was done with you. I want you out of here."

"You want me out, I want to talk." Inog picked up a jug on the side of the bath, and poured the hot water over his neck. "Give me what *I* want first and I will be on my way."

Kada stared at him for a moment. Physically removing a god from the building could prove difficult. It would also likely make more noise than she was comfortable with. Inog chortled as if he could read her mind.

"Very well," Kada said. "Tell me whatever it is you need to tell me."

"No problem. While I talk, would you mind doing my back?" He held out a brush to Kada.

"I really hope you're joking." She didn't move, staring daggers.

"I just want to get properly clean." He shrugged his shoulders, an impish grin stretching his lips.

"I saw you roll around in the mud often enough to doubt that." She crossed her arms. "Now out with it."

"Worth a shot." He leaned back in the bath. "Very well, here it is."

"I'm all ears."

"I want you to still visit me."

Kada couldn't help but laugh, in spite of herself.

Inog looked hurt, and with a start she realised he was serious.

"Well, that is an obvious no," she said.

"And why is that?" His hand shot out of the water, and he grabbed Kada's wrist.

"Let go." Kada kept her voice level, speaking between clenched teeth.

"I know you want me." He pulled her a bit closer. The heat from the water steam hit her face. He locked eyes with her. He pulled her closer still, till her face was mere inches from his. Inog stood up in the bath, and stepped out, the water dripping on the floor, pouring along the lines of the hair covering his body.

He grabbed a handful of her hair and pulled her head to the side, exposing the lifeline of her neck. He let his mouth hover above it and let out a growl, a low, rumbling animal sound, warming the skin just below her ear. The water shone in the low light as it trickled down his tan skin. The small hairs on Kada's neck rose up as she breathed in his smell. "I know what you like, and I know what you need. And you need this." His lips brushed against her earlobe. A shiver ran down her spine and she fought against herself. She wanted to push her hips against his, to taste the salt of his sweat on her tongue. She remained very still. "You need me."

"If I did, I would have you still," she said.

He chuckled, a rush of breath in her ear which made her close her eyes, to shut out the sight of him, of his skin and the muscles on his chest, and the dark line of hair running from his navel. "I know you, Kada. You're a creature of magic and power and the forest. You will die here, locking yourself from the rhythm of the world." He let go of her hair, and she let out a sigh, a small sound, which he took for disappointment, for he moved his fingers towards her collarbone, pulling on the string holding together the neck of her nightgown.

The steam from the *banya* made the fabric stick to her skin, and Inog let his eyes wander along the lines of her body, unhurriedly. He stroked her collarbone with his thumb, studying the curve of her breast, her waist, her hips. A smile stretched his lips as he rested his eyes on the darkness of the hair between her legs, visible through the damp fabric.

"You think you want something else, and you think this fat merchant can give it to you." He lifted her hand to his lips and kissed the inside of her wrist. "You haven't given me the chance to give you those things first. And I can give you so much…"

"You have nothing to offer me that would make a difference," Kada said. She shook her head and kept her eyes fixed on his face, refusing to look down. His body was so close she could feel the heat emanating from it. If she took half a step forward, she'd be in his arms. But he kept the remaining distance, hopefully, expectantly, and she would not close it.

"I disagree," Inog said. He raised one eyebrow, mocking Kada's attempt at composure. "I think you like what I give you more than you like the lukewarm embrace of your employer."

"You think very highly of yourself." Kada raised her eyebrows. "Perhaps I like him more than I do you."

Inog laughed, a loud booming noise bouncing off the walls of the *banya*. He released her wrist and instead wrapped his hands around her ribcage, his thumbs resting just below her breasts. "You're a better liar than that! At least try to convince me."

"And what *would* convince you?" She placed both her hands on his chest. He inhaled, a broken, raspy breath, as she stood on tiptoes, bringing her mouth close to his. "Do you need me to tell you *why* I like him better? Maybe I like how he kisses my neck, how his thumb draws a pattern around my nipple when he cups my breasts?" Inog let out a low warning growl, but Kada ignored him. "Perhaps I like how he feels between my legs, how his tongue feels when he moves it inside me–"

"Enough!" Inog roared. He seemed to grow taller, anger flashing in his eyes.

Kada pushed at him with both hands. He slipped and fell backwards into the bathwater.

He came right back up, spluttering. He stared at her, teeth lengthening.

"And what are you planning on doing with those tusks, oh mighty God Inog?" Kada crossed her arms and threw her head back, as if the man in front of her wasn't strong enough to rend her apart. "I thought gods did not get jealous?"

"I'm not jealous." Inog swept his wet hair off his face. "But no god likes others taking what's theirs. That goes for all the gods."

"That's very well, because I was never yours to begin with."

"Perhaps not," he said. "But you have taken what wasn't yours to take, didn't you?" He narrowed his eyes. It gave him an unpleasant, sly sort of look.

"Nothing you say makes sense anymore. I'm leaving." Kada spun around towards the door. "Bannik, don't forget to clean up this mess," she threw over her shoulder.

"Not so fast," Inog said. "I know what you've been hiding."

"I hide many things," Kada said, pausing at the door. "For instance, I will have to hide this visit from the people in the house."

"I know of the man Secha put in the ground, Kada–"

Kada didn't look at him. She held her breath. She hoped that would be all. But hope was for children and for fools.

She shut her eyes, trying to steel herself for what she knew would come next.

"–I know Secha wasn't the gift you claimed she was."

Kada could hear bones cracking behind her as Inog transformed from a man to a boar. She stood very still.

"You can't steal from the gods, Kada," he said. His boar voice was harder to make out, more guttural than his human speech, but Kada could still feel his hurt and resentment. "Sooner or later, we come to collect."

"There is nothing of yours here." Kada pushed open the door. "And I want neither your warnings nor your help."

"And so, you will have neither." She heard him say as she walked back out into the night air.

# CHAPTER 38

A week or so had passed since Gorcay's engagement to Kada, when Artek Lelechek walked up the long road through Torlow, and knocked on Gorcay's door.

He walked in with his head lowered, like a wolf stalking an unfamiliar prey. Lelechek didn't ordinarily come calling on people. They would usually come to him, paying homage to his wealth and status. But that day something shifted. His back was stooped, his eyes bloodshot from the lack of sleep. As he walked into Gorcay's hall, he looked around dazed, as if unsure of where he was.

"My dear Lelechek!" Gorcay came down the stairs, his hand outstretched. He smiled warmly, though his guest knew he despised him, a feeling thoroughly reciprocated. "What brings you here this morning?" Gorcay made a broad gesture, pointing to the small sitting room to the left side of the staircase where he liked to entertain, for it had the most extravagant furniture in the house. He winced as he shook Lelechek's hand, so cold were the tips of the man's fingers.

Lelechek followed Gorcay and sat awkwardly in one of the tall-backed reed-woven chairs. The room had tall shelves filled with books, a point of personal pride for Gorcay. The servants would burn incense in the room every morning, at first because Gorcay heard it kept the mould at bay, and now because he enjoyed the lingering scent too much to do without it.

Gorcay pulled on the bell rope, conveniently installed by his chair, and instructed the thus summoned serving girl to fetch refreshments from the kitchen.

Artek sat in silence until the servant came back with a slice of bread, salt and a glass of spiced milk, which was customary to offer morning guests. Gorcay filled the silence with prattle about the fields and the state of the roads and all the usual nonsense which took little from his concentration and allowed him to observe his guest.

"So what brings you here?" he asked again, once the servant had gone.

"My son," Lelechek said in a hoarse voice. "He's missing."

"So I've heard," Gorcay said, scratching his head. "But I wouldn't worry, Artek. Botrik is a hot head, much like my own Makail, and the two of them have in fact gone off to who knows where many a time in their short lives. So many times, in fact, that if I'd been pulling my hair out each time it happened, I'd be as bald as you!" He rubbed his forearm, the silence falling heavy after his attempt at humour. "Look," he said, suddenly serious. "I know you worry, but Botrik is a big lad, he can take care of himself. And he's not exactly on the straight and narrow, between the two of us. He might be holed up drunk with some of his friends, or off wenching in the nearby towns. Zemya knows I barely hear from my own son about his comings and goings. At some point a father has to learn to let go and trust his children will be alright."

Artek Lelechek listened to that in silence, his eyes fixed on the thick rug beneath his feet. Finally, he raised his eyes to meet Gorcay's. "Have I ever, in all the years you've known me, appeared to you a man prone to hysterics?"

Gorcay shifted uncomfortably.

Artek nodded. "There then, now that's settled, I haven't come to you for handholding, or for words of empty comfort. I have sent my men far and wide. Botrik's closer associates are all accounted for. He's not in any inn, tavern or brothel within fifty miles of Torlow, by any road. He has simply vanished. And wealthy young men don't just vanish." He took a sip of the warmed spiced milk and wrinkled his nose at it, as if he'd forgotten what he was drinking. He took a couple of deep breaths to steady himself, while Gorcay waited in uncharacteristically respectful silence.

"I've asked Vedma Kada to help me already," Artek said.

"I see…" Gorcay shifted a bit, a movement which didn't go unnoticed by his guest. "And?"

A shadow of amusement crossed Artek's face. "She didn't tell you?"

Gorcay kept his face impassive. "She doesn't tell me her vedma business. I don't think those she helps would appreciate me sticking my nose into their private matters."

"No, I suppose they would not," Artek said after a moment. "But the problem is, she promised me help, yet didn't deliver."

"Zemya is a capricious mistress."

"That might be so, but my son's still missing. How he's found doesn't interest me as much as that he *is* found…" Artek's mouth twitched, and he closed his eyes for a moment. He lowered his head into his hands.

Gorcay stood up, and, with hesitation, placed his hand on Artek's shoulder. "I've never seen you like this. Now, man, take heart. He is fine, I'm sure he is."

Artek pushed Gorcay's hand away. "Don't, Sobis. We've known each other too long to pretend we're friends."

He looked up, a tear welling up in the corner of his eye. "I know your opinion of Botrik. I won't even pretend it's undeserved. Zemya knows, my son is not the best of men. He's greedy, entitled and untruthful. I have spoiled him and now it's too late to undo the damage. But he is my son. I would do anything to see him home safe. I come here to your house, to ask *you*, my rival, to help me look for him. Your resources are greater than mine. Your men are many, and your betrothed can speak to the spirits of the land. She might not do her best for me, but surely, if you ask her, she will try again." The room seemed unbearably warm, and Gorcay stood awkwardly over Lelechek.

"I will help you, Artek. Of course I will help you." He held out his hand, and Lelechek, standing up awkwardly, clasped it in his. This they were more comfortable with. This agreement between men, masking the pain and the pity between fathers.

A small noise in the doorway made them both spin around, as if a ghost passed above their heads.

"Who's that?!" Lelechek croaked.

Huddled beside the door that stood ajar, Tula shrunk into herself, holding onto the doorway.

"Oh." Gorcay raised a hand. "Don't worry, Artek, it's just the girl my son's lover took on as her charge. Tala, or Tola, or something."

"Well, she should be whipped, listening in doorways, like a thief!" Artek turned red in the face, any sign of vulnerability gone. "You hear me, child?" He took a step forward, hand raised as if he were going to slap the child who watched him wide-eyed.

Gorcay stepped between them. "Calm yourself," he said. "She's my guest. And look at her, she's just a child, and a mute as well. She won't be telling anything to anyone." He turned back towards Tula, and sat on his haunches, bringing his face to the same level as the child's. He reached out and tucked a lock of her hair behind her ear. "You heard voices and were curious, didn't you?"

Tula pursed her lips and nodded.

"That's alright." Gorcay smiled. "Tell you what, why don't you go to the stables? My stable boy said one of the hounds had a litter of puppies. Why don't you have a look. Maybe your guardian will even let you pick one. As a gift from me"

Tula's eyes went wide, and a smile lit up her face. She nodded and ran off.

When she was out of earshot, Gorcay stood up and turned towards the grim-faced Artek. "I will speak with Kada. We will look for Botrik and find him if he's to be found." He nodded towards the door. "I will walk you out."

# CHAPTER 39

The trees swayed, whispering to each other with the crackling of the bark and the susurration of the leaves.

"Thank you all for coming." Artek Lelechek stood in front of the crowd. "I'm humbled by the love and the concern you all feel for my son. With your help, I hope we can bring him home." His words choked in his throat, and he paused before turning to Kada. "Our own Vedma Kada is here to lead us, to show us where to look, better than any hounds can. To help us succeed, she has promised to use her magic, to call upon one of the spirits who serve her."

"No pressure then," Gorcay whispered to her, barely moving his lips. He looked at her and winked. "The stage is yours, Kada."

She nodded at him and took a step forward. The forest seemed dark to her, darker than usual, though the sun shone, with no clouds in sight. She was trespassing, she knew that. She could feel it in the way the air twisted around her, and how the very blades of grass beneath her feet bent away from her.

Kada could feel the eyes of the townsfolk on her back, the crowd unnaturally quiet, waiting for her to do something, to show them something beyond their own world, a window into something more. That was why they were there, most of them. Not for Botrik Lelechek, certainly, the stupid, vain and brutal son of an unpopular man. Botrik was known in the town for his drinking and his gambling, and for darker things; rumours circled in half whispers, the way crimes of the powerful often are.

And yet here they all were, the good people of Torlow, come to see their vedma's miracles. And more than them, the guests of Gorcay's household had joined in, for the lack of proper entertainment, she thought. A little bit of a vedma show to brighten up the lazy rhythm of their days. And among them stood Sladyana, beside the perpetually grinning Makail. It was Lady Goroncheva's eyes Kada felt on her neck most of all, a shiver of tension which hung on the air. Sladyana wanted to see this miracle, to see Kada's power once more for herself, to keep her hopes alive.

And so Kada had to agree to this. And yet a shiver of revulsion travelled down her spine as she opened the sack she brought with her. A bright-combed rooster struggled inside, its eyes swivelling wildly as it tried to see the one who had trapped it. The bird shrieked and flapped its wings, the blades of its talons tearing at the sack.

A pinch of a bluish powder was blown towards the rooster's head, and it went limp, the fight for its life over before it began. Kada took the rooster out gently, tenderly almost. The rooster opened its beak, a protest of the helpless. Its eye met Kada's. It was a young bird, the comb on its head barely having filled with colour. It had won no battles; it had fathered no chicks.

Its neck cracked loudly, like a walnut shell giving way. Kada pulled out a small paring knife and cut a deep line into the bird's neck, blood dripping onto the ground. She scattered a handful of dried fern flower. It bloomed for an hour one night of the year only and Kada had found and picked it herself. She begrudged having to waste it on a performance, but there were more important things at stake here.

She dropped the rooster to the ground with a sense of relief. But it was not the bone roots that came to claim it. Kada could feel the great tree's displeasure, Zemya's jealousy over the gift.

The tall grass swayed and parted ahead of Kada, as a shape slithered towards her.

A gasp from behind her made Kada chuckle. She saw in the corner of her eye that Gorcay took a step forward, an arm outstretched, as if he meant to pull her back, but she raised one hand and he didn't dare touch her.

"People of Torlow!" She raised her voice without turning around so that everyone in the crowd could hear her. "See before you a znajdnitza! The patron-spirit of lost things. Her, who you so often ask for help in your muttered prayers. Today, you all get to see her for yourselves."

In front of her a figure rose up from the ground. The creature took on the form of a woman, pale and golden-haired, her skin shimmering with a hint of scales, though she could have just as easily taken on any other form. What looked like a wide lace collar around her neck rose up, a snake's mantle growing from her pronounced collarbones. She was naked except for a spiderweb dress, strands of which flew away on the wind. She smiled at Kada and narrowed her eyes.

Kada gave the creature a curt nod and spoke up again. "Znajdnitza, the lady of the forest and the field, the helper of the lost and the finder of the forgotten, will you help us this day?" Kada turned towards Gorcay and gestured for him to step back, which he did with clear reluctance.

The snake woman's forked tongue flicked out of her mouth, as she tasted the air before deciding to speak. "Vedma Kada! You have called me and so I come!" the creature spoke, a hiss building up in her throat. She leaned forward and whispered, so that only Kada could hear her. "You know who I really am. I know you do. I see it in your eyes. And I know you called upon me because you know I delight in misleading, and tricking. But how can you be so certain I will mislead those fools" –she nodded towards the cowering people of Torlow– "And not you?"

"You like the rooster's blood just as much as you like your tricks," Kada said slowly. "And you can't break the promise of a blood gift, should you accept it." Kada smiled as the creature's eyes darted towards the dark pool of blood at Kada's feet.

"Very well," the snake-woman said, and she darted towards the ground.

The crowd let out a collective gasp, and Gorcay called out in alarm, doubtless thinking Kada was the creature's target. But the fear turned to disgust and dismay as the creature began lapping up the cooling blood.

Kada cleared her throat and once more raised her voice so all could hear her. "One among us is lost, a young man, Botrik Lelechek. I implore you to help us find him, to bring him back home to his father!" Kada paused to take a breath. She bit the inside of her cheek to steady herself. The eyes of Artek Lelechek were fixed upon her back and she felt them, choking her with the intensity of the father's hope, as much as if he had his very hands around her throat.

The creature at Kada's feet raised her head, the rooster's blood trickling down her chin. She wiped it away carelessly with her forearm, smearing it further. "I understand," she said in a whisper. "I will look for him, Vedma Kada!" the creature said loudly for the crowd's benefit. "I will track his steps and find him if he *wills* to be found!" She smiled a crooked smile at Kada, exposing one long fang. Kada fought the bile rising in her throat at the hidden meaning.

"Follow me, those who dare!" the creature shouted and then turned to Kada with a mocking smile. "How was that little Vedma?" she hissed out.

Kada nodded, her lips tightened to a line.

The creature brought her serpent's face toward Kada and whispered. "I can feel his bones crumbling in the ground, his flesh stripped clean. But I will take them all far, those fools who trust you."

"Do what you do, blednitza," Kada replied, shutting her eyes tight.

"Oh, don't close your eyes, little one," blednitza laughed. "You chose this. You keep what's not yours to keep. What did you think was going to happen?"

Kada took a step back and turned towards those gathered. "People of Torlow, I have called upon znajdnitza, the kind guiding spirit, to find Botrik. She will use her power to find him, if he can be found. Nobody can do more than that." She turned to Artek Lelechek. "Zemya go with you. May you find your son!" She walked up to Gorcay and let him offer her his arm.

"Take me home, Sobis," she said.

He looked at her quizzically, before casting one last glance at the serpent woman, who led the people into the forest. He frowned, before turning towards his carriage. They walked past his son and his guest. Gorcay bowed his head towards Sladyana, who watched Kada with a different kind of curiosity in her eyes.

"So that was really a znajdnitza?" he said, when they were seated inside, and once Gorcay's servant's whip cracked above the horses' heads.

Kada looked up sharply. The horses' hooves beat on the dry dirt road, and the carriage wheels turned with a creaking. Nobody but Gorcay would hear the next words she said.

She searched his unsmiling face for a moment. "That *is* what I said," she said. She leaned her head against the side of the carriage, the painted resin wall feeling pleasantly cool against her cheek.

Gorcay laughed mirthlessly. "I know what you *said*." He rubbed his left hand, in the place between the palm and the thumb. "I asked if that was really a znajdnitza you have called for us."

"Who else?" Kada tried to smile and failed.

"I don't know, Kada." Gorcay leaned closer. "You tell me."

When Kada remained silent, he sighed, and said, "I know you have your own reasons for marrying me, and I know they are unlikely to be very flattering to me." He raised his palm up as Kada opened her mouth to protest. "No, don't worry, I don't require comforting lies. I'm getting you, after all. What right do I have to complain about why the universe chooses to provide me with what I want?" He smiled, a little sadly. "I care for you, and if I can't have your love, or your desire, at least I hope I have secured your respect. So, believe me, I don't need you to comfort me, and I don't need you to even tell me all your secrets, of which I'm sure a woman such as you has many. But I ask you this: please do not lie to me when I ask you straight."

Kada leaned forward and took his hand in hers. "You don't ask for much."

"I disagree," he chuckled and stroked the top of her hand with his thumb. "Asking you for the truth is asking for a lot, I know."

Kada opened her mouth and shut it again. She looked out the window. The carriage drove down a bumpy road, the familiar landscape rolling past. The golden wheat, the marshes with their deceptive green algae. Kada wished with all her heart to be out there instead of in this carriage, calmly observed by this man.

"Lelechek isn't going to find his son, is he?" he said when the silence lengthened.

"No, he's not." It felt good to tell the truth, just once. Even if she was likely to regret it later.

"A truth at last." Gorcay turned towards the window. "So, what was that creature?"

"A blednitza."

"The thing we scare kids with, so they don't go wandering off?" Gorcay rubbed his chin. "The one drunks blame for getting lost after they've had a few too many?"

"The same."

"It has something to do with Secha, doesn't it?"

She snapped her head back towards him, all blood draining from her face.

"I've noticed..." Gorcay paused, searching for the right words. "I've noticed Secha's different lately. And so are you, watching her like a hawk." He shrugged. "Maybe it's the mysterious man from your past you told me about, or... Well, truth be told, Kada, I wonder if your own Secha isn't the wolf at your door that's keeping you so afraid."

She said nothing, instead thinking of the knife in her pocket, still stained with the rooster's blood. She thought of the herbs in her pouch, which she could blow into Gorcay's eyes. She thought how easy it would be to twist the rope from the blinds at the carriage window around Gorcay's neck. Secha would be safe then. They could disappear, the two of them.

Gorcay's expression didn't change as he took in Kada's tensed body, the wild look in her eyes, her hand slowly moving towards her pocket. Kada felt like his steady gaze was peeling the very skin off her bones. And she knew he could see her thoughts. He sighed and leaned back. "When you're ready," he said, and closed his eyes. After a moment he began snoring.

Kada sat very still, looking at this man she'd promised to marry. This man who knew, who *knew*, and yet he chose to trust her, closing his eyes to the threat of her.

*Like a fool*, she thought. But Gorcay was no fool. He knew she wouldn't kill him, even though he understood enough to condemn them mother and daughter both, should he choose. It would be smart to kill him now. She looked at her hands. Any moment now, she'd pull a knife, she'd bring out the poison, she'd…

She watched his face, with his mouth ajar. His hair flopped over his forehead, making him look younger somehow, like a boy tired out from a day at the books.

He was a danger to Secha, she reminded herself. He might not have threatened her, but how long before he threw his knowledge in Kada's face.

Gorcay snored and twitched in his sleep. Kada smiled, in spite of herself.

Gorcay opened one eye and said, "If you're not going to kill me, do you mind not staring at me? Makes it hard to nap." He closed his eyes again and a crooked smile twisted his lips. "There'll be plenty of time for you to have your wicked way with me once we're married."

Kada opened her mouth and closed it again.

"Speechless? That's a change." Gorcay muttered, before drifting back to sleep.

Kada sat back in the seat and stared out the window, motionless, till they arrived at Gorcay's house.

# CHAPTER 40

The baskets were packed and the blankets were folded and tucked away in the carriages. The servants, both Gorcay's and those his children brought with them, hurried around, nudging each other in the subtle power struggles between the powerless – who packed a basket where it would be least likely to overturn, who would sit by the driver and who would be left behind. All those little confrontations and arguments were held quietly, subtly, and out of the earshot of the employers.

Kada adjusted her sun hat, self-conscious under the curious gaze of the maids and the stable hands. Even before her engagement, she had occupied the space between servant and master, bridging the gulf with her knowledge and her power. She was used to making those around her uncomfortable with this perch she had chosen for herself. Paid, yet beholden to nobody, intimately involved in the life and the decision-making of the rich, but never one of them. It was a space she was content in, a role she had carved out for herself. But this new role she was stepping into felt as uncomfortable as a pair of new, pinchy shoes.

She wasn't Gorcay's wife, yet she was there, living under the same roof as him. She was a vedma and so beyond the control of men, yet she had made promises to the contrary of that. Not a servant, not a mistress. An in-between.

This new dress she was wearing, with its fine billowing sleeves, so impractical for any activity beyond lounging, made her feel like an imposter, a spy of some kind. The overdress was made of dark teal silk, picked by Gorcay, as if Kada were a doll to be dressed up however his fantasy dictated. Which she supposed she was now, she thought, casting a dark look towards her betrothed, who was seemingly in a great mood, chatting away with his son.

A stable boy offered his hand to Kada to help her get into the open carriage. She frowned and was about to wave his help away, when she realised the long heavy skirts of her gown would make it impossible for her to climb up on her own. Once seated she waved to Secha, who, unlike her mother, seemed very happy with her elevated status.

"May I join you?" Sladyana asked, startling Kada.

"Of course!" Kada moved to the side, glancing towards her daughter, who was already seating herself beside Bratyava and her brood in the other carriage.

"The men will travel on horseback, and so it will just be us and Tula, I think," Sladyana said.

Kada smiled weakly.

Once they were all seated comfortably, the driver clicked his tongue and they rolled along the path. Many people of Torlow stuck their heads out from their windows or from behind their doors to catch a glimpse of the fine clothing and the painted carriages pulling the party along. Kada shrunk under the gaze of those she served, as they both marvelled at the way she looked, and perhaps wondered if she meant to abandon them and their care once she married.

She hated it all, but a glimpse of her daughter's red hair ahead calmed her, centering her on what was important.

"What are you so very deep in thought about, Vedma

Kada?" Sladyana asked suddenly. "This is a light-hearted occasion, yet you look so serious one would be forgiven for thinking it's a funeral we're attending."

"Not at all," Kada said. "I'm just tired from last night."

"Why, what happened?" Sladyana said with a smirk.

"I delivered a baby." Kada forced a pleasant smile to her lips, pretending not to catch Sladyana's meaning.

"Is that so?" the woman raised her eyebrows. "I would have thought you'd be done with all that." She groaned as the carriage wheel slid into a groove in the road, making its passengers jump in their seats.

"And why would you think that?"

"What's the point of marrying above your station if not to drag yourself out of other people's muck?"

"I beg your pardon?" Kada gave Sladyana a withering look.

"I can't quite see dealing with the bodily functions of others as a particularly pleasant occupation, you see." Sladyana petted Tula's hair. "Not for one who can avoid doing so, in any case. I hope I didn't insult you?" She turned her head to the side.

"You haven't," Kada said. She looked out at the fields rolling by. The grain had turned golden and was nearly ready for the harvest. A worker noticed the carriages and paused in his labour, admiring the fine procession. Kada turned back towards Sladyana. "I don't consider a vedma as below a rich man's wife. In becoming the latter, I don't cease to be the former. A man in my bed doesn't change what I hear or see, or what I can do for that matter."

"Very well." Sladyana nodded. "In a way, that is exactly what I hoped you'd say."

"We're nearly there!" Makail appeared to the side of their carriage. He rode a fine mare, speckled white, with patches like bruises on the side of an apple. He patted the beast on the side of the neck.

Kada sighed with relief, happy for the distraction. She only half-listened as Gorcay's son flirted with Sladyana.

Kada let herself be lulled by the rhythm of the wheels, their metal spokes creaking as they rolled along the bumpy country road. There had been little rain in the previous weeks, and the air smelled of dust and dry grass.

A pair of brown eyes, fixed on Kada, drew her attention.

Lady Goroncheva's foundling girl was staring at Kada from across the carriage, with a serious expression oddly unsuited to the small face. The child couldn't have been older than five or six, but there was something in her gaze Kada found unsettling. She tried smiling at the girl, but it only made the child's eyebrows knit together.

Once they arrived at their destination, Gorcay helped Kada get down from the carriage. He beamed with pleasure noticing the dress she wore. Kada didn't think she should begrudge him. Such a small claim really, to be able to give her this. But she thought of Inog's hands on her shoulders and she shivered. The claims could so easily escalate from a gift to a demand.

"While the men direct the setting up of the picnic, why don't the two of us have a walk!" Sladyana slid her arm under Kada's elbow and pulled her along.

Gorcay cast them a confused look, but Kada smiled and shrugged her shoulders.

The picnic spot picked for the occasion was on a small hill not far from Torlow, overlooking the woods on one side and the town on the other. A small grove of silver birches shimmered in the sun, their already yellowing leaves fluttering along the lines of the long weeping branches.

"I was hoping you'd have something to tell me by now," Sladyana said. She had kept her voice level, but Kada could feel the tension in her.

*What did I think, that she would forget?* Kada nodded. "I'm sorry, as you know there was the matter of the young Lelechek I had to attend to."

Sladyana gave her an odd look. "And how is *that* going? I haven't heard of him being found."

Kada frowned. "I can only do so much. I have called upon znajdnitza. If the man doesn't wish to be found, then that is outside of my control."

"Oh, I don't believe *that!*"

Kada's mouth went dry, and she stopped for a moment, searching Sladyana's face. "What do you mean?"

Her companion shrugged. "I simply think you are giving yourself too little credit."

"I'm just being realistic."

Lady Goroncheva threw her head back and laughed. "Realistic?" She shook her head, the sheer gauzy veil protecting her hair from the road dust reflecting the light, the braids beneath rubbing against the fabric, catching on the thread. The woman glanced at Kada. "Your vision of what's 'realistic' is somewhat different to most people's. I had no child, and you found my daughter, for me to pluck from a tree no less. You command creatures of the earth and the air. You speak to the bone roots of the Great Mother. No. Your reality is very different from mine, Vedma Kada."

"I fear you judge me too powerful," Kada said. They had reached the birch grove, and stood in the green grass, turned away from their companions, who were already getting comfortable on the blankets. The white and pink flowers clustered on the long stalks of yarrow released their pungent sweet scent into the air. Kada's hand brushed against their tops, and squeezed gently, enjoying the feeling against the skin of her palms.

Sladyana's shoulders went up as she breathed in deeply, seemingly to steady herself, clearly dissatisfied with Kada's reply. "You also have powerful friends," she said, fixing her eyes on Kada.

"Allies, mostly," Kada said slowly.

"Oh, surely more than that!" Sladyana laughed. Across the small distance, Makail raised his head, curious, and Sladyana wiggled her fingers at him. She played the flirtatious debutante role well, Kada thought, but the woman's gaze was steely when it turned back upon her. "I saw him visit you in the *banya*, you know."

Kada's mouth felt dry. "What do you mean?"

"Oh please, it's just us here, Vedma Kada, no need to pretend." Sladyana reached and brushed an invisible speck of dust off Kada's shoulder. "I heard you that night and followed you to the *banya*. There's a small window in the building, you know. And in the dark, with the light inside, I saw it as clear as day."

"I don't know what you think you saw–"

"Don't demean yourself by lying to me, Kada." Sladyana shook her head. "I saw his hands on you. Don't think I blame or judge you at all!" She smiled. "That must have been the best-looking man I have ever seen. And I have seen many."

Kada narrowed her eyes. At least that she could well believe.

"I moved away then, of course, not wishing to observe you in such a state. But I did stay at a distance. And I saw a different creature altogether leave the *banya*."

Kada stared at Sladyana in silence.

"You will help me find my Luba?" Sladyana said.

"I already said I will try."

"Botrik Lelechek might not wish to be found." Sladyana kneeled down among the low bilberry shrubs. Most of the indigo berries were dry and wrinkled from the heat, but she pushed the little tear-shaped leaves apart till her fingers found one still plump from the moss-held dew. "But my daughter does."

"How can you be certain?"

"I know." Sladyana looked at the berry against the light, rolling it between her fingers, then popped it in her mouth. "A mother knows. And I want you to find her and bring her back."

"We can only be hopeful," Kada said slowly, shielding her eyes against the sun.

Sladyana narrowed her eyes. "I hope you don't misunderstand my meaning when I say, I am heartily sick of waiting and hoping."

Kada held Sladyana's stare. "Yes," she said. "I suppose you are."

"And what are you going to do about it?"

The two women stood in the shade of the grove, as still as statues.

"I will try something else."

"Now." Sladyana held her hands clasped together, so tightly Kada could see the white on the skin where the woman's fingers dug into her own flesh. "Not a week from now. Not in a month, not in three days. Now, Vedma Kada. Show me *something*." There was a hint of desperation in her voice. And Kada could use that.

"Very well. Let's go to the group."

"No!" Sladyana actually stomped. "Here."

"Just a moment, Lady Goroncheva," Kada said. She raised her hand and brushed her fingers against Sladyana's shoulders. "I need a few things from there. I will show you something now. Something real."

Under Sladyana's watchful gaze, Kada went to the picnic blanket and picked up a piece of bread, a slice of cured meat, and a small slab of cheese. She wrapped them in a handkerchief and picked up a glass bottle of vodka as well.

"Are you two having a picnic away from us then?" Makail asked. "At least leave the liquor so we can mourn the loss of your company."

"Sorry, Makail," Kada said with a wink. "This is women's business. We'll be back in a moment."

"Oh, are you to perform some of your vedma tricks!" Bratyava piped in. She started to get up, her large belly making the movement awkward. "I want to see!"

"No, daughter," Gorcay said. His tone surprised Bratyava enough that she sat back down. "I believe Vedma Kada has private business with Lady Goroncheva. Isn't that right, *moya mila*?"

Kada rather suspected Gorcay considered everything his business. So, the fact he didn't insist on being part of the conversation was a respectful gesture. One whose value she appreciated. Kada nodded. She stood up and started walking back to the grove.

Gorcay blocked her way momentarily, leaned forward, concern written on his face. "Is everything alright? Is she causing you any trouble?"

"No." Kada's eyes widened in surprise. She looked into his blue eyes and saw nothing there to cause her alarm. No curiosity or anger, just worry. Something suspiciously like affection gripped her heart. She pushed it down. "Any trouble that's to be had, Sobis, is to be had with me."

"I believe that," he said, then moved towards the rest of the company. "Since we're being so brutally abandoned by the two ladies, what say we start with the honey cake to sweeten the day?" Tula clapped, bouncing on her knees. "There now," Gorcay said and mussed the child's hair. "I knew it was a good idea as soon as it popped into my head!"

Kada walked back up towards the small grove, ignoring her daughter's questioning looks.

She glanced at Sladyana. Lady Goroncheva could barely contain her excitement, her whole body tense. So hopeful.

"Let's move to the other side of the grove," Kada said. "I need the quiet."

"Whatever you need, you shall have." Sladyana lifted up her skirt and followed Kada through the undergrowth, uncomplainingly, though her fancy embroidered slippers wouldn't be fit for wear after.

The two women emerged on the other side of the birch grove, and Kada knelt in the grass. She opened up the handkerchief and took the bits of food from the inside. "Do you have anything of Luba's?" she asked, raising her eyes.

Sladyana flinched, startled.

"It's fine if you don't, but it will make it easier."

"Her hair," Sladyana pulled a small locket necklace from under her dress. It was fine silver filigree and was likely costly. But Kada knew its real value lay in its contents, as she watched Sladyana open it with trembling hands. Inside was a cutting of soft soot-black hair, tied with a red thread.

Kada took a few hairs from it and gave the rest to Sladyana, who was visibly relieved at not having to part with it all. "Now, you should probably stand back," Kada said.

Sladyana shook her head. "Not in this. I want to be a part of it." She kneeled next to Kada with a determined look on her face.

"Very well." Kada breathed in deep and dug her left hand into the ground. She felt the tickling of the bone roots, as they moved beneath her, the tips of the tendrils touching her fingertips. With the other hand she took out a small pouch from a hidden pocket in her skirt and emptied the contents onto the ground.

"What's that?" Sladyana craned her neck to see better.

"I need to focus," Kada said. Chastened, Sladyana once more sat back in her spot, still too close for Kada's liking.

Kada half-smiled as she felt the bone roots receding from the bite of the herbs she'd spilt.

Her left hand still in the ground, she pulled the stopper of the vodka bottle with her teeth and poured some of the contents on the ground, wrinkling her nose at the smell.

She mumbled a few words, trying to crumble the piece of bread onto the earth. The bread was freshly baked and too wet to come apart, so in the end she just pulled off little bits of it and placed them onto the earth. With her right hand she dug a little hollow in the earth, put the piece of cheese and meat inside, and covered it up with soil.

Sladyana and Kada waited in silence for a moment. Kada could feel Sladyana's excitement and impatience, like a vibration in her gut. But the woman said nothing, too afraid of breaking the spell Kada was weaving.

Finally, their patience was rewarded, as five straight bones, yellowy-white and sharp-ended, stuck out of the ground and grasped Kada's left hand, which was still dug into the ground.

Sladyana gasped, her hand flying to her mouth.

"Don't worry," Kada whispered. "It's still Mother Zemya. It's the bone roots that are deeper to the heart of her tree."

"They look different," Sladyana whispered. Her eyebrows were furrowed, and her face went a deathly white.

"None but vedmas ever get to see these," Kada said. "This is not the surface of things. This is the heart of Fiesna, and your best chance to reach your daughter. Now, the hair."

Kada picked a few of Luba's baby hairs she took from Sladyana's necklace and placed them in the ground.

"Dearest mother, hear my plea," Kada said, her head thrown back. "Help this mother find the child you have gifted her. Please bring her to us, the stolen child Luba, and damn the fox who stole away your own gift!" She chanted, swaying her body from side to side. Then, suddenly, she stopped. The bone fingers receded back into the ground and Kada turned to Sladyana with a grin.

"Did it work?" Sladyana looked to the ground then to Kada. "Will Zemya give my Luba back to me?"

"The Great Mother has listened," Kada said. "She will search for the fox, and, if your daughter is to be found, she will be brought back to you."

Sladyana's face fell.

"Did you think Zemya would just produce your child here and now?" Kada shook her head, as if disappointed at the other woman's ignorance. "The plea has been accepted. Now you must wait. And the Great Mother will bring you your child. But be careful." She raised a finger in warning. "Zemya doesn't reward the unworthy. Make your offers and gifts to her generous, make your prayers earnest. Hide nothing. For, if you offend Mother Zemya in any way, if you don't prove yourself worthy, she will bring you nothing but grief."

"Oh, I will!" Tears stood in Sladyana's eyes. She suddenly threw herself into Kada's embrace and kissed both of her cheeks. "I will not let my child down. Not for a second time. I will be worthy now. Thank you, Kada, thank you." She grabbed both of Kada's hands and placed a reverent kiss on them. Then she stood up and brushed the dirt off her dress. She turned to go. "Aren't you coming?"

Kada shook her head. "I need to pray a bit more. I will be with you all in a moment. Sladyana nodded, and, beaming at Kada, she practically danced off.

For a moment, only a moment, Kada felt ashamed. But hope in itself is a comfort. And that is what she gave Sladyana. Hope. For now, at least.

"That trick must be getting a bit boring," a voice came from behind Kada.

"Why?" she said. "Do you bore of the food I give you?"

"Oh, don't mind my words, no complaints here!" A creature dug its way out of the earth. Its hands and arms were bare bone, with half the flesh rotting off its worm-like body. Its orange eyes glowed deep within the cavernous sockets of its too-large head. "Isn't it some kind of a blasphemy though?" it said, packing some of the dirt-covered cheese into its mouth. "Not for me, as damned as I am already. But for one such as you, don't you worry?"

"My worries are my own," Kada said. "And why would Mother Zemya bother with words and broken promises. She has the whole world growing from her roots. She gets her own, and I get mine. And you can serve my needs, or you can be discarded, miecnik.

"Oh, I know!" The miecnik laughed. "I know what you did to some of my brethren."

"Do you grieve them?" Kada glanced at the creature.

"Not in the least. They chose to burrow in the land protected by a vedma, more fool them. I'm not as stupid as some of my kind." The creature gave Kada a sly look. "Of course, you might not be a vedma for much longer, not if you keep disappointing your people."

"Are you giving me advice now, miecnik?"

"Merely making an observation." Using the tapered bone of its fleshless index finger, the miecnik picked at something stuck in its teeth.

"Noted. Now go back whence you came." Kada stood up and looked at the canopy of trees above her. She needed another moment, just a breath to compose herself again.

"And that other woman?" the miecnik asked, stroking its long, scraggly beard with its bone fingers.

Kada didn't reply and walked off, the creature's laughter ringing in her ears.

# CHAPTER 41

"I can pick anything I like?" Secha clapped her hands together like an excited toddler. She and her mother stood in Gorcay's warehouse, the large brick structure smelling of perfume, and the herbs meant for keeping away the moths from the costly garments stored in large chests of reed and lacquer. Before Secha lay rolls upon rolls of fabrics. Fine brocade, with gold-thread detail. Delicate muslin, as sheer as a drop of water and as light as a baby's breath. Silks, painted and embroidered, in a rainbow of colours. Secha's fingers hovered over this bounty, not quite daring to touch it.

Kada chuckled and rubbed her hand on her daughter's back. "Sobis says yes. He wants you to have a fancy dress for the wedding."

"Huh." Secha glanced at her mother, a mischievous grin on her face. "That's the first time I have ever heard you call him that unprompted."

"Is it?" Kada raised her hand to her hair self-consciously. It was braided by Sladyana's own maid, sent under strict instructions to treat Kada to the finest courtly hairstyle. Kada felt ridiculous, but it wouldn't do to insult Sladyana. Lady Goroncheva was wholly consumed by the false hope Kada gave her. It wouldn't last, though. Power doesn't impress as much when marked with failure. But by the time suspicion swelled, Kada and Secha would be living a very different life, a protected one.

"You know what I think?" Secha turned Kada's attention back to the fabric. "I think Gorcay's growing on you."

Kada glanced at the warehouse assistant and motioned with her chin. Luckily the man had the sense to make his getaway. "I think you shouldn't read too much into things," she said, once she was certain nobody was listening in.

Secha gave her a look. "He *is* growing on you! Like mould on a curd cheese!" She cast her hand over her eyes. "I can see it now! You will fall in love with him and cast your daughter away, as a reminder of the squalor of your previous life!"

Kada scoffed. "Don't be ridiculous." She paused, pretending to inspect a piece of gold and yellow silk. "I do like and respect him though. And you should too. There is more to him than meets the eye."

Secha rolled her eyes. "He's nice enough, I suppose."

Kada frowned. "Nothing wrong with nice, you know." She pinched Secha's chin and looked into her daughter's eyes. "Or kind, or gentle. It's something you'd do well to remember, my girl. Especially now, when we're so close. So close to safe and happy."

"I know." The grin disappeared from Secha's face, and the pretence of mischievous humour with it. "I like him, Mama. I like him and I like that you like him. I'm just scared."

"What are you scared of my baby? What do you have to be scared of with me to keep you safe?"

Secha didn't answer. She just watched her mother for a moment with her leaf-green eyes.

"I thought I'd find you here!" Gorcay's voice came from behind them.

Secha's face transformed, all of a sudden the very picture of child-like cheekiness. "We're savouring the moment!"

"I can see that!" he said, placing his arms around Kada and Secha. He leaned forward to look at the fabrics on the table and frowned. "Gniv! What is this that you have brought out!" he called out to the warehouse assistant. "This is my daughter-to-be! You think me so stingy? Bring out the good stuff! No, not that!" He scoffed and looked at Kada. "Never mind, I have to show him." He walked over and pushed the terrified-looking Gniv aside. "Now here, this one just came from Noskow, you know they have the best weavers, yes and that one too!" He beamed at Kada. She smiled back, all the while thinking back to their ride in the carriage. He hadn't mentioned it since, and she knew how much it pained him to keep silent on it. He was not a man who liked to be kept in the dark, but he would not hurry her.

"These fabrics Gniv showed us are really some of the finest I've ever seen," Kada objected weakly. Gniv shot her a grateful look.

"Nonsense," Gorcay waved it away. "There is a difference between good and what merely *looks* good. And a good merchant can tell." He locked eyes with Kada for a moment before striding towards Secha and leading her towards another table. "Now this!" he made a sweeping gesture, nearly knocking poor Gniv off his feet. "*This* is worth looking at!"

Secha touched the glittering silks, as delicate and smooth as a butterfly wing. "I like this one," she said, pointing towards a blue damask.

Gorcay pulled it out, heedless of what was knocked over in the process. "What do you think, *moya mila*?" He turned to Kada, holding the fabric against Secha.

"It's beautiful," Kada said, turning her head to the side. "But I think this feels more true to you." She stepped towards the table and picked up a silk, plain and unembroidered. It was the green of birch leaves held against the sun, as lush as a spring morning, with thread glittering, as if sprinkled with dew drops. Kada put it against Secha and held her breath. Her daughter's eyes sparkled against the shadows on the folds of the fabric, and her red curls showed up even brighter next to it. Secha nodded. Her teeth flashed so white, so sharp, against her red lips. The playful child of the moment before was gone and Kada felt like a stranger watching her.

"She looks beautiful! Like a rusalka," Gniv whispered, staring open-mouthed.

"What are you staring at?" Gorcay spun around. "Get to work folding the rest, my boy. She'll be having this one." He cleared his throat. "Very well. Now the trimmings." He walked off to shout at another warehouse boy, leaving Kada and Secha alone.

"I will turn sixteen in this dress," Secha whispered suddenly. She took her mother's hand in hers and placed her forehead against Kada's. "I will be yours forever then. I believe it now."

"As you should have before." Kada laughed uncomfortably.

Secha nodded. "I should have."

"Kada, come pick some muslin for Secha and yourself!" Gorcay called out.

"Coming!" Kada laughed and took Secha's hand.

# CHAPTER 42

"What in the name of the Great Mother are you doing?" Makail's voice came suddenly, startling Sladyana from her meditation. She'd secluded herself in Gorcay's household shrine, a small room at the back of the house. It was rarely used, in spite of its beautiful furnishings, and so Sladyana didn't expect to be interrupted. While the master of the house made sure the room was sumptuously decorated, he was not a pious man, the gods playing small role in his life.

"Ah, it's you. Good morning, my friend."

"Good morning indeed!" Makail stood over the kneeling Sladyana. "I like the nights, for the company and the drinking, but you are usually in bed at this hour. With me, preferably. Yet I find you kneeling by the dirt like you're a chicken looking for grubs."

"I suspect there's a point somewhere in there?" Sladyana raised her eyebrows.

"I was hoping you were going to take it for an invitation," Makail said. "But if not, I suppose you could at least satisfy my curiosity. What are you doing here?"

"Praying."

Makail scoffed derisively. Then he paused. "You're serious."

"Deathly." Sladyana opened the little hinged door covering a round hole in the floor tiling: The chapel's direct link to the soil, and by extension, to Zemya's roots. The woman pulled a slice of bread and crumbled it before her. She then carefully took off the top off the tin milk jug and poured some milk onto the soil.

"And may I ask why?" Makail scratched his head. "I thought we've come here to enjoy each other's company, not to indulge in yet more ridiculous rituals that achieve nothing."

"I've seen what Vedma Kada can do," Sladyana interrupted him. "I've seen the heart roots of Mother Zemya, and they demand devotion and gifts. I must prove myself worthy for the goddess to help bring my daughter back."

"The heart roots?" Doubt creeped into Makail voice. "Never heard of them."

"Well, of course not," Sladyana said. She watched as the bone roots pushed out of the ground, sluggishly, and lapped up the milk. She'd prayed for the best part of the night, and this lazy acceptance of the offering is all she'd been rewarded with. "You're not a vedma. It's not everyone that gets to see the miracle of the Great Mother."

"I suppose not," Makail said. "But this new-found devotion – did Vedma Kada tell you how long you're expected to keep it up?"

Sladyana went silent.

"I didn't think so." Makail sighed and looked through the glass-paned window towards the East, as the rising sun painted the sky pink. "So ever since you saw the fox by your home, you've had signs, and messages, and small miracles, some of which you've told me about, some I suspect you kept to yourself. You had a glut of them, in fact, in the last few weeks. And yet there's one thing that you're still to see."

"What's that?"

"Results," Makail said, leaving her alone to her thoughts.

# CHAPTER 43

Makail groaned. "Are we to sit here for the rest of the afternoon then?" He paced the floor and stared out of the window. "Such a waste of daylight!"

"What would you have us do?" Sladyana asked, as she turned the page of the little poetry book she'd found on Gorcay's shelves. It was full of insipid little rhymes, but she supposed it was calming to read about tulips and spring chickens.

The day was of the sort that sat heavy on one's head, and made the thought of movement somewhat unappealing, but Makail was not used to boredom, and the sheer youth of him despised the calm and quiet.

There was no entertainment planned for that day, and so he'd complain and cajole till some was arranged for him.

"Let's go on a ride," he said, eyes twinkling. "My father keeps a palfrey that'd be perfect for you."

"I suppose so." Sladyana turned to Tula, who was playing with a spinning top on the floor next to her chair. The girl yanked on the string and watched with rapt attention as the toy twirled. "Tula, you stay behind. You can play with the puppy Gorcay's so kindly gifted you." The child nodded, and bumped her head against Sladyana's hand, almost like a cat. Sladyana smiled, and stroked Tula's hair. The girl smiled at her. Sladyana felt a pang of guilt at leaving the child in a house where nobody understood her. Maybe once Sladyana got Luba back, she and Tula would become friends. Sladyana indulged in a moment's daydreaming, imagining her daughter and Tula, two girls playing together in the sun. She shook her head. But of course, when Luba was returned, she'd be nearly sixteen. Practically a young woman, and not a child. Still, Tula was a charming companion. Luba would surely grow fond of her.

"And what about me?" Bratyava piped in, breaking Sladyana out of her reverie. She'd been sitting in the corner, playing some fashionable single player card game Sladyana thought looked terribly dull. "Will you just leave me all alone?"

"I believe your husband's somewhere around." Makail smiled sweetly, pulling Sladyana up to her feet. "Surely he's the best company for you!"

Bratyava rolled her eyes. "Of all the mean things you have said to me, Makail, I believe this one is the meanest."

"We're doing you a favour." Makail patted his sister on the shoulder as he led Sladyana out. "Once we're out of sight, think how much easier it will be for you to complain about us!"

He ducked to avoid the fan thrown by Bratyava and he and Sladyana left the room, laughing.


Sladyana adjusted her seat on the saddle. It was a particularly beautiful one, with a thick hand-woven fabric stretched over the rigid frame. It matched the blanket under it. But of course it did. Gorcay's house was the most deliberately decorated one Sladyana had ever seen. The man had been the architect of his own fortune, by and large, that much she knew from Makail. But unlike some of the newly rich folk who had entered Sladyana's circles on the wave of their wealth, Gorcay did not fill his house with an assortment of gaudy, yet expensive status symbols. Instead, he opted for the highest quality in virtually every item, from the linens to the buckets used to fill the *banya's* bathtub. It was the kind of precision that Sladyana appreciated. Which made his relationship with Kada all the more puzzling. What would a man like that want with a wife who could not be controlled or moulded to fit into a carefully thought-through role in his life.

"Are you ready?" Makail rode up to her, his tall felt hat matching the blue of his eyes. She nodded, and they both pressed their heels into their horses' flanks.

Sladyana's riding skirt draped beautifully over the side of the horse, the red tones of the fabric contrasting nicely against the chestnut palfrey's coat. Those sorts of details were important, she knew. Makail's admiring glance would have told her so if she didn't. Her hand rose to adjust her simple embroidered headdress, which kept her hair out of her face.

They took the shortest way out of the town. The sky was overcast, and the air itself felt somewhat heavy. They rode through the path leading across a field where farmers were transferring the harvested haystacks onto wide carts. Those would take the dry hay with its precious cargo of golden grain to the granaries and barns. A couple of the men bowed their heads in greeting as Makail and Sladyana rode past, a couple of women glancing at Sladyana in curiosity.

Most of the town was helping out with the harvest, the threat of the imminent rain spoiling the crop heavy on everyone's mind. Even small children carried the wheat sheaves, while the men and women loaded them up onto large carts. It was hard work, but nobody, not even the smallest among them, complained. Sladyana tightened her grip on the reins, suddenly self-conscious of her and Makail's indolence and entertainment. It would pass, that feeling. But for now, she fixed her gaze firmly ahead.

Would she even know her daughter now? If she saw her among the people of Torlow? If Luba was among those women with their sleeves rolled up and their hands tanned by the sun. Sladyana liked to think so. But as her aunt Kasimira would hasten to add, she would also like to think many things. That the apples from their orchards could turn gold, that the brass figurine of a bird could sing, that drinking nettle tea could roll back the years on her face. Kasimira could think clearly about things, no matter how hard or painful, and Sladyana sometimes envied her aunt the skill.

"Look over there!" Makail called to her, tearing her from her thoughts.

She shielded her eyes from the light and, over the field, in the largely barren stretch of land used for pasture, stood an old man, his hair wild, and his back bent. The man Makail pointed to stared towards the woods, praying or crying, Sladyana wasn't sure. He held something in his hands, a garland of flowers, and a jug.

"Do you recognise him?" Makail said.

Sladyana shook her head.

"It's Artek Lelechek himself!"

Her jaw dropped. The man she saw in that field bore little resemblance to the man she saw when Kada called upon the znajdnitza to search for his missing son two weeks before. That man was straight-backed, and clear-eyed.

"The poor man," Makail said, rubbing his chin. "It appears his son doesn't want to be found, after all, for whatever reason. He was a good-for-nothing so that shouldn't surprise anyone. But Artek took it hard."

Sladyana shot Makail a strange look then clicked her tongue and trotted up towards the old man, forcing the horse off the path. The beast whinnied and tried to pull her back towards the more comfortable road, but it obeyed when she pulled back on the reins.

"Where are you going?" Makail called after her, then swore as his horse stumbled. Sladyana didn't look back.

She dismounted and left the palfrey to graze as she walked up to the old man, who was now kneeling in the grass, swaying backward and forward as if in a trance.

"Artek Lelechek?" she said softly when she was right by him.

The man's flint eyes shot up at her. His brows furrowed. "Do I know you?"

"Not exactly," she said. She felt awkward standing over the old man, so she sat next to him. She tensed her jaw as she saw a hidden thistle leaf catch on the fine fabric of her skirt. "I have met you briefly, but you wouldn't remember. It was during the search for your son."

"Yes." Lelechek nodded. "I'm sorry, I usually remember people."

"I understand." Sladyana heard Makail get off his horse and she gestured for him not to approach.

"Ah, but I do know *him*," Lelechek said, pointing to Makail with his chin. "You're staying with Gorcay, aren't you?"

"Yes, I–"

"Did Vedma Kada ask you to speak to me?" Lelechek

interrupted her. His face brightened for a moment. "Did she find out anything more about my Botrik?"

"No," Sladyana said. "I'm sorry," she added, as the old man looked down.

"I'm doing what she told me, you know," he said. "I don't skimp on my offerings to Mother Zemya. I pray, I chant." He patted his bare head self-consciously.

Sladyana gasped as she saw the many criss-crossing lines cut into the skin on his hand. A little blood seeped through the sleeves of his shirt as well, the dark markings on the light linen.

Lelechek looked away, embarrassed. "Mother Zemya will accept the mead and the honey, and the flowers. But none of it worked!" He stared towards the woods. "Vedma Kada told me to pray, to be diligent. She said it might make the difference."

"I thought your son didn't want to be found..." Sladyana said.

"How could that be?" He shook his head. "His home is here. Many were happy to abandon the search after that first attempt failed. I can't exactly blame them. Botrik was not always as I'd have wished him to be, that is true. But a father's heart knows." Artek balled his fist and thumped his chest. "He would not stay away from me unless he had to. Unless something kept him. So, I went back to see Vedma Kada, after we didn't find him in the forest. I went back and I demanded she ask Mother Zemya for me. And she did, to her credit." He nodded, his eyes closed. "She did, though I was less than courteous with her. She poured the mead on the ground and some other things, though I didn't get what you'd call a proper look. And the bone roots from the very heart of Zemya came out, wouldn't you know."

"From the heart of Zemya?" Sladyana repeated the words, a strange feeling coming over her.

"Yes." Artek Lelechek smiled at the thought. "Different to the bone roots we see at the surface. Not the white wriggly things, but yellow bone, like fingers, popping out of the ground!"

"And what happened then?" Sladyana fought to keep her voice level. Her fingers grasped a bunch of her skirt's fabric and tightened around it, till the muscles in her arms ached.

The man didn't seem to notice, evidently glad to be able to tell this to someone who listened. "She said Mother Zemya would bring him back to me." He looked at Sladyana, his eyes gleaming wet. "That the Great Mother would help me, if I believed hard enough, if I stayed true and prayed diligently. And I try, I really try." He wiped his eyes with the back of his hand. "But I fear I'm failing. I fear my faith is not strong enough. For I have nothing else to give, and yet my boy is still not with me." He paused, a raspy breath caught in his throat. "But I can't give up now, can I?"

"No, I suppose you cannot," Sladyana whispered. She stood up and placed her hand on the man's shoulder. "It looks like it will rain soon. You should go home."

"Oh no." He shook his head. "I think I will stay a while longer. Thank you though," he added.

"For what?" she asked.

"For listening to an old man. It makes it easier somehow."

"I'm not sure anything can make it easier," she said, her eyes turning to the forest. "But you're welcome. I wish you luck."

But Artek Lelechek wasn't listening anymore. He went back to swaying back and forth, humming a prayer.

Sladyana walked towards her horse, holding up her skirt

with one hand. She placed one palm on the animal's neck, the warmth and the smell of it oddly soothing. She waited wordlessly as Makail walked up to help her climb on.

"You're upset," Makail said, grunting as she stepped into his laced hands and hoisted herself up. He watched her for a moment. "What did you talk to him about?" He smiled and shook his head. "He's just an old fool and that idiot son of his will surely show up one day, with a hole in his pocket and some foreign pox on his ass. Not worth your worrying over!"

"Be quiet," Sladyana snapped, her eyes flashing as she looked down at Makail. She softened at the shock in his face. "The man lost a child," she said. "I know well what that's like."

Makail had the good sense to look ashamed of himself, so she rewarded him with a brush of her fingertips on his cheek. "Let's go back," she said.

He nodded and mounted his horse.

Before they rode back, Sladyana glanced once more at the old man in the field. She bit her lip hard, as the cuts on her own forearm throbbed under her long sleeves.

# CHAPTER 44

Secha hummed to herself, letting the honey drip from the strip of honeycomb, heavy golden drops falling into a big jar. She breathed in deeply, the sweet smell filling the air. The bees were calm that day, some settling on her shoulders as she worked.

A movement in the corner of her eye attracted Secha's attention. As if sensing her alarm, the bees flew up in a small cloud above her head, only to settle back down when she laughed. "You're Tula, are you not?" Secha called out.

Tula peeked out from behind a tree in Gorcay's garden. The girl, clearly deciding Secha wasn't a threat, stepped out. She did so tentatively, as if any sudden movement on Secha's part would cause her to run away.

"Do you like honey?" Secha asked. The thinly veiled promise of a treat was too much for the child, as Secha knew it would be. Tula walked up, nodding vigorously.

"You don't talk," Secha said. It wasn't a question.

Tula shrugged her shoulders.

"Don't worry, I know how to listen," Secha said. She broke off a small piece of honeycomb and held it out to Tula. The bees buzzed, their suspicion filling the air. Tula's eyes widened. Secha knew that even from a few paces away Tula would be able to sense the vibration of the thousands of little wings, splitting and slicing the air.

Secha grinned and whispered a word. The nervous buzzing subsided. She then held the piece of honeycomb above her lips, her face towards the sun, and took a bite. The sticky honey dripped down her chin, and she giggled like a small child.

Tula cocked her head to the side, a serious expression on her face. But the honey smelled so sweet, of blossom and the forest and the heather growing in the hills. The scent clearly pushed away her concerns till she took a step forward, then another, her little hands outstretched, her desire for the treat written all over her face.

Secha held out another piece of honeycomb and allowed Tula to take it, gingerly, with her fingertips so that she only got as close as absolutely necessary.

Tula took a bite, stuffing the piece into her mouth quickly, as if Secha was about to snatch it right back. Her shoulders relaxed, and languid contentment spread across her face like a smile.

"There you go," Secha said. She sat down in the dirt, stretching her legs, her feet bare, like a peasant girl's. She raised her eyebrows at Tula and wiggled her toes.

Tula, the dreamy spell of the honeycomb unbroken, laughed soundlessly. She sat next to Secha and, after a moment's thought, pulled her own slippers and socks off.

"That's right, little one." Secha nodded. She held out another small piece of the honeycomb towards Tula, who didn't hesitate this time.

They ate together, honey dripping on their clothes, staining them. The bees scurried to collect their carelessly scattered treasure, as Secha watched the child from the corner of her eye.

Secha tapped the ground with her index finger, once, twice.

A tendril of the bone roots shot out of the ground and wrapped itself around Tula's wrist. The child made a shocked sound and looked up wide-eyed at Secha.

The child struggled, but the roots held firm.

Secha turned onto her knees and crawled up closer, till her moon face was inches from Tula's. "I know," she said, exposing her very white, sharp teeth.

Tula's eyes turned perfectly round, and she shrank into herself.

Secha placed her hands on Tula's shoulders and repeated, "I *know.*" She turned her head to the side. "I don't know what it promised you. But it's all lies. The fox always lies. *Especially* to small children."

Tula shook her head violently, a tear trickling down her cheek.

"You don't need to be afraid of me, do you understand?" Secha suddenly pulled the girl into her arms, a tight hug against the thrashing frame. "But you *do* need to be afraid." She pulled away, finally letting Tula push her off with her one free hand.

"I will not surrender, do you understand?" Secha said, a cold note entering her voice. "And I'm not unprotected." She clapped and the bees all rose in the air, their buzzing deafening. Secha stared at the child before her, her green eyes bright, a strange expression on her lips.

Tula covered her head and sobbed, curled on the grass.

Suddenly, the buzzing ceased, and Secha whipped her head up, covering her face with her hands. "Oh no," she looked at Tula, and a look of horror entered her eyes. "I'm so sorry!" She touched the bone roots, which receded back into the ground. "I didn't mean to scare you, little one... I just–" She tried to touch Tula's back, but the child recoiled, the look of fear replaced by a sudden fury, a soundless scream stretching her lips. The little hand found a small stone, which she flung blindly at Secha. The stone hit Secha's cheek, painting a line across the skin, biting just below the surface.

"I deserved that," Secha said with a sigh.

Tula, heedless of the fact Secha couldn't understand her, was gesturing wildly, the emotions demanding to be expressed, the silent words' intent clear in its intensity. Suddenly the child froze. Her hands suspended mid-motion, she stared at Secha, at the line on Secha's cheek, which welled up, not with blood, but with gold sap.

# CHAPTER 45

"I can't see it!" Sladyana called out. The rain began to fall, sparsely, the heavy drops darkening the fabric of her clothes. A late summer storm was growling out its arrival somewhere over the horizon, as the day was slowly coming to an end.

"I've lived here my entire life almost," Makail said through gritted teeth, "and when I tell you we need to turn right on this road, then we turn right."

Sladyana squinted. The road stretched straight ahead only, the path darkening with patches of wet sand. To the right there was nothing but a gulf, a cliff edge with a slope's jagged stony edge falling nearly vertical all the way to the bottom.

"My horse can't go down that cliff!" she said. "Where have you taken us?" She tightened her hands around the horse's reins.

"What cliff?" Makail threw his arms in the air. "We've been riding for hours, you as sullen and quiet as a woodcutter passing over the roots! You insisted on going round and round in circles. Have you gone as crazy as Artek Lelechek? What next, Zemya preserve us!"

"Crazy? Me?" Sladyana scowled. "I'm not the one trying to turn my horse into this abyss! But go ahead, be my guest, and if you feel so confident your horse can scale it, then lead the way, and break your neck while you're at it!"

"Damn your nonsense woman!" Makail swore and turned his horse towards the cliff. He clicked his tongue.

Sladyana screamed as the horse trotted right over the edge, but the scream froze in her throat, as both the horse and Makail disappeared.

"Makail?" she whispered, panic rising in her chest. The cliff was still there, and so were the jagged stones on its side. For a moment her vision went blurry. Makail was nowhere to be seen. "Makail!"

"Are you coming or not?" Makail's irritated voice came through the nothingness before her.

"I can't see you!"

There was a moment's silence. "I'm right in front of you."

Tears of frustration stood in Sladyana's eyes. "I can't see you!"

"Hold my hand." And out of nowhere, Makail's hand appeared, surrounded by mist. A glimpse of a horse's flank appeared in the air, like an apple bobbing in in a pail of milk.

Sladyana hesitated, seeing the chasm before her. A part of her wished she could just turn around and ride away. Go back to her home, back to her house of mourning. But Tula was still at Gorcay's, with *her*. With the red-haired vedma, lying, hiding. Well, she wouldn't be able to hide for much longer.

Sladyana reached out and clasped Makail's hand. "Lead me back," she said.

A breath caught in her throat as her horse stepped forward. She closed her eyes, half-expecting to fall. But the horse walked onwards. She dared open one eye and saw Makail's half-amused expression. Their horses stood abreast on a path, shaded by trees on either side. Ahead the smoke from the town house chimneys snaked up towards the sky.

"You really saw a cliff then?" he said. "You weren't tricking me?"

"I'm too old for such tricks." Sladyana looked around her. They were once more on the path towards Torlow.

"Did you anger some spirits here?" Makail let go of her hand and scratched the back of his head under his hat. The moment his hand let go of hers, the landscape changed again. The world whirled before her eyes until Sladyana saw nothing but a stretch of arid land, dry bramble tendrils snaking their way across the ground, twisting and rising to form an impenetrable wall. Suddenly a bull appeared in front of her, foam at its mouth, its horns gleaming and sharp. It noticed her and wore at the ground with its hoof, kicking up the dust, before charging at her.

Sladyana screamed and pulled at her horse's reins. Makail's hand shot towards hers again, and the moment their skin touched, the vision before her disappeared.

"Give me your reins," he said. "I will take us back."

She nodded, and closed her eyes, holding onto the saddle front. They rode in silence, each deep in their own thoughts. She hated having to rely on Makail like this, hated her own eyes betraying her.

It was evening when they arrived back at Gorcay's house. The building cast a long shadow over the road. The air smelled of rain.

Gorcay came out of the front door. "Where did you two go? Did you get lost, son?" he said. "I meant for you to come to the warehouses with me. I came back just now."

Makail helped Sladyana off the horse, waving away the stable hand. "Where's Vedma Kada, father?"

"Why?" Gorcay's face turned serious. His eyes turned to Sladyana. "Are you hurt, Lady Goroncheva?"

"Some spirit trickery, I'm afraid," Makail said before Sladyana could open her mouth. "It might be a blednitza latched onto her, or some other creature. But whatever it was, it kept leading Lady Goroncheva away from the house. Vedma Kada would know."

"I'm sure she would." Gorcay's expression was thoughtful, as he turned to Sladyana. "We will ask her, but for now, please lead our guest to her room, son. You must be so tired, Lady Goroncheva," he said.

Sladyana nodded. "I am, thank you." A flicker of movement made her turn her face towards a window of the house. A curtain twitched, and Vedma Kada's pale face appeared, made almost ghostly by the changing evening light. They locked eyes, for a moment. There was no surprise or concern in Kada's face. And Sladyana made sure to not let her rising fury show in hers.

"Where is my ward, Tula?" Sladyana asked, attempting to put on a casual tone.

"Oh, I saw her somewhere in the garden earlier," Gorcay said. "She was playing with the cat, as happy as a child gets."

Sladyana took Makail's hand, as she looked to the house.

In that moment Tula ran through the garden gate, half stumbling under the weight of a large cat in her arms.

Tula gestured with one hand, making the cat almost slip from her arms. She adjusted her grip and laughed soundlessly. The animal mewed a protest, then climbed onto the girl's shoulder, balancing with an impossible grace.

"It's rather prettyish, isn't it?" Makail said, his head cocked to the side. "I think I've seen it around." He turned to Sladyana. "There's this funny superstition in the local country here that cats can protect the home. I suspect it's

Kada's then. Our very own domovoy!" He grinned and scratched the cat behind the ears.

Sladyana looked at the animal, which purred as Tula rubbed her face in its silver fur. "A superstition? Do you not believe in it then? Even when you've seen some of what Vedma Kada can do?"

Makail shrugged. "I just don't know if this particular cat is a domovoy is all. It's hard to doubt the existence of creatures and powers you've seen first-hand." He bent down and brought his face close to the domovoy. "So, kitty, are you my protector as well?" He laughed as the cat stared back with its golden, wide-pupiled eyes, unblinking. "Not sure it likes me very well."

Tula frowned at Makail's laughter and turned a little away from him, bringing the cat closer to her chest.

Sladyana shivered as the creature in Tula's arms looked towards her. There was a sort of alien intelligence in its face, and she couldn't help thinking it was laughing at her. "Put it down," she said.

Tula's eyes widened in an unspoken question.

Sladyana laughed mirthlessly, and even she was surprised at the sharpness of her tone. "I just don't think the animal should be handled quite so roughly. Let it go and come with me, *slonechko moye*." There was an urgency in her voice, and a need in her, which made the child obey without question. The cat's expression seemed mocking somehow. It just sat there, more still than any cat Sladyana had ever seen. Kada's creature. Kada's spy.

# CHAPTER 46

Kada stared silently for a moment at Lady Goroncheva's back. Barely a day had passed since the bastooks tried to stop Sladyana from returning to Gorcay's house. In that time Sladyana made no attempt to talk to Kada about it, though Makail did consult with her, in his careless sort of way, after which he promptly forgot the whole thing. It took barely a few hours for the whole incident to be laughed off as a navigational failure on Sladyana's part, and Makail's too. "So much time spent gallivanting abroad, my brother can't even find his way around his own home!" Bratyava commented, and that was the matter settled as far as everyone was concerned.

But Kada had noticed that Sladyana hadn't left the Gorcay house for her usual morning walk, and she only went into the garden, holding on tight to Makail's arm.

"Good morning, Lady Goroncheva," Kada said.

Sladyana spun around and smiled tersely. "And to you, Vedma Kada." She bent her head in greeting. "The cook's been looking for you. I believe there were some final details of the wedding feast he meant to discuss with you?"

"Thank you," Kada said. "I'll go find him."

"An interesting man, that cook. Motik, is it?" Sladyana said.

"Yes?" Kada raised an eyebrow.

"We got to chatting, him and I. Very loyal to the house." Sladyana smiled. She walked over to the backless chair by the wall and sat down in it.

"He's been working for the Gorcay family for a long time." Kada bent her head to the side. *Was there a point to this?*

"So have you." Sladyana smiled. "Yet Motik didn't seem to know all that much of you and your girl."

"He knows enough," Kada said. "I've been a friend to him and this town for over seven years now."

"So he said. Hardly a family in Torlow that hasn't benefitted from your services over the years. Still." Sladyana picked up the china cup on the small side table, and stirred the spoon, more for the effect than out of real need, Kada suspected. "It's hard to really settle into a place like this. One is always an outsider in a way. Especially with powers as great and strange as yours."

"They are only strange to those who don't understand them." Kada shrugged.

"Most people, then." Sladyana let out a mirthless chuckle. "I, for one, am still mystified by how the heart of Mother Zemya herself can fail to find my child, for instance."

"Ah." *There it was.* Kada frowned. "I understand your frustration, Lady Goroncheva."

"Do you?"

Kada stiffened. "Have you been performing the prayers and offerings, as we discussed?" She shook her head. "That part, unfortunately, I cannot help with. Mother Zemya promised her help, lest your devotion be judged insufficient. I'm just a vedma and it isn't my place to question the gods' judgement in this matter."

"Was Artek Lelechek's devotion insufficient as well?" Sladyana said.

"Mama?" Secha's voice carried into the room, followed a heartbeat later by the girl herself. She bounded in, twigs and leaves in her uncombed hair, her feet bare.

"Secha, what are you doing?" Kada started. She hated that Sladyana would see her daughter in this state, and she was about to reprimand Secha, when she saw the small scratch on the girl's cheek, barely sealed. Her eyes widened. She hastily pulled a small handkerchief out of her pocket and in two steps she was by her daughter, pressing the fabric to the cut. Secha's mouth hung open, and her eyes darted to Lady Goroncheva.

"Go upstairs and put a poultice on this cut, Secha," Kada said tersely. Secha nodded and left, leaving behind her a faint smell of moss and honey.

Kada didn't turn around for a moment. From the silence she knew Sladyana had seen it. The glisten of rich reddish sap, drying to amber on Secha's cheek.

Kada heard a rustle of Sladyana's skirts, as the woman stood up and slowly walked up to Kada.

The two women locked eyes. "I had guessed she was from Zemya's tree," Sladyana said finally. "Of course, I only had eyes for my Luba that day, as the goddess intended. But the other baby, my girl's twin… You took her. I would be the last person to begrudge you this, of course. But her blood… Is that what you've been hiding? Is she bleeding sap because she wasn't intended for you?" She looked the vedma all over. "Now I understand."

"What do you *think* you understand?" Kada reminded herself that disposing of a body when the body in question was one of her fiancé's guests might prove too difficult a task, even for her.

"The sign Zemya sent me through Tula. The drop of sap."

A pause, before the words were said out loud. Before the world shifted. "Secha's not yours."

"She *is* mine," Kada said. For the briefest moment, her teeth flashed in a snarl, before she brought her face back under control. "You can't look at her and not see that."

"But we both know, Vedma Kada." Sladyana stood there, close enough that Kada could smell the woman. "We both know how looks can deceive."

And with that the woman turned around and left the room.

# CHAPTER 47

The servants were roused from their sleep by a desperate howling from the back of Gorcay's house. By the time Sladyana and Makail joined the people outside, the screaming had largely stopped, replaced by guttural cries and wails.

"Kada, what's happened?" Gorcay himself had gone out in nothing but his nightshirt and some hastily pulled on breeches. He was breathing heavily from the exertion, and he clearly favoured one leg, but such was his concern, that he had half-run ahead of the group to find Kada rocking Secha where the hives had been.

The members of the household all gasped and called out in outrage at the sight of the devastation before them. All but three of Secha's hives had been destroyed, their husks enveloped in flames.

Makail bent down and picked up a bottle of spirits, doubtless filched from the kitchens. "Whoever did it used this to burn the hives," he said to Sladyana, pointing at a ribbon of burnt-out grass leading from hive to hive.

"Who would have done it?" Sladyana said. She was looking at Kada, who held the screaming Secha in her arms. The girl and mother's curly hair was all tangled together, so that they looked like a twisted candle, whispering, crying, comforting.

"That's a bit of vandalism," Bratyava announced, finally rolling up to the group. "But Zemya protect us, what is the girl doing?"

And indeed, Secha was muttering incoherently, her face bent low to the ground.

"Who's she talking to?" One of the servants behind Sladyana whispered. Gorcay must have heard him also, for he turned on his heel and roughly ordered everyone back in the house.

"Has the girl gone mad, do you think?" Sladyana whispered to Makail as they walked towards their rooms.

"Wouldn't surprise me." Makail shrugged. "She's always been a bit touched in the head, the way I saw it. She was only a child when she came to my father's house with her mother. But even then, she was odd. Didn't join in the play, or dances, or anything else a normal girl might be interested in. Folk didn't pay it any mind, for she was a vedma's child, and so a bit of strangeness was to be expected. But I remember there were occasions when she'd be seen talking to insects, or playing with Zemya's roots tied around her fingers, like that string game, you know." He wriggled his fingers in the air, miming a game of cats in the cradle.

"And nobody seemed bothered by it?"

"She never hurt anybody." Makail rubbed his ear. "And she's a pretty girl, and was a charming child. People are willing to forgive a lot if you're pretty and charming."

"As *you* well know," Sladyana said, patting his shoulder.

He laughed. "Indeed."

"And her mother was useful to the townsfolk too," Sladyana added, so quietly he barely heard her. "People won't care how odd you are, as long as you deliver their child safely and ease their rheumatism. Speaking of," she stretched her back, "I'd best be back in bed. The cold air does me no favours."

"Why don't you let me warm your old bones then?"

She gasped, feigning outrage. She laughed then and took his hand. They scaled the steps in the house and were about to turn towards his room, when a thought hit her. "I'll be with you in a moment. I need to check up on Tula."

Makail's face fell. "The child will be asleep. Why bother?"

Sladyana kissed him quickly and stroked his cheek with her knuckles. "I want to put my mind at rest."

The bedroom the child was given was small but comfortable. The curtains were drawn, so that only a sliver of moonlight penetrated into the chamber. Sladyana tiptoed towards the narrow bed. She felt the warmth emanating from the girl's small body before she saw her. Something about the child's breathing felt strange though, too irregular. Sladyana leaned and smelled the ash on Tula's hair and saw the earth-stained tips of her fingers, clutching the pillow.

# CHAPTER 48

"And that child of hers! I hope my father knows what he's doing, Lady Goroncheva, I really do!"

Sladyana only half listened to Bratyava's grousing. She looked on as Gorcay's stout maid poured tea from a silver samovar. The girl seemed nervous, but whether it was because of what Sladyana had witnessed in the garden or because of what Bratyava was saying, was yet to be determined. Sladyana turned back towards Bratyava who, she realised with a start, had been waiting for some sort of a response.

"Yes, quite," Sladyana said, hoping it would do the trick.

And it did, of course. People like Bratyava only ever asked for an affirmation of their words, not an actual conversation partner.

"Vedma Kada is herself, of course, a fine woman," Bratyava said quickly. "But if my father has sense, he will find a husband for her offspring as soon as he can!"

The maid dropped the sugar spoon and shot a nervous look around to see if anyone had noticed.

"Secha *is* unusual, isn't she?" Sladyana said, not taking her eyes off the maid. "One could say unpolished in her manners, which should of course be expected."

"Unpolished?" Bratyava scoffed. She took the teacup from the maid and rolled her eyes before taking a sip. "She is feral! We all saw her by those hives of hers. There is something unnatural about the girl, I'd swear it! She walks around with that long pipe, like some hedge *babushka*."

Sladyana stood up, a faint smile on her lips. "It is bound to make people uneasy, Secha's performance last night," she said. "And the hive destruction itself: if one dares raise a hand to a vedma's child, what does it say of her power and position?"

"*And* by extension, my father's." Bratyava nodded. "Since he's chosen to align himself with her."

"A vedma who can't protect her own, can hardly protect the people she's meant to serve," Sladyana added thoughtfully, still watching the serving girl like a hawk. "And if she can't serve them now, did she ever truly serve them in the first place?"

"How am I supposed to show that to my friends? Can you imagine?" Bratyava returned to her favourite subject. She rolled her eyes, "'Dearest Lady Slavotna, this barefoot creature with moss in her hair is my stepsister!'" She mimed, then burst out laughing.

"When Bratyava's laughing, you can bet there's somebody about to cry nearby!" Makail said, coming into the room. "How are you, dearest sister?" He leaned forward and gave Bratyava, who seemed not in the least affected by his words, a peck on the cheek. "Ah, yes! Some good black tea. Pour me a cup, girl, will you?" He said to the serving girl, who studiously kept her eyes down. She curtsied and went to pour another cup. Sladyana noticed how graceful the girl was, in spite of her farm-raised musculature, so desirable among the peasants, and so distinctly unadmired among Sladyana's own sort.

"Your sister was discussing your soon-to-be stepsister,"

Sladyana said, her eyes still on the serving girl who flinched. Interesting. "And what's to be done about her."

"What's to be done?" Makail brought his hand to his heart and feigned a swoon. "I sincerely hope nobody intended for me to do anything! For one, I don't know what one could possibly expect me to do with a beautiful young woman..." He winked at Sladyana. "Nothing that's decent to talk of in any case."

A cup crashed to the floor. The serving girl reddened and mumbled an apology, gathering up the shards and collecting them in her apron pocket. She hurried out of the room.

"I'd better go and have a talk with the girl." Sladyana stood up and half-smiled at Gorcay's children. "I suspect the clumsy thing will forget to prepare the *banya* for me tonight if I don't remind her."

She needn't have bothered. Bratyava and Makail weren't listening, already engaged in some good-spirited teasing.


"Wait a moment!" Sladyana called out after the girl, who turned towards her with a surprised look on her face.

"Yes, Lady Goroncheva?" The girl's cheeks reddened, and she fidgeted, her calloused hands lacing and unlacing their fingers in front of her, like she was playing some fleshy form of cats-in-the-cradle. Sladyana frowned. She disliked fidgeting and fidgeters both. But instead of scolding the girl for her feckless appearance, she plastered a smile on her face and didn't speak till she was close enough to smell the girl. "I have a need to talk with you. Will you walk in the garden with me?"

She turned to the stairs without waiting for the girl's reply. What answer could there be, after all, except compliance, immediate and unquestioning. But, to Sladyana's surprise, the girl lingered.

The woman turned "What is it?" *Be patient, be calm.* She reminded herself that if she spooked the girl, she would get no answers.

"I–" the girl looked up. "Only, what was your ladyship wanting to talk to such as me for?"

"What's your name, girl?"

"Aleenka, my lady." *She actually curtsied.* Sladyana winced.

"Very well, Aleenka, would you ask me why I'd have you clean my sheets, or draw my bathwater, or make my breakfast?"

"No, my lady." The girl tightened her lips.

"Then why do you question that I might want a word with you?" Sladyana smiled. "Perhaps I'm interested in your thoughts as well as your work, did it not cross your mind?"

Aleenka looked up sharply, a smile twitching in the corner of the mouth. "No, my lady, it didn't."

"Smart girl," Sladyana nodded. "Now let's get a breath of fresh air together. I can hold your arm, if it makes you feel useful."

Together they walked towards the gardens, the orchard's trees heavy with their fruit. They didn't speak, and Sladyana used the time to look over the girl. Aleenka was much like any other servant hired from the field. Heavy-set, with muscles hardened by work. With a body made for action, not lounging in sitting rooms. There was an odd grace about her. Not the kind admired by the high society of Fiesna, but something altogether healthier.

The girl was watching Sladyana herself, every now and then stealing a sly glance from under her long pale lashes.

There was a tension in her, like she was ready to break into a run at any sight of danger. *Not stupid then.*

"So," Sladyana said, once they reached the orchard. "There are some things in this house that puzzle me, you see, and I dislike the sensation. I hope you can help me understand." She sat on a cast-iron bench, not releasing Aleenka's arm, thus forcing the girl to sit next to her.

"My lady?"

"I've noticed you are close to Vedma Kada's child, the pretty little Secha."

*There it was.* The girl's whole body stiffened, like she'd swallowed a broom handle.

"I'm a servant, my lady. I'm no closer to her than to any other in the house."

"But she wasn't always in the house, was she?" Sladyana said. "Before Vedma Kada became your Master Gorcay's betrothed, she and her daughter were merely employed by him, same as you."

"*Not* the same as me," Aleenka said, then, evidently feeling she'd said too much, closed her mouth.

"No, I suppose not the same as you," Sladyana said. *There is anger there, in this child, a sort of resentment. And resentment is a useful tool.* Kasimira had taught her niece well, and so Sladyana proceeded cautiously. "That difference... It might make you want to keep certain things secret. But I promise, you can trust me."

Aleenka raised one eyebrow.

Sladyana laughed. "Very well, maybe not entirely." She patted the girl's hand. "But there is something odd about that girl, and I wish to know what it is. And if you tell me, I promise you will be safe."

"There is nothing." Aleenka kept her voice level and her

face blank. "I draw Miss Secha's bath, and I help prepare her breakfast. I wash her clothes too, as she forgets such things." A hint of bitterness crept into the girl's voice. An emotion that was easy to exploit.

"It must bother you that one who was of a similar station to you be elevated like that?" Sladyana tried. But Aleenka looked genuinely puzzled. Not jealous, then. Change tack. "She seems such a lively, pretty little thing. There's a dreamy kind of gentleness to her, wouldn't you say?"

Aleenka's face twitched, as in pain. Sladyana was getting closer.

"She might *seem* so, alright," Aleenka said before she could help herself. Her face whitened and she made as if to stand up. Sladyana grabbed her wrist.

"What do you mean by that?"

"Nothing, my lady, please forgive me," Aleenka said. "I need to get back to the house."

"And you will, once you tell me what I need to know. What is it about this Secha girl that you almost said? What's sitting at the tip of your tongue? You tell me, girl, for I wouldn't hesitate to pull it out of your mouth for you!"

"She's cruel," Aleenka said finally, the stricken expression of shame and hurt on her face saying much more than her words.

Oh. "So, you were lovers," Sladyana said, instantly disappointed. "Is that all?" She scoffed. *So much effort wasted on a lover's spat.* But something else in Aleenka's face told her there was more to it. "By cruel, do you mean she threw you over for someone new?"

Aleenka shook her head. "She isn't as she seems. Maybe it's the vedma in her, I don't know. But she is not right. There is an animal in her, one that eats at her day and night, here." She pointed to her temple. "You saw how she was when she saw her hives burning."

"It's her livelihood. So she cried, what of it?"

"It's more than that." The young woman stiffened. Resentment bubbled just under the surface with that one. She seemed to consider her next words for a moment, before arriving at the decision. "She talks to the bees and the roots and it's all very well, till she turns on you."

"What did she do to you, child?" Sladyana asked, her voice softening at the girl's sadness.

Instead of replying, Aleenka pulled open her blouse, revealing deep cuts and bite marks on her shoulder, barely healed. It looked like an eagle's talons had ripped into her flesh.

"*She* did this?" Sladyana asked. Her face was calm, but her voice trembled.

"She or that animal that nests in her head." Aleenka pulled the blouse up. "Either way, I don't care to know. As soon as I can find another position, I'm leaving."

"Make sure you call on the Goronchev estate," Sladyana said. She hesitated, then took the girl's hand in hers and gave it a little squeeze. "I have a feeling my aunt might be needing a new girl servant in her old age." Noting the girl's surprised expression, she said. "I did say you would be alright if you talked to me."

"Thank you, my lady!" Aleenka brightened.

"Walk with me to the house." Sladyana took the girl's arm and allowed her to lead her right up to the bench hugging the house wall. It wouldn't do to let the vedma's tricks get her lost in her host's own garden. If Aleenka found this strange, she made no sign of it. "Now go. I need to think, and I can't do that with you hovering." Aleenka nodded, and ran back towards the house, leaving Sladyana alone.

Kada could play her games, but Sladyana knew the rules now. And she was not afraid to break them to get what she wanted.

# CHAPTER 49

Kada pressed the palm of her hand against the wall. It was past midday when she finally walked downstairs, and she still felt groggy. Secha had taken a long time to fall asleep, and only Kada's herb tea finally managed to calm her. But even now the girl muttered through her sleep, strange sing-song words. Kada would keep her in their room for as long as she had to. For as long as it took to make sure the fox was still away.

She passed Sladyana in the corridor, an unwelcome surprise, but for once the woman didn't say anything loaded with meaning. Just a mocking smile danced in the corner of her lips. It took a great deal of Kada's self-control to not slap the smugness off the woman's face.

She had noticed Lady Goroncheva had ceased with her daily prayers and offerings. The flame of devotion didn't burn for long. Still, Secha's birthday was coming soon. Just a day after her mother's wedding, barely a week away. It wasn't long to wait, and after that Sladyana wouldn't be able to do anything.

The kitchen was dim, the clouds blocking out what little light usually entered the basement room.

Motik was standing with his back to Kada when she entered, a row of neatly formed *pierogi* on the flour-dusted counter next to him. He added to them quickly, his fingers pinching out the braid edge of the meat-filled dumplings.

"Good afternoon, my friend," Kada said softly.

Motik jumped up, the *pierog* in his hand hitting the floor with a wet sound.

"Oh, dear me, you startled me!" He exclaimed, shaking his head as he picked up the spoilt food. He avoided Kada's gaze, and looked to the side, wiping his hands on his apron. "What do you need, my lady?"

"'My lady?'" Kada cocked an eyebrow. "Since when? 'Kada' was good enough yesterday, it's good enough now."

The old man moved his head in a way that could mean either yes or no. He stood there silently for a moment, clearly struggling for something to say. "I hope Secha's feeling better?" he finally managed.

"Yes, she's calmed down a bit. But I wanted to bring her some food. Is there any bread left?"

Motik gestured to the basket on the table. He continued standing awkwardly, his hands folded in front of him, as Kada cut generous slices for herself and Secha. Finally, she'd had enough. "What is the matter? Why are you acting strange all of a sudden?" *Like she didn't have enough to worry about. Was it too much to ask for the most consistent parts of her existence to remain so until the fires that currently made up the rest of her life were put out?* Motik acting out of character was no less confusing and frustrating than if a chair decided to suddenly serve as a teacup.

"I'm sorry, am I being strange?" He didn't meet her eyes. "I didn't mean to be."

Kada put the bread down and walked up to Motik, leaning towards him over the work counter so he had to look at her. His eye twitched, when faced with Kada's gaze. "Talk." She jabbed a finger into his chest.

He sighed and looked up towards the window, as if looking for answers there. "It's just, Secha's behaviour yesterday made people uneasy," he said finally. He shook his head and picked up a round of the dough, stuffing a spoonful of filling in with renewed vigour.

"What people? And uneasy how?" Kada crossed her arms. "She loves her bees, and somebody came to destroy them."

"Well, that's true enough," Motik said, though he didn't look like he was agreeing at all.

"But?"

"But, people talk, Kada. It's not natural how Secha talked to those bees. Not normal, like. And maybe, someone has had enough of it."

"Who?" Kada gripped the edge of the worktop. "You know who did that?" She would find that mysterious 'someone' who was so uncomfortable with her daughter, and she'd show them the real meaning of the word 'discomfort'.

Motik put down the *pierog*. "I don't know. I'd tell you if I did. But you have to admit there's something strange about how Secha behaved last night."

"She was upset."

"There is upset, Kada, and then there's what we witnessed last night." Motik finally looked her in the eyes. "But she wasn't even crying. The sounds she made; it was like a curse." He made a face, and if he'd been anyone but Motik, Kada suspected he would have spat on the floor then.

"You've known Secha since she was a child, Motik," Kada said.

His eyebrows knitted together, and he looked at the wall. "In fairness, Kada, you are a vedma. And if Secha turns out to be a vedma too, then I suppose it's Zemya's blessing on all of us in Torlow. But she is in that in-between space now, when you don't know what you're rightly looking at. She's not quite like the other maidens, and she's not a healer like you either. She's just strange these days, and folk don't like strange."

"Strange!" Kada seethed. "You know what's 'strange'? That the town I have given seven years of my life to, would judge my daughter for her sorrow. That ingratitude *I* happen to find very strange."

To his credit, Motik actually looked contrite, but Kada was not in a forgiving mood. She snapped up the plate with the bread and, after a heartbeat's hesitation, picked up a honey jar as well. "You wouldn't want any of this *strange* honey, I'm sure?" She held it up in front of the old cook's nose. "Wouldn't want to offend you with our *strange* vedma offerings!" And with that she walked out of the kitchen.

At the top of the staircase, she bumped into a servant on her way down. The woman actually squealed, and practically ran past Kada, her shoulders raised as if she wanted to hide her head between them.

Kada swore, rolled her eyes and strode upstairs to her bedroom.

She closed the doors behind her, the tray propped against her hip. Secha was still in bed, covers pulled over her head. But Kada could tell Secha wasn't sleeping, and so she sat down next to her and rested her hand on the bump that was her daughter.

"I brought you some food."

"I'm not hungry," came the muffled reply.

"And yet you will nourish your body regardless." Kada pulled the cover off Secha's face, and her daughter looked at her accusingly, eyes red and lids puffy from crying. "Come now," Kada said, cupping Secha's cheek. "I will comb your hair as you eat."

Secha grumbled but she scrambled up, and pulled the tray closer to her, as Kada picked up the comb from a small stool. She pulled Secha's tangled hair all back, so it rested on the girl's back. Kada worked slowly, from the ends, humming a wordless tune.

"Who did it, do you think, *mamusha*?"

Kada stopped for a moment. "I don't know."

"Can you find out?" Secha turned her face towards her mother.

Something about her tone sent a shiver down Kada's spine. "Leave it," she said.

Secha shook her head.

"Listen to me," Kada said. She placed her hands on Secha's shoulders and pulled her daughter towards her till Secha rested the back of her head against Kada's chest. "You need to lay low for now. There's too much that could go wrong."

"And *this* is not wrong?" Secha's voice cracked. "I could feel them burn."

"Feel who?"

"My queens." Secha's finger wore a hole in the slice of bread Kada brought her. "I could feel them calling me. They wanted me to protect them. I let them down, *mamusha*."

"No, Secha, you didn't." Kada hugged her. "But this must be dealt with the normal way, not the vedma way."

"How?"

"I will speak to Gorcay. We will try to find whoever did it. But I can't have more talk of magic and you together. You're not a vedma yet, not properly, and folk are bound to think you're stepping outside of what's allowed." She hesitated. "And be careful of Lady Goroncheva."

"Why?" Secha looked up. "She's been very nice to me."

"Has she?" Kada narrowed her eyes. "When?"

"The other day. After you put the poultice on my cheek. She bumped into me outside."

"What did she say?"

Secha shrugged. "Just wanted to know about where we lived before. She was chatty, not like that stuck-up Bratyava. She said my hair was pretty." Secha paused, then chuckled. "You know, she said a strange thing then."

Kada's ears pricked up. "Strange how?"

"She asked if I ever dyed my hair. Isn't that an odd thing to ask?"

"Yes," Kada said. "Very odd." She gently pushed Secha upright and braided her hair in a crown around her head. "Stay away from her for now."

Secha looked at Kada strangely but nodded.

# CHAPTER 50

"Come in," Gorcay said.

Kada came into the room carrying a small tray. He smiled at her over his shoulder, then went back to gently shaking off the excess pounce powder from a letter, right back into its container to be used again. Kada put the tray on the writing desk in front of Gorcay and waited as he carefully folded and sealed his letter. She smiled at the small, neat handwriting. Gorcay wrote like a merchant: clearly, legibly, and without flourish.

"You're staring," he said, without looking up.

"Do you mind?" She lifted the top off the teapot and smelled the tea. Judging it had brewed enough, she poured a small cup.

He put the letter down and turned towards her, resting his elbow on his desk. "Not at all," he said. "As long as you're – I'm not conceited enough to say 'happy' – let's say, as long as you're content with what you see."

"Would I tell you if I wasn't?" She placed her hand on his cheek.

"Of course not," he chuckled. "My unkind woman. You're no good for my vanity, you know."

"Vanity is overrated," she said. "Confidence is a different story. And you have that in abundance, which I find a lot more attractive."

"Attractive now, am I?" He raised his eyebrows. "Very

well, but kiss me first, before you ask me whatever favour it is you want of me."

She laughed, in spite of herself. "You know me well."

"Better than you think," he said, resting his hand on her waist. "While you and Secha were sleeping, I've been busy. I just wrote to some local officials reporting the damage done to Secha's hives." He patted the letter on his desk. "I have already instructed the carpenter to piece together the finest hives Secha has ever laid eyes on, and some of my men will be asking around town. I'll do my best to catch whoever did it, but I can't promise more than that."

"I prefer an honest promise to bluster, always," Kada said, and kissed him. He smelled like soap, and fresh linen, and she found herself leaning into him. The pleasure of it startled her and she moved away, suddenly. Gorcay noticed but said nothing.

"But there is something I need to talk to you about," Gorcay said, scratching the stubble on his cheek.

"Yes?" Kada passed him the cup. Some steel returned to her eyes, and she avoided his.

"It's about Secha, obviously – what did you put in this?" He scrunched up his nose at the smell of the drink.

"What *about* Secha?" There was a warning in her voice.

"People have been uneasy about her lately," he said, taking a sip. "And you can't pretend you didn't notice yourself. She was always a lively girl, doing as she pleased, and it was charming, even. But charming and eccentric becomes strange very quickly in the minds of people."

"I've noticed." Kada sighed. "Motik's informed me of the same this morning. But I can handle it. The folk are overreacting. Secha cares about her bees." Kada folded her arms. "She was upset."

"There's upset, and then there's whispering to the wind, muttering spells into the earth, and dancing barefoot in the night." He leaned back in his chair, wincing as it creaked. "You persist in behaving like nobody will notice anything. If I have noticed then others have too, Kada."

She knitted her eyebrows and walked up to the window. The sun was high, but the air smelled wet. The street was filled with people of Torlow, going about their daily lives. An old woman walked past, her back bent. She walked slowly, observing all around her. She idly looked up and locked eyes with Kada. Her lips tightened into a line, and she hurried off, the basket bouncing off her elbow. Kada sighed. "What do you suggest?"

"That depends."

"On?"

"On what you're not telling me," he said. There was no anger or impatience in his voice, just weariness. "I can't help if I don't know the true problem. Is this who Secha is, or will it pass? Do I need to pretend, or can we seek help?"

"Help with what, Sobis?" She turned back and looked at him. "With changing my child? I happen to love who she is."

"Help with keeping her from harm." He drummed his fingers on the lacquer desk. "And is this who she *really* is, Kada? Was the joyous, charming child I knew a pretence? Is this new, crazy-eyed, muttering sprite here to stay?" He raised his hands defensively at the anger in Kada's face. "You misunderstand me, Kada. It doesn't matter to me which one it is. But I need to *know*. Look around you." He made a sweeping gesture with his arm. "What do you see?"

"I'm not in the mood for games, Sobis." She tucked an errant curl back under her scarf. "It's your bedroom. Fine as always."

"Yes, fine it is." He nodded. "Every room in this very fine house is very fine indeed. I leave nothing to chance. Not a detail too small. But do you think this is the sort of house I grew up in?" He raised his eyes to hers. "I was raised the youngest among four brothers, in a house that could not afford to feed even one boy properly. Not that anyone I do business with will ever get a hint of that. I know people, Kada, and I know how to be who they're comfortable with." He stood up and faced Kada. "Let me help you. We both know you're not above using me." He laughed at her expression. "Don't deny, it, Kada, for I don't mind. It's a fool who wastes a good tool, and I wouldn't marry a fool. But use my skills here." He placed his hands on Kada's arms. "The harvest is near done and so the dozynki celebrations are coming up. Let's make them a truly extravagant affair. We will show what we want and dazzle the good folk of Torlow. And Secha will be the most dazzling among us. People will forget their whispers. You just need to redirect their attention where it benefits you."

Kada stared at him for a moment. "You're an interesting man, Sobis."

"I have to be." He grinned. "I wouldn't dare bore a woman like you."

# CHAPTER 51

Walking the familiar street through Torlow shouldn't have felt like this. Kada straightened her back. There was a quiet that accompanied her. Whenever she turned her eyes on one of the people walking by, they would lower their gaze, or mutter a hasty greeting, before scurrying off. Before, all she had to do was step one foot outside Gorcay's house and scores of the townsfolk would descend upon her, asking her advice and assistance. Not today though. If not for Motik's words, Kada might have ascribed this change to the elevation of her status. People didn't like change and it would make sense for them to be distant at first. But if this was all due to Secha's behaviour, then she had to intervene. Out of fear and confusion, anger grew. And she'd nip it in the bud, if it was the last thing she did.

Kada brightened somewhat when she saw the familiar bald head of Rotik Moglovy. The little man was talking animatedly to the bored-looking vegetable seller. The woman nodded politely, eyeing another customer, who was checking the quality of the eggs by making them spin between two other eggs. Only those that twirled satisfactorily would be selected, to the seller's growing irritation. "I've *told* you; these are all fresh, Tilkova!" she said, finally, waving away Rotik.

"Some of 'em, maybe," Tilkova said, without even looking

in the seller's direction. She lacked a lot of her teeth, in spite of not being much older than fifty, and she moved her jaw like her tongue was getting in the way.

The seller bristled. "I never sold you a bad egg, and you know it! Don't blame my wares for your poor cooking!"

As the two women bickered, Kada approached the group. "Good morning," she said with as pleasant a smile as she could muster.

The change in the atmosphere was abrupt and complete. Tilkova nodded at Kada and quickly tossed the coin for the eggs to the seller, who pocketed it without counting.

"I wanted to check up on you, Rotik, but I haven't had the time, what with the wedding and everything," Kada said. "I hope the tonic I've sent you helped?"

"Why, yes, Vedma Kada," the man said, pulling on the fraying ends of his belt. "It's very kind of you to remember. I'm feeling much better, yes, but you know I don't like to complain."

"No, of course not." Kada nodded. "Let me know if you have any more trouble."

"Oh no, no." Rotik laughed nervously, casting a glance at the seller, who kept her eyes on her cabbages, which she began rearranging like she was a florist for the Tsarica herself. "I'm not such a relic just yet, Vedma Kada. I can't complain really. My health's never been better."

"I'm glad to hear that." Kada turned to the seller. "For the harvest celebration this year, Gorcay thought to do something extra special. His household will be donating cakes and pastries. And we wouldn't dream of ordering eggs from anyone else in Torlow. If you come to speak of the details with Motik at the house, we can figure out an arrangement."

"That's mighty fine of Master Gorcay," the woman said, still gazing intently at her baskets.

Kada waited for more, but both the seller and Rotik stood there, waiting for her to leave. She nodded at them curtly and turned to go. As she was walking away, she heard their feverish whispers.

"Motik is a good man, wonder how he can stand that house now–"

"–heard the latest–"

Kada ground her teeth. She looked up at the dove-grey clouds chasing the sun. They were nothing much now, but by the afternoon they would bring a storm. Kada knew the feeling. It moved her from place to place in those early years. But she was very young then. And Secha's birthday was so close. If only they could fix this.

She cleared her throat, chasing away the emotion welling up. Was this fixable? Sobis seemed to think so, but Kada wasn't so sure. But then she never used to stay long enough to find out before.

She was glad Secha didn't go to town with her that morning, in any case. She was so fragile now. Two days since the hives were destroyed had done little to calm her. She stayed in their room and ate little. And those damned birds. They kept flying to the window and staring at Kada's daughter. They didn't touch a crumb of what Secha threw them. Just perched there, watching. Kada shuttered the window in the end, but she knew they were still there. That Zemya was still there, everywhere, watching.

"Kada!" A voice called her back to herself.

With shock she realised it was Gorcay, hurrying up the road behind her. He caught up with her, breathing heavily. "I've been calling you all the way from the butchers. Didn't you hear me?" His eyes twinkled, as he offered Kada his arm. "This is not for you, but so you can hold *me* up," he whispered. "I'm not used to running, you know. Hardly dignified."

Kada laughed, in spite of herself. "What are you doing here?"

"I heard from my daughter you'd gone out by yourself after breakfast, and I wanted to accompany you. Is it so strange I might want to take a walk with my intended?"

"Yes." Kada nodded. "Yes, it is."

"Very well, so I'm coming to offer support." He ran his finger along his eyebrow. "My daughter, for all her many sterling qualities, does rather enjoy the gossip. So she didn't fail to inform me of the whispers going through Torlow. And I'm having none of it. We will quash them together."

"Secha being upset at her hives alone should not have caused this, even if she were acting a bit strange," Kada whispered. "I know these people. I treat them, I help their children come into the world. You'd think they'd have more faith." Gorcay's uncharacteristic silence made her turn to him in suspicion. "But there's something else, isn't there?"

Gorcay sniffed. He smiled and nodded at a silversmith walking past, who tipped his hat in respect, before hurrying off.

"Tell me, Sobis."

"It's going to pass."

"Sobis."

"Very well." He sighed and took a moment to arrange the words in his head before speaking again. "It's about Artek Lelechek. Seems somebody's been talking, spreading suspicion like a disease."

"Suspicion of what?" She looked at the neat little brick

homes of Torlow, like a row of teeth, ready to crush her bones and chew up her and Secha both. Kada could feel the beads of sweat form between her shoulder blades, and she wished, not for the first time, for her simple linen shirt, and her comfortable wide trousers. Gorcay's finery weighed her down, a snare that limited her movements, and made her as visible and vulnerable as a struggling hare.

She turned to Gorcay who remained silent. "Well?" she said again. "What do they suspect?"

"The folks here hold you in great regard, Kada," he said. He smiled at a passing worker. Gorcay glanced at her. "You might be a victim of your own popularity, in fact. You're seen as so powerful, that when your powers fail – in this case, by not finding Botrik – people assume there must be more to it."

"I see."

"As far as I know nobody has dared accuse you of anything or implied anything they oughtn't. But somebody *did* dare destroy Secha's hives. Which implies somewhat of a dip in the community's regard."

As they walked through the street, Kada couldn't help but feel impressed by how easily Gorcay could charm people. He smiled at everyone, flashing his white teeth, scattering compliments around like grain to voracious crows.

She found herself drawing comfort from Gorcay's arm holding her own. The realisation made her try to pull her hand out, but Gorcay only pressed his elbow closer to his side, so she couldn't step away without struggling. After a pair of two elderly sisters who ran the Torlow mill passed them, Gorcay turned to Kada, and, lowering his voice, said, "I won't hold you if you don't wish it, Kada. But don't move away from me because you're afraid of relying on my help."

Kada's jaw hung open. For a moment she found she had nothing to say. Instead, she squeezed the sleeve of Gorcay's *kontush* with her free hand.

"I'm not used to it, Sobis."

"I know," he said. "But isn't that rather the point of marrying me?"

She remained silent.

"Think of me as an ally then. You have many of those!"

"Yes, but spirits are easier in a way," she said. "The creatures of the other world keep their word. They follow the rules. So as long as you understand them, you can predict their actions. Humans..." She forced a smile when passing a Torlow merchant. "Humans are more complicated in my experience."

"And what promises would you be content for us to keep?" he asked. A heavy drop of water fell from the awning of a shop they passed and turned a spot on his shoulder darker. "How about 'I trust you, and you trust me?'"

Kada nodded, sensing tension in Gorcay's voice. She stopped and brushed at the wet spot on the fabric of his *kontush*. "Trust doesn't come easy to me. But I can try."

"Lean on me and I will lean on you?" He leaned forward, his lips close to hers.

"I will," Kada whispered. "I will try to."

# CHAPTER 52

The fox coughed and hacked as the sharp fumes scratched at its throat. The fires were not real, it knew, and yet they burned. The fox's eyes darted sideways at its unexpected companion, a dark shape in the forest. The creature, whoever it was, made no attempt to speak to the fox, made no sign that it intended to attack, or hurt it either. It just watched, from between the trees.

The fox should have run. It knew that. And yet, there was something intriguing in the way the roots responded to the stranger. They twisted at its trotters and wove their way up the creature's tusks. A strange decoration. White on white, bone against bone.

The wild boar was the largest the fox had ever seen. His flanks were lean, and the rough fur on its neck stood up like a snake's mantle. He watched as the fox attempted again and again to cross through the barrier. He moved not a muscle to help. But he didn't try to kill the fox either, which in itself was helpful, all things considered.

As the boar seemed to present no immediate threat, the fox once more turned its attentions to the illusions of the small ground creatures. It could smell them, beneath the earth. Could hear them too, their scurrying and scrambling, their digging and scarring the earth with their drawings, with their obscene magic that kept redrawing the very reality before the fox's eyes, every time it tried to go where it must. It was the sort of trickery the fox was not used to being on the receiving end of, and it was aggravating beyond belief.

It'd been a while since the fox could smell the child though. The one who called out through the roots, with a voice so clear. The voice of one of Zemya's chosen. The girl had gone quiet, and the fox worried it might not hear her again, but it would not give up, not when it was so close. Not after it had given so much, offered so much for the promise.

And so, the fox tried to push through the invisible brambles, as they mussed rather than tore at its fur, and walked the clear path that turned to mush beneath its paw pads. It had done worse itself, so it could appreciate a job well done, even as the illusions grew more vicious with each passing day, as the fox's hatred grew.

It was tired now, so tired and hungry.

Suddenly the boar moved. The fox danced light on its legs, stepping sideways, its eyes swivelling in surprise, a gurgled hiss boiling in its throat.

But soon it calmed, as the bone roots cushioned each step of the huge creature, until he stood high above the fox. The boar could rend it now with his tusks, if he so wished.

"Come with me," the boar spoke with a human voice, and he trotted away. He paused, briefly, at the edge of the treeline, waiting for the fox to follow.

They walked in silence for a while. Then they stopped by a field. It smelled sweet, of flowers which didn't grow there. The fox gave its companion a questioning look. The boar seemed to hesitate. Hesitation is a strange thing to witness in a creature as powerful as that. A show of weakness that defies the strength of his body and the brutal power behind his muscles.

But then the boar seemed to come to a conclusion. He sniffed the ground, letting his nose lead him. With one fluid motion he tore into the earth, splitting the soil like it was warmed butter, the tusks drawing deep grooves. The fox was confused for just a moment, until an ear-piercing scream came from the ground, and blood sprayed on the grass.

The boar lifted his head, a small body of a bastook impaled on his tusk. The boar shook his head, spraying the ground with blood and guts, till the lifeless body of the guardian spirit slipped off and fell to the ground with a sickening crunch.

The boar grunted, and the bone roots rippled like a wave beneath the ground. Zemya responded, lifting up the other bastook out of the ground. His small black eyes stared in horror at the boar.

"God Inog!" The creature fidgeted, the sides of the bone root platform that lifted him up digging uncomfortably into his sides.

"You will let my friend here pass," the boar said. "You will not block my path or anyone else's who serves Zemya."

"Well, of course," the bastook said. He pulled his hat off his head and kneaded it nervously. "I'd never work against the Great Mother, none of us would. Not ever. Yes." The bastook had the size and the posture of a child, but his crafty face bore little resemblance to humankind. The bastook glanced at the fox. "This is just a promise, a little promise made, but to Zemya's own servant, the Great Mother wouldn't mind a promise made to her own?"

"Do you think Vedma Kada is closer to Zemya than Zemya's own son?" Inog leaned forward, his trotter wearing the ground, angry snorts escaping his snout.

The bastook seemed taken aback by that. "Well, no, of

course no. We didn't know, we had no idea. We just..." His small face drooped suddenly. "You didn't have to kill Torto, you know. We are peaceful folk; we just help our friends. You didn't have to do this."

"Do what?" Inog chuckled, as the bone roots rose up around the fallen bastook, wriggling through his wounds, the little worms of them knitting what had been torn and broken, till Torto was sitting up, looking around him in confusion.

"Remember what I can do, and remember who helped you," Inog said. "Now, you will let my mother's servant pass."

The two bastooks bent their heads and, with an unnatural speed, dove into the upturned ground and disappeared from view.

The fox had been watching all this with cautious interest. It had no experience of allies and friends, and so did not trust this creature, this god. But Goddess Zemya had many children, and it was not hard to imagine this great beast of a boar might be one of hers.

But gods never did anything without cause, and so the fox stayed where it was, watching Inog.

"Well, off with you," Inog said without turning around. "Claim what you need."

The fox sniffed the air. There was the stench of the spilt blood, and the soil and the moss. And the hitherto masked stench of the human town, which was just there on the horizon. The fox stood up and trotted past Inog, giving the boar a wide berth. The dark line of Torlow was there, just within reach.

# CHAPTER 53

Sladyana smiled as Tula twirled in front of her, delighted with her new dress.

"It's lovely, isn't it?" Sladyana said, as she beckoned for the girl to approach her. "I also got you a ribbon for your hair. Have a look!" She dug into her purse and pulled out a length of pale blue ribbon, which she unrolled and held out as an offering to the twinkly eyed Tula.

The girl laughed soundlessly and briefly covered her mouth in excitement, before her fingers once more began their dance.

"Yes, I will tie it in a bow on your plait." Sladyana nodded. "Yes." She placed a hand on Tula's hands, to cut off the flurry of questions. "It will be a very big, very pretty bow."

A knock on the door made them both turn. Makail was leaning against the doorframe, watching them. Tula looked down sullenly. The girl begrudged having to share the few private moments she had with her guardian. Sladyana found herself squeezing the child's hands as reassurance.

"You're both looking lovely!" Makail said, grinning.

"Do you like it?" Sladyana straightened up, better to show off the shiny folds of her orange and red dress. "I bought the dress directly from your father, you'll be pleased to know!"

"Very well, keeps it in the family," he said. Tula scowled at Makail's presumption, but he ignored her. "Are you ready?" he said, his fingers drumming the doorframe. "My father's eager to not delay the proceedings. This year, Torlow's Dozynki are going to dwarf all of Fiesna's festivals, harvest or otherwise. And we are all to be paraded like prize peacocks in Tsarica's menagerie."

"I wonder why that would be," Sladyana said with one brow raised mockingly. *Go, I'll meet you downstairs*, she signed to Tula, who nodded and dashed past Makail.

"I'm sorry." Makail looked self-conscious all of a sudden. "If you don't want to take part, I'm sure you don't have to. I invited you so we could enjoy ourselves, but things have turned more complicated than I'd have wished. If you wanted to return to your home before the wedding, nobody would blame you…"

Sladyana looked Makail up and down. Then she walked up to him and patted him on the shoulder. "And why wouldn't I stay, you silly man? I assure you, I find this all very diverting, and you haven't failed in your duties as a host. Just make sure you stay close by, in case of any unexpected developments." She winked at him and took his arm.


Most of the household was already waiting in front of Gorcay's house. They would all travel on foot, with the exception of Bratyava, who, due to her state, was to stay behind and wait for the procession to return for the party.

Sladyana watched Makail and his sister get into one of their mocking little arguments. Gorcay was clearly reassuring the somewhat anxious-looking Kada, who stood with her arm resting on her daughter's back. Tula stood next to the two of them, watching them with a serious expression.

A sudden dread squeezed at Sladyana's heart. She would have pulled Tula back towards her, but there was no way to do it without causing a scene. Something about Tula's expression caught her guardian's eye, however. The girl's eyes were focused on Secha's face, and the usually friendly girl seemed... Sladyana wasn't quite sure. Angry, perhaps? Sladyana hadn't ask Tula about the hives, hoping the child would come to her with the story herself when she was ready. Perhaps that was a mistake.

As for Secha herself, the girl seemed to not be very much concerned with what was going on about her. She wore a narrow flower wreath, with yellow ribbons trailing down her back. Sladyana narrowed her eyes, as she saw the girl's hands fidget, nails scraping bits of skin off from around her nails.

A purr, like the grinding of a mill stone rumbled somewhere next to Sladyana's leg. She looked down, into the domovoy's golden eyes. She glanced about, but nobody was paying her any mind. "Did your mistress send you to spy on me?" she whispered. She felt silly, all of a sudden, talking to the little beast. But the cat stretched lazily, digging its claws into the ground, making a strange gurgling noise deep within its throat. For a moment, Sladyana thought it was purring, but then the cat gave her a sly little look and deep within herself she knew it was laughing at her.

"Get away from me, twisted little beast," she said through gritted teeth, aiming a kick at its flank.

The domovoy sidestepped, avoiding her boot easily. It hissed, the fur on its neck standing up like a mane.

"You're not fond of cats, are you, Lady Goroncheva?"

Sladyana froze and turned slowly towards Kada, who watched her with cold eyes.

"I came to ask if you'd be willing to have Tula take part in the dozynki celebrations along with Secha?"

Sladyana opened her mouth to refuse, but something in Kada's expression gave her pause. "Why?"

Kada shrugged. "Secha asked. It's customary for the young girls of the prominent households to take part. I understand if it's not to your liking."

Sladyana and Kada stared at each other for a moment as Sladyana tried to divine what Kada wanted, so she could do the opposite, but the vedma's expression was inscrutable. And so, the only thing to do was to agree. "Very well," she said.

Gorcay called Kada, who took his arm, and they led the way, followed by Gorcay's household, except for those who were helping Motik set up for the feast later.

The families of Torlow joined the procession behind Gorcay, swelling the group till a river of people moved through the town, at a slow ponderous pace, pouring through like molasses.

The girls wore ribbons down their hair, with wreaths of meadow flowers, while their mothers wore colourful scarves, tied under their chins, the fringed edges draping softly over their shoulders. Every one of them wore multiple strings of red beads, of distant coral, painted bone or rowan berries.

The men were no less finely attired, even the poorest among them wearing their finest shirts, with colourful woven belts. The rich wore heavy *kontush* jackets, embroidered on the sleeves, with silk belts tied at the waist.

Each family carried a loaf of home-made bread, made from newly harvested grain, with patterns cut into the golden crusts. The loaves would be blessed, and shared with the forest, and would hopefully bring a year of good fortune to those who made it.

A few of the town musicians, with their simple fiddles and carved reed flutes, brought music into the procession, and soon some of the children and young couples broke away from the crowd, dancing on the outskirts of the stream of people, to twirl and laugh for a moment, before they were once more pulled into the unstoppable tide of bodies moving towards the fields.

The day was bright and there was no sign of the recent rains, except for, perhaps, the lack of dust that so many feet would normally kick up from the road.

The mood was joyful, infectiously so, and even Sladyana felt buoyed up by it, though she still held Tula's hand, somewhat over-anxiously.

Makail was in his element, shoulders linked with two of his friends from the town, kicking their heels in an athletic dance display aimed to impress. Tula laughed and clapped, delighted by everything and everyone she saw. Something like guilt gripped Sladyana, seeing the child's joy. Perhaps she had kept the child too close, too isolated back in her house. There was comfort in that, a great comfort, of course. For Tula spoke only to her, smiled only at her, loved only her. *Needed* only her. But as Tula glimpsed the life outside, and saw that there was more, would she resent the seclusion her guardian's love demanded?

The thought was unpleasant and Sladyana shook it off. She couldn't be blamed, she decided, for learning from her mistakes. The mistake of feeling safe, of feeling too happy, too content, too open. When the fox stole Luba, it was able to do so only because Sladyana suspected nothing, feared nothing. She floated on her soap bubble of joy, and how easy it was for the thief to sneak up on her. She tightened her hand around Tula's fingers. She would not be such a fool again.

The procession reached the harvest field, where a patch of grain by the road was left uncut. Somebody brought a folded stool towards Gorcay and set it up in front of him. With his son's help, Gorcay stepped up, so that all could see him. He cleared his throat and then spread his arms wide, as if he was bringing the whole town into a hug.

"My dear friends!" he began. "Another year has passed, and our Mother Zemya blessed us once more with good harvest!" The people cheered, as many of them remembered the lean years. He waited for the noise to calm down.

"As you all know, I have my own special reasons to be particularly grateful this year." He nodded towards Kada. "And so, I have spared no expense in my contributions to this year's dozynki feasts!" The men stomped their feet and hooted as the women clapped. "Even now, my good man Motik is turning the spit, pouring on the *sekacz* cake rings, as his helpers carve the hams and pour the mead, made from my future stepdaughter's honey!" There was cheering and clapping, though more muted, Sladyana noticed with some satisfaction. Gorcay must have noticed as well, for he coughed, and once more raised his voice, overcompensating somewhat with an excess of joviality. "And now, the young and the beautiful among us will give our thanks to Mother Zemya, may her roots grow ever strong!"

Secha stepped to the front, a deer-like expression in her wide, frightened eyes. She was joined by a few other pre-selected girls from the village, and Tula, who Sladyana led right up to the line.

Secha reached towards Tula, but the child shrank away from her, and moved to the other side of the line. Sladyana watched Tula's expression with interest, and a part of her was glad, strangely, that the two did not clasp hands.

The girls formed a circle around the unharvested grain, and joined hands, waiting for the music to start. As the notes carried on the wind, the girls moved to the left, then to the right, a few of the ones with stronger voices lifting them up in a song to Zemya. Tula shot a look at Sladyana, who tried to encourage her with a smile.

The child knew none of the steps to this dance, but she rallied well, trying to match her movements to those of the girls around her. The dance grew more complicated, with squats and jumps added to the repertoire, but the rhythm of them felt natural, soothingly predictable even. Sladyana let herself relax, watching Tula's happy grin. The child held hands with a Torlow girl, similar in age, who laughed at her own missteps, of which there were many, and the child's good humour rubbed off on Tula, who laughed soundlessly at her companion's expressions. The other child enjoyed Tula's attention, and so she exaggerated the moves for her new friend's benefit. There was something so good-spirited about the whole thing that Sladyana laughed, and leaned her head on Makail's shoulder, as he stood by her side.

"You approve of our little peasant customs then?" he asked, clearly delighted at the change in Sladyana's mood. "If I'd known, I would have brought you out of your fine house sooner!"

She didn't reply, allowing herself to enjoy this brief moment.

After the song was finished, Kada walked up to the girls and pulled a knife from her belt. "We thank you, Mother Zemya, for the blessings you have lavished upon us!" she called out, brandishing the knife high.

The happiness from the moment before bled out of Sladyana, and she felt the small hairs on her neck stand up, as her eyes locked with Kada's. Tula was there, unprotected, alone. Sladyana took a step forward, but Makail held her back. "Wait," he whispered.

Sladyana snarled, and she would have screamed, but then the vedma grabbed the sheafs of wheat in her hand and cut them off with one smooth movement.

As Kada stepped away from the girls and towards the crowd, Sladyana let out a breath she didn't know she was holding. A woman Sladyana didn't recognise approached Kada with a small, neat loaf on a large platter, decorated with garden flowers. With a practiced movement, Kada twisted the long sheafs of wheat into a simple wreath, which she then placed on the platter around the loaf.

Kada faced the town. "We will place this bread by the edge of the forest, our gift to Leshy and Borovy, so that the woods so close to Mother Zemya may flourish, its saplings grow in harmony alongside our children."

Did Sladyana imagine it, or did Kada shoot her a look at the last word?

After the offer to the forest was complete, the procession went back to town, in joyful anticipation of the feast and dancing awaiting them there.

The xylophone and gusla players were waiting by the long tables set up in the street, and the air was filled with the mouth-watering smell of roast meat. Cheese and bread were prominently displayed on the tables, with sausages doled out by Motik's helpers. The afternoon light fell softly on the people of Torlow, and it would have been difficult to find one sour face in the crowd.

The hard work of the year was done, and the brief respite

from life's worries was to be celebrated. For a moment, all was well, all was goodness and calm. It was a feeling Sladyana didn't trust, not with Kada's green eyes flashing at her, not with the memory of Luba's face striking her heart. Still, in a crowd of happy people it was hard to fortress up her emotions. Not with Tula close and Makail asking her to dance.

The mead was poured generously, and Sladyana's head swam. Makail pulled her up and into the dancing circle.

"I don't know this dance!" she said, looking at the faces around her. This was a peasant dance, unlike the more stately affairs of her own circle. Though the energy and the pure joy of the crowd was hard to resist.

"I will help you, don't worry!" Makail called over the din. The music stopped for a moment, as the dancers all arranged themselves in a circle, the women on the inside, facing their partners. Makail grabbed Sladyana's hands and nodded an encouragement. "See how the real people of Fiesna dance!"

Sladyana was aware of the Torlow people around her casting her curious glances, but Makail's confidence was irresistible.

The music started, slowly at first. The women began singing, a song well-known to them but new to Sladyana. The circle started moving, a few steps to the left, a few steps to the right. The men's voices joined in the song, which was now gathering pace. The rhythm was punctuated by the stomping of feet and the clapping of onlookers' hands.

"Now the fun bit starts," Makail called to Sladyana, who only had the time to open her eyes wide in surprise, as Makail turned her around and grabbed her by the waist. They side-stepped and then he shouted "Jump!" into her ear.

She obeyed and he lifted her up, and twirled her around, using the momentum, before setting her back on the ground. It knocked the air out of her, but there was no chance to collect herself before the music grew faster and wilder, and the figures more complicated.

It seemed like no time at all before Makail led the red-faced and out-of-breath Sladyana back to her spot at the table.

"I thought you were going to squeeze the life out of me!" She laughed as she sank to her chair. "Get me some water, will you?"

"As you command!" He leaned forward and kissed her on the lips before going off on the errand.

Sladyana chuckled. The sheer exertion of the dance did much to restore her spirits, and she sipped her mead, and chewed on a piece of crusty bread, sliced for her by the woman sitting next to her. As she waited, she cast her eye about, searching for Tula. She didn't feel any alarm, as the child had been playing with her companion from the dozynki blessing. The two girls were no doubt giggling about something or other in the crowd. It was the blessing of that age that they needed no common speech to understand each other perfectly. As Sladyana swirled the dark golden mead in her cup, she wondered how it was that communication was so much harder when she had so many more words at her disposal.

From where she sat, she could see Gorcay's cook, putting the finishing touches on the *sekacz*, the cake so called as it looked like a tree trunk, its many rings knotted round. The cook was explaining something about his technique to the young children crowding around him, more for an early chance to taste the cake than because of any will to learn, Sladyana suspected. But there was something rather fascinating in the process, she had to admit, as Motik carefully poured a thin layer of the mixture over the slowly spinning cake. As soon as one layer cooked over the fire, the next was poured on, the thin, golden-brown rings creating a pattern best suited to honouring Goddess Zemya on this day.

"And what are you thinking about, looking so dreamily at our cook?" Makail's voice made her look up. "Should I be jealous?"

"Perhaps." She laughed and winked at Makail, who was bringing a water jug and a fresh cup for her. "Thought I'd have to send out a search party."

"As if I could be kept away!" He smiled. "I'd be drawn back to you no matter where you were!"

Sladyana snorted. "Your lines are getting better," she said, not without affection. She drank deeply of the water, and then traced her fingers along Makail's cheek.

"I have my fiercest critic to practice on," he said, leaning in. "A man can't help but improve."

"Yet so few ever do." She put down the cup and laced her fingers on the back of his neck.

A commotion interrupted them, as an anxious voice rang out in the crowd, joined by more voices. "Lenka!" The words reached Sladyana's ears above the mind fog caused by her drink. She looked about but couldn't locate the source of the call.

"Who's Lenka?" She raised her eyebrows.

Makail shrugged. "Some child sneaking away to grab extra treats, no doubt. In the crowd, with the dancing and all, it's easy to lose your companions. Unless," he grinned, leaning in for a kiss, "they shine as bright as you, of course."

But something about what he said struck Sladyana and

sobered her up. She stood up and walked towards the source of the commotion. A nervous-looking woman was being comforted by a group of her companions, as she was looking around her.

"What's the matter?" Sladyana said.

The woman turned her eyes to the newcomer and, noticing Sladyana's fine clothes, curtsied. "My girl, m'lady, my Lenka, is gone somewhere, and I can't find her."

An older woman standing next to the mother added. "Nothing for you to worry about, m'lady. The child will be found soon enough, for sure."

"Are you the mother of the brown-haired girl in the blue dress, from Gorcay's house?" A hawkish-looking man asked, staring at Sladyana.

"I am," Sladyana said, not bothering to correct him. "She was playing with another child dancer from the blessing."

"Oh, but that is my Lenka!" The first woman seemed relieved. "I knew the child had gone off somewhere! Would you mind pointing me to where I might find her, m'lady, if it pleases you?"

Sladyana opened her mouth and closed it again. All blood drained from her face.

"What's happened?" Makail came up behind her, and placed his hands on her shoulders, to comfort or support her, she wasn't sure, for she likely needed both.

"Tula," she whispered. "Tula was with this Lenka. And I don't know where they are."

It wasn't long before the news spread through the crowd. The music stopped, and the calls rang out across Torlow.

Sladyana wandered around, calling Tula's name, in spite of Makail asking her to sit down and wait for the child to be brought to her.

As Gorcay organised several search groups to comb through the town in search of the girls, Sladyana saw Kada approach her with hesitation. A fury built up inside Sladyana, and the vedma, who must have seen the warning signs in her, stopped a few paces away.

"I'm sure Tula will be found soon enough," Kada said. She folded her hands in front of her, giving her a look of a strange sort of modesty, incongruous with what Sladyana knew of her. "I wish I could help."

"Why don't you then?" Sladyana spat out. "Oh yes, a vedma's help is not worth much these days, is it?" She was aware of curious looks, but she had no self-restraint left. "Maybe it's better that you don't assist us. After all, these days asking your help in a search for lost children seems the best guarantee they're not found!"

Kada's eyes grew cold. "I can only do my best."

"And has Artek Lelechek experienced your best?" Sladyana seethed. Kada's collected expression infuriated her further. *How dare she be calm. How dare she not look down in shame.* "I swear, Vedma Kada, if I find you've had something to do with Tula's disappearing!"

Kada opened her mouth to respond, but they were interrupted, as Makail ran up to Sladyana, pushing people out of the way. "She's found, Sladyana, she's found!"

Sladyana followed him immediately, leaving Kada in the middle of a suddenly sullen-looking crowd.

There she was, in the arms of a Torlow man, her new dress torn. Sladyana screamed at the sight of the child, who had a ragged cut running along her leg.

"I found her on the edge of town," the man carrying her said to Sladyana who snatched Tula out of his arms and held her tight, as the girl wrapped her legs around her waist, clinging to her like a limpet. The man scratched his head. "I tried asking where she went, or who hurt her, but she wouldn't say a word to me. I told her I have children of my own, and she has nothing to be afeared of, but she must've been too frightened to talk to a stranger."

"She's mute," Makail said to the man, patting him on the back.

Sladyana wasn't listening to them. Instead, she went to her knees, and gently peeled Tula's arms from around her neck.

*What happened?* She signed to the child. She wiped some dirt off the girl's cheek with her sleeve.

Tula lifted her hands then let them fall down again, as she looked towards her shoes, heavy tears falling to the ground.

"And my Lenka?" The woman from earlier approached the man who brought Tula. "Where is my daughter, did you see her?"

"I'm sorry, Milena, I haven't, not for want of looking," the man said. "I'll go back there; she might be hiding somewhere. Whatever hurt this one," he pointed at Tula, "might have frightened off the other."

"It's the fox! It must be." An old man hobbled towards the front of the crowd. "Who else?"

Sladyana tightened her grip on Tula, staring at the man who swayed from side to side, like a reed on the wind. "The fox? The fox is here?" she whispered.

"Fairytales," someone scoffed.

"I tell you, on dozynki, a child is taken, it can be nothing else, it is nothing else, and nothing is what you will find now." The old man scowled.

Lenka's mother sank to her knees with a wail. Her friends crowded around her and began to talk over each other, some seeking to quieten the man's prophesying, some trying to comfort the distraught mother.

"I saw it!"

The crowd turned like one towards a lonely figure standing by the bonfire, her red hair loosened from its braids, a strange, dreamy look on her moon-face. A murmur travelled over the crowd, curiosity mixed with suspicion in the townsfolk's eyes.

"It's the fox, I saw it!" Secha said, her hands clasped in front of her.

"Where?" Milena demanded, breaking away from her friends. "Where is my child?"

Secha looked towards the woman, confused, like she was trying to place her. The girl's striped skirt moved, as if of its own accord, though there was no breeze.

Sladyana squinted and gasped, as she saw the bone roots crowding around Secha's feet, like a pile of white maggots crawling over carrion. They slithered up the girl's feet and legs, pushed at the fabric of her skirt, then sank back in the ground, only to rise up again a heartbeat later.

From the collective gasp, Sladyana understood the crowd noticed it too.

Secha, seemingly oblivious to the shifting mood, looked at Tula, and said, "I saw the fox. But to be the gift, the fox needs a gift, but an ordinary one won't do, will it?"

The missing girl's mother snarled and grabbed Secha by the shoulders. "Are you mad? What are you saying? Where is my girl?"

Makail swore and jumped to Secha's rescue, trying to pull Milena away. "She's just a girl," he said. "She must have drunk too much of her own mead." He looked around, trying to feign a smile, but was met only by sullen expressions.

"The fox's magic is strong!" Kada walked through the crowd, which parted for her as if there was an invisible force around the woman. *Which there might as well have been*, Sladyana thought.

Kada stood in front of Secha and faced the crowd, her brow furrowed and her lips in a tight line. "The *fox* is the enemy. My daughter has some of my gifts, which all of you benefit from. It's no wonder she can sense the fox's evil wishes, just as well as I do." She placed her fingers to her temple then shook her head. She glanced at Sladyana. "A child was stolen. We don't know why one was chosen over the other, but–"

Someone – Sladyana couldn't tell who – interrupted Kada. "What about this one?" The crowd's attention turned towards Tula. Sladyana brought the child closer to her chest.

"Yes, she was with Lenka!" Milena moved towards Sladyana. "Ask her! Where is my daughter!"

Tula hid her face in Sladyana's dress, shrinking away from the approaching people.

"I'll ask her!" Sladyana said. "I'll ask her, give me space!" Makail moved as if to approach them, but Sladyana shook her head. A crowd this agitated was a dangerous thing. A spark could turn desperation to fury in a moment. She kneeled in front of Tula, and stroked the child's hair, making soothing, cooing noises. "That's alright, *slonechko moye*, don't worry, I'm here."

She carefully peeled the girl's arms from around her neck and held Tula so that she would look at her. "Your little friend is missing, *moya mila*, and her mama is so worried." Sladyana spoke gently, punctuating the words by kissing Tula's tear-stained cheeks and hands. "If you can tell me what happened, we might be able to help. I know you want to help your friend, don't you?"

Tula bit her lip and nodded.

"That's my girl, my brave, brave girl," Sladyana stroked Tula's hair, ever aware of the hawkish gaze of those surrounding them. "Tell me what's happened."

Tula hesitated, then seemed to arrive at a decision. She lifted her hands and began talking, her nimble fingers moving so fast, even Sladyana had trouble following.

"What is she saying?" Lenka's mother demanded.

*Shhhh!* Somebody silenced her. But Sladyana wasn't looking at them.

At long last the child finished and gazed up, hopeful, at Sladyana.

The woman stood up and faced the crowd. "It was the fox," she said.

Milena sank to her knees and wailed, her cries filling the air as the rest of Torlow stood stunned.

"The fox dragged Lenka towards the forest," Sladyana said. "If you organise a search party, she may yet be found."

Sladyana locked eyes with Kada, each wordlessly daring the other to betray what else they knew.

Finally, Kada turned to those assembled. "The time is short! The fox is wily, and we must be too! Gather what weapons you can. We must go now!"

All doubt was put aside as the people of Torlow began organising, some bringing gardening tools as weapons with them.

Makail stayed behind with Sladyana. When there was nobody about them to hear, he turned to her. "That was a lot of signs from Tula just to say 'fox'." He turned his head to the side.

"The child is scared. She spoke a lot to tell little." Sladyana put her hand on Tula's shoulder and led her towards

Gorcay's house. Not even to Makail would she admit what she concealed from the people of Torlow. For the fox did not come for Lenka, and Tula was not safe.

# CHAPTER 54

"Can you really do nothing?" Gorcay paced the room, struggling to keep his voice level.

Kada shook her head. "I have few options." She sat on Gorcay's chair by his desk and propped her head on her hand. She was tired after the sleepless night. The bastooks didn't answer when called, and she couldn't go see to the bozhontkas, not when the town's eyes were on her.

"What about Mother Zemya? Can you ask the roots?"

Kada snorted. "The fox is hers. She will not interfere."

"How do you know that?" Gorcay stopped his pacing and looked at her. "All *I* know of the fox is that it's an evil child-stealer. That's all *anyone* around here knows. You mean to tell me the mother of our land, the goddess of our soil, who we toil and offer thanks to, is also responsible for the kidnapping of Fiesna's children?"

Kada straightened up and drummed her fingers on the desk. She didn't mean to say so much, and if she hadn't been so tired, she wouldn't have. "Yes," she said finally. "The fox serves Zemya. Though in this case its business is its own. But then, why should it surprise you?" She looked into Gorcay's eyes. "Decay nourishes the soil, just as the rain and the sun bring new green. You can't have spring without winter. Mother Zemya gives generously, but she takes too."

Gorcay took a step towards Kada. She couldn't decipher

the look upon his face, as his penetrating gaze seemed to analyse every hidden part of her.

Finally, he spoke. "You're a vedma, and so you belong to Zemya too…"

Kada did not reply.

"Make sure the fox's alliance with the goddess is the furthest thing from the townsfolk's mind. If they think you're in any way responsible, none of your powers can protect you."

"What do you suggest?"

He fell silent for a moment and looked out of the window. "There's people at my door," he said flatly. He rubbed his eyes, then reached a hand towards Kada. She hesitated and wrapped her fingers around his. "Do what you must, Kada. Try to help the child. But if you can't–" He nodded, as if coming to an agreement with his own conscience. "Then put on a performance, if you must, to show you're trying. Anything to keep the town's anger away from you." He pulled Kada up from the chair. "And do your best to be convincing. Because they're downstairs, and they want blood. Even yours would do under the circumstances."


They descended the stone steps together. Kada paused at the last step, and squeezed her eyes tight, as the blood rushed to her head. She could feel the pounding of her own heart, and her mouth felt as dry as sand.

"You can do it," Gorcay whispered, squeezing her hand. "You've done it before."

"Secha…"

"Secha is safe under my roof. I've charged my son-in-law with keeping an eye on her. He wouldn't dare fail me."

She nodded, though the words brought her little comfort. Nobody else could keep Secha safe, she knew. The fox got through Kada's defences; it was close, too close. And no mob could cause her as much dread as that knowledge.

Gorcay motioned to his manservant, who opened the front door, letting a number of the most influential townsfolk in. Kada knew them all. Some whose children or grandchildren she helped welcome to the world. A woman whose heart complaint Kada treated. A man whose hand Kada saved after an infection set in, and many were ready to cut it off. But there was no familiarity or gratitude in their faces. It was as if they stared at a stranger when they looked at her. A situation she would have to rectify if she and Secha were to survive this.

"What news?" she spoke first, her voice confident, her eyes compassionate. She moved towards the town representatives, and gently placed her hand on the shoulder of one of them, a man, who instantly took his hat off, as if shamed for his boldness.

"We're still searching, Vedma Kada," the man said, his eyes fixed on the tips of his shoes.

A woman behind him seemed irritated by his sudden meekness, and she stepped forward, elbowing him out of the way. "The folk of Torlow are all doing their bit, Vedma Kada! And where are *you*? Hiding out here in this fine house, while the rest of us trudge through the marshlands and the woods, searching for the poor child."

Kada gave the woman a cold look. "I've been here, working in my own way, searching for clues. My work is different to yours, and more dangerous in many respects."

"Of course, Vedma Kada," the first man said quickly. "We know you are helping all you can. But the folk get restless.

If they could see you out with us, so we could observe and take comfort from your magic, it would bring such comfort."

"I will come," Kada nodded, though the thought of leaving Secha made her blood run cold.

"And your daughter, Vedma Kada?"

Kada snapped her head towards the voice, which had seemed to mirror her own thoughts.

"What *about* my daughter?" she said, more sharply than she meant.

The woman who spoke lifted her chin and folded her arms on her breast. "You said last night, your Secha has some of your powers. I say what better time to use them than now? If she's a vedma like you, then let her help! Unless–" she made a sweeping motion with her hand. "Unless she's too *fine* for the likes of us now."

Kada fought the urge to spit in the woman's eye and smiled instead. "Secha is in a delicate state."

"Who isn't! You think Lenka being stolen didn't shake the rest of us to the core?"

"Like I *said*." Kada was grateful for the sudden cool breeze from the open door. Without it, she might have slapped the woman. "Secha is only now coming into her powers. It is a difficult time. She wouldn't be much help."

"Did Secha call this on us, Vedma Kada?" Another man rushed forward. When faced with Kada's cold stare, he suddenly stopped, almost ashamed. "I'm sorry to speak so plain, Vedma Kada," he said, fiddling with the edge of his shirt. "But many in the town noticed that your girl's been acting mighty strange of late. And when someone destroyed her hives, there are many that heard her strangeness and spell-casting."

Gorcay moved as if to intervene, but Kada raised one

hand, stopping him in his tracks. "Spell casting, Boslav?" She straightened herself up and, though the man was easily a head taller than her, her confidence seemed to make her tower above him. "You hear a girl crying, a girl wronged, and your first thought is 'spells'? Is that the kind of man you are?"

The man shifted uncomfortably, but a woman next to him, irritated at the lack of progress, stepped to the front. "It's not just that, Vedma Kada. You can explain it away all you like, but Secha's been acting like she's half a striga and no mistake. Everyone saw her yesterday, talking about the fox and the gifts. How would she know anything of the sort, if she wasn't consorting with the thief? Are you protecting her because she's your daughter, or because you had a hand in the theft as well?" The woman looked very satisfied with herself, and the tension hung heavy in the air.

Kada held her breath. This was it. One wrong word, one show of weakness and the home she'd built over the years would collapse over her head.

"I have served this community faithfully for years," she said. "I have guided, healed and protected you all." She laughed mirthlessly. "You disappoint me. Your lack of gratitude and faith disappoints me. Very well." She lifted her chin and squared up to the woman. "I will do my best to help find the unfortunate child, as I have always done my best for the people of Torlow. But," she raised a finger, "that is it. See how well you do without a vedma to cater to your every need."

"Now, Vedma Kada, there's no need for rash words," another member of the group piped in, as the bravado of the town representatives weakened, each weighing in their mind the consequences of Kada's words.

"Get out of my house," Gorcay said quietly. "Kada will do what she can for the missing girl. You all take your time thinking about how you can gain her forgiveness."

When the two of them were left alone, Gorcay walked up behind Kada, and placed his hands on her shoulders.

She exhaled and leaned back, for once happy to be supported by him.

"What will you do?" His words reached her over the rush of her own blood.

"What I planned to do in private must now be done in full view of people, who will not forgive me for it," she whispered.


She didn't announce her plans to the town. She had hoped to leave unnoticed, though that was a vain hope, of course. As soon as she stepped out the back of Gorcay's house, a crowd began to follow her at a distance. The privacy usually afforded her was gone; the people she'd served for years now demanding a proof of her loyalty, a proof of her power that would assure them once and for all of her allegiance. She didn't doubt that if they were satisfied, Gorcay's house would become overrun with apologetic supplicants within an hour, all swearing they had never doubted her or Secha. But success was measured not only in the end result, but in the methods too. And nobody in the town had dared question her methods before.

She reached the end of the fields. By then, it seemed the whole town was gathered behind her. Gorcay was home with Secha; she wouldn't have trusted anyone else with her child, not now. That she even trusted Sobis was a surprise to them both.

The people following Kada out of town did so with a grim determination. None spoke to her or each other. The sound of their many footsteps hitting the path behind her sounded like a war drum, bringing ever closer the answer to whether she could hold onto the life she had built.

Her best bet at success were the bozhontkas. Yet she shivered at the thought of the townsfolk seeing them. Some aspects of her powers, or the spirits she had dealings with, were acceptable to the simple people. Some less so.

Kada held her arm up, gesturing for those who followed her to stop. They obeyed. There was an unspoken understanding passing between them. They would watch from the distance, bearing witness to what she was about to do, without interfering.

Kada climbed on top of a boulder, and took out dry poppy seedpods, their light, black carcasses sitting comfortably in the palm of her hand. She shook them, the soft rattling of the tiny seeds inside barely loud enough for her to hear, though she knew they were as loud as a bell to the lonely creatures listening among the grasses.

"I've come again, *moye male*," she said, straining to see the pale auras of the child spirits, taking shape in the dusk. She set the poppy pods down, then, taking a small, sealed jug from her bag, poured some milk into the palm of her hand.

The bozhontkas appeared before her in the half-light, crowding, the strands of the light that made them weave in and out as each tried to get closer to her.

The townsfolk gathered by the road called out and screamed. Kada ignored them, focusing all her attention on those clamouring for it.

"*Shhh*," Kada soothed and stroked the small heads, and smiled at the hopeful faces. "I am so glad, so happy to see you all. I worried for you. The fox has come." She looked at the bozhontas' faces and singled out one who seemed the most solid among them. She beckoned to him with a smile and rested her hand on his half-translucent cheek. The spirit let out a satisfied sigh before speaking.

"We saw the fox. We held it, but it was strong, too strong and it escaped."

"And the girl he stole?" Kada's heart turned cold. If the spirits couldn't find Lenka, then the consequences would be dreadful.

"We have her!" the little spirit replied with a grin. "We keep her with us! She said she would come play with us anyway! But we know she would go. If we keep her, then she's safe, then the fox can't get her. And then she will be one of us soon, and then she is safe for good!" The other bozhontkas nodded approvingly.

"Where is she?"

The spirit who spoke furrowed his eyebrows. "Safe and hidden."

"Where did you hide her?

"You won't show the fox, will you?"

Kada sensed a discomfort among the bozhontkas. They were easily spooked after all. And once they went, there'd be no getting them back. She smiled her sweetest smile, and once more stroked the spirit's cheek. "I keep children safe, remember? The fox is my enemy too. But the girl needs my help now that she's had yours. Will you take me to her?"

The spirit's chin quivered. "But if you take her away, she will be gone, and not our friend anymore."

"She will always be your friend," Kada said soothingly. "As will I."

The bozhontkas seemed to reach a decision. They joined

hands and hovered a little above the ground, then shot in a flash of blue light over towards the path, where the Torlow people were.

The crowd of onlookers scrambled to part as the spirits hovered about, waiting for Kada, who was struggling to keep up. Kada steeled herself against the townsfolk's reaction. She wished that the years of her service could be her armour against the people's suspicion and anger. But she was a vedma, and so knew better than most that people seldom stay grateful for long. Not when they could choose to be resentful instead. Especially towards those more powerful than them.

A woman in the crowd screamed, as one of the bozhontkas paused in front of her, watching her with a wide-eyed wonder.

"Palinka?" The woman said, her hand raised to touch the girl-spirit's face.

The spirit twirled, and planted a kiss, no more solid than a light breeze, on the woman's cheek, who burst into tears.

"It's my sister Palinka, my baby sister, gone these thirty years," the woman cried, as some of those present struggled to focus on the bozhontkas' faces, as they faded in and out of view.

Kada swore under her breath, and called out to all present, alive or otherwise: "They will take us to Lenka! Follow me, people of Torlow!" Then, as the bozhontkas once more shot over the field, she broke into a run, the townspeople behind her.

The bozhontkas swirled about, leaving a blue trail behind, a shimmering ribbon flowing through the air for a brief moment, before dissipating in the evening breeze.

Not all could follow at the pace set by the spirits, but Kada ran with a grim determination, closely followed by Lenka's mother, whose eyes the vedma felt like ice on her neck.

The evening's shadows grew, and the grey hour had set in. The bozhontkas seemed to sense the weariness of those behind them and slowed down, filling the air with echoey laughter, this being the first game they had been able to play in a while.

"There!" Kada stopped abruptly, her arm outstretched.

In a small grove, between the large roots of an ancient tree, she saw the gaping maws of a burrow big enough to fit a young bear. The lights of the bozhontkas were already fading as the night settled in. They hovered about the entrance to the hole.

Lenka's mother saw it too, and she rushed ahead, heedless of her friends' warnings.

Kada exhaled as the woman's happy cries carried across the field.

There, in the burrow, Lenka was found, tied with ivy branches and covered in scrapes, but otherwise seemingly unharmed.

Her mother tried to tear the ivy with her hands and teeth as she laughed and cried, relieved to find her daughter alive.

"Let me," Kada said softly, and she pulled out her knife to help free the child.

"Get away from her!" Lenka's mother turned to Kada suddenly, the fury clear in her face.

Kada's mouth grew dry. "I'm only offering to help. We found her–"

"*Found* her? Who *are* you? You control the spirits of the dead. They tied Lenka up in this hole! They waited for her to die, and if we hadn't forced you to come here, you would have *let* her die!"

"And that was my sister among the spirits!" Another woman called out from behind Kada. "How did my dead sister come to be in your power, vedma?"

"That was my Yurek!" An old man approached Kada, fury clear on his face, so much so he was held back by a couple of his companions. "My own child died forty years ago, but I would know his sweet face anywhere! Is he your prisoner?"

Kada held her hands up. "Bozhontkas are not my prisoners, they're not mine to command."

"And yet they do as they're told!" The man showed his teeth. "And yet they answer *your* call, though I called my boy's name many a night, me and his mother both!"

"Some don't rest, I cannot change or control it," Kada said.

"And who knows if what you say is true?" Lenka's mother said, bringing her girl out of the burrow. She lifted the child up, the girl's arms tight around her mother's neck. "Your daughter seems to know things you're not telling us." She jutted out her chin, contempt dripping from her voice. "And the things you're not telling us tear our very children from our arms. How do we know we can trust you, vedma?"

Kada stood there, silently, no answer ready on her tongue, as she was left in the grove, to make her way back alone in the dark.

# CHAPTER 55

Kada entered the chamber where Gorcay sat vigil next to Secha, who lay curled up in the wide cushioned seat. The curtains were drawn, and the only light came from a flickering candle on a side cabinet. The room smelled like melting beeswax and the bitter herbs Motik had prepared, which were now cooling on a small, tile-mosaic-topped table next to Secha.

"How did it go?" Gorcay stood up when she entered the room.

Kada softened at the concern in his face and brushed her knuckles against his cheek. "The child is safe."

He eyed her carefully. "But?"

"But the town's distrust of vedma magic and, by extension, me, is growing." She walked up to Secha. She pushed an errant curl off her daughter's face, thinking her asleep. She was startled when she realised Secha was awake, staring emptily ahead. "Has she been like this all evening?"

"Since the sunset." Gorcay nodded.

Secha's green eyes were wide open, as she muttered to herself, her fingers picking on the thread of the chair's fabric.

"Here, *moya slichna*, here, my beautiful one. What is the matter?" Kada cooed, and coaxed, finally turning Secha's face towards her. "Why won't you talk to me?"

"She's talking to me and wants me to listen." Secha smiled, a strange haze over her eyes.

"Who is talking to you, Secha?" Kada pulled the girl up and wedged herself beside her, heedless of the mud sticking to her clothes. "I'm here, talk to me."

Secha frowned and shook her head. "She is *here* too." She tapped her chest. "And she doesn't have what she needs."

"And what is it that 'she' needs, exactly, Vedma Kada?" Sladyana's voice made both Gorcay and Kada snap their heads towards the door. Kada instinctively placed one arm protectively over her daughter.

"Lady Goroncheva," Sobis stepped between Kada and Sladyana and bowed his head. "I'm afraid this is a family matter we're discussing. If you would perhaps be so kind as to join my daughter and son in the Yellow Room, I believe they are playing 'Eight Man Draft' and they'd be glad of your company."

"Thank you, Gorcay," Sladyana said. "But this affects me too, as my Tula was very nearly taken as well. And if there is an answer here, I will have it."

"I must insist—" Sobis started, but Secha interrupted him, her face brightening at the sight of Tula, half-hidden behind Sladyana's skirt.

"*She*! She is the key!" Secha pointed at Tula, who shrank away from the young woman's feverish gaze. "The day is coming, and I'm here, so if I'm here, another might help, but another doesn't want to help, and yet another is no help at all!"

"What is your crazed child talking about?" Sladyana's face darkened, as she tightened her grip on Tula. "Is the fox after Tula? Is that why the other child was released?"

"And why would the fox be after Tula specifically?" Kada watched the woman with interest. "Is there something *you're* not telling *us*?"

"I have lost one child to the fox, as you well know."
Sladyana narrowed her eyes. "If the creature is after Tula,
and you know something that would protect her, speak so
now."

Kada and Sladyana stood very still for a moment, each
keeping their child behind them.

"I don't know why Lenka was taken, or why Tula was
spared," Kada finally spoke. "Secha's mind is unsettled, and
I can no more glean what she's seen than you can."

Sladyana nodded. "You're lying, of course."

"Lady Goroncheva!" Sobis reddened and stepped in front
of Kada. "May I remind you that you are a guest in my
home, and I will not tolerate your accusations towards my
soon-to-be wife!"

Sladyana opened her mouth to respond, but then Tula
yanked at her guardian's sleeve. The woman looked into
the child's eyes, and, whatever she saw there, made her
reconsider. She took a breath then faced Gorcay and Kada
again. "I'm sorry, you're quite right. I'm driving myself half-
mad with worry. I'm glad the child Lenka is well."

Gorcay rushed to accept the apology, once more the
model host. But Kada spoke. "How did you know Lenka
was fine? I haven't told anyone but Gorcay yet."

Sladyana froze in the spot, then turned her eyes on Kada.
"Tula told me. The fox didn't want the other child."

"Not the right gift, not the needed one, not the wanted
one." Secha piped in from behind Kada.

They all turned to watch the girl, as she nodded to
herself. And then Kada saw what Secha had been picking
at, what she'd thought was the fabric of the chair. The bone
roots had crept their way from the vine growing outside the
window, along the wooden floor, in a single thin tendril, like

a rivulet of poured milk. And that single tendril of Zemya's bone roots wrapped itself around Secha's fingers, twisting and squirming under her touch.

# CHAPTER 56

Sladyana moved quickly through the streets of Torlow, half-dragging Tula who struggled to keep up. But she would not leave Tula behind, would not let her out of her sight. The child did not complain though, instinctively understanding her guardian's feverish fear.

Sladyana felt the eyes of the townsfolk on her. She was a guest at Gorcay's house, and so expected some of the hostility. But her goal was to reach the crowd gathered right on the outskirts of the town, the one Aleenka told her about in hushed tones. The girl was scared, and with good reason. But she had placed her fate in Sladyana's hands, a fact they were both more than conscious of.

And there it was.

The raised voices and animated whispers, which carried if not the thoughts, then the emotion on the wind. It was not a united group, not yet. So far, in twos and threes, people had gathered driven by a common sense of unease, if not yet a purpose.

Some of the people stopped talking as soon as they saw Sladyana. Others did the opposite and whispered with increased fervour, watching Tula especially with a hawkish curiosity.

Sladyana cleared her throat. Another woman might have lost her nerve, but she had the accumulated confidence of generations of women bred to give orders. "Good day to you, good people of Torlow," she said, putting on her most commanding smile. That failed to have the effect she'd hoped for; the people of Torlow did not seem impressed by her.

"I understand you are all concerned by the recent events," she tried again. "As you know, the child under my care was too almost taken by the fox, though she luckily escaped."

"Yeah, so she did!" A woman Sladyana vaguely recognised from the dozynki night stepped forward. The woman placed her hands on her hips and lifted up her chin. "Found same night, unscathed, while my niece Lenka was captured for a night and a day, held by the spirits controlled by your friend, Vedma Kada!" The woman turned back to the crowd. "How interesting that they who live in the Gorcay house, are so often so much *luckier* than the poor folk."

"Poor or rich, that has nothing to do with it!" Sladyana scoffed.

"Says a rich woman, about to gorge herself at the vedma's wedding feast," a man, clearly the other woman's husband, piped in, placing his hand on his woman's back. "While us here fret over a child thief on the loose!"

"And was Artek Lelechek a poor man?" Sladyana asked, her head to the side.

The crowd seemed stunned for a moment. "What does Lelechek have to do with the fox? His boy was a grown man, and the fox don't steal grown men," somebody said.

"So where is he?" Sladyana asked. "Where is his son? If the fox didn't take him, then how is he not yet found?"

"The vedma said that the znajnitza can't find those who don't want to be found..." Lenka's aunt said, but the conviction was fast draining from her voice.

"Vedma Kada seems to say a great many things," Sladyana said. "Yet many of them seem to come to nought, except where it serves her. She promised Lelechek to enquire among the spirits of this land but has so far brought no answers." She looked around her triumphantly. "And did she bring him no answers because she had none to give, or because she *would* not give them?"

"Why would she not want to help find Botrik, if it were in her power to do so?"

"Botrik wished to marry Vedma Kada's daughter, did he not?" Sladyana looked up, as if the thought had just occurred to her. Aleenka had proven a fount of information once she felt confident of Sladyana's assistance.

"Secha's a good girl," a young man said, a brick-maker, by the look of his clay and red-dust-covered clothes. "She'd not do anything wrong, not on purpose."

"And of course *you* would say so, as you watch her day-in, day-out, mouth all agape, like a calf staring at a painted gate!" an older man scolded the boy. "She is no more interested in you than the grass is in last year's snow!"

"Yes, and we all saw her at the dozynki night! She knew the fox was around!" another woman cried out.

"Vedma Kada says her daughter can see things! Yet Secha didn't help find Lenka!"

"And why did Kada wait so long to help?"

"And what happened when she did help?" Sladyana added. "Isn't it true she tried to hide the terrible powers at her disposal?"

"The children!" a man cried out. "The spirits of our children, of *our* dead. Why do they answer *her* call, and not ours? My boy, my dear boy, dead and gone these forty years. I saw his face as clear as I see yours. Yet she could have called on him any time, and never thought to before!"

Sladyana nodded, her face the picture of sympathy. "Not until it served her."

# CHAPTER 57

Kada lay very still, thinking how the morning light shining through the window filtered pink through her closed eyelids. She listened to her daughter's steady breathing beside her. It would likely be the last time they slept like this, sharing a bed. From that day on, Kada would be sleeping beside her new husband. *How strange.* For all the time Kada had spent worrying about Secha, she never considered how great a joy it was to at least have this comfort in the night, of being able to reach out, and reassure herself that her daughter was safe, sleeping, at peace. She would miss it. But that was what all mothers did, was it not? Mourned each moment past, while struggling to survive the present.

But the day would not tarry on her behalf. So, reluctantly, Kada sat on the side of the bed she shared with Secha. "Are you awake?" she said, brushing the hair off Secha's face. "The sun is up high, it's your birthday and the day I marry. Will you not come back to me, *moya mila*?"

Secha turned around and looked into her mother's eyes. There was a confusion in the girl's face, which nearly broke Kada's heart.

"I have some helpers still to keep us safe for now," Kada said. "And from tonight you will bleed red, and the fox won't be able to harm you anymore. Its grasp on your mind will grow less and less, and soon you will be whole again."

She leaned forward and kissed Secha's cheek. "But you must come back to me now." A tear fell from Kada's eye and splashed on her child's face. Kada realised with a start she was crying. She moved to wipe her tears away, but Secha lifted her hand and held her mother's.

"I am trying, *mamusha*." Secha's leaf-green eyes focused on her mother's face. "It's hard."

"I know it is." Kada nodded, relief washing over her like a wave. A movement caught her eye. Behind the glass pane on the window a bone root twisted and tested the glass, trying to push its way in. Kada stood up and closed the curtain. She turned back to Secha. "Fight for one day more. Our enemies are trying to confuse you. You must stay close to me today. Tomorrow it will become easier, I promise."

A knock made them both turn towards the door.

Kada moved as if to open it, but Secha stopped her. "I know what it is. I will open it."

Kada looked in Secha's face, suddenly alarmed. But her daughter's eyes were clear and her speech unslurred.

"Just a moment," Secha called out, quickly pulling on her skirt and vest.

She opened the door and there stood Gorcay, flanked by the exhausted-looking Bratyava and Makail. In front of him he held a small silver box. His eyes widened in surprise to see Secha, but something about her appearance reassured him, and he grinned.

"And who comes knocking on Vedma Kada's door?" Secha said, with some of her old energy.

"Sobis Gorcay, and his kin," he replied.

"And what do you bring?"

"A string of pearls for my betrothed's hair!" He opened

the box and presented a folded string of fresh-water pearls, pinkish white, beautiful in their imperfection.

"We thank you for–" Secha shut her eyes tight, as if a sudden fog came over her mind. Kada rested her hand on her daughter's shoulder, and Secha rallied. She looked to her mother for encouragement, then nodded. "We thank you, Sobis Gorcay. Vedma Kada accepts your gift!" She exhaled, exhausted by the effort.

Bratyava sniggered behind her father, but one look from Gorcay silenced her.

"I will see you both downstairs," Gorcay whispered, to Kada this time. "When you're ready."

Once the door shut behind them, Kada embraced Secha. "You did very well, *moya mila*. Now, help me with these pearls?"

They sat back on the bed. Secha brought out a bone-comb and began brushing her mother's hair. She first undid the braid her mother wore for comfort and loosened the curls with her fingers. Kada closed her eyes, the pleasure of the touch calming and comforting. A sleepy sort of sensation washed over her, and she began to hum under her breath. Secha picked up the tune, and their voices blended in a wordless song. Kada's hair, greying, but still thick and glossy, fell in a wave over her back, as Secha used the sharp handle of the comb to divide the hair into sections for braiding.

When she was ready, she pulled the shimmering string of pearls from the silver box, and wove it into Kada's braid, so that it would catch the light whenever Kada moved her head. The string symbolised the union between Kada and Gorcay and Secha touched it gently with her fingertips once she was finished.

Kada turned to her daughter, trying to guess her thoughts.

They touched foreheads and stayed still for a moment, before they both felt ready to turn to the day's task.

Secha helped Kada put on her fine embroidered gown and carefully placed the flower wreath on her mother's head.

"I sooner expected to perform this task for you," Kada said.

Secha didn't answer.

Kada stroked her daughter's head. "I know what it's saying to you, Secha," Kada said. "And it's all lies. You deserve this. I've been with you every day of your life, and nobody deserves this world more than you. So don't listen to the thief." She lifted her daughter's chin, so Secha was forced to look at her. "Listen to me, only to me."

# CHAPTER 58

Sladyana pinned a flower just above Tula's ear, and pinched the girl's cheek, before lifting up the small hand-held mirror so the child could admire her reflection.

A knock came on the open door and Makail stood there, leaning against the frame. A yearning took Sladyana's breath for a moment. Her young lover looked so different, so serious, in the traditional *kontush*, heavy with embroidery.

"The flower suits you, Tula," he said.

The girl opened her eyes wide in surprise, then she looked to Sladyana, who shrugged with a laugh.

Makail seemed to take offence. "I can't give a compliment?"

Tula's hands flitted in a quick succession of movements.

"What is she saying?" Makail folded his arms.

Sladyana suppressed a chuckle. "Just that usually you never say anything nice to her." She glanced at Makail. "She's not wrong."

The young man seemed suddenly embarrassed. He looked to Sladyana. "How do I tell her 'sorry?'"

Sladyana stared at him for a moment. She'd never been asked to share her and Tula's secret language. She looked at the child, who watched her, expectantly, and she felt shame wash over her.

"Like so," she demonstrated the word to Makail, who

copied it. Tula clasped her hands to her mouth and jumped up with excitement.

Makail laughed and mussed the girl's hair. "We'll be friends yet," he said.

Sladyana shook her head in wonder. "So, when is the celebration going to start?" she asked.

"As soon as my new stepmother and Secha come downstairs," Makail said with a shrug. "My father's barely sat down all morning. He's making the servants run around like there's a slew of nocnice behind them, and he's even dared to lock horns with our cook over the stew, which takes guts."

"It's a wonder he survived," Sladyana said, trying to force a laugh.

"I looked for you in the morning," Makail said, eyeing her closely. "Where were you?"

"I went to the town on an errand," she said.

"If you say so." He scratched his head and looked away. Then, seeming to have arrived at a decision, he turned back to Sladyana. "I know there are things between you and Kada, more than you are saying. I'm not blind, you know, or stupid."

"I never said you were." Sladyana was taken aback by his words. Her fingers absent-mindedly followed the line of embroidery on the back of Tula's vest.

"Is there going to be trouble, Sladyana?" He watched her carefully. "You know I care for you. But this is my father's wedding. I don't care for the vedma myself that much, truth be told. She is secretive, and even a child could see she's dangerous. But she seems fond of my father, and he has decided on her. So whatever business you have with her, tell me now."

"My business is ever my own." Sladyana locked eyes with him. "And what can I possibly do to hurt anyone here? You think if I had the power to wring the answers from that woman, I wouldn't have done so already? Vedma Kada lied to me, *and* to Artek Lelechek. She lied to us both about our children, giving us false hope, to hide what?" She shook her head and brought Tula closer. "Kada knows what happened to my child, or perhaps her daughter knows. The fox tried to take Tula from me too. And Secha, now carefully hidden from view, has the answers as to why." She softened her voice and reached for Makail.

He hesitated and moved forward. "I'm not your enemy, Sladyana." He motioned to Tula. "Or hers. Wait till after the wedding. I will talk to my father; we will get you your answers."

Sladyana stroked his cheek and smiled. He looked so young, so earnest. *He so badly wanted to help. He was innocent enough to think he could.* Who was she to take this away from him this soon? "Thank you," she said and kissed his lips. "I trust you."

And for the briefest moment, she could almost convince herself she did.

# CHAPTER 59

Sladyana looked towards the sky. The weather would hold, it seemed. The clouds rolled at an unhurried pace, and birdsong filled the air, as if the news that the summer was over had not yet reached the natural world. The rows of guests stood up, and all turned towards the path leading up to the spot where the ceremony was to be carried out. Kada was led by the women of the household, in this case Bratyava and Secha. Vedma Kada looked beautiful, Sladyana had to concede. She wore a traditional Fiesnan long skirt with a richly embroidered vest over a snow-white blouse. Her curly red hair was braided with a string of pearls woven through it, so in the light it seemed like dew drops had settled on her head. The clothes were not fashionable, something a rich farmer's daughter might wear perhaps, but they suited her.

Sladyana suspected this nod towards the traditional country dress was deliberate. The vedma was trying to remind those gathered that she was still one of the people. That marrying a rich man didn't sever her link to the people she served. Sladyana wasn't fooled. *Kada served only herself.*

Kada locked eyes with Sladyana, for only a moment, before looking away again. She imagined herself safe. The vedma thought, no doubt, that Sladyana was done with her. That there was nothing more she could do. But while

Sladyana might not have been one of those blessed by Zemya, Kada would soon find there were other weapons a clever woman could wield.

But for now, Sladyana joined in, clapping politely as Kada was led towards the flower-decorated trellis. There she was awaited by her intended and a town elder summoned to perform the ceremony, a small corpulent woman, dressed in her finest kaftan for the occasion, embroidered at the neck, and overlong, so that the hem of it was already grey from the dust. Behind her burned a small bonfire, washing over those gathered with waves of almost unbearable heat whenever the breeze blew.

Sladyana dabbed a handkerchief on her forehead before crumpling it in her pocket. The smell from the flower decorations was cloying and oppressive. She wished she could turn around and leave. But she was better trained than that, and so few would be able to tell the smile on her face was less than genuine.

The ceremony itself was short, as those things go. *Thank Zemya for her small mercies.*

There were many guests, some of whom Sladyana vaguely recognised from the engagement party, though she recalled none of the names, unsurprisingly. She smiled politely and shook hands when offered, never losing sight of Kada.

Behind Kada, her daughter Secha stood in a green silk gown, simply cut and unadorned, with crimson beaded necklaces hanging from her neck. The girl seemed more settled than Sladyana had expected, so to a casual observer she might have appeared no different to how she was that night Sladyana first laid eyes on her.

The town elder cleared her throat, silencing the crowd. "We are gathered here, friends and kin, to witness the promise Sobis Gorcay and Vedma Kada wish to make to each other," she said in slow ponderous tones. Her hands were folded, resting over her stomach, and she paused every other word to check that people were listening.

"This will take a while," Makail said out of the side of his mouth, leaning towards Sladyana.

"What are the promises you wish to make to one another?" The priestess turned to Gorcay and Kada with a stern look. Gorcay seemed amused by her tone, though Kada kept a neutral expression.

"I promise to be with you for as long as you'll have me, and to keep my word to you and your secrets for as long as my shadow is long," Gorcay began. "I promise to share with you in good luck and bad, and to never willingly bring sorrow into your life."

"And your promise to Sobis Gorcay?" The priestess turned to Kada.

The vedma seemed to hesitate, a pause so short it was almost imperceptible to any who weren't watching her as closely as Sladyana.

But when she spoke, the vedma's voice was clear and confident.

"I promise to remain by your side for as long as you'll have me. To share my secrets–" Her voice cracked, as she looked at Gorcay. He smiled at her and gave the tiniest nod. Sladyana glanced at Makail. They were more alike, father and son, than either wished to admit, she thought.

Kada coughed and continued. "And to keep yours. To share in your fortunes, good and ill, and to help you through life's sorrows."

Secha stepped forward and passed a bright red ribbon to the priestess. The woman tied it around Kada and Gorcay's clasped hands, and they threw a cup of mead and a slice of bread on the fire.

The newly-weds turned towards the crowd and lifted their tied hands for all to see.

"*Gozhko! Gozhko!*" Someone to Sladyana's left called out, and in a moment the whole crowd was chanting. *Gozhko*, for life is bitter without some kisses to sweeten each day.

Gorcay, suddenly shy, looked at his wife. Kada laughed and, putting her hand on the back of Gorcay's neck, pulled him in for a kiss, to the delight of the crowd.

Some of the guests then took the especially prepared willow-reed brushes and began sweeping the path between the newlyweds and the house, so that no sharp stone might spoil their first steps as a married couple.

Gorcay and Kada smiled at the crowd and took the first step towards their home, when a rotten tomato flew through the air and splattered in front of Kada, spraying its juices on the edge of her skirt.

"Vedma Kada!" A voice carried across the suddenly silent crowd. "The people of Torlow would have a word with your daughter!"

# CHAPTER 60

Kada stood, too stunned to speak. She looked at the crowd, but she could only see the wedding guests, all as shocked as she was. She scanned their faces, till she locked eyes with Sladyana, who showed no surprise.

"Who was it?" Gorcay grew red in the face and stepped in front of Kada. "Who dares?"

The crowd of the wedding guests parted and behind them Kada saw a sea of faces, pouring in from either side of Gorcay's garden. She knew them all, the good people of Torlow, who she'd cared for, listened to and advised all these years.

"Apologies, Master Gorcay. Some folk are overexcited. We want no trouble, not really," a man leading the mob said loudly, in a voice which showed he meant the opposite. "But the vedma denied us the right to hear the truth. Her daughter knows about the fox thief." He pointed towards Secha, who stood as white as a sheet behind Kada.

"I have only ever told you the truth of what I know!" Kada said, loud enough for all to hear. "I've served you all near on eight years, and you repay me with this outrage?"

Kada's words failed to have the desired effect on the townsfolk, who watched her sullenly.

"All we want is a word with your daughter, Vedma Kada!" somebody called out.

Kada could hear Secha's stifled whimper behind her.

"And that's how you come asking for it?" Kada demanded. "With threats and insults?"

"And what of the insult to *us*?" a young man with a round red face said. He pointed at Secha. "The insult of bringing her among us! Your lies have been exposed, Vedma Kada! Secha's not one of us!"

"What is this nonsense, man?" Gorcay squeezed Kada's hand.

"It's true! She's Zemya's spirit! She bleeds sap!" An ale-seller, a garrulous woman prone to taking offence, folded her arms and cast a triumphant look over the wedding guests. "No wonder we've been having the trouble we have. I bet she called the fox herself!"

"That's nonsense, woman! How much of your wares have you consumed before coming here?" Gorcay said. He faked a smile, trying to diffuse the atmosphere which hung as heavy and thick as molasses.

"Nonsense, is it?" a familiar voice came from the crowd. Artek Lelechek, leaning on the arm of one of his serving men, hobbled to the front of the mob. Kada heard Gorcay suck in a sharp breath. She didn't blame him. Artek Lelechek was near unrecognisable. Never a big man, his emaciated frame had so little meat left, it was a wonder he could walk at all. His clothes were dirty and worn at the knees. But when he looked at Kada, his flinty eyes were clear, and filled with the kind of hatred that burns. "My Botrik was to marry Secha. He proposed to her, against my better judgement. And then he just disappeared!" He pointed an accusing finger at Kada's daughter. "And our vedma made many promises to me, so many! She would help me find my son, she said."

"I told you I couldn't help you if he–"

"Oh yes, I know," the old man jeered. "If he didn't *want* to be found. Then you put the burden on me, making it out as if my faith was too weak. And I *believed* you. I tried so hard to–" A sob escaped from his throat, and he covered his eyes.

The man supporting Lelechek cleared his throat. "Botrik's sabre was found in the linden grove. It was buried deep in the ground, with only a piece of the pommel visible among the grass."

Lelechek sucked in a long breath and shook his head. "So, tell us, vedma, how did your roots not know, why didn't they tell you, where my boy was buried?"

# CHAPTER 61

Through it all, Sladyana watched Kada's face. The vedma's eyes flitted across the crowd, no doubt looking for a face that wavered. Someone so deeply in the woman's debt they could turn the tide in her favour.

Makail's hand squeezed Sladyana's shoulder. An unwelcome intrusion on her thoughts. She turned to him, only to see suspicion in his eyes.

"Did you have something to do with this?" His whisper had a desperate edge to it, and she realised he was afraid, as of course he would be.

"The vedma's actions are her own," she said, pulling her arm out of his grasp. "She knows where my daughter is. She has lied to me again and again." She gestured towards Lelechek. "Like she did to him. And if Secha is able to give me the answers I need, I don't care if the mob tears her to shreds after."

Tula shrank under the force of Sladyana's words, who just held the child closer.

"Why didn't you tell me?" Makail said, but before she could reply, the leader of the Torlow people stepped towards Kada.

"Let the girl talk to us, Gorcay!" The man, puffed up by the tacit support of the crowd behind him, tucked his thumbs behind his wide belt. "We won't hurt her. But she will tell us all she knows."

"You will burn for what you did to Botrik, vedma!"
Lelechek stumbled forward, impatient with the first man's
lack of fire.

Sladyana narrowed her eyes at Kada. Secha was the answer,
she was sure of it. The girl of the same age, of the same tree.

"You come to my wedding and threaten my child?" Kada
stepped forward, eyes blazing. "You address my husband
like I'm not here? You forget yourselves, people of Torlow."

"And what's a hedge witch going to do?" someone jeered.
"You think you can take our children and work for the fox
and that we won't find out?"

"The fox is all our enemy!" Kada threw her arms up in
frustration. "Fear is dimming your eyes!"

"No." Sladyana was surprised to hear herself speak, and
so were the people around her, who stepped away as if she
carried the plague.

"What are you doing?" Makail hissed next to her but they
both knew he couldn't do anything to stop her.

"The fox is my enemy." She paused, and spoke in a calm
tone, a trick of power that quietened the crowd. "With
Kada's help, sixteen years ago, I had a baby. The fox stole
her from me soon after, but by that time the vedma had
disappeared." She looked at Kada and it was as if there was
nobody but the two of them there, their hatred finally given
the space to breathe and grow, like an ember thrown on dry
grass. "And now, I find her here, with a daughter same age
as mine should have been, though her belly was as empty
as mine when I last saw her. I've had little but lies from her
since then. Now the fox has tried to steal my ward as well."
She gestured to Tula so that everyone could see. "Secha has
the answers. So, tell me, Vedma Kada." Her mouth went
dry, her heart beating hard in her chest. "Tell me why you

won't let us have the truth. Tell me why you won't give me back my child."

A panicked look passed over Kada's face. *Surely the vedma was expecting this to happen eventually?* She must have. Or perhaps not. People like that got used to having their lies accepted. The poor and the obliging, desperate for her small favours. None of them ever dared challenge her.

"I know nothing of your daughter," Kada said. Gorcay, standing next to his wife tensed his shoulders. Sladyana wondered briefly if he knew it was a lie.

"So you keep saying," Sladyana said. "Nobody here believes you anymore. You can't keep the answers from us – from me – anymore."

"Step back!" Kada shrieked, as the crowd advanced. She whistled, two fingers in her mouth. The piercing sound made the mob stop in its tracks.

People looked around, watching out for the consequences of the vedma's spell, or summoning. Then, when nothing happened, they exchanged satisfied smiles. They moved forward again, emboldened, now only a few steps away from Kada and Secha.

Something brushed again Sladyana's skirt. The tip of a fluffy silver tail swished as the domovoy cantered towards Kada.

It stood in front of its mistress and licked its paws, unhurriedly, its contempt for the people watching complete.

"Is that all the power you can muster, vedma?" Somebody laughed, breaking the tension. "I have one just like that at home. Warms my feet at night and steals the cream."

Many joined his laughter, which died down when Kada smiled. "Remember who gives you your gifts, friends," she said.

And then Sladyana saw it. Dozens of domovoys coming forward, hissing and growling, jumping from the trees, swarming on the path. All coming to their mistress, who stood very still, arms wide.

Sladyana shook her head, as if she couldn't quite trust her eyes. The domovoys grew as they came closer to Kada, their claws lengthening, their shoulders getting broader, till they were each the size of a lynx.

"They're *our* domovoys, they're supposed to protect *us*," someone in the mob whimpered.

"And who gave them their form?" Kada spoke. "Who saved them from the marshes?"

"They won't hurt us, vedma!" A man in the mob spat on the ground. "Everyone knows, domovoys protect the families they serve!"

"That's true, of course." Kada turned her head to the side. "But your neighbour's domovoy?" As if to reinforce her point, one of the house spirits next to her stepped towards the man who spoke and hissed, the fur on its back standing up.

"I have been your friend for years," Kada spoke again. "I brought your children into this world, and I saw your loved ones off on their last journey, taking away their pain and comforting them. And I will continue being your friend. But not if you threaten my child." She raised one hand and the domovoys closed in on the mob, which seemed to collectively lose its resolve.

"Go home, people of Torlow!" the vedma called out.

And they were going to, Sladyana realised. They were just going to leave. And she would never get her answers. Kada was going to win.

"No!" Sladyana moved as if to throw herself at Kada, but

the silver domovoy of Gorcay's household stepped in her way, except now it was as big as a calf, its swirling golden eyes fixed on Sladyana's.

Sladyana covered her mouth in shock as the creature released a growl.

Kada shot Sladyana a satisfied look. *This was the end. Kada had won.*

The mob was dispersing now, the huge cats shepherding the people away, the gardens emptying slowly.

Angry tears stood in Sladyana's eyes.

"Do you think a cat will stop *me*, lover?" A deep voice cut through the noise like a hot knife through butter.

A tall, broad-chested man walked between the stunned townsfolk, towering above them. He was naked, as if it was the most obvious and natural thing in the world. Sladyana felt a shiver go down her spine when he suddenly looked at her, just for a moment, one eyebrow lifting. *Was it mockery?*

The newcomer stood before Kada, ignoring the domovoys' warnings.

"It is time, Kada," he said. "Secha must return to Zemya."

# CHAPTER 62

"So, is this one of your secrets I have somehow promised to keep?" Gorcay said next to Kada. "I wish the naked truth was a bit less naked, to be honest with you." Kada ignored him.

"Give me Secha," Inog said.

Kada stared at him. "If you think I'd do that then you must have been gorging yourself on wolf berries."

"I suspected Secha belonged with the forest before," Inog stretched his shoulders, casually, the violence of his body's power an unspoken threat. "But now I realise you had lied to me."

"Many times," she said, her chin up. The jibe hurt; she could see it did. There was some small satisfaction to be found there, she supposed.

"Yes," he said after a moment. "I suppose you did."

"Never about Secha, though," Kada said. "She is mine. *My daughter*. That's the only thing you or your mother need know. She's mine and I won't give her back."

"But she's not really yours, is she?" Inog laughed, his teeth lengthening into tusks. "You stole Zemya's share of the fruit, and you thought you could escape."

"*Mamusha*, what is he saying?" Secha's small voice made Kada close her eyes for a moment.

She turned to her daughter. "Lies. You were a gift from Zemya. You were mine; you chose me."

"She couldn't have, Kada!" Inog said triumphantly. "The choice wasn't hers to make!"

Gasps and cries of horror spread among the guests and the townsfolk still gathered, as Inog inclined his head. A shape, small and sleek, emerged from between the trees.

The fox sat next to Inog's leg and watched Kada with its blue eyes.

"You would bring the thief to my door, Inog?" Kada said. The fox sat very still, watching her. Its fur was matted and its sides sunken. A thick black stripe ran down its head and back.

"You're the thief," the fox said with a voice unused to human words. "You stole my life after all."

Kada wouldn't listen. She wouldn't let Secha listen. The words had to be stopped, the bleeding stemmed, the milk unspilt.

She lifted her hand to her face. Then with a flash of sharp white teeth, without hesitation, she bit into her own palm's fleshy meat, cutting through the skin. Blood poured down and soaked the earth.

Inog threw his head back and laughed. "We know the truth, Kada! You think you can continue lying to my mother, lying to *me*, with your little blood offerings? It is too late!"

"It isn't for you," Kada said, her own blood smeared on her chin. "For what you've done, your blood too will fall today."

A breeze lifted up Kada's braided hair, bringing with it a scent of decay and rot. The ground trembled, and the wedding guests and town's people ran screaming, as the rumble of thunder rolled across the earth.

Someone slipped his hand into Kada's, and she realised with no small amount of surprise that Sobis still stood by her side, though his face was as white as flour. Kada couldn't blame him.

In front of them, the dust and the earth itself rose up, pulling in to form bone and muscle and sinew. Long limbs covered by white-green skin, as glistening as a frog's back, stretched and pulled and bent till the creature was complete. Taller even than Inog, with yellow-grey hair streaking in greasy strands down her back, she stood. Her breasts hung thin and long over her chest, their empty sacks dripping pus across her distended abdomen. Everything that was life, that was health, that was goodness, shrank before her.

"It is good to see the sun on my scythe again," Baba Cmentarna said. She gave Kada one nod, an agreement reached. Then she flew at Inog, her weapon raised.

Inog transformed into the boar in a moment, but not before Baba Cmentarna's blade cut deep into his arm, shaving a sliver of muscle off. Inog's tusks bore a hole in Baba's stomach, a fact she seemed barely to notice, though maggots slipped out of her wound and squirmed upon the ground.

The fox dove to the side, as the two giants fought. It ran, stomach close to the ground, drawing a circle around Kada, who was ready for it. Gorcay's domovoy turned on the fox, in a flash of teeth and claws. The fox fought where it could, and ducked between the guests' legs, as fast as a thought.

Inog charged at Baba Cmentarna, knocking her to the ground. The creature screamed as she landed heavily, a cloud of dust rising as her body hit the soil. Inog jumped on top of her, and, putting one foot on her throat, pinned her down.

He turned his dark eyes towards Kada. "Has it truly come to this, lover?" he said. She steeled herself at his words. "I would never hurt you, Kada, you know that. Secha needs to return to my mother, for the good of us all."

"You would take my daughter from me." Kada laughed, shaking her head. "And you dare say you don't wish to hurt me? You'll forgive me for not thanking you, for this attempt to tear my heart out of my chest." She hesitated. "You can still walk away, Inog. If you ever cared for me, just walk away now."

"It's done, Kada." Inog shifted his weight, squeezing at the Baba Cmentarna's windpipe. The creature beneath him squealed, her eyes rolling back in her head. "You've tried your best. But I'm a god and you're a human. And humans don't get to dictate terms to my kind."

"Very well," Kada said. She closed her eyes for a moment and took a deep breath. "You've made your choice. Baba Cmentarna, finish this."

Even in his boar form, surprise was clear on Inog's face, as Baba Cmentarna turned a sharp-toothed grin on him, and pushed him off her, with a force which made him slam into the flower-decorated trellis, under which Kada and Gorcay had exchanged their vows moments ago.

Inog struggled to stand up as Baba Cmentarna flew straight at him. He lowered his head, hoping to impale her on his tusks, but was easily avoided, as his opponent turned her scythe and sliced off a part of his ear.

Inog roared in pain. Kada steeled her heart to his cry. He *chose* this.

The Boar God fought, blood gushing from deep cuts on his body. The earth beneath him was torn and carved, his mother's bone roots swarming beneath him while his blood soaked the earth. His Goddess mother's powers seemed suddenly weak and useless, just when her son needed her the most.

Kada pulled Secha towards her, to shield her daughter's eyes.

Inog weakened. And when the inevitable blow came, there was no fight left in him to withstand it.

"Enough!" Kada called out. Baba Cmentarna looked at her, her corpse face neither amused nor caring.

"Our business is done, vedma," the creature said, and, just like that, her body turned back into a cloud of dust, blown away on the wind.

Kada nudged Secha towards Sobis. "I trust you," she said to him, and she found that it was the truth.

She walked towards Inog, lying on the ground, staining it rust red. His body changed and shrank, till Kada once more stared at the god's human eyes.

She knelt next to him.

He looked up at her, blood foam collecting at the edge of his mouth.

"Was it worth it?" he asked. "Killing me?"

Kada rested her palm on his cheek. His eyes closed.

"It was," she said, pulling a small knife from an inside pocket of her vest. "For Secha I'd kill you again and again." And with a smooth, fluid movement, she slid the knife's edge across her lover's throat.

# CHAPTER 63

Sladyana sagged to her knees. Tula wrapped her arms around her guardian's neck, pushing her face into the woman's dress, trying to hide from the horror they just witnessed.

"Come out, fox," Kada said, standing up. Her face was turned to the ground, her shoulders hunched. She still held the blood-stained knife in her hand. "Your ally is dead. You're too late. You know you're too late."

"I'm not." The fox's voice was strange to Sladyana's ears. The child-thief spoke as if the human words strained to come out of its throat and had to be spat out. "I'm here, and the usurper is here, and she still bleeds sap."

The fox stood between Sladyana and the domovoy, who protected Sobis and Secha.

Kada laughed and turned back. "She might. But you don't."

Sladyana watched the fox tense its body.

"I plucked you from the tree a day before Secha. When the sky was high this morning, your blood turned true red, thief. Secha is beyond your grasp now." Kada's face twitched as she smiled. Were the vedma's teeth always so sharp?

"It doesn't matter," the fox said. "Secha is still Zemya's. If I return her, the Great Mother will give me back my life."

"Wait!" Sladyana said. She looked at the fox, who turned towards her, indifference etched into its sky-blue eyes. "Tell me, thief. What does she mean she plucked you? What is –" A truth too terrible to consider dawned on Sladyana. She wished she could not know it, not face it, not acknowledge it. But she had to know. "Where is my daughter?" It was no more than a whisper, but they heard her, the fox and the vedma both. There was something like pity in Kada's eyes. Sladyana swallowed back her tears. *How dare the vedma pity me. I don't want it, I don't need it. I just asked for the truth, just asked for–*

"Don't you know me, *mamusha*?" the fox said. There was no kindness, no affection in the words. Nothing but resentment and contempt and pure, undeniable truth.

"Mother Zemya's child-bearing tree grows twin pods. You didn't look inside the other, so focused were you on mine," the fox said, slowly. "One seed for a mother, one to serve Zemya. That is the law."

Sladyana looked to Kada, who watched her in silence.

"Unless someone gets greedy," Sladyana said, weakly.

"Not greedy," Kada shook her head. "Secha was mine, I could hear her calling to me. I should have plucked her pod first. It was different. *My* parents were greedy, not satisfied with the gift of me. They had to have a son too, to carry the name, to pull the plough."

"Your brother, *mamusha*," Secha spoke, more clearly than she had in days. Her eyes were wide open, and Sladyana knew within herself the child had been kept innocent.

"My brother was growing in the second pod." Kada's voice was devoid of emotion. "My father wouldn't stop thinking about it, the son he could have had, had he spotted him a moment before my mother cut the stem of my pod. He went back to the tree, later. To get the boy, the boy meant for Zemya. And I could feel it when my father pulled him from the tree. It changed me. Turned me."

"You were the fox..." Secha said. "The fox who took your brother." She walked up to her mother. "What happened to him... How did you turn back?"

"Her brother belonged to Zemya..." the fox said, looking at Sladyana. It grinned, its blue eyes narrowing.

"...So, I put him in the ground," Kada finished. Her voice was low, but the words carried in the sudden quiet.

Secha gasped, staring at her mother. Kada looked at her daughter, silently pleading. Sladyana thought Secha would reject her mother then, reject her for this crime. But instead, to Sladyana's surprise, the girl's expression softened, and she embraced her mother, the murderer, the thief. Offering love and acceptance to the one who denied the same comfort to Sladyana.

Disgust twisted Sladyana's insides. "So you *knew*!" she screamed. "You knew all along what it would do to Luba, if you pulled the second child off the tree! You knew she would become this fox." She walked up to the fox, who was swishing its tail at her. "Luba?" Sladyana said. "Can you? Why didn't you come back to me? I would have helped... I'm your mother... I would have–" She flashed her eyes at Kada and Secha. "You stole my daughter's life, vedma. But you'll pay for it. I will kill your Secha myself if that's what it takes!"

"You can try." Kada bared her teeth. "I have just killed a god, woman. You think you can get past me?" Kada looked at the fox and laughed, like she was mad. "Besides, it's too late. Luba's blood is red now, you can't swap my daughter for yours anymore!"

"But my twin is not yet sixteen, is she?" Luba, the fox, said. She took a step towards Secha, but the Gorcay's household domovoy got in her way.

"It won't make a difference." Kada shrugged. "Your form is set. Even if you could kill Secha, it wouldn't give you your body back."

Sladyana's heart sank. She looked at the fox, at her Luba. "Is it true?"

"You have the domovoy with you now," Luba said, to herself more than anyone else. "But do you think you can keep my sister away and safe forever?" A toothy grin stretched the fox's maws, and a strange noise escaped her throat. With a start, Sladyana realised Luba was laughing. "I have grown and learnt these sixteen years, vedma. I will keep chipping away at your precious daughter's mind. We are one, she and I, and only one can live on this land."

"You're out of time," Kada said, and in the vedma's strained voice, Sladyana recognised the truth. It was too late. Whatever damage Luba has been causing Secha, driving her mad, was coming to an end.

"I'm out of time, unless I buy some more. There is another way," Luba said. The fox wasn't looking at Sladyana. Her ears twitched, and then, so quickly, Luba pounced towards Tula, teeth bared. Sladyana barely had the time to pull the child behind her.

"No!" Sladyana kept her body between the fox and the terrified child. Luba jumped away and began circling the two. "Luba, what are you doing?"

"The child feels the roots. She's a vedma, or as close as they come." Luba's words came out as a growl. "She is of the tree, and Zemya might accept her still. She might give me time."

"That's why you tried to kidnap her?" Makail surprised Sladyana by coming between her and the fox. "That's why you took the other child?"

"She was not the right gift," Secha said, just loud enough that Sladyana heard her.

"The roots wouldn't take her," Luba said with a growl. "But this one… This one will be the gift I need. She will give me time." The fox looked up at Sladyana.

Her eyes were still the same blue. The blue Sladyana saw each day when she looked at her own face in the mirror. She was hers, there was no denying it. It was her Luba.

"We'll find another way…" she pleaded.

The fox jumped up and sank her teeth in Makail's shoulder, then leaped off, before he could react. Makail sank to his knees, blood gushing from the wound. Gorcay screamed. The silver domovoy hissed.

"You don't get to stand between us," Luba said to the man simply, circling around, getting closer and closer to Sladyana. "Now, *mamusha*…" There was mockery in the word, a taunt. "You failed to protect me before. Now you have the chance to redeem yourself. Give me the child."

"No!" Sladyana kept turning around, keeping Tula behind her. "She's innocent, just a child!"

"I'm *your* child," the fox spat. "She's just a mute, a nobody. But the roots listen to her. Her blood will give me a chance to live. A chance to claim my life back."

"I can't…"

"Don't you love me?" the fox mocked. "Don't you want to help me?"

Sladyana stared into her daughter's merciless eyes, and her heart broke. But behind her Tula held onto fistfuls of her skirts, and even through the fabric Sladyana could feel the child's shivering. To give Tula's life? *Her* Tula? Her little girl? Her *slonechko*? Sladyana straightened up. "No. Not like this."

"Then on your head be it." Luba bared her teeth and jumped, high, towards Sladyana's exposed throat. The woman held up her arm just in time, though the weight of the fox made her fall backwards, falling on top of Tula.

Luba slashed the skin on her mother's forearm to ribbons with her sharp teeth, even as Sladyana tried to push at the fox's throat.

A thump and the fox flew off Sladyana. Gorcay stood over them, a stick in hand. But the fox stood up quickly, still reeling from the force of the impact, glaring at Sladyana and Gorcay.

Then something caught the animal's eye, and a grin stretched her blood-soaked mouth. She broke into a run, and, too late, Sladyana realised that Tula had managed to scramble away.

"Tula! Come back!" she screamed, but the child, gripped by blind terror, broke into a run, the fox close behind. Tula stumbled, the skirts of her dress tangled between her legs, and she fell heavily to the ground.

Through the haze of pain, Sladyana watched as the fox's whole frame coiled, her powerful hind legs bent, ready for the final jump.

Then a flash of red curls appeared as another fell on top of the fox.

*Kada?* Sladyana saw a glimpse of the moon-round face, of the flaming hair, but no, the vedma stood apart.

It was Secha who held on tight to the fox, even as she scratched and bit.

"Let go, thief-twin!" Sladyana heard Luba's hate-filled words, as the fox twisted and writhed, trying to grab onto Secha's neck.

Cuts and bite marks appeared on her skin as Secha's sap

blood slowly pooled on her arms, her shoulders, her chest.

"Secha, let go!" Kada ran towards them. "She will kill you!"

"I'm sorry, mama." Secha shot her mother a look and smiled. "My blood... still runs true... to Zemya." She wrapped her legs and arms tight around the fox.

Sladyana and Kada realised at the same time what Secha meant, as the bone roots shot out of the ground, called by the girl's blood. In a moment, they enveloped both the fox and the girl, weaving a white cage around their bodies.

Kada screamed, an inhuman, keening sound, as she fell towards them, using her bare hands to rip and pull at the roots. Some broke off, cutting into the vedma's hands, but more took their place.

Sladyana, helped up by Gorcay, stood on shaking legs and hobbled towards Tula, who still lay in the grass, her little hands over her head.

Kada cried and pleaded, trying to pry open the bone roots. And through the lacework of it, Secha pushed out her hand.

"Please, Secha, please..." Kada laced her fingers with her daughter's, collapsing over the domed roots.

# CHAPTER 64

Kada watched helplessly as Secha's eyes grew dimmer. "Please, no, please…" Kada pleaded and begged as Secha's fingers, laced with her own, were finally pulled out of her grasp. Who she was begging, Kada didn't know herself. She killed Mother Zemya's own son. The goddess would not listen to her now.

The place grew silent. No sound came from within the bone root dome over Secha and Luba. Kada climbed over it, trying to peer through, trying to pull the strong bone lacework apart.

Then something shifted. The roots moved once more, softening, wriggling apart, opening up.

Kada knew what was inside before she saw it, yet she forced herself to look.

Dust, nothing but dust, in the patch of soil with no grass, no living thing within it. The dust painted the shape of Secha and Luba's bodies, a grey outline on the ground.

The roots sunk back into the earth, exposing the patch of ground to the breeze, which took away the last mark of where Kada's daughter was moments before.

Kada sank her hands into the ground and screamed. She swayed from side to side and scratched at her own body, watching the blood drip and lie unclaimed on the ground.

"Stop it, stop it!" She heard the words, though she didn't grasp their meaning.

She was trying to stop it. The pain and the loss, she was trying to stop it all. Why did strong arms hold her hands to her sides, stopping her from opening her veins to Zemya?

She looked around, confused, as a familiar face hovered near hers. "It's done, Kada, it's done." She recognised the man. Sobis, it was Sobis. He was still there, he hadn't gone. But he didn't understand. She had to make him understand.

"Zemya won't take me," Kada whispered. "I'm telling Zemya to take me instead, but she won't do it."

"Mother Zemya won't listen to you now." Makail stood next to his father, his hand pressing down on his shoulder wound.

"But she must..." Kada looked to Sobis, to *her* Sobis. "She must bring her back. Or take me. But she must do one or the other." She raised a hand to Gorcay's cheek, and he let her. It was hard to focus, hard to understand the meaning in his eyes. And suddenly she understood. "She's gone," she said.

"She's gone." There were tears in Sobis' eyes.

"Gone..." Sladyana's voice repeated Sobis' words. Kada looked up at the woman, her rival, the mother she wronged. Kada met her gaze. Something like anger flickered in Sladyana's eyes, and then it went out. Replaced by something else, something Kada couldn't quite recognise.

Something rested on Kada's shoulder. A small hand, a child's hand. But what child would touch her? Her own child, her Secha, was gone.

Slowly, Kada turned towards Tula, who watched the vedma, cautiously, as if Kada was a wild dog. The girl pointed to the place in the ground where Zemya pulled the twin sisters into the soil.

Tula rested her hand palm down on the ground, and the

small tendrils of Zemya's bone roots came out, wriggling playfully around the child's fingers. Tula closed her fingers over something and lifted it up to show Kada.

And there, in the child's dirt-stained hand rested a seed. As smooth and dark as a river pebble, its skin glistening in the sunlight.

Kada looked at Tula, a question written on her face.

The girl looked to her guardian, who approached them slowly, blood dripping from her fox-savaged arm. Tula made a gesture and then nodded, waiting for Sladyana to interpret.

Kada and Sladyana looked at each other. There was no more hatred in their eyes. No forgiveness either. Just... understanding.

"It's for you," Sladyana said. "Your daughter sacrificed herself for Tula. So Tula asked Zemya on your behalf." She looked away. "You don't deserve it. But I suppose I got more than I deserve" –Sladyana placed her hand on Tula's head– "So who am I to deny you?"

Tula placed the seed into Kada's hand and nodded. Then the child stood up, brushed the dirt off her skirt and took Sladyana's hand.

The child and her mother left then, leaving Kada on the ground, the promise lying light and glistening in her palm.

# EPILOGUE

Sladyana sat next to her aunt on a stone bench, surrounded by the blossom-filled gardens of her ancestral home. She held a yellow dandelion in one hand, her fingers absent-mindedly playing with its petals.

Tula chatted with Makail, who was patiently trying to explain to her how to hold a bow. More than once, Makail had to ask the girl to slow down the movement of her hands, so he could interpret her words.

Once back in her home, Sladyana insisted on teaching the servants, as well as her aunt and Makail, some of the language between her and Tula. Kasimira grumbled at first, but Tula's relentless affection softened the old woman somewhat, even if she'd never admit it.

"Why are you grinning like a cat that got the canary?" Kasimira narrowed her eyes at her niece.

Sladyana didn't reply. Instead, she reached out and squeezed her aunt's wizened hand.

"Now then, enough of that," Kasimira grumbled. "You're growing soft on me."

But she didn't pull her hand away, Sladyana noticed.

◇◇◇◇

The bees buzzed in the deceptively warm, late spring sun.

Kada moved quietly in the garden, taking in the smells of

the woken earth. She squinted, looking at the sky, judging the weight of the clouds marring the blue. Her broad-rimmed straw hat fell off her head and hung by its ribbon on her back.

She could hear Sobis' voice, as he spoke to his daughter. Bratyava and her newest child, who lay on a blanket within Kada's sight, stayed more with them now, helping with her father's business. With the woman's endless energy thus directed, she spent less time complaining, and Kada had found herself, if not actually liking Bratyava, then at least tolerating her reasonably well.

A bee, heavy with pollen dusting its body, rested on Kada's sleeve. She smiled and held out a finger for it to crawl on. She took it towards a large stone pot in the middle of the garden, carefully tended.

Within it grew a single plant, barely a sapling, with a twin flower blooming on its single stem. Kada carefully placed the bee inside the blossom. She knelt next to the pot and rested her arms and head on its rim. She closed her eyes and smiled, her fingers brushing against the new life.

# GLOSSARY

*Baba Cmentarna*    A malevolent female spirit, taking the shape of an ugly old woman, haunting the burial grounds. Enjoyed digging up fresh graves and scattering the bones around.

*Bast shoes*    Woven shoes, made from the fibres of tree bark, most commonly from linden trees. Not particularly durable, they were generally worn by the poorer classes in the forested areas of Northern Europe, prevalent in Russia, Belarus, and among the Balts

*Bastook*    Small of stature, these creatures living in "miedza", the bit of grassed land between the neighbouring fields, were always open to being bribed with bread and meat. Thus paid, they would protect the farmers' harvest, and sometimes steal a bit of the neighbours' grains too, to boost their benefactors' stores

*Blednitza*    A malevolent female spirit, delighting in confusing travellers and getting them lost.

*Bozhontka*    The spirits of dead children

| | |
|---|---|
| *Domovoy* | A helpful house spirit. Protects the home and the family, in return for a crust of bread and a spot of milk. Often takes on the form of a cat. |
| *Kokoshnik* | [Spelled "kokosznik" in Polish, "кокóшник" in Russian] A traditional Russian headdress most commonly worn by married women, usually crescent-shaped, though the styles of it varied greatly throughout history. It was worn in its various forms from the 10th century |
| *Kontush* | [Spelled "kontusz" in Polish, Lithuanian: "kontušas"; originally from Hungarian köntös, meaning "robe"] A traditional long outer robe worn by Polish and Lithuanian nobility, common in the 16th century. Long, with open sleeves, it was usually brightly coloured, tied at the wait with a belt. |
| *Miecnik* | A monster living in "miedza", the stretch of land between fields. |
| *Moya mila* | [Moja miła] My dear |
| *Moya slichna* | [Moja śliczna] My pretty one |

| | |
|---|---|
| *Nalevka* | [Spelled "nelewka" in Polish] A traditional Polish alcoholic beverage, often used as medicinal tinctures. Nalewka is created by macerating or infusing fruits, spices and herbs in neutral spirits. Nalewka is generally strong (45-75% alcohol content) and often sweetened with honey |
| *Pashtet* | [Spelled "pasztet" in Polish] A type of baked meatloaf, made with a variety of cooked meats and vegetables, mixed with bread and liver. My grandmother's wild boar's pasztet was the stuff of dreams |
| *Piekna moya* | [piękna moja] my beautiful one |
| *Sekacz* | [Lithuanian "šakotis" or "baumkuchenas", Polish: "sękacz", Belarusian "bankucha"] A traditional Lithuanian, Polish and Belarusian cake, golden in colour, cooked over an open fire on a rotating spit |
| *Shvitzosh* | [Polish spelling "świcorz"] Monstrous humanoid spirits of the dead, often found by the riverbanks and swamps. They waited for someone willing to listen to their story, and to forgive their crimes, thus releasing them from their torment |
| *Slonechko moye* | ["Słoneczko moje" in Polish] My little sun |

| | |
|---|---|
| *Vedma* | ["Wiedźma" in Polish] A witch or "hag". Sometimes understood as a female magic user, sometimes a demonic humanoid creature resembling an old woman. |
| *Znajdnitza* | A spirit helping to find those who are lost. Entirely made up by Kada, as well as myself. |

# ACKNOWLEDGEMENTS

This book is in your hands thanks to the hard work and help of so many people. While I can't list them all here, I'm deeply grateful for all their support.

And so I wanted to offer special thanks to:

My husband Cameron, who is the most thoughtful person I know. Thank you for always standing beside me and for standing up to me when I need it.

My clever, cheeky daughters, Scarlett and Sienna. I would burn down the world for you.

My supportive and endlessly enthusiastic agent, John Baker, who goes above and beyond every single time. This book would have made a lot less sense without his input. Also everyone at Bell Lomax Moreton.

My writing companions, the very talented Nadia Idle and Rachael Twumasi-Corson, who I simply can't do without anymore. Your friendship means a great deal, and our conversations guide me, teach me, and keep me on my toes.

My dear friend Caroline Hardaker, whose talent I envy, and whose wisdom I rely on. There's hardly anything in my life these days I don't talk through with you, and long may it remain so.

My friend Katarzyna Chruszczewska. I would be a very

different person had I not met you when I did. I'll be forever grateful for your friendship.

Kathy Choi. I've known you for most of my adult life, and you have taught me so much. Thank you for being my friend and for all our "heart exchange" conversations.

My family in the UK and abroad. I love you all.

The teachers of my youth: Anna Kramek-Klicka, Urszula Siuta and Wiesława Brama, who I wish was still with us.

Finally the Angry Robot team who believed in this book and helped make it a reality: Eleanor Teasdale for offering on *The Bone Roots*, my editor Gemma Creffield, Amy Portsmouth, the marketing team with a special mention for Caroline Lambe, the mistress of scheduling, the reaching-out guru, and ever the optimist, which you kind of have to be in this industry. The Angry Robot designer, Alice Coleman, for creating a cover I instantly fell in love with.

And finally, thank you, reader, for picking up this book.

# CHAPTER 1

*Clang*

A slender hand hit the table, the iron rings on the fingers ringing out as they touched the wood. There were no words spoken after that. Everyone knew that Miriat had made her decision and no amount of talking would change it. The women crowded in the small room watched sullenly as Miriat took off her rings and bronze bracelets one by one. She made a point of lifting each item for everyone to see before putting them on a small pile in the middle of the table. You could only take the clothes on your back when you made the choice to go to the strigas' nest.

Miriat approached a narrow bed in the corner of the room and picked up a small, warm bundle. She pressed it to her chest. A cry came from inside the folds of the fabric, and a woman in the corner spat with disgust. Miriat ignored her and walked past with her head held high.

She paused only for a moment, just as her foot was about to pass the threshold. A young man stood outside the door, his hands fidgeting as if he was cold, though he stood in the still-warm autumn sun. His dark eyes watched her impassively, and perhaps Miriat was the only one who could notice the furrow on his forehead and the twitch in the corner of his lips. He said nothing though, and she replied with a silence of her own. Without breaking eye contact, he undid the clasp on his woolen cloak and wrapped it around Miriat's shoulders, his hands pausing for a brief moment as they brushed past her arms. Some of those back in the house muttered disapprovingly. Moments earlier they'd been family and friends, comforting and coaxing, drawing a vision of a life filled with joy and love. If she would only relent. If she would only let them take her child away. Now they begrudged her even the comfort of a warm cloak.

Miriat took a deep breath and stepped out, leaving her life behind.

She walked down the road, trying not to look at the people watching her go.

Aurek the baker, who had hoped to woo Miriat when she was but a girl, now spat at the sight of her and drew his wife closer to his chest. Gniev, the old shopkeeper who had a soft spot for children and would sometimes give them a chewy sweet or two from the big jar on one of the shop's shelves while their mothers weren't looking, twisted his amiable face and shouted an obscenity that Miriat would never have accused him of knowing.

She pulled the cloak closer around her little bundle as the wind blew. A rotten apple flew through the air and splattered in front of her on the stones, its juices spraying the hem of her long skirt. She looked at the crowd. It could have been anyone. Any of the women who, only a few days ago, would spend long hours chatting with her companionably, on the long daily walk bringing the men's lunches to the mine. Any of the men who drank with her husband to celebrate her pregnancy, or who patted him on the back after they married. Their faces, so familiar, and yet now so strange, like a nightmare that puts the face of a dragon on your child's head to frighten and confuse you. *This cannot be real.* She jutted out her chin with a defiance she didn't feel.

As was custom, the whole town had gathered to see her go. Three Dolas came down from the mountains in the morning to see the law was obeyed, and they stood now, silent, at the edge of the crowd. Their ceremonial cloaks had hoods drawn across their faces, so nothing but their unsmiling lips were visible. She was grateful for their presence. They were there for her safety as well.

*Save the tears for later.* She gritted her teeth.

A woman, a skilled pastry maker who'd made the cake to celebrate Miriat's wedding, and would accept no coin for it, ran in front of her and swung her arms wide. Miriat only had a moment to turn her back on the woman, protecting the baby as a bucketful of kitchen waste was emptied onto her back. The crowd whooped and laughed as the half-decomposed potato peel and bits of rotten onions and chicken bones slipped down Miriat's hair, the pungent juices trickling down her neck and under her collar.

"Rot to rot, striga," the woman said, nodding with satisfaction.

Miriat yearned to hit the woman, or else to throw the betrayed sisterhood in her face. But a glance at the crowd froze her mid-word. They hungered for a reaction. Any excuse to tear her to pieces. If Miriat hit the woman now, then all the Dolas of Prissan wouldn't be able to help her.

Miriat straightened her shoulders. "As you say," she said, turning away from the woman. As she continued down the road, Miriat's arms tensed, though she prayed none could see it. They would sniff out her fear, even under the stink of the rotting food caked in her hair.

Miriat left the town and walked down the muddy path leading towards the forest through the terraced fields. The last of the year's crops had been harvested, and the ground looked bare.

At the end of the road, just at the edge of the tree line, stood a small hunched-up figure of a woman. Miriat's heart sank, but she walked on.

"Are you planning on talking me out of it?" Miriat asked. There was no defiance in her voice, only resignation.

"No."

The older woman pulled the shawl lower over her forehead. She leaned on her walking stick, which some kind hand had decorated with a crude carving of twirling leaves. White, unseeing eyes turned towards Miriat.

"I won't ask you if it's worth it, either. Only you can answer that."

"It's worth it. It's worth it for me," Miriat said.

"Then there is your answer." The woman pulled out a pouch from the depths of her apron and proceeded to fill a small pipe. The two stood quietly for a time as she lit it and took the first two puffs. She coughed and said, quietly, "You could have other babies though. Later."

"Yes, but not this one," Miriat said.

"No, not this one," the woman replied, her voice making it clear that in her opinion that wouldn't be an altogether bad thing. "You can't come back, you understand."

"Good. I don't want to."

"Not even if it dies." The woman brushed the greying hair

out of her face. "You're leaving forever. And the forest will never release you."

"And what would you have done?" Miriat asked. "If it were you in my place, what would you have done?"

The older woman puffed on the pipe and, as she exhaled, a circle of smoke wafted above their heads briefly, before dissipating into the air. She nodded. "You'd better be off then."

Miriat hesitated and leaned towards the old woman, planting a kiss on her cheek. "Goodbye, Mama."

Miriat pulled her child closer to her chest and walked towards the forest, never once looking back.

There was only one town in the Heyne Mountains. It was an ancient collection of houses and farms held together by law, tradition, and a single road. The houses were small but warm, built to withstand the winter cold. Most of the doors were painted pale blue, both to ward off evil, and to please the eye. The landscape was cold and unforgiving, and it bred a cold people. And sometimes it also bred strigas.

Sometimes in Heyne Town, a child was born with two hearts. Though no one knew why, everyone knew what was to be done about it. After each birth, a Dola midwife would put a hollowed-out horn to the baby's chest, place her ear to the narrow point, and listen. Most of the time the steady beating of a single heart would bring a smile to her face and reassure the anxious mother. But sometimes the baby's eyes would watch the midwife carefully, as the little thud-thud of a double heartbeat sealed the infant's fate.

The Dola would then take the child to the edge of the forest, tie a bit of red leather around its wrist and leave it there, never looking back. The family would mourn the child, burying their grief and shame in an empty grave.

But once in a while, a mother would refuse to let go of the child. And if no reasoning could convince her otherwise, she'd join her baby in its exile. The two of them would then seek a different life in the striga village high up in the mountains, never to return.

Miriat looked around her. The trees domed above her head swayed, their trunks creaking like a rusty hinge. She held her baby closer still and kissed its forehead. A happy little sigh rewarded her, before the baby's face screwed up with a threat of an imminent cry. "Oh no, little one, no no, hush, sweetling…"

She rocked the baby from side to side as she walked towards where the forest path led westward. The air was cold and felt wet, chilling her in each breath she took. The soft whispers of the forest did nothing to alleviate Miriat's fears. She knew nothing about how she might reach the strigas, whom she'd been taught all her life to avoid and fear. And would they accept her, or just tear her baby from her arms? She shivered. She would not let that happen. She would face them all if she had to.

The baby's screams pierced the air. Miriat sat down underneath a tall oak and put it to her breast. The baby's mouth screwed up in anger as its little arms flailed about her mother's chest.

"You should probably learn to keep it quiet," a high-pitched voice said from somewhere behind Miriat, sending her into a panic. She whipped her head around but saw nothing. Only the leaves moved in the breeze. "I could hear you from the other side of the Hope Tree," the voice continued, "and you're in the bear country now, you know."

"Where are you?" Miriat said, fighting to keep her voice level. "Show yourself. I have no fear of you."

A young girl of no more than twelve slid down the very tree Miriat was sitting under. She had dark eyes and dark hair with a hint of red. She jumped off a low branch and landed next to Miriat. For a moment, it seemed like two girls were standing side by side. But then Miriat blinked and there was just one.

"I'm Maladia," the girl said, eyeing the baby in Miriat's arms. "Can I see?" She reached out one hand towards the child.

Miriat stiffened and pulled the baby closer.

Maladia chuckled. "What, you scared of the big bad stigoi? You think I'm going to gobble you up? You're one of us now, better get used to it." She cocked her head to the side and waited.

Miriat resented the barb. Still, the girl was right. She unwrapped the baby, exposing its small face.

Maladia put two fingers on the baby's neck. Miriat sucked in a sharp breath as she fought the urge to push the girl away.

"A striga, sure enough," the girl said after a while. She turned her attention to Miriat's clothes. "You do realize it's almost winter, right? You didn't think to bring anything else with you?" Miriat only shook her head.

Maladia shrugged her shoulders. "It's your bum to freeze off, I guess. Some girls hide extra blankets around the edge of the forest before they're due. Just in case... you know."

Miriat looked down miserably. So stupid. She knew some girls took precautions, but in the past months the worry just seemed so distant; Miriat refused to even consider her firstborn might be born a striga.

Maladia took pity on her. "Let's look around. I bet there's some long-forgotten blanket tied to a tree somewhere. We can take the time and look for a bit."

Miriat tried to smile.

"So, what's the baby's name then?" Maladia asked as they walked along the treeline.

"Salka," Miriat said. "I named her Salka."


"Are we getting close? I need to feed her," Miriat said, as she and Maladia walked between the pine trees. They'd been walking for most of the day, and Miriat had to stop often. The walking was both painful and exhausting so soon after the birth, but she didn't complain, even though her impatient guide kept racing ahead, visibly bored with their slow pace. Salka began squirming in the cold, in spite of the woolen blanket Miriat had eventually found in the branches of a tree.

The girl laughed and smacked her forehead. "Right. Sorry! The critter must be starving. Here, sit down." Maladia skipped over to an old string bark aspen, growing solitary between a pile of large boulders. She looked encouragingly towards Miriat, who sat on the ground with a grunt.

Suddenly, a blue egg fell from the tree's branches, bounced off a moss-covered rock with a faint crack, rolled down and bumped against Miriat's boot. For a moment, the baby stopped crying, and Miriat and Maladia both looked on as a featherless creature squeaked weakly from inside the broken shell. To their surprise, it had survived the fall, the cold air waking it as it strove to free itself from what remained of the egg.

"A cuckoo hatchling must have pushed the poor thing out of the nest," Maladia said, looking up at the branches. "I've never seen a chick survive a fall like that. Must be an omen," she said, turning to Miriat. She cocked her head to the side and said, "It won't survive though. It'd be a mercy to kill it."

She stood without a smile and for a chilling moment, Miriat wasn't sure if Maladia was talking about the bird.

Miriat reached out to the chick and picked it up, and cradled it gently within the palm of her hand. The creature hopped and turned its open beak towards Miriat. At that moment, Salka stirred again, and looked at her mother.

"It will die anyway," Maladia said again, watching Miriat with interest.

"No, it won't," Miriat said. "There is enough of me for them both."

After Salka had been fed, and a grub had been dropped down the hungry chick's mouth, the three continued their slow climb towards the striga village. Maladia offered to carry Salka once, but the look Miriat gave her taught her not to repeat the offer. So, she carried the chick instead, and allowed Miriat to stop frequently. As the day wore on, they finally came up to a large wooden gate, which, if looked at from any other direction but the one they were approaching from, would have seemed a mere scattering of twigs and dry logs.

Maladia knocked. A raspy voice from above said, "So they kicked another one out, did they?" They both looked up and a plump face looked back from between the branches of a large tree growing on the other side of the gate.

"Stop your chattering and open the gat[...]
We're tired and cold! Have you no shame?" M[...]
out with a broad smile on her face.

"Not much, goat-voice, not much. Shame[...]
And it doesn't satisfy curiosity, either," th[...]
slipping down the tree. Moments later the ta[...]
open.

The new girl was pleasant-looking, roughly[...]
as Maladia, with a cheerful wide face, and warm[...]
The girls embraced. Maladia's friend had more[...]
bones and a soft look which spoke of an easier[...]
than three leather pouches were tied to her be[...]
with colorful patterns, and her tunic had a sm[...]
embroidered thistle around the collar. Her cloth[...]
seem familiar, though Miriat was sure she'd no[...]
face before.

"Are you a striga?" Miriat asked, carefully.

"Hah!" Maladia laughed. "She's a Dola. Can[...]
the airs she gives herself?" Maladia said, her[...]
crossed. Her friend made a pretense of kicking[...]

"Dola?" Confusion crossed Miriat's face "Bu[...]
young? All the Dolas I've ever seen were old[...]

"Some of us are old, but we don't exact[...]
mothers' wombs that way." Dola said with a[...]
made her cheeks shake. "My work tends to be[...]
side of the mountain, so you wouldn't have[...]
Heyne Town."

"Your work..." Miriat turned her head to t[...]
couldn't help but feel skeptical.

"'Work' she calls it" Maladia scoffed. "Don't bo[...]
she says. She's barely an apprentice." The Dola ga[...]
look.

"And what do they call you? I mean, what's your name?" Miriat asked. The lighthearted banter between the two girls raised her spirit a bit. There was comfort in the everyday.

"They're all called 'Dola,'" Maladia said, rolling her eyes. "And they all tell the future. Some with less competence than others..."

"'There is one fate and so one name is enough for those who read it,'" Dola said with mock solemnity. "Anyway, you're in luck. The West Stream Dola is inside, attending a sick child so she can see you after. Saves us a trip down and up the mountain!"

Miriat shifted uncomfortably, casting a look at the tall gate in front of them. She tried to peek over Dola's shoulder to catch a glimpse of her new home.

A shiver ran down Miriat's back as she saw two quiet figures, observing her from the open gate. A middle-aged woman stood there with her hand on a dark-eyed boy's head. The boy was looking at Miriat with unabashed curiosity, his very dark brown hair hanging low across his forehead. His mother's hand tenderly swept it to the side. The woman locked eyes with Miriat, but she didn't smile.

Instead, she just said, "If you're bringing a new striga with you, Maladia, don't you think you ought to report to me rather than just stand there gossiping?"

The two young girls squealed in surprise and looked towards their feet. "Yes, Alma. Sorry, Alma," Maladia said, and gestured to Miriat to follow her. Dola trailed close behind. She leaned forward and whispered, "Maybe after you meet Alma and have the West Stream Dola look over you, you and I can have a talk? I'm a good talker. And a game of chance, perhaps?"

"Don't," Maladia said, rolling her eyes. "She cheats."

"I do not!" Dola said, indignant. "Not my fault if I can predict the outcome."

"Right. Knowing the extra bones you keep stashed in your sleeves must help with the predicting." Maladia ignored her friend's less than convincing show of outrage and nodded towards Miriat, "Take my word for it: with a Dola, even when you win, you lose."

The first thing Miriat noticed were the goats.

They were everywhere: nibbling on drying clothes, unwillingly giving an insistent child a ride, and fouling up the path and the entries to the houses indiscriminately. They were all clearly well-tended, their long coats glossy from brushing. They gave the air a distinct sour milky aroma that made Miriat feel nauseous and very hungry at the same time.

She followed Maladia and the woman called Alma, cradling her daughter in her arms. She became aware of a pair of eyes staring at her intently. The boy she saw at the gate was trotting beside her, clearly trying to catch a glimpse of Salka. Miriat noticed the difficulty with which he walked, one of his feet seeming to give him pain, as it twisted inwards at an odd angle. As they walked through the village, they were watched by its inhabitants. One by one, the villagers all followed them in a small procession of solemn curiosity.

Miriat's heart sank as she looked around at what was to be her new home. Though she'd expected hardship, nothing had prepared her for the squalor and the poverty now surrounding her.

The houses in the village were little more than round huts, and Alma led them to the largest one. Miriat spotted a small, raised vegetable garden and a few goats tied to a pole. The goats stared at the women impassively as they entered.

Inside the hut, herbs and dried cheese necklaces hung from the ceiling, and there were a couple of elevated pallet beds with a space underneath each for the livestock. The house was surprisingly organized and clean, though the smoke from the fire burning in the middle of the room made Miriat feel light-headed.

Alma called for everyone else to come inside, and she waited for the villagers to take their places along the walls before she spoke. Miriat looked at those around her, and a shiver ran down her spine as she saw a few once-familiar faces. She felt like she had crossed into the afterlife, with the ghosts of her past about to stand in judgement of her.

"So," Alma said, sitting down in a leather-covered wooden chair. "Sit yourself down and tell me why I should let you stay." The striga leader leaned back and steepled her fingers in front of her face. Alma had the lean wiry frame of someone who habitually worked harder and ate less than was good for them. Her face was pleasant enough to look at, though there were hard lines around her mouth and between her thin eyebrows, lines that spoke of hard choices made and much pain endured.

Miriat wasn't sure what was expected of her. She turned towards Maladia, but the girl avoided her eyes and busied herself stroking the bare head of the hatchling in her hand.

"What's that? Give me this!" the dark-eyed boy demanded, with all the greed and tact of toddlerhood.

"Leave it!" Maladia said sharply, doing her best to shake

the boy off as he pulled on her sleeve. "It's Miriat's! She found it and it's hers!"

"Oh, indeed?" Alma chuckled, her sharp eyes taking everything in. "Looks to me like that bird will be dead soon. So, townswoman," she turned towards Miriat. "You have nothing to say for yourself?"

"You know why I'm here," Miriat said, inwardly berating herself for the quiver in her voice. "My daughter was born a striga. And I couldn't let them take her from me. So, I came here. To join you."

"Have you now?" Alma raised her eyebrows. "Oh, how very brave of you." A few of the strigas in the room sniggered.

"So, tell me now, girl. What else is there to recommend you to us than the minimum of a mother's feeling?" Alma raised her hand and the room fell silent again. "You haven't abandoned your child, which is all very well, but why should we take you on? As you see, we have plenty of mouths to feed as it is."

Miriat looked around. The men and women lining the walls were watching her. The room felt oppressive, the air was thick with the smell of these people, with the shadows dancing strangely on the walls.

"I have nowhere else to go," she whispered, her head down. *They will send us away,* she thought, *they will send us away to starve in the woods.* The courage of the morning had now left her, and hot tears fill her eyes. She wiped them with the back of her hand. "I don't know what I need to do for my daughter, but you do. I've no kin now, no friends to help or shelter me. So, I've come here. And if it's my blood and flesh you want as payment, you may have it. But my child won't survive Heyne winter unless you take us in."

"Your 'blood and flesh'?" a man standing in the corner scoffed. "Because what else would dirty stigois want, right?" Miriat shrunk as he used the word. "Who do you think we are, girl?" The other strigas in the room tensed. Clearly the taint of the word had power over them still, even in their own home.

"Mordat, show some manners." Alma looked upon the man fondly, though her words silenced him. "Our guest seems unaware of our customs. Which is not her fault, I'm sure," she added, though she gave Miriat a look as if to note that last point was yet to be decided. "Girl, we have no designs on your life. You'll find no striga here who'd follow the dark impulses of their second heart."

The strigas in the room all nodded and made small gestures by their chests, as if to ward off evil.

Alma rubbed her temple and paused before announcing, "You can stay." The crowd of strigas visibly relaxed, with some smiles exchanged shyly across the room. Alma raised her finger. "But one thing must be made clear. You're no hero. How many children have you seen left at the forest's edge? How many women did you see make that lonely journey into the night, with never so much as a 'fare thee well'? What did you do then, what did you say?" She paused, allowing her words to sink in, but expecting no reply. "I'm sure there are some among us who could answer that for you, if they so wished." Miriat shrunk within herself. Alma sighed and said, not unkindly, "But you have given your child a chance, and so we can do no less." She continued, "I see the chick in Maladia's hand. See it survives." Alma looked Miriat in the eyes and gave a curt nod. "That will be the right thing to do."

* * *

Miriat was ushered into a small hut no larger than her tool shed back in Heyne Town, with the young Dola she'd met by the wall trailing behind her. The woman referred to as the West Stream Dola was waiting for her inside and gestured towards an elevated straw and moss mattress, positioned by the back wall of the tiny room. "Come in, come in," she said with a smile as Miriat sat down.

"Pass me my bag, child," the older woman said to the younger Dola. The midwife rummaged through it and took out a small glass phial. She pulled out the cork with her teeth and poured a few drops into her palm. She passed the phial back to her young apprentice, without looking in her direction and rubbed her palms together. A sharp smell filled the room. Though not unpleasant, it was strong enough to make Miriat's eyes water.

"I see you've met my young friend here." The West Stream Dola pointed to the young girl who winked at Miriat. "She will observe, if you don't mind. I need to check the state of you."

Miriat nodded and allowed the older woman to place her hands on her stomach. "Not much more than two or three days since the little one came, I'd say," the old midwife said, gently kneading Miriat's flesh with her plump fingers. She shook her head. "Their love didn't hold out long enough for you to heal, did it?"

"They hoped mine wouldn't either," Miriat said, looking squarely into the old Dola's face.

The older woman nodded and placed a reassuring hand on Miriat's shoulder. "Well, you're safe now, at least. Though I'll have a talk with my fellow Dolas. The Heyne Town folk seem more and more impatient with their own. I'm not sure we'll be able to achieve much with the council, but perhaps the next time they throw a young mother out, they will wait for her wounds to heal at least. Lean back for me please."

Miriat couldn't help but feel reassured by the old midwife's quietly competent demeanor. It brought a sense of normality to the day which had been anything but. The young Dola gently took Salka from Miriat's arms so that she could lie down. The West Stream Dola hitched up Miriat's skirt and waved at her apprentice to watch what she was doing.

"This hut is not much, but at least it's a dry place to sleep," the old woman said. She noticed Miriat's expression. "It's nothing to what you had, I know..." Clearly nobody had lived in this hut for a long time, and the mud walls were crumbling, revealing the support branches underneath. The door was a half-rotten animal skin, stretched out and hooked on the sides of the doorframe to keep out the cold. But there was a lit fire pit in the middle of the room, with a stack of wood and peat for fuel in the corner. While Miriat was being interrogated by Alma, somebody had hung half a dozen or so of the cheese necklaces she'd seen before from the ceiling. Their dried squares glistened white in the firelight. In the corner there was a single clay pot with a roughly carved wooden spoon, and a single cup and a bowl, similarly fashioned out of wood. The floor had been swept and some kind hand had sought to fill the holes in the walls with moss. Either the hut had been kept ready or, more likely, the villagers knew Alma wouldn't turn Miriat away and, while their leader was putting her through the wringer, they had furnished her with the basic necessities quietly, without ceremony. Something stuck in Miriat's throat. Those people, strangers to her, would not allow their first kindness to be a debt.

"It's more than I expected," she said.

The midwife nodded with approval. "I'm glad you feel so. I had told Alma to prepare for your arrival. The bones told me you'd be coming, and a young mother needs a safe place to sleep." She watched Miriat carefully. "And to mourn, I suppose."

Miriat realized she was crying. She wiped the tears with the side of her hand, not trusting herself to speak.

The old Dola finished her examination. She pulled out a couple of sealed clay jars from her bag and put them on the mattress. "For your wounds and the bruising," she said.

Miriat's eyes opened wide. "But I have nothing to pay you with…"

"When you do, you'll pay me." The old woman raised her hand. "You will have to rely on others' help in the coming months. And in time, you will repay it. Make sure you do so. The strigas look after each other… to a point. But they will watch you too. Just because you can't see the tally, doesn't mean it's not kept.

"Now, for your child, make sure to keep her warm," the midwife said, gently passing the infant from her apprentice back to her mother's arms. "The child will learn to control the other heart in time, but you must stay vigilant as well. An infant cannot be expected to have any self-control. You must give the other heart no reason to assert itself."

The old woman smiled at Miriat and left the hut. Her young apprentice lingered for a moment and surprised Miriat with a quick hug before, she too, left.

Miriat looked around her new home. Salka gave a content sigh, wriggling in her mother's arms.

"We can make this work," Miriat said, smiling at Salka. "I can make this work."

For more great titles, check out our
website and social media

angryrobotbooks.com
@angryrobotbooks

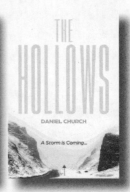

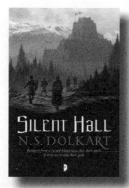
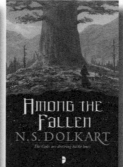

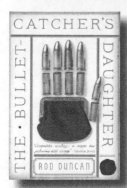

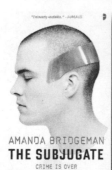

We are Angry Robot

angryrobotbooks.com

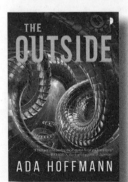